Close to a hundred thousand people gather in the London Olympic Stadium. Billions more watch on televisions around the world. There is a commotion near the main gates. The crowd begins to cheer as a single figure appears. A young woman, her head held high, her right hand higher as it bears a shining rod aloft. The top of the rod glows and flickers with a bright flame. The Olympic torch. She runs across the stadium's field, the cheers rising all about her as she approaches the platform set there in its center, and the wide, shallow brazier it holds. She stops short, ten feet away, and, with a practiced overhand toss, flips the burning torch toward the brazier. It lands squarely in the center, and the oil there ignites at once, a rich blaze springing up—

—and then the blaze bursts into a blinding light. Those in the crowd shield their eyes, blinking and squinting and staring as the light pours forth—

—and gleaming, golden figures leap from the flames.

At first the crowd thinks these are holograms, laser displays, some form of special effect, and they roar their approval as the powerful, handsome figures turn and survey the scene. They wear togas and robes cinched with heavy brooches, laurel and olive wreaths atop their oiled and curled hair, sturdy sandals upon their feet. They are beautiful, commanding, and their very skin glitters like gold.

Then the central figure steps forward. He is taller than the others, broader-shouldered, his beard full and his deep eyes wise and arresting. He raises a hand and the cheers stop as if a shroud had fallen, cutting off all sound. And into that silence he speaks.

"I am Zeus," he declares, his deep voice rolling out across the stadium, across the country, across the world. "The father of the gods, the ruler of the sky and the land. I am he who slew his father Chronos, shattered the Titans' might, and laid claim to the world. You know me, for you have worshipped me since your earliest days."

"I have returned." He raises his arms wide to encompass his companions and his audience. "We have returned. And now we will accept your worship once more."

Crazy Eight Press is an imprint of Clockworks.

First edition

ReDeus
Beyond Borders

EDITED BY
ROBERT GREENBERGER
&
AARON ROSENBERG

CRAZY 8 PRESS

Contents

Dear Diana,

Thank you for your friendship and support. Your belief in me means more than you will know!

David McD

Introduction

When Aaron Rosenberg, Paul Kupperberg, and I conceived *ReDeus* some years back, we thought it would be a fun playground for the three of us to explore. Then in 2012 we decided to invite our friends to come play with us, resulting in *ReDeus: Divine Tales*, an anthology of eleven stories that debuted at Shore Leave, marking Crazy 8 Press's first anniversary.

When we first approached the writers and then discussed it with the fans, everyone got very excited at the notion of a world where all the gods from all the pantheons had come back to pick up where they left off. Based on the stories we received, our instincts proved correct—this was a different Earth, and wonderful to explore.

We had so much fun with the project, and received such excellent response from readers in person and online, that we decided to keep going. But with a world so rich we needed to really expand our scope. As a result, we determined that for 2013 there would be two volumes, one focusing on domestic matters and one with an international theme.

Given that the best known mythologies hail from Europe, starting with the international stories made the most sense—and offered up a whole host of possibilities. After all, the realms the various pantheons controlled do not necessarily match current national borders. Many of them overlap, with certain areas bowing to one pantheon in one era but another a century or two later. Now that all of them had returned simultaneously, who controlled which lands and where did people cast their loyalties?

We invited all of the *Divine Tales* authors to come back and most readily agreed. Some wished to continue the adventures of the characters they'd introduced in that volume. Others were eager to explore different opportunities. We welcome back the 2013 Nebula-nominated

Lawrence M. Schoen, Scott Pearson, Steve Wilson, Dave Galanter, Phil Giunta, and William Leisner.

But other authors had been interested but unable to participate in *Divine Tales* for one reason or another. And still other authors had come to our attention as people we thought would really enjoy writing in the ReDeus universe. We extended new invitations, and several more heeded the call—we welcome first-time ReDeus authors Kelly Meding, Janna Silverstein, David McDonald, Steve Lyons, and Lorraine J. Anderson. It's very exciting adding new voices to the mix, and *Beyond Borders* is stronger and more diverse as a result.

For the cover, Aaron brought Lorraine Schleter to our attention and she delivered an outstanding image that got all the writers very excited. The gods do enjoy their iconography!

In the second half of 2013, the gods will be back for *Native Lands,* which will explore the North American pantheons—and those others trying to gain toeholds on the continent. After that we expect to continue exploring the first decades after The Return and see how people do (or do not) change their ways, how the pantheons seek to manipulate their worshippers (and vice-versa!), and how gods maneuver for supremacy over other gods. Close reading of the first two volumes hints at great conflicts to come, and we look forward to seeing where those beginnings take us.

For those back for a second helping, we thank you for your continued support. For newcomers, we say welcome. And of everyone we ask: If all the gods returned, who would *you* worship?

—*Robert Greenberger*

What Remains Is Light

by Aaron Rosenberg

"Work, curse you! Work!"

Hiroto Fumiji pounded the small, curved keyboard, but impotently—still it failed to respond. The transparent, visor-like screen had lit, but refused to coalesce its brilliance into the desired image of the desktop. All around the long conference table, his investors looked on, irritation beginning to show behind the usual masks of intent concentration. No one said anything, of course—that was not their way. But he saw the glances, the minute headshakes, the notes jotted down on pads or typed quickly into phones and tablets.

He was losing them.

"Just a temporary glitch, gentlemen and ladies," he assured them as best he could, schooling himself to his own polite mask. He was just as Japanese as any of them, he knew how to play this game. But beneath the façade he could feel his control slipping. He had worked too hard, lost too much—brief memory flash of a face he tried hard to forget, and another he did his best to ignore—to have this fall apart on him now! He gestured for Arata Matsuo, his head technology officer, to join him there at the head of the table and see if he could spirit the recalcitrant machine to life, but before Arata could reach him something else happened. Something unexpected.

A rich golden light seemed to fill every inch of the sleek room, beaming down from above. It was outside as well, Hiroto noticed through the long windows forming the room's outer wall, looking for all the world like the sun had chosen to burst forth even though it was past seven at night.

Except the cheery light was radiating down upon him and the board as well. Right through the paneled ceiling, and the roof above that. And he could see that the hallway behind the conference room was equally bright. As if whatever was projecting this intense illumination would not tolerate any sort of barrier.

But how was that even possible?

He had his answer an instant later, when the light grew still brighter, still warmer, making his cheeks heat and his fingers tingle—

And then it spoke.

That was how it felt, at least. As if the light itself had been given voice—a beautiful, soft, sweet, resonant voice, a woman's voice as warm and encompassing as the light from which it emanated.

And this is what it said:

"Hear me, O my people," it intoned, its wording stilted, old, almost formal for all the warmth of its tone. "I am Amaterasu-ōmikami, she who shines in the heaven. I have returned, and all my kin alongside me. We are home, here in our land of the rising sun, and we are pleased to once more resume our rightful places as your leaders, your rulers, your gods. We must reacquaint ourselves with the world, with our lands and our people, but once we have, we shall lead you into a new age of peace and prosperity and prayer. That is all."

The voice faded slowly, its words still echoing in the corners of the room, and the light began to filter out along with it—it was no longer radiating down through the ceiling but still that golden haze clung to chairs and heads and screens, curling about them possessively before slowly, reluctantly releasing its grip and dissipating back into the normal sharp, cool light of the lamps and bulbs all around.

At once a murmur sprang up, everyone there so stunned by this strange event that they set aside propriety and conversed openly about what had happened and what it meant for them.

Hiroto set the flexible, portable, wearable prototype computer down in front of him, all but forgotten, and then leaned forward, elbows on the table's polished surface, hands in his hair. He didn't know what all this meant either, but he had a feeling it was not going to be good for him.

"You cannot do this!" Hiroto saw the pencil-thin crease appear above Ichiro Kato's brow, and hastily moderated his tone. Mr. Kato was the majority investor in FlexTech, and had always made it clear that he expected his contributions to net him a corresponding level of awed respect. Normally that was not a problem for Hiroto. But this latest news, coupled with the events of the past week, had rattled his customary calm and cracked his usual efficient, polite, driven demeanor. "Please," he tried instead, hating to plead but willing to if that was what it took. "Please do not do this!"

"It has been decided," Mr. Kato replied, which of course really meant "I have decided." "We must recoup as much of our costs as possible, which means acting without delay. If we hesitate, we are lost."

"We don't even know what they will say yet!" Hiroto pointed out desperately. "They might not care!"

That did not seem likely, however.

In the weeks since The Return, everyone had been watching and listening to news from all around the world. The gods truly had returned, and not just Amaterasu and the rest of the kami. Zeus and Heracles and Poseidon were back in Greece and Rome, Anubis and Set strode across Egypt once more, Odin and Thor stalked about Germany and Sweden, Raven and Coyote skulked about North America—everywhere you turned, there were gods. As Amaterasu had said, they had all seemingly come back to reclaim their rightful places as gods and rule over all their people.

Only, some of the gods were a bit nicer about taking up the reins again than others. Some had simply stepped in and demanded worship, but others had seized control of every aspect of their people's lives. And the gods' understanding of humanity, its needs, its desires, its capabilities—they were all hundreds, even thousands of years out of date.

And that was particularly true when it came to the many things mankind had created since they had last seen their gods.

In many ways, it was a wholly different world than it had been back then.

And not all of the gods approved of the changes.

It had started with the Egyptians—Geb and Osiris and the others had banned the Internet from their domain, and had swiftly followed that with additional decrees: no cell phones; no email, no digital cameras and so on. It was like living in a police state. Worse, it was like a police state from the middle of the previous century, back before there had been a global community.

The Greco-Romans had swiftly followed suit. Several of the smaller pantheons did as well. There were entire nations that already had no electricity, no Internet, no phones. Many of them no longer allowed television from beyond their own borders, though thus far it seemed radio was still universal. Radio was an older technology, though, and it seemed that bothered the gods less than many newer inventions. Perhaps it was simply because the gods could appreciate the idea of one's voice being heard everywhere at once, but the concept of digitizing images was too much for them to grasp. No one knew for certain.

And everyone—not just Mr. Kato—was afraid of what would happen here if Amaterasu passed the same sort of decree those other pantheons had. She had yet to say anything—in fact, she and her brethren had remained utterly silent since her first declaration—but everyone in Japan knew it was just a matter of time.

None of which changed the fact that Hiroto wasn't about to let anyone—even Mr. Kato and the other investors—tear his company apart and sell it for scrap. Not after he'd worked so hard to put it all together in the first place. This had been his entire life ever since . . . well, for quite a while.

"Just give me a little time," he asked now. "We are so close to getting the FT-1 fully functional. Once that is done, we can market it to those countries still allowing technology—including our own. With our first shipment, you will make back your money tenfold. Why take a fraction now when you can have many times the amount so soon after?"

Silence, then, as the older gentleman studied him. Mr. Kato was a shrewd businessman, Hiroto knew—his father had been a fisherman and as a young man Mr. Kato had leveraged the family's one boat into a small fleet, then into a fishing company, and then had expanded out into other foods, transportation, pharmaceuticals, and more. He understood risk, and respected courage—so he had told Hiroto when they had met, two years ago at the first FlexTech investor meeting. Now he proved it again by nodding, once, a sharp gesture that matched the gaze he leveled upon Hiroto.

"Two weeks," Mr. Kato warned. "You may have that much and no more. If the FT-1 is not ready in two weeks, we will shut this company down—lights, water, everything. We may get only a fraction then of what we could get today, and even that is barely a tenth of what we have invested here, but I have stood by you this long, I will give you that much longer to prove I made the correct choice."

Hiroto bowed his head. "Thank you. I will not let you down."

He only hoped he was right.

● ● ●

"Did you figure it out yet?" Hiroto demanded as he stepped into the main lab. Arata and several of his techs were clustered around the FT-1 prototype, studying the diagnostic monitors they had hooked up to various parts of its assembly. One of them, a tall, slender young man with a thick mane of hair, glanced over as Hiroto entered but quickly turned back to the monitors, and Hiroto frowned. The youth did not look familiar, and he knew every one of his employees. Indeed, after all they had endured together, he could no longer think of them as strictly workers. They were like family.

"We think it is the linkages again," Arata replied, prodding one such connective point with a thin metal wand. "They're still having trouble keeping the data stream intact."

Hiroto resisted the urge to scream. That had been one of their biggest hurdles all along. How did you build a fully flexible, completely wearable computer? Your components had to be lightweight, obviously, and needed some degree of ductility to bend with your movements. Most wearable computer designs had standard solid components linked by wiring, but that was really just taking a regular computer and stringing it across your body like a high-tech utility vest. Hiroto's idea had been to alter the components themselves, making them completely flexible as well. It had taken them the better part of two years to work out how to do that, but unfortunately with increased mutability came decreased data cohesion. The FT-1 had been plagued with static, faulty connections, fuzzy signals—it was exactly like taking an old radio and spreading its components across a long table, then expecting it to still work the same way it had when everything was tidily packed into a small case. He'd thought they'd solved that problem, but evidently not quite yet.

"Can you fix it?" he asked finally.

Arata sighed, then shrugged, his broad, honest face troubled. "Not sure," he admitted. "And even if we do, I don't know that it won't fritz out again the second someone puts it on and bends their arm too much or turns a little too far to the side." He lowered the wand. "Sorry. What did Kato say?"

"We have two weeks." Hiroto found himself studying the young man again, but still couldn't place him. "Do I know you?"

"Oh! Yes, sir!" The young man finally turned to face him, and offered a wide, toothy grin that instantly made everything seem better, even a little funny. "I'm Taka, remember? Taka Mikato? I'm here to study and learn?"

Hiroto frowned. Something about that did sound familiar, despite the odd phrasing. "You're . . . the college intern?" he said, struggling to pull together a hazy memory of a quick conversation with someone, weeks before.

"Yes, exactly!" Taka bowed. "The college intern! Thank you so much, sir, for this opportunity! I'm really excited to be here!"

Hiroto couldn't help but laugh at the young man's obvious enthusiasm. "Of course. Well, welcome aboard, Taka. I'm sorry you came to us at such a difficult time."

"Such an exciting time, you mean," the intern corrected gently, his smile still firmly in place and still seemingly genuine. "Mr. Matsuo here tells me this amazing device of yours is very nearly working! That's fantastic!" He turned to admire the FT-1 where it hung on its display mannequin. "Such a clever idea!"

"Thank you." There was something about the way the boy expressed himself, so openly admiring, that set Hiroto at ease. Why hadn't he remembered about the internship right off? Clearly he was too stressed to think clearly. Probably too tired as well—it was late, and once more the day had run away from him. "Let's hope Mr. Matsuo is correct." He waved a hand at Arata. "Carry on." Then he turned and headed for the door.

Perhaps a little sleep would help. And some food. But definitely sleep.

Sliding open the front door, Hiroto listened intently. All was quiet. Good. He stepped in, set his shoes in their customary place along the low rack just inside—ignoring as best he could the still-empty space beside them—and eased the heavy panel shut again behind him. Then he moved as silently as he could toward the kitchen, his socks making faint swishing sounds across the woven mat floor. The lights were all out but he didn't need them to find his way about, and he didn't want to disturb anyone else. It was later than he'd thought.

Entering the small, familiar kitchen, the same one he'd grown up in many years before, Hiroto spotted a small covered bowl sitting atop the stove, a low flame from one burner keeping it warm. Ah! Reaching carefully for the bowl, he lifted it and carried it over to the table, enjoying the way the heat nearly burnt his fingers and palms. A teapot was waiting at the table, a single cup beside it, a pair of chopsticks resting in a napkin before them, and Hiroto allowed himself to sigh as he sank into the chair and set the food down as well. The sigh deepened, lengthened when he lifted the lid and the smell of beef negimaki wafted up to him.

"The tea is cold. Let me warm it for you." The voice emerged from the shadows and Hiroto jumped, then settled, chuckling at his own foolishness.

"You don't have to, oka-san," he assured the short, stout woman who slid up alongside him, her sturdy, wrinkled hands already claiming the teapot. "Cold tea is fine. I'm sorry I woke you."

"Eh." She shrugged off his concern. "I sleep light, you know that. And I was listening for you." One hand rose to push the hair back from his forehead, and she smiled fondly at him. With him seated, they were close to the same height. "You look tired."

"I am," he admitted, letting himself relax into his mother's touch. "It was a long day."

"You're close to finishing it, though?" She took the teapot and carried it over to the stove, and Hiroto decided to concentrate on eating rather than argue with her again. "And then you'll be home more?"

"I hope so." He thought that was true, but he couldn't be entirely sure. Nor did the one guarantee the other. And judging by her reaction, his mother didn't entirely believe him, either.

"She was asking for you again today," she said instead, over her shoulder. "I tell her you are working hard, that you are nearly done, but I am not sure she understands."

Hiroto bowed his head, the fatigue catching up to him again—that, and something more. A grief still so raw, so powerful, he could only bear it by pushing it away. "It is true. I am working hard."

"I know." His mother turned to study him in the dim light from the stove. "But that is not the only reason." As always, she understood him far better than he might have liked. He couldn't meet her eyes, and after a second she nodded—not angry but sad. And perhaps a little disappointed. Then she brought the tea back over and poured a steady stream of the now piping-hot liquid into his cup.

"A girl needs her father," was all she said before setting the teapot down and disappearing once more down the hall to her own room.

The words lingered behind her, settling upon Hiroto's shoulders with a weight that nearly sent him crashing to the floor. Grief, mixed with guilt, swirled about him as he mechanically finished his now tasteless food and dragged himself off to bed. There, blissfully, he escaped into a deep, dreamless sleep.

When he arrived at work the next morning, Hiroto found Taka already there. The young intern was with Midori Ghoda, who was part graphic designer, part advertising person, and part sales rep. She was clearly in the process of giving him the grand tour when Hiroto caught up to them.

". . . had to be fully portable, of course," Midori was explaining, gesturing toward an array of micro-cell solar dots, "and most of the standard battery options had the same drawbacks as old computer parts: too bulky, too heavy, too stiff and awkward. Plus we wanted to avoid having to plug in to recharge, if at all possible. That's why we went solar instead."

"Ah, the power of the lovely, life-giving sun!" Taka commented, glancing out toward the windows where the first rays of dawn were just beginning to creep across the horizon. Something in his tone made Hiroto think the younger man was mocking, but who, exactly? The sun?

Midori didn't seem to notice. "Exactly!" she agreed, her long hair flowing over her shoulders as she tossed her head. "But even standard solar cells weren't right—they were too fragile, and too limited in capacity." The smile she gave Taka looked half flirtatious and half conspiratorial, and for a second Hiroto felt as if he were intruding, though he shook that off quickly. This was his company, after all! Still, he kept motionless to avoid distracting them as Midori continued, "our engineers figured out a way around that, however."

Hiroto fully expected Taka to ask what that was, but the intern surprised him by simply nodding and accepting the bold statement at face value. The pair continued on, then, heading toward the company's small but efficient manufacturing center, and Hiroto watched them go. In a way, he found having Taka here surprisingly uplifting. He and the others were already so heavily invested in FlexTech and its product, so focused on making everything just so. It was nice to have someone around who could still see the wonder in it, and could admire all the hard work they'd done to get here without being worn thin by the effort it had taken.

As he turned toward his office and the day's reports, Hiroto found himself humming beneath his breath, and walking with a slight bounce to his step. He stopped that quickly before anyone could notice, but he was still smiling as he slid behind his desk.

"Sir?" His phone buzzed, startling Hiroto. He had been focusing on the latest set of projections, and eagerly hit the Reply button, glad for anything that would tear his attention from those depressing calculations. Two years ago, when he had first announced FlexTech, they had been considered one of the best and brightest of the new cutting-edge high-tech start-ups. So why was it that now, only a couple of years later, they were thought of as has-beens, could-have-dones, and even never-weres? How had they so quickly gone from a highly anticipated, eagerly watched company to a longshot most people assumed would never pan out?

"Yes?" he answered, trying to shake off the depression that had crept higher and loomed larger with every number. "What is it, Ishi?"

"Sir, there seems to be some . . . trouble down in the testing rooms." The way she said it, he got the clear sense that his assistant hadn't wanted to tell him at all, but had felt she must.

"Trouble? What sort?" He was already out from behind his desk and striding toward the office door. Ishi sat at her workstation just beyond, her compact grace and pretty features the perfect concealment for her sharp mind and brisk efficiency, and looked up as he slid the door open and approached. "What's happened?"

"I don't know exactly," she answered, rising to meet him. "Just that Jiro called and said there was trouble." That simple statement curdled in Hiroto's stomach, changing everything from lighthearted concern to serious worry. Jiro Nigata was in charge of security, and he wasn't the type to concern anyone else with the smaller stuff. If he had called up, whatever was going on was big.

Hiroto was already marching out into the hall toward the stairs. Ishi was right behind him. FlexTech had spent a fair chunk of its investors' money on this state-of-the-art facility, everything in it completely up to date. But the first floor, that was the showcase area, what the investors and potential distribution partners and other businessmen saw during tours and presentations and meetings. It wasn't where most of the technical work got done.

That was in the basement.

"No fire alarms, security sensors, nothing?" Hiroto asked as he walked. Beside him Ishi shook her head. Interesting. He thought that might rule out sabotage or industrial theft. Which left what, exactly?

Taking the stairs two steps at a time, Hiroto was crossing into the basement level only seconds later. This was where all of the labs were located, in windowless concrete rooms both for security and for safety. He continued past the labs, and stopped at a long expanse of windows that looked into the largely empty rooms just beyond. The testing rooms. Several employees were clustered there, pointing and laughing and having a grand time from the look of things. They fell quiet the minute he appeared, and parted before him like a curtain, disappearing in his wake. Only Ishi was still beside him as Hiroto got his first clear look through the glass—

—and froze.

What in the world was going on here?

Inside the room, two men danced about each other. Literally. Hiroto thought he recognized a few breakdancing steps, along with what might have been the meringue and a bit of the foxtrot. Taka was in there as well, leaning against the wall, arms folded over his chest. He looked utterly delighted by this little spectacle.

And it was most definitely a spectacle. Because bad enough that the two FlexTech personnel—Hiroto recognized day shift manager Ryu Watanabe and second technician Kana Mori—were engaged in some impromptu dance competition in the middle of the workday, and especially during the current crisis. But both men's limbs flickered with light as they moved, and more shimmers and flashes appeared across their torsos as well.

Because each of them was wearing one of the early versions of the FT computer.

They were literally prancing about with two years and several million yen worth of blood and sweat strapped to their bodies.

After a minute, Hiroto shook himself out of his stunned daze. Stepping closer, he pounded on the glass. The competitors inside stopped at once, their wide grins fading quickly to abashed grimaces, their heads falling, shoulders slumping. They moved toward the door but Hiroto beat them to it, yanking it open from his side.

"What is the meaning of this?" he demanded.

Neither man would meet his gaze.

"Sorry, sir, sorry!" That was Taka unfolding himself and shifting to one side as he approached, thus somehow putting himself between Hiroto and the two embarrassed workers. "It was all my idea! Mr. Watanabe was showing me the early versions of the FT—fantastic job, sir, really! The idea of a computer you could wrap around you like a robe is just brilliant!—and how, even though they couldn't really do much in the way of computing, they still proved the concept of a wearable computer." He shrugged like it was no big deal, and oddly Hiroto felt some of his anger melting away. "I asked just how much you could really move while wearing one of those, and so they set out to show me. It's pretty incredible, sir!"

The youth's effusive praise robbed Hiroto of the rage that had been bubbling up inside him at the shameful display. After all, wasn't everyone here as invested in the company's success as he was? Weren't they entitled to blow off a little steam from time to time? And where better than within the building, where they could do so without impugning the company's reputation? And if they could demonstrate one of the FT's selling points at the same time, so much the better!

"Well, tell me next time you decide to put on a demonstration like this," he warned the two men, who both nodded quickly, the relief clear on their faces. "And talk to Midori—we may be able to incorporate your idea into our next presentation. 'A computer so light, so flexible you can dance with it!'" He chuckled at the thought, and a ripple of uneasy laughter from the others joined him.

Thinking about that, and places they could market that aspect, Hiroto turned and began retracing his steps. A small part of him felt that he should have been more upset about what had just happened, but the rest of him responded that nothing had been damaged, they had all learned something, and they had gained a potential new marketing approach, so, really, what did he have to be angry about?

That night, Hiroto made a point of leaving work at a more reasonable hour. He could not bring himself to go straight home, however. Instead he wandered the streets of Tokyo for a while, letting its bright lights and bustle wash over him before turning down a side street away from the busy commercial areas. He wasn't really paying attention to where he was going, but made several turns out of old habit, and when he finally stopped it was with a pang as he recognized the small, homey little sushi restaurant before him. They had eaten here all the time, the two of them. Back before FlexTech. Before—

The memories welled up, so painful he had to blink back the tears that stung his cheeks, and Hiroto almost turned away. But he was hungry and he was here, and so he went in anyway.

"Ah, so good to see you!" The proprietor called out, making his way over and bowing welcome. "It's been a long time!"

"Yes, it has." Hiroto bowed in return. "I hope you are well?"

"Doing fine so far," the owner replied, laughing, and gestured behind him. Many of the tables were full. "The gods won't stop us from eating, I don't think!" Then he glanced behind Hiroto, toward the door. "You're by yourself? Where's—?"

"Yes, just me," Hiroto cut him off. "I'll just sit by the counter, if that's okay."

"Of course, of course." It was clear from his face, and the concern in his voice, that the older man wanted to ask. But he didn't. He just escorted Hiroto to the counter, and told the sushi chef there to "make sure our old friend here has everything he needs." Then he left Hiroto to dine in peace.

The food was every bit as good as he remembered, but Hiroto still had trouble choking it down. Coming here had been a bad idea, he could see that now. Every painting, every candle sconce, every chopstick and cup and napkin ring hit him like a bullet train, buffeting him with bitter blows. He ate quickly, paid, and left with barely a good-bye.

It was dark when he reached home, but his mother padded out to see him as he was straightening from placing his shoes. She was already dressed for bed, not only in her nightclothes but in the frown that hung about her face.

"We waited up for you," she explained, the disappointment clear in her tone. "But eventually she fell asleep. I could wake her for you, so you could say good night." The way she said it, it was clear she already knew his answer, and Hiroto hated himself for proving her right by shaking his head, yet it was all he could manage right now.

"No, no," he responded softly, his throat tight. "Let her sleep. I will try to be home earlier tomorrow."

Yet as he turned toward his own room, they both knew he would be late then as well.

Some things were just too painful to confront. Both memories, and the living reminders of those who had wrought them.

Two days later, Hiroto was talking with his chief financial officer, Sachiko Ehime, when they were disturbed by a commotion out in the hall. Irritated, he leaned past her and stabbed at her phone.

"Ishi, what is all the noise?" he asked.

"It's . . . you'd better see for yourself, sir," she replied.

"Ah," Hiroto muttered under his breath as he glanced at Sachiko, who shrugged and shook her head. "How are we supposed to get any work done with all this?" He pushed his chair back and rose to his feet. "Well, let's go see what's causing it." Together they exited her office. It was along the same hall as his own, at the front of the building and on the ground level, and so when they emerged they had a clear view of the lobby beyond—and of the employees streaming out through it, disappearing into the midday sunlight like mirages flickering away in the heat.

"What?" Hiroto picked up his pace, almost sprinting, and reached the lobby just as the last two crossed to the front doors. "Marco!" he called out to the man. "Danielle! Where is everyone going?"

Both of them turned back toward him, frowning, though he didn't think they looked angry. Not at him, anyway. "Sorry, Mr. Fumiji," Danielle answered, glancing down at her feet which shuffled back and forth as if eager to be in motion once more. "But we need to go."

"What do you mean? Go? Go where?" Hiroto looked at her and at Marco for an answer.

"Home," Marco replied. "Or at least away from here. We don't belong here." Danielle nodded, and together they turned toward the door again, but Hiroto darted past and interposed himself.

"Don't belong here? You've been here since day one!" Which they had, both of them. Marco was a talented software designer. Danielle was a mechanical engineer. They had been among the first to sign on with the fledgling company, back before they'd even had any funding, when it had just been Hiroto and Arata and one or two others and a crazy dream. "Is it because of the deadline?" he asked them. "We can beat it! You know that! We're so close! Can't you just have faith a little longer?"

At the word 'faith,' however, both of them stiffened, and Hiroto bit back a curse as understanding flashed through him. This wasn't about whether they believed in the company. "Ah," he said softly. "You are being called back home."

Both of them nodded, and Hiroto sighed. He had heard on the news, of course, about how the various gods had begun summoning their people back to them. Some were subtle about it—Amaterasu remained silent, but more and more Japanese people were returning to the island nation from other countries, saying they had simply felt like they should be back here where their ancestors had hailed from. Others were more blatant, issuing decrees and causing all those descended from their ancient followers to feel a powerful compulsion nothing could deny. Marco was Russian by blood, Hiroto remembered, and the dark, cold gods of that region were said to be among the most aggressive at reclaiming their followers. Danielle he knew was Native American, and her gods were being gentler but no less insistent.

Still, one thing confused him. "Why now?" he asked. The gods had begun calling their flocks weeks ago, and neither employee had shown any inclination to leave. Nor had any of the others. What had changed?

Danielle shrugged. "I don't know," she admitted, and Marco nodded. "We were just having lunch, and talking. That intern, Taka, he was asking where everyone was from, and said it was surprising we were still here, with everything that was going on. And suddenly it felt like I needed to get back to the U.S. right away."

"Same here," Marco agreed. "When he asked that, it was like I could feel Perun reaching out to me and demanding my return." He shook his head. "I'm sorry, sir. I hate to cut out on you like this. We all do. But we have to go."

"I understand." And he did, though he wasn't happy about it. But what man could stand against the wishes of the gods? Hiroto held out his hand, first to Marco and then to Danielle. "Take care, both of you. Tell the others, as well. Perhaps we'll meet again, some day."

"I hope so." Marco shook hands with him, but Danielle surprised Hiroto by embracing him tightly.

"Take care," she whispered. "And good luck." Then, with one last, quick smile, they were through the doors and following the others, who had already vanished down the street. The lobby was empty again, except for him—and the sound of feet approaching softly from behind.

"Wow, sorry," Taka said as he neared. "I didn't mean to send anyone away. I was just curious where people were from, you know? I was really surprised you had people here from all over the world." He scratched his cheek. "I guess they were resisting the call of their gods or something, and they just couldn't hold out any longer."

"I suppose not," Hiroto agreed, but he stared long and hard at the young intern. What was it about him that things kept happening in his presence? Strange, unsettling things—not always bad, though this one was certainly not good—but definitely confusing. He started to ask something, what exactly he didn't know, but Taka grinned at him and the thought slid away.

Well, whatever had happened, Hiroto decided after a second, there was nothing he could do now except pick up the pieces. He was already running through the company roster in his head as he turned away from both Taka and the lobby, trying to remember which employees were pure Japanese and thus likely to still be here. It was a depressingly small number, and he wondered if they would have enough to keep going.

But they had to. Anything else just wasn't an option.

As he'd feared, FlexTech had lost more than half its staff from the strange, spontaneous exodus. Halls that had bustled with activity, with movement and conversation and laughter, now echoed between long bouts of silence. Inboxes that had filled up every day from progress reports, questions, updates, queries, demands, and quick, casual conversation now sat as empty as many of the offices and cubicles and workstations, the occasional ping of a new message replacing the near-constant patter that had been a background susurration for so long. As Hiroto walked about the building a few days after everyone's departure, he couldn't help but wonder how much of the place's new emptiness was due to the loss in numbers and how much from the sudden forced purity of its occupants. From the start he had been open to hiring the best people, the brightest minds, the sharpest skills, without regard to such antiquated concerns as age or gender or religion or race or orientation. FlexTech had been a small, jumbled, happy microcosm, Africans working alongside Middle Easterns, Italians arguing with Russian, Scandinavians sharing equations with Chinese, Americans laughing arm in arm with Brazilians. Now there were only the Japanese, and it felt so quiet, so hushed and still, the people who had stayed so formal and soft-spoken and unobtrusive, there were times he felt like shouting just to wake them from their disciplined half-stupor. But of course they would simply go right back to being polite and mild-mannered and self-effacing. It was their way.

All except for Taka.

Perhaps it was because there were fewer of them now, but it felt like everywhere Hiroto turned, the tall, shaggy-haired intern was there. He seemed to be around every corner, in every room, and talking with every employee. He was poking a finger at the chemical tanks where they grew the solar micro-dots and the silicon chips. He was sketching lines with the visual designers. He was studying numbers with the accountants and finance officers.

And then there was the day that Hiroto walked into the main lab and found Taka and Arata and the two other remaining techs surrounded by wires and components and chipsets—which he immediately recognized as the guts of the FT-1.

"What have you done?" Hiroto demanded, though what had started in his head as an angry roar muted itself to a hushed whisper in the face of such devastation. All their work, all their effort and planning and sacrifice, and now it was scattered about the floor like so much digital refuse!

His chief technical officer didn't look at all concerned. "Taka here was curious how it all fit together," Arata explained with a shrug. "This way he can see all the linkages, all of the connective points, and it all makes sense."

"It does," Taka agreed with an easy laugh, that same humorous note that always seemed to rob Hiroto of his rage. "Not that I understand all of it, of course, but I can see now how all the pieces fit together. Truly it's marvelous!"

Hiroto resisted the urge to smile, nod, and turn away. Instead he gritted his teeth. "Put it all back together," he ordered quietly. "Now."

He was pleased that everyone jumped up immediately. "Of course," Arata promised. "Don't worry. A few hours and you'll never know it was apart." He attempted a small smile. "We may even be able to pack some of the linkages in better this time around, give it a smoother motion, a little more range of movement. And we'll check every connector as we go, make sure they're all good and tight."

The rest of his statement he left unsaid: "So that the blasted thing might actually work this time around."

Hiroto just nodded, once. Then he did turn to go. But evidently not quickly enough.

"Mr. Fumiji! Wait, please!"

Despite himself, Hiroto found his foot hovering in mid-stride. Mustering his will he succeeded in lowering it flat to the ground again, but he still couldn't take the next step. Instead he swiveled his head to look up at the tall young man now bearing down on him. Taka's thick hair streamed behind him as he jogged closer, his dark eyes flashing, and for a second Hiroto felt a slash of fear tighten his belly. Then it passed. Afraid? Of an intern? Really?

Still, he eyed Taka coolly as the young man slowed to a stop beside him. "Sorry, sir," the intern began, not even breathing hard. "I just wanted to ask you about something."

Hiroto sighed. He supposed this was the price of having an intern at all—you opened yourself up to being asked questions and expected to have some answers. "Very well." He led the way back to his own office.

Taka fell into step beside him. "Yes, well, what you're doing here it's really impressive, I mean it really is. But what I was wondering was, you see, how exactly did you get started? What made you decide to do this?"

They'd reached the office now, and Hiroto led the way past Ishi and settled into his chair, gesturing for Taka to take one of the seats across the desk from him. It was a fair question, he had to admit, even if it did skirt close to certain topics he had vowed never to revisit. So he steepled his fingers in front of him and took a second to compose his thoughts, laying them out neatly in his own head before replying.

"I have always been fascinated by computers," he began. "My own father brought one home when I was just a boy, and I thought it was the most amazing thing ever. You could play games on it, and write on it, and do math problems or keep lists with it—it was like magic." He smiled, remembering those early days. "We got them in school next, and had classes on how to use them. I did well at those. Then one day at home I tripped and dropped the books I'd been carrying. They knocked the computer off the desk. There was a sound like glass shattering. When I picked it back up, it wouldn't turn on." He frowned, though that soon became a grin. "I was terrified. My father would be furious. I had to do something! So I got some tools and I took the computer apart and I did my best to fix it. And it worked! He never noticed anything was wrong. But now I knew there was a whole other side to these miraculous machines, and I was hooked."

"You didn't want only to use what these devices offered," Taka guessed slowly, his body still for once, only his eyes alight. "You wanted to control what they offered."

"I suppose I did," Hiroto replied. "I tinkered whenever I could. I took classes in computers but also in auto mechanics and shop. Once the Internet began, I researched online. I taught myself as much as I could, and then I went to university and asked others to teach me more." He couldn't help but laugh at that mental picture, himself at eighteen, all spindly legs and gangly arms and bristly hair. There was another image right after that, though, an associated memory, and he was quick to brush that one aside.

"After college, I got work as an computer engineer," he continued. "We were creating a newer, lighter, stronger laptop. But you can only go so far with that. The case and the screen and the keyboard mean you'll never be able to get down below a certain size." He grinned at Taka, who grinned back. "Which is why I knew I had to change the game."

"So you started FlexTech and began work on the FT-1?"

Hiroto laughed again, though he thought there was the tiniest bitter aftertaste. "Oh no, that took many years. I worked for several other computer companies first. I learned what I could from them, everything I could, until I was ready to put it all to use." And it might have sat there in his head all this time, he admitted to himself, moldering away, doing absolutely nothing, just another pipedream. If not for . . .

But no. He forced himself not to think about it. Again. To push it back into the corner. Again.

"One day," he continued, his voice harsh and jagged in his ears, "I decided life was too short. And that there was no point sitting back, playing it safe, never going for it. We might fail, of course, but it was that or never doing anything at all." He tried to shrug but couldn't quite pull it off. "That was when I quit my old job. I found some other people who wanted what I did. I talked to investors and sold them on the idea." He waved his hands around them. "And this is the fruits of that labor. Such as it is."

Take leaned forward. "Yes, but why this? This exactly?" For once there was not a trace of humor about his face, eyes, or voice. He was deadly serious, to a degree that was almost frightening. "What made you say that this endeavor, of any you could choose, was worth the sacrifices, the pain, and the devotion?"

Hiroto smiled again, a practiced smile, his mask once more firmly in place. "The world always wants something bigger and stronger, or else lighter and smaller. I wanted to combine the two—the strongest computer possible, but so small and light you could carry it easily. Then as I thought about it I realized, why carry a computer when you could wear one instead? That was when I knew what I wanted to do." Other thoughts crashed in on him—youthful dreams, playful boasts, shared plans, a tear-soaked promise—but he pushed those back. Those were his, not anyone else's. Not anymore.

His intern nodded. "Thank you, sir. That was most enlightening. I had best let you get back to work." He rose to his feet and strode from the room. And Hiroto realized as he watched the younger man go that Taka had done all that without smiling once. There was still no humor about him, just a strange somberness instead.

Almost as if he'd somehow known he was being lied to.

The next few days passed all too quickly. Everyone worked long hours, trying to do the impossible, but even if they'd still been fully staffed Hiroto wasn't sure they could have managed. With only the handful who remained, they seemed doomed to failure right from the start, but they all refused to give up. There was too much riding on this.

Still, two weeks after his meeting with Mr. Kato Hiroto found himself in his office, staring at his monitor and the dismal status update it displayed. "Data stream still not steady," Arata had noted. "Full operation still not sustainable."

That was it. Hiroto slumped in his chair. They had failed.

It was over.

He heard noises coming from the hall outside, but couldn't muster the energy to care. Until they grew louder, more discordant.

Angry.

"Now what?" he muttered, pulling himself upright and stepping around the desk for what he feared might be the last time. "As if anything else needs to go wrong?"

The tumult assaulted his ears as he exited his office, and he turned to ask Ishi about it, but for once her desk was empty. Suddenly worried for some reason he couldn't name, Hiroto picked up his pace and all but trotted down the hall. But when he reached the lobby he stopped suddenly. In part because what he saw there stunned him into immobility.

And in part because there simply wasn't room to go any further.

From a quick glance, it looked like everyone left at Flex-Tech was there in the lobby. He spotted Ishi across the way, and Arata, and Midori, and Ryu, and Kana, and Sachiko, and even Jiro. And, in front of them all, his back to the door, backlit by the afternoon sunlight streaming in, was Taka.

"We don't have to let him tell us what to do!" The intern was saying loudly, waving his arms, his usual lighthearted smile replaced by a look of fierce intensity. "It is our choice, not his! This is our company, not his! What happens next is up to us!"

"Yes!" The others roared back, raising their own fists and pumping the air, and Hiroto felt both surprise and sorrow at the sight. Had they all turned against him so easily? After everything they'd been through? Then Taka spotted him over the crowd. "Mr. Fumiji!" he shouted, pointing one long arm at him, and Hiroto felt skewered as every gaze swung in his direction. "The time has come! We are taking Flex-Tech back! It is ours, and we will no longer let others tell us what to do!"

Several of the people there, people Hiroto had hired and worked with for years now, started toward him, and Hiroto raised his arms to shield himself, stunned. How had this happened? Why had they all turned against him? And why had Taka done this, after he had always seemed so enthusiastic, so supportive?

Jiro was the first to reach him, one powerful hand lashing out to catch him by the wrist. The short, stocky, chief of security tugged, pulling Hiroto toward him, and then the serious, no-nonsense, former military man—

—hugged Hiroto tight.

"We are all with you, Mr. Fumiji," he told the dazed Hiroto in his gruff voice. "Every one of us."

Others were beside him then, clasping his hand or clapping his shoulder or hugging him, and Hiroto found himself being moved to the front of the crowd, one quick embrace at a time. He was still trying to process it all when Taka reached out and laid a warm hand on his arm. For once the young intern seemed to have set aside his youthful eagerness, and the smile he gave Hiroto was a little mischievous but at the same time wise and kind.

"We believe in you, Mr. Fumiji," he said gently, though loud enough for his words to carry. "We believe in all of us. Mr. Kato cannot tell us what to do. He cannot decide when we are done. Only we can."

Hiroto nodded, feeling some response was called for but unable to think clearly. He was touched, however, by the devotion evident on every face and in every voice. Even in Taka, who had been here such a short time. Everyone fell quiet then, waiting for him to say something, and Hiroto's mind raced, trying to figure out what that should be. "I—" he began, then stopped himself and took a deep breath. "We—" he started again, the thoughts slowly coalescing, a vague plan beginning to form.

But that was as far as he got.

Because suddenly, all the lights went out.

There was a momentary pause, there in the half-gloom. Sunlight still floated in through the windows, but it was now late enough that those beams were heavily slanted, and the shadows were starting to push them back, sweeping away the daylight and bringing dusk in their wake. The back half of the lobby was dark, and the halls beyond darker still. They were also quiet, Hiroto realized. Too quiet. There was no steady hum, no gentle hiss.

Kato had done it. He had shut them down. Literally. He had turned everything off.

And the realization of exactly what that meant, crystallized Hiroto's previously scattered thoughts, even as a cold trickle of fear slid its way down his back.

"Everyone needs to get out of here, right now!" he announced.

At first no one moved. Then came the protests, the arguments, the denials. Beside him, Taka was shaking his head, but Hiroto didn't give the young man a chance to argue. "No, you need to go," he repeated. "Immediately! It isn't safe!"

Halfway across the room he saw Arata's eyes go wide, and then Ryu's and Kana's as well. Now they understood. The three of them nodded and turned to their respective neighbors, and Hiroto could see them talking quickly. The tenor of the room shifted.

"Sir!" Taka declared, clutching at Hiroto's arm. "Don't do this! We don't have to give in to him!"

Hiroto shook him off, and turned to face the tall intern. "You don't understand," he explained quickly. "Listen, you studied the chemical tanks, yes?" He didn't wait for Taka's nod before continuing. "Those processes, they're delicate. Unstable, even. They have to be carefully maintained, especially the temperatures. If they are not—"

At last he saw understanding crash across Taka's face, horror trailing behind it. But "we need to get everyone out of here" was all he said. When Hiroto nodded encouragement, the younger man turned his attention to the other employees still huddled before them. "Listen, everyone!" he shouted, raising his voice. "We are not giving up! But for now, it is imperative everyone exit the building at once!"

That did the trick. They all rushed forward like the morning crowd on the subway, instinct and mob mentality and fear taking over. The doors were shoved open and people streamed past, pushing and shoving their way out into the twilight. In mere minutes the lobby had emptied, leaving only Hiroto behind.

And Taka, who had remained beside him.

"What do we have to do?" the intern asked, his tone urgent but unafraid, and Hiroto admired his calm.

"There are emergency shutdowns on each tank," Hiroto explained, quickly leading the way toward the stairs down to the lower level. "They may have activated when the power went out, but we need to be sure." He took the steps two at a time, and started down the long, dark hall at once, only the dim emergency lighting showing the way. "And we have to hurry, because if those chemicals overheat—"

He started to say "they will explode," but that turned out to be unnecessary.

Because the chemicals said it for him.

There was a tremendous boom, first. The sound of it came crashing down the hall toward them, powerful enough pick them off their feet and hurl them back like a fierce wind. Then behind them came a hammer blow of pure force, toppling them a second time. The heat smothered them next, and a flash of light. A massive crack followed, and then Hiroto felt someone grab him and slam him to the ground. He had time to think "Asami," though even he couldn't have said if he meant it as a summons or a plea, followed by "Mitsuko," which he understood all too well, right before a deluge of dirt and dust and debris buried him in darkness.

"Uh." Hiroto stirred, reaching up to wipe at whatever was covering his face. It was heavy, whatever it was. And warm. Solid. And when he brushed at it, it moved.

"Sir?" The word was close to his ear. "Sir, are you all right?"

"Uh," he managed again. He blinked, but still there was nothing but dark all around. He took a deep, shuddering breath, and coughed on dust and particles, but even the thick, close air helped to clear his head. "I think so," he responded finally, his voice a bit shaky. "You?"

"I think so." With a grunt Taka heaved himself upright, shoving away whatever had fallen on top of him, and then reached down and hauled Hiroto to his feet. The young intern had been the object covering him, Hiroto realized. Taka must have pushed him down to shield him from . . . whatever it was that had happened to them.

"What happened?" he asked, blinking and trying to see anything at all. It was no use. The emergency lights were down, and there were no windows down here, no other light sources.

"The chemicals exploded," Taka replied, a hand fumbling for his shoulder and telling him where the intern was. "Part of the ceiling came down. We're lucky to be alive."

Hiroto knew that was true, but right now he was too concerned about their current predicament to fully appreciate that. He'd be grateful—among other things—later. If they made it out of this.

"We need light," he said. "So we can find a way out of here." With the power off, there was no air circulation. And if the stairs had been sealed, they'd suffocate before terribly long.

"I agree." He thought he actually heard a hint of humor from Taka. "Unfortunately, I do not have any. You?"

Hiroto shook his head, and regretted that as it sparked with pain, no doubt from his recent impact with the floor. He reflexively glanced around again, then sighed. That wasn't going to help. Instead he shut his eyes. Where had they been when the chemicals had exploded? They had left the stairs but hadn't reached the testing rooms yet, which meant they were right near—he reached out and grabbed for Taka, finally finding the intern's shoulder. "Did you get it put back together?" he demanded.

"Sir?"

"The FT-1," Hiroto explained. "After the other day, when you and Arata and the others pulled it all apart. Did you put it back together?" He was sure they must have, given the reports he'd seen since, but he had to be sure.

"Yes, yes," the intern replied. "Why?"

Hiroto smiled. "Because we are right next to the main lab," he said. He turned to his right, stepping carefully, letting each foot glide along until it found secure purchase, one hand out in front of him, the other holding onto Taka's shoulder. After what felt like hours his questing fingers made contact with a solid vertical surface. The hallway wall. Then he felt along it until he found a slight protuberance. The doorframe. From there it was an easy matter to drop his hand to the accustomed level, brush against the doorknob, grasp it, and push the door open. The change in air was noticeable at once—the hallway tasted cloying, dusty, while the air in the lab was still mostly cool and clean. "Follow me," he warned, "and be careful. We don't know what's been knocked over inside."

Step by step Hiroto led the way into the room. He kept his eyes closed, moving by memory since sight was useless. Several times his foot brushed up against something, some sort of obstacle, or his hand encountered some barrier, and he had to work around it. But he kept going, inch by inch, Taka right behind him—until his hand encountered something upright but narrow, with rounded contours and a smooth texture.

The display mannequin.

Hiroto pulled his other hand free from Taka and let both hands roam the model, and his pulse quickened as fingers entwined with a telltale weave of wires and cables. It was tricky working by feel but he had practiced this maneuver enough times for presentations, and so it was with a surprisingly small amount of fumbling that Hiroto managed to remove the FT-1 from its mannequin and don the wearable computer himself.

Once it was on and latched securely, he let the fingers of his right hand caress the controls—and hit the power switch.

"FT-1, operational," the computer's voice declared, and Hiroto almost laughed with relief.

Taka did laugh. "Smart!" he said. "Can it tell us the way out of here?"

"No," Hiroto had to admit. "But it can show us. Computer, displays brightness at full." Obeying his command, the small display screens built into the FT-1's control bracers lit up brighter and brighter, until they were glowing like tiny suns. They cast more than enough illumination for Hiroto to clearly see Taka beside him, the intern dusty and dirty but otherwise apparently intact, and the now-bare mannequin, and their immediate surroundings.

"That is brilliant," the intern breathed, and then he grinned, his teeth gleaming in the light. "Literally."

"It's just an overgrown flashlight," Hiroto argued, some of his elation fading. The FT-1 was still a failure.

But Taka put a hand on his shoulder, and in the reflected light the young man's eyes almost seemed to glow. "No," he said softly. "It is much more than that. It is a little piece of the sun you can carry with you, bearing her light wherever you go."

He smiled, then, the same warm smile he had cast about him so many times over the past two weeks. And for the first time that day, Hiroto felt as if everything might be all right.

With the FT-1's light to guide them, finding their way back out through the rubble and debris proved a simple if slow matter. The main stair had indeed been sealed off by the explosion, which had collapsed much of the main floor on top of them, but between the two of them Hiroto and Taka were able to wrench open the metal fire door at the hall's far end, and the emergency stair behind it proved to be intact. Thus, an hour or so later Hiroto was standing outside his damaged headquarters, explaining the situation to the firefighters who had gathered there. Medics checked him out and declared him largely uninjured, then sent him home. Taka was cleared as well, and waved cheerfully as Hiroto turned to leave, still wearing the FT-1, though he had powered it down for now. Not that it didn't have energy to spare—the tiny, coated solar micro-dots that it ran on could go for days on a single charge.

Hiroto staggered home, and for once he did not have to make excuses to avoid his daughter. His mother had seen about the explosion on the news, and after hugging him tight she had left him alone to wash away the dirt and dust and soot and then collapse into a deep, surprisingly restful sleep.

"You have someone here to see you." His mother's voice through the door was soft, wary, concerned, and something else, something Hiroto hadn't heard in a long time. It took him a few seconds to realize what that something was, as he sat up and shook his head to clear it. Then he remembered. He had heard that same tone the day his daughter was born.

It was awe.

Pulling himself slowly to his feet, wincing from the pain of bruises he'd sustained that had blossomed overnight like subcutaneous flowers, Hiroto grabbed a pair of yoga pants and a T-shirt, pulled them on, then tugged his robe on over them. Then he dragged himself to the door. His mother stood just beyond it, her eyes wide but shining, cheeks ruddy.

"In the sitting room," she told him. "Go. I will bring tea."

Making his way slowly down the hall, Hiroto heard an excited chatter coming from the sitting room. This time his wince was not from the bruises—at least, not the physical ones. He had a lot to make up for, he knew. When the lights had gone out on them last night, some things had become clearer by contrast. He knew he had made many mistakes. And that he had to fix them.

Sliding open the sitting room door, Hiroto was unsurprised to see his daughter there, speaking in her rapid little-girl speak, her face alight with interest. What did astonish him, however, was the visitor to whom she spoke, the tall, lithe but broad-shouldered man who turned his youthful face to regard Hiroto with a bright, piercing gaze from beneath thick, shaggy hair.

It was Taka.

Only—it wasn't. Not exactly. It was still the same intern whose presence had so filled FlexTech these past two weeks, but at the same time there was something different about him. His playfulness was still there, and his curiosity, shining out of his eyes. But, as had happened last night when they'd spoken in the main lab, there was something more beside them. This man's eyes all but glowed with wisdom, and his entire body radiated power, despite the delicacy with which he held Hiroto's daughter's hand. Everything about him shouted majesty, and finally something clicked in Hiroto's head. Now he understood.

He dropped to his knees at once, pressing his head to the floor. "Forgive me," he intoned, his words muffled against the woven mats.

A gentle hand came to rest on his shoulder, and with a nudge Hiroto was encouraged to sit back, to look up. The hand offered itself now, palm up, and Hiroto found himself drawn to his feet as easily as he might lift his daughter. Who still clutched the god's other hand and gazed up at him adoringly with the trust and joyous wonder only a small child could possess.

"There is no need for forgiveness, Hiroto Fumiji," the god informed him, his smile a kinder, quieter version of the exuberant grin "Taka Mikato" had flashed so frequently around the offices. "You have done nothing wrong." His words contained echoes of themselves, a deep booming within them like ocean waves beating upon the shore. Which was only fitting. For Takehaya Susanoo-no-Mikoto was the god of the sea and the storms. He was also the trickster god, the adventurer god, and the younger brother to Amaterasu, the supreme goddess of Japan. Amaterasu, who was the sun.

"Why?" Hiroto asked, wondering at his own boldness, though Susanoo's smile told him it was all right. "You pretended to be a lowly intern. You spent the past two weeks with us. Why?"

"Why?" The god laughed, releasing their hands to spread his arms wide, and in his laughter there was lightning and thunder but also gentle rain and playful surf. "This is a new world, my friend. A world we do not know. My sister was content to sit back and wait, but not I." Some of his wildness returned to his grin, and to his eyes. "That was never my way." Susanoo laid one long finger against his nose and winked down at Hiroto. "I wished to know what this strange new technology was, what it meant, what it might do for us—or to us," he confided. "I chose your company to show me its potential." Now the grin was back full force, and clearly the god was his sister's brother, for his smile contained all the radiance of the noonday sun after a storm, light peeking out from behind fading clouds. "And I am well glad I did!"

Hiroto couldn't help but laugh, though it turned bitter at the end. "You chose a struggling company that ultimately failed to deliver," he pointed out, unable to meet the god's bright gaze any longer. "I can't see how that's a good thing."

"But you did not fail." The sincerity throbbing in those words brought Hiroto's eyes back up, to find Susanoo studying him, his face serious but kind. "Not at all." From within his robes—which only now Hiroto realized were dashing and elegant, the epitome of the rich adventuring prince of a bygone age—the god produced a scroll, which he handed over with a flourish.

Unrolling it, Hiroto read quickly: "This is to declare that Amaterasu-ōmikami, she who shines in the heaven, hereby grants the company Flex-Tech an exclusive privilege to produce shizuku tenpi blessed with her own divine radiance." Glancing up again, he frowned. "I don't understand. The FT-1 doesn't work. And what is a shizuku tenpi? A sun drop?"

"Of course." The god waved his hand. "Your computer does not function completely, it is true. But do you remember what I said to you last night?" Hiroto did: "It is a little piece of the sun you can carry with you," the man he had thought was only an intern had whispered; amazed, "bearing her light wherever you go." And now that made sense.

"The micro-dots," Hiroto said softly.

"The micro-dots," Susanoo agreed. "When the woman Midori told me of them, I did not understand. I had seen batteries at work by then, and thought these little more than a play upon that theme. But that night, when you lit the room, I could feel my sister's presence with us. It was not merely light you gave us, but radiance, illumination. Majesty." He smiled. "When I spoke to my sister, and told her that we had a way for her to touch all her people, to light their way, and to provide us with power for everything we might need . . . she was impressed." His hand settled upon Hiroto's shoulder like a benediction. "As was I."

Hiroto nodded slowly, still processing all this. The micro-dots were one of the few parts of the FT-1 that had worked out exactly as planned. Better, even. There had been lots of research into better solar cell technology the past few years, the two most promising being the idea of solar cells comprised of tiny micro-dots and a technique for coating solar cells with a layer of organic minerals. Hiroto and his staff had figured out a way to combine those two, producing coated micro-dots that offered more than fifty times the power of a normal solar cell in a significantly smaller size and could retain their charge for weeks without loss. He had only ever considered them part of the process to get the FT-1 up and running, so focused on that project and his vow to achieve it, but now Hiroto could see the full ramifications. "Energy independence," he whispered. And especially now, at a time when foreign resources would be even harder to come by—the idea that he could help make Japan self-sufficient was astounding.

"Each of the sun drops will be stamped with her own divine image," Susanoo told him then, and of course Hiroto nodded because what else could he do? "They will be my sister's blessing made manifest, granting all our people light and power without end." He winked at Hiroto. "And you, my friend, have made all that possible."

Hiroto found himself smiling. He had, hadn't he? True, the FT-1 didn't work, but these micro-dots would revolutionize their nation, maybe even the world if Amaterasu decided to share them. And he had done that. He had not fulfilled his promise, not exactly, but perhaps he had not failed entirely after all!

It was as if the god beside him could read his thoughts—which maybe he could—because he nodded now, his shaggy hair flowing about him like a roiling storm cloud. "You did not fail," he affirmed. "Sometimes you need only look around you and see what remains. When you do, you may find that the best things are those you had not previously considered."

The smile the god gave him now was a tender one, a little sad but hopeful. As he turned to the side, and with his other hand presented the little girl beside him.

Hiroto dropped to his knees before her. For a moment all he could do was stare at her, her big dark eyes, her waterfall of silky hair, her little upturned nose. She stared back, and the pain of the resemblance washed over him as it always did, but this time he did not turn away. Instead he allowed himself to accept, and to grieve. She looked so much like Asami, seeing her always reminded him, and that reminder only served to emphasize his loss. But this time, through the pain and the sorrow Hiroto saw joy and hope as well. Yes, her mother was gone, long gone, dead these several years, ever since that fateful accident. But here was his little girl—*her* little girl—and she had her mother's eyes, her mother's face. Here was Asami's last gift to him, the greatest gift she could have offered. Like Amaterasu's sun drops, here was his love's radiance made manifest, her own image for him to cherish and nurture.

He held out his arms.

And watched, breathless, as his daughter's face transformed. Her lips curved up into the biggest smile he had ever seen, her eyes shining like the sun, and she leaped into his embrace. "Oto-san!" she whispered into his shoulder, and that one word brought tears to Hiroto's eyes. Never had he heard anything more wonderful, and as he hugged his little Mitsuko he wondered why it had taken him so long to understand. So much time he had wasted!

Then a hand squeezed his shoulder again, and Hiroto looked up into the kind, wise eyes of his god. "Do not worry about what has passed," Susanoo advised. "Enjoy what there is now, and take delight in what is to come." The words lingered, their echoes filling the room even as the god himself disappeared, blurring like a rain-smeared photo and fading away. Hiroto knew he would be back.

But right now, none of that mattered. Instead he stood, lifting Mitsuko with him, and leaned back to look her in the eye. "The sun is out," he told her softly, smiling as he brushed her hair back from her face. "Let's go outside and play."

She squealed with delight, and together they stepped out into the light.

The Wanderer

by Robert Greenberger

Three Weeks After The Return

Andrin had wanted to drink his beer in peace. Despite the mild August weather, he was feeling the storm clouds that colored the mood of the entire country. It had been nearly a month since the gods returned and people were rushing about in a frenzy, debating where they needed to go to worship. Or was this some cosmic hallucination? Some checked their genealogy for the first time in their lives, trying to determine if they were Norse or Celtic or hung on some other branch of the European family tree. While they were panicking, Andrin was quietly operating his fishing company, a fleet of four boats that brought in herring by the ton and he made a good, honest living.

He was a pure-born Norwegian and therefore knew his allegiance was to the Norse Aesir and if they would let him fish, he'd be happy to switch from novenas to one entity to another. It all didn't really matter that much to him. He just wanted some peace, of which there had been precious little since the Olympics. Around him, people were going on and on about this god or that, how they've lost contact with far-flung family and who just moved away. He'd already lost several of the crew, but just as readily hired new people as the migration churned about him.

"What're you having?" the bartender asked as a stranger took the stool to his right. The Bien Bar was busy but not packed as the sun set and night arrived. A handful were dining but most ringed the bar and the one man on duty was busy enough. The stranger was tall and thin, in a great blue cloak and a dark navy slouch hat that he seemed uncertain what to do with. Finally, he took it off, and nearly white hair fell to his shoulders.

It was then that Andrin noticed the man wore a black eyepatch that stood out against his pale, weathered skin and white beard.

"A beer," he replied in Danish, then paused. "You pick which one." The last phrase was in Norwegian. The accent was good, but he was clearly not a native.

The pint was dark with a golden, foamy head the stranger admired before picking up the mug. He gestured in a friendly manner towards Andrin, who nodded in return.

"Long day?" the man asked, keeping to Norwegian. His voice was smooth but deep.

"Long enough," Andrin replied. Great. A stranger and a talker. Still, he'd be polite enough, maybe get a free pint out of it. The man seemed off somehow and the fisherman studied him closely. He looked old but in remarkably good shape. He was clearly fluent in multiple languages and definitely was not from around here. The eyepatch got him to wondering.

"You're a fisherman." The man stated it as a fact.

At that Andrin cocked an eyebrow.

"You have rough hands and the scent of fish remains. You can never really scrub it away if it's your life," he said.

Andrin nodded at that truth and drank. "You new to town?"

"Just passing through. I've been walking the coast, trying to soak in the atmosphere."

Andrin nodded. "The coast is lovely. You should see it at sunrise. Gorgeous."

"I have at that, and you're right. Have you lived here long?"

"My whole life," Andrin replied, finishing the pint. Sure enough, the man gestured to the bartender to come and refill their glasses.

"This is good. What's it called?" the man asked the bartender.

"Haandbryggeriet Odin's Tipple," came the reply. At that, the man snorted, earning him stares from Andrin and the bartender. To Andrin, the sour look on the man's face was an alert of some kind. He was definitely more than he appeared.

"Odin didn't drink beer," the man said unhappily. "Sometimes ale. Certainly the song-mead, but rarely. His name is being misappropriated."

"You one of those worshippers?"

"Yes," the man said. "Although I seem to be in the minority. Did not the gods want us all to return to our homelands?" Andrin was no fool.

He knew how to read the signs, when the sun would keep the water calm or when the fish were running. This man was far more than he seemed. While his language was fluent, there was a stiffness to it, as if he were unused to talking with people.

"Sure," the bartender said. Andrin nodded in agreement and tipped his refilled glass in gratitude. The man nodded.

"Has Odin been so forgotten that his name is used so carelessly?" A curious question and one that provided a piece to the puzzle that Andrin had been forming in his mind. He grew tense at the possibilities that he was sitting next to a god. *The* god of the Aesir. He gripped his glass tightly and began ordering his thoughts. If he was wrong, he could feel foolish on the way home, but if he was right....

"That's been around since before those gods returned," Andrin said. "It's one of Norway's most popular brews so I doubt they'd change the name now."

"Truly? What if Odin objected?" There was a dark tone to the question that set Andrin on edge. He seemed genuinely offended by the beer's name and certainly seemed to know plenty about the god's personal tastes.

"Let him take on the corporations," Andrin scoffed.

The bartender checked a bottle and reported, "It's made by Haand Bryggeriet, near Oslo. If you're wandering about, you can always pay them a visit."

"Oh?" There was that curiosity about something so obvious. If this was Odin, and the eye-patch sort of confirmed that for Andrin, then he wouldn't understand such basic concepts as modern day commerce. If Odin was here for information, Andrin would be foolish not to try and impart some of his own wisdom. Wisdom for an ale, not a bad exchange. If he recalled, Odin gave up his eye for wisdom; too steep a price for the fisherman.

"Well, as I see it," Andrin said, feeling somewhat emboldened, "the gods left and for the last few thousand years worship has changed. So has power. Now it's in the hands of those with the most money and that's the big businesses. And it's gone global, so I sell my haul to a conglomerate with offices in Norway but is really based in America. The brewer also ships his Odin's ale to America." There, let him chew on that.

The man took a sip, making a face at the beer he previously liked.

The name really made it unpleasant for him. "Does it bother you to dance to so foreign a master?"

"Like I said, I sell to the local guy so America is just a distant concept. The money is good and I make a living." Which was true and he didn't want to jeopardize that. He had no idea how business would run if the gods severed ties between countries. He had a family to provide for and all he knew was how to fish.

"Enough to provide for your family?"

"Yes."

"Wife. Children?"

"A boy, two girls."

"So few?" He sounded sad about that, which caught Andrin by surprise.

"To some, that's too many. I'm out on the water ten hours a day, or working to sell my catch. I have payroll to meet, dock masters to make happy, and unions to worry about. I try and get home to see them for a bit, but there's never enough time. So yeah, three can be too many." Andrin had been racking his brain trying to come up with tidbits he could recall about Odin, but was coming up short. He couldn't shake the first notion was that he looked or spoke nothing like Anthony Hopkins. He tried in vain to come up some memory of how many children Odin is said to have had but kept stopping after Thor and Loki.

"I've seen that most now have two or three," the man said. "And I see how stressed everyone has become. Both parents working. That's not a good thing. It unsettles the mind and soul."

"A philosopher are you," the bartender asked as he wiped the nearby counter. Their conversation was largely ignored by the others around the bar, which might have been for the best. If there was a buzz over the need to relocate, it would have become utter madness had they realized the Allfather was sitting among them. "How many do you have?"

"As you said, 'too many'. Some remain loyal, others are bastards…"

"That's not a nice thing to say about your children," the bartender said in anger, something Andrin had never heard before. There was something charging the air around them so maybe it was best he headed for home.

"Just trying to understand the world," the man said. Sure, if you were to rule Scandinavia and Germany, you need to know how everything fits. Andrin was feeling lightheaded and it was not the beer, not matter how good the poorly named beer tasted.

"Good luck with that," Andrin said. "I don't think it's made sense in a long time."

"Then it's a good thing the gods are back, to restore peace of soul," the man said. "Right?"

"I can't say it's a good thing or not," Andrin admitted with some heat to his voice. "They just announced themselves and expect blind obedience. Go back from where you came, they said, and there's no explanation for where they've been or what they want."

"They want to be worshipped and not see their name blasphemed," the man said, holding up his mug higher as an example. *Ah ha*, Andrin thought.

"Maybe," Andrin said.

"You think otherwise?"

"What I think doesn't really matter. What they do will tell me more than what they say."

The man drank from the glass, savored the taste once more, and put it back down. "You speak wisely. And you suspect they want something else."

"Maybe. It's not like they've said much since they returned. They're focused on cutting off technology or herding people to their ancestral lands. Why doesn't seem to enter into it."

"And removing the technology is a bad thing? I would think it simplifies things."

Andrin had to pick his words carefully. After all, he liked his technology and wanted to find a way to convince the Norse Gods to accept the Internet and cell phones and satellite television. Already he'd been hearing horror stories of how some countries literally went dark overnight. And he was feeling anger seep into his previous comments and the last thing he wanted to do was piss off Odin. "I just think they don't understand it and therefore ban it before trying to comprehend it. We're told we fear the unknown and maybe that applies to the gods too."

The man carefully put down his glass, hand wrapped tight around it. Andrin appeared to have struck a nerve.

"I truly doubt the gods fear anything."

"What about Armageddon or what the Norse say is the end of everything…it's called…"

"Ragnarok," the man said softly.

"Right. That they fear."

"As they should. But I truly doubt they fear electronics."

"I hear they shut it down without question," Andrin said, feeling sure of his position, emboldened by the beer.

There was a dark look in the man's eye. "Has it happened here?"

"No, not yet," Andrin said. "In fact, we haven't heard much from Odin. Or Thor or the others."

"That will change. I have no doubt of that."

I bet you don't. "I hope they learn so they can rule…wisely."

The man studied Andrin's face. There was a glint in his good eye. The charade had run its course and each knew the truth.

"This cutting off of technology. Would that truly harm the world?"

"It certainly reinforces the borders between lands and that's never a good thing."

"How so?"

"People look over the border and see something they want and if they can't easily get it, they try to take it and then it's a war."

"Is war so bad?"

Andrin studied the man, measuring his words carefully but letting some of his emotions come through. "For those who suffer. For those who mourn their lost ones. If the gods want to fight one another, they should not wipe out their worshippers in the process."

"An interesting point," the man said, still not coming out and admitting his identity.

Andrin had finished the beer and put the empty glass on the bar. There was more he wanted to tell Odin, more he needed to say on behalf of his wife and his friends. But he really didn't have the words. He was a fisherman who didn't want his way of life upended. "I have to be getting home. I want to catch the children before they go to sleep."

The man thrust out his hand.

"You speak well, Andrin. And your words have not fallen on deaf ears. A good night to you."

They shook and Andrin left the bar, just as a fight was breaking out in the back. He refused to look back, glad to be gone from that place. With every step, he felt lighter, the dark gloom that cast a pall over the conversation was lifting. He had traveled a block, replaying the conversation in his mind when it occurred to him, he never gave the man his name but he knew it nonetheless. Stifling a shiver that ran from head to toe, he hurried home.

Five Weeks After The Return

Gerd was completing a phone call when she saw movement from her peripheral vision. Since she was alone with her son Svein at the playground, she cast a quick glance in his direction to make sure he remained safe. The five year old was climbing up a ramp, nattering on to himself as was his wont. Once more she looked towards the object emerging from the forest at the edge of the Mt. Fløyen. She didn't hear the Fløibanen cable car that brought people to the top of the mountain so this was one hardy hiker.

The tall, thin figure, in deep blue robes and tall, pointed hat came into view from the forest and she noted he used a walking stick to balance on. She was impressed that someone clearly a senior was making the journey to the top by foot. Still, his presence sent the hairs on the back of her neck up and she suddenly felt an urge to gather up her son and their things. She willed herself to remain still since he was not presenting any danger.

Still, she couldn't shake the feeling that he was something else.

To avoid the gnawing sensations rising from the pit of her stomach, she scrolled through messages on her phone, focusing on that with all her will. Her ears, though, remained on the alert and she heard his footsteps atop rock and crusted snow.

"Good afternoon," he said in a voice that betrayed no threat. In fact, he sounded stronger and younger than she imagined. Gazing his way and nodding in greeting, she studied him. Tall, easily two meters, but very thin, with a long, white beard and the slouch hat covered his eyes. He didn't appear to be wearing gloves and the chill seemed to have no effect on him. For a brief moment, she was reminded of Father Christmas and her inner alarms instantly silenced.

He took a bench near her own and sat, resting. His head swiveled about, taking in the beauty of their surroundings.

"This is lovely," he said at last.

Looking up from her phone, Gerd said, "It is. Did you read the sign at the bottom? This was designed by Ketil Dybvik."

"I don't know that name," he said.

"I didn't either until I read up on him. He's quite the artist and this playground is one of his best known works."

"An artist designs play areas," the man repeated. "Interesting."

Gerd once more glanced at Svein, now clambering over notched logs and returned to studying her phone.

"What is your boy doing?"

She studied him for a moment and replied, "When he's on the logs he's either walking the plank, about to turn on the pirates, or tightrope walking between two tall buildings, practicing his balance."

"He's a brave one, then. Good." The man watched the boy at play, still and silent, as if he had become a stone statue. Gerd mentally shrugged and replied to a text from her husband.

The two sat in silence, each taking in the cool air and the sun, which was beginning its descent ever so slowly. Gerd continued to catch up on personal email, checking on Facebook, and ignored the man. He, in turn, studied his surroundings, seemingly communing with nature.

"Where is everyone," he finally asked.

"Pardon?"

"This forest, atop this mountain. It's magnificent. More people should be here to play and pray. Why are we the only ones here?"

"It's a school day," Gerd said. "They're just getting out so some may be up later. Svein had a doctor's appointment so we made it a day off."

"You bring this boy here and then ignore him?"

The disapproving tone hurt. She wasn't ignoring her son. In fact, she took a day off from work too, ensuring he got the first appointment with the doctor to check on his asthma. As usual, there was a wait, then the examination, and the consultation. He was fine, for now, and would stay that way with the help of an inhaler. She decided to make a treat of things so they went out for a late, fat breakfast before doing some shopping and coming up here for the afternoon. Svein loved the view and the cable ride even if the thinner air bothered him now and then. It didn't stop him and she tried not to be an over-protective parent. She wanted to give him his freedom and now this stranger was accusing her without cause. There was definitely something about him; since he sat down, the air suddenly felt heavier. She scanned the clear blue skies for storm clouds, seeking a source.

"I'm not ignoring him, I am letting him play."

"A parent's bond with a child is a sacred one. You should not be focused more on that device than on him." Clearly, he didn't approve of her phone, but then again, many seniors didn't like modern technology, usually because they struggled with mastering it. Her father certainly did and harrumphed every time Svein, at five, demonstrated some feature that baffled the retired man.

"Are you a parent?"

He nodded. "Many times over."

"Did you always bond so closely with each of them?"

The man hesitated, mulling over the question and she hoped it stung him in the same way. Finally, he said, "With some, yes. I was less...successful with the others."

"Too busy with work?"

"You could say that."

"I try and find a balance, but it's not easy with him and his two sisters."

"And where are they?"

"At school. My husband will collect them soon and we'll meet up for dinner." She felt defensive which tended to make her argumentative. Why did she feel hostility from the man? Was she divulging too much information? He seemed amiable enough but her inner senses continued to shriek a subtle warning and she couldn't figure out why. She decided she would have to be more forceful.

"You both work?"

"What family doesn't have both parents at work? The economy is tough and gotten tougher since the gods returned."

"Oh?" The one word, the tone, everything about it set her on edge.

Still, this was safe territory to discuss, far less personal so she decided to extend this stretch. "At first, people panicked and didn't come in so that backed things up. There was a market panic as well, it was in the news." Damn, there was condescension in her tone.

"I was preoccupied and only caught the highlights," the man acknowledged.

"I just hope you're well invested and spread out your accounts," she said, trying to sound friendly.

"I have much invested in gold," he said. "You understand finance?"

"I'm a market analyst in the utilities field," she said. "Anyway, once the gods set up shop in their homelands, people began relocating so the job market was thrown upside down. We lost a lot of people who suddenly felt they had to move."

"As they should if that is what the gods want, who are we to argue?"

"You make it sound so simple," she argued. He gazed at her and for the first time noticed he had only one eye, and it had a piercing gaze.

"Is it not?"

Again, she was feeling hostile and feisty which was not her nature. "You know, there are so many mixed heritages today, people have been uncertain where to go. An Italian/Greek would go where to worship? I was just reading how Eva Longoria is related to Yo Yo Ma; she's Mexican and he's Chinese. How's that going to work out? There's no clearing house, no god to make these determinations."

With two hands now wrapped around his walking stick, the man stared ahead, deep in thought. After a while, she thought he was annoyed or something but finally he turned her way and said, "I don't think the gods had any idea how much inter-breeding there had been."

Gerd nodded in agreement. "Atop that, you have some gods turning off the Internet, others turning it on and off, and still more exploiting it. It's hard to conduct global commerce when you don't know, day to day, which countries you can communicate with."

"And you can do that from your...phone?"

How old was he? She started to speak and forced herself to modulate her tone. "Sure. It's got a terrific data plan and the signal remains strong until someone in Asgard decides to shut us down, too."

"I've been hiking the country and I've noticed how few people are stopping to enjoy this view. Or gaze out at the water. Or watch a sunset. Instead, indoors and out, they seem fixated on their phones."

"Let me guess, you have a rotary cell phone," she cracked.

He stared back at her, clearly not getting the joke.

"Never mind. Lots of seniors remain off the grid," she said. "Yeah, we like our phones and have grown accustomed to accessing information or each other all day and night."

"Does that not distract you from your other responsibilities, such as playing with your boy?"

"Svein's playing and doesn't want me interfering with his stories. He knows exactly what's going to happen and if I try to participate he gets grumpy. And I am keeping watch. When I don't have to watch his every move, I am also trying to keep up on the news, the shifting fortunes of the companies I track. People still need electricity...so far."

"You fear the gods?"

"I fear they will want us to return to the way things were a thousand years ago," she said, truly fearing this.

"Or more."

"Or more," she agreed. For the life of her, she couldn't remember when the Norse gods vanished. It was after the Greek and Romans, she knew, but mythology wasn't emphasized in school these days. Of course, that was about to change. Maybe she should invest in some university press.

Svein was clambering up a ladder, giggling, the sound echoing among the trees.

"I wonder: have people grown so accustomed to comfort and instant gratification that they have forgotten to work hard for things that matter like heat and food?" What an odd question, she thought.

"We still work hard, just for different things. The world's changed a lot, don't you think, and the gods can't expect it all to be the way it was."

She paused, realizing how many colleagues had left her office and how many acquaintances had gone silent.

"Can they?"

"That is to be determined," he said. "They've just returned and there are still ebbs and flows to their worshippers and their whims. Change is always hard, especially a change of this magnitude."

He rose, using the walking stick for support.

"I know this: not all change is for the worse. Worrying more about our families and friends who are close by is not a bad thing. Less impersonal interaction may actually be a blessing."

Gerd studied him for a bit. She still felt the internal alarms and tension in the air but if he was leaving, no harm had come to her or Svein. What was troubling her so?

He nodded once more towards her and then turned his back and headed in the opposite direction of his initial approach, clearly heading deeper into the forest.

Svein continued to play so she pulled out her cell phone once more and noticed its battery had gone dark. It was powerless.

A part of her felt she had failed the old man in some way but it was a diffuse feeling, and one she couldn't articulate in a text message or a dinner conversation as she learned in the following hours.

Eleven Weeks After The Return

The train left the station and was picking up speed when the man entered the car and sat beside Astrid. Since the train was crowded, she didn't think twice about it, giving him the briefest of looks as he put his walking stick in the overhead and settled into the cushioned seat beside her.

When he turned to look past her out the window, she noticed he was handsome, despite missing an eye. He had a neatly trimmed brown beard but somewhat shaggy hair. The man was actually rather striking even if he was at least a decade older than she was. Astrid had dated older men before so that wasn't a barrier; but this man, seated as he was, radiated something special. She felt instantly drawn to him, which was unusual as she normally took time warming up to men. This would either turn out to be a fun train ride or an excruciating one.

He seemed to just look out their window as the city faded behind them, then at the countryside. Periodically, he would turn look through the window on the other side of the aisle. Since he was ignoring her, she concentrated on her tablet and the book she was reading. This was her time and she cherished it, shoving thoughts of the man's presence from her mind. Or trying to.

About thirty minutes after leaving Myrdal, he finally seemed satisfied and leaned back in his seat, staring ahead.

His silence was growing vexing since she inexplicably wanted to talk to him. If he wasn't going to speak, then she would have to go first, especially with the fifty minute trip rapidly drawing to its close. "It's a wonderful morning to be on the Flåmsbana," she said.

He turned and his cool blue eye seemed to bore deep into hers. His smile broke the odd sensation and the smooth, mellow voice replied, "A glorious day, I would think, although it is well past midday already."

Midday? Who said midday anymore?

"I'm Astrid," she said and offered her hand.

"Bölverk," he said and the warmth of his hand was pleasant. She couldn't believe how magnetically drawn she was to him and all he did was sit there.

"What brings you to the valley?"

"Me? I wanted to walk where the brochures said we could experience 'historical traditions reaching back to pre-Christian times'. That interests me greatly. What about you, Astrid?"

Hearing him say her name was electrifying. She cursed herself while also thrilling at the encounter.

"I'm a photographer and want to shoot the sheep at Flåm Valley. There's about one hundred and fifty of them so I am hoping to get some interesting configurations." And sell them to printers for post cards and calendars to cover the next month's rent, but that was too much information to share this early. She mentally shook her head, how could she be thinking of a shared future already? Astrid did not recognize herself.

He nodded without seeming to fully understand what she was saying, which normally would have bothered her. Instead, she liked the notion of playing teacher. She spent the remainder of their ride until they arrived at Kårdal explaining about her training and work as a wedding photographer but her real passion was in other types of free expression. She omitted the rush of cancellations as the return of the gods threw more than a few weddings off the rails as some couples split over where to relocate for worship. While she liked snapping the sheep, she really needed the cash. Bölverk listened in silence, asking few questions, and he kept his gaze riveted on her. The attention was welcome although she felt nervous, as if she were back in grade school and she mentally chided herself for that.

It had been a while, though, since any male paid this much attention to her and that helped her spirits and encouraged her to keep nattering on, even as they began strolling the mountain pastures. The sun was warm against her skin, which was already feeling hot to being with. This was proving to be a most unusual day; first the unseasonable weather and then this bewitching man. With two different cameras slung around her neck, she switched from one to the other, grabbing shots of the gorgeous location and the sheep milling about. She wanted to take some with Bölverk in them, but he always seemed to vanish from the viewfinder just as she pressed the shutter. She made due, though, with other tourists petting or making faces with the placid flock. Their bleating sounds filled the crisp air and made her smile.

Bölverk strolled about, soaking up the scenery rather than pay attention to the sheep. She did note that two large, black birds, crows maybe, flew nearby which was uncharacteristic. They landed on the meadow near Bölverk and he knelt down to study them, the first living things that seemed to capture his attention. He remained low for a while, almost as if the three were communicating but all she heard were the sheep.

Once the birds flew off, Bölverk resumed wandering but his shoulders were hunched, his gait slower. Something seemed to be troubling him.

With a shrug, she hurried through more shots before they had to reboard the train. Every now and then, she looked for him and saw him walking which was good. But she also could hear a number of arguments breaking out, shattering the pristine feel to the place. Maybe there was not enough time for some of these tourists.

Reboarding the train, she noted that people seemed edgy and agitated. There was even one scuffle over the seating. They settled back in their seats and talked about the pastures, the birch trees surrounding the area and the sheep. They spoke easily but she realized that she was revealing far more about herself than he was.

Soon after, the train stopped at Kjosfossen, with its magnificent waterfall. The pair stepped from the train and admired the high up mountain, watching the water rush off the side and come crashing below. Bölverk smiled at the sight and, feeling inspired, she snapped off several pictures.

"Have you seen this before?"

"Yes, but a long time ago," he answered. "It sounds like a battle, the kind when men fought one another up close. Today it's all so remote and impersonal."

"You sound like you are a war hawk."

"My dear, there is always a time for battle but also a time for peace. I am equally comfortable with both," he said. Then he slipped his hand into hers and there was an electric thrill that ran through her.

"Which do you prefer?" she asked, unwilling to give him a chance to break contact.

"It depends upon the circumstances," he said. "When challenged or threatened, obviously, I am ready for a fight. But, when I stand amidst nature with a beautiful woman, I am apt to recite poetry not do battle."

A poet? He's too good to be true, she thought.

They fell into silence but suddenly he began to recite a poem, an old one from the sounds of it.

Wealth is a source of discord among kinsmen;
the wolf lives in the forest.

Dross comes from bad iron;
the reindeer often races over the frozen snow.

Giant causes anguish to women;
misfortune makes few men cheerful.

Estuary is the way of most journeys;
but a scabbard is of swords.

Riding is said to be the hardest for horses;
Reginn forged the finest sword.

Ulcer is fatal to children;
death makes a corpse pale.

Hail is the coldest of grain;
Christ created the world of old.

Need gives scant choice;
a naked man is chilled by the frost.

Ice we call the broad bridge;
the blind man must be led.

Harvest is a boon to men;
I say that Froði was generous.

Sun is the light of the world;
I bow to the divine decree.

Týr is a one-handed God;
often has the smith to blow.

Birch has the greenest leaves of any shrub;
Loki was fortunate in his deceit.

Man is an augmentation of the dust;
great is the talon-span of the hawk.

Waterfall is a River falling from a mountain;
but ornaments are of gold.

Yew is the greenest of trees in winter;
it is wont to crackle when it burns.

"What is that?"

"You would call it a Norwegian Rune Poem," Bölverk said. "It's very old."

"You mentioned, Týr," Astrid said. "He was one of the Asgardians who returned."

"Indeed he was," the man said. "I hear he was dispatched to bring the true born back to their native lands. Last I heard, he was in America."

"Have you seen the gods?"

"I have. And you?"

"Just reports on television. What do they look like?"

"Men and women, larger than life and filled with energy and purpose," he replied.

"Thankfully, we still have that and the Internet to follow them, unlike so many other countries," she said.

"You value the technology that much?"

"I have friends I can't contact," she said. "And we're not getting the full sense of what is happening around the world. I never realized how much I miss the news."

Bölverk seemed thoughtful and turned to her, still holding her hand. "Tell me, is it that important to know about the doings in faraway lands? The gods asked people to come home to worship them, what difference does it make what Americans or Japanese do?"

Astrid glanced up at him, seeing the inquisitive nature in his good eye and the serious look on his attractive features. He was being genuinely serious about this, regardless of how ridiculous the question sounded. Before she could answer, though, they were called back to the train for the last stop.

Walking back, still hand in hand, she replied with a question of her own. "Are you an isolationist?"

Now it was his turn to look at her, studying her features.

"The global economy appears to have caused many, many problems. Maybe keeping to ourselves would be for the best."

"Every country's economy is dependent on trade. I love my coffee every morning and we don't grow it. My favorite fruits come from Spain. I would miss those terribly if all we had to dine on was fish and game."

"Food does not interest me as much as it does you, but I understand your point," he admitted.

Once more they headed for the train and Astrid couldn't help but notice the people pushing and shoving, the occasional argument breaking out and the weird tension to the air, In fact, everyone seemed out of sorts except her and the alluring companion. He radiated charm, made her feel all squishy inside, which seemed to intensify as they drew nearer, making each leg of the train ride all the more powerful.

They resumed their seats and they continued to discuss the pluses and minuses of international relations. She increasingly realized that he was taking a hard, isolationist stand, as if trying on a new coat. He was testing it and seeing how often she could poke holes in the argument. She hadn't had this sort of intellectual debate since she was at university nearly a decade ago. It was stimulating and showed depths beyond his good looks.

She knew if he asked, she'd sleep with him. From the moment he touched her, there was a sexual desire growing within her she had never felt previously. He did nothing untoward or salacious, but she was melting.

Finally, the train pulled past Reinungvatnet, the lovely mountain lake near the Vatnahalsen Hotel. She gazed at it and mentioned its world-renowned reputation, "something we wouldn't know if we stuck to our borders and kept to ourselves."

He leaned closed and whispered in her ear, "Sometimes, sticking to ourselves can be most desirable."

She turned her head and impulsively, hungrily kissed him. The passion she had been feeling rise within her had cracked through her resolve. Astrid's tongue darted into his open mouth, meeting his. Their hands wrapped around one another and the kiss lingered as their bodies grew closer.

It wasn't long before they broke contact and Bölverk suggested that when they reached their destination, they get a car and drive up to the hotel. Astrid agreed without thinking.

A week after that one day magical encounter, Astrid opened her front door and found a small, ornately carved wooden box. Within it was a small heap of golden coins, the likes of which she had never seen before. She hoped it was from *him*; regardless, it would more than pay her debts and keep her flush until things sorted themselves out.

Fourteen Weeks After The Return

The normally boisterous pub was even louder and more crowded than usual. That made sense to Carl since he and his friends were among the many laid off when Falbygdens Ost had cut their staff by a third earlier in the day. Pissed off as he was, it made sense given the dramatic drop in demand for their cheese. The entire second shift was sent home with meager checks, a half-hearted apology from the owners and a case of cheese. Most dropped the cases in the garbage between the factory and the nearest pubs. Finding other work was going to be difficult given the small size of Falköping. As a result, there was despair in their slurred voices.

Carl, on his third pint, could name just about everyone in the bar, except maybe the old geezer in the stupid hat, sitting in a corner. Most were drinking and bitching, complaining about the same thing: the money won't go far, there would be bills to pay, and children to feed. Their wives will wail the loudest and berate them endlessly, which is why most everyone from the shift had crowded into the pub. Misery most certainly loved company that day.

"No one's getting any tonight," Gottfrid said, gesturing for a refill.

"I'd take a pity fuck," Carl responded. Of course, it had been a while but that was entirely beside the point. But now that his friend had mentioned it, he wouldn't mind some physical comfort beyond the buzz from the beer.

"You'd take any kind of lay," the bartender said as the pint was placed beside Gottfrid.

That turned the conversation from their miserable lot in life to their second favorite topic, women. There were the rude and derisive comments usually reserved for the less attractive female members of the second shift, including Maria, the shift supervisor who somehow managed to keep her position.

"That bitch is probably blowing the owner," he said. "Only way that incompetent woman could keep her job."

"So, you blow the owner and keep your job," Gottfrid said.

"I hear he's not as good at giving as he is at receiving," Johann, one of the line workers, jibed from the other side of the bar.

"And I've heard otherwise," Kirsten said. She was one of the attractive ones, tall, with long blonde hair usually nicely piled atop her head. Yeah, Carl wouldn't mind giving it to her. He elbowed Johann, making him spill some of the beer, and moved closer to the woman, who was speaking with Clara, an almost-equally attractive friend. They once had an overly long kiss under the mistletoe at one of the holiday parties a year or two back. She'd do nicely. They could both use a pity fuck.

While he moved towards them, Gottfrid and Kettil, his other close buddy, began some argument with Johann, which he couldn't follow. Gottfrid was squat, dark-haired, and was in his usual black sweater while Kettil had shaggy hair and was wearing the red and black striped jersey used by the Falköpings Fotbollklubb. In fact, Carl noticed, there were a lot of arguments beginning to break out. No doubt the anger and the beer helped.

"Ladies," he said as he settled onto the stool next to the women. They nodded but more or less ignored him, which he found rude.

"Buy you a round?" he asked, figuring that would loosen them up.

"Thanks, Carl," Kirsten said. She gestured with two fingers to the bartender and he grabbed fresh glasses.

The three chatted amiably enough, but Carl was not picking up a vibe from either woman that they were possibly interested in finding other ways to deal with their unemployed status. With each passing minute, he was getting more frustrated and angry with them.

His next biting comment was toward them was halted when he heard a shout. Sure enough, the first fight of the night had broken out.

In rapid fashion, the two men brawling turned exponentially into more men punching, kicking and even biting. Glass cracked, tables splintered and the bartender was on the phone to the police. Carl barely noticed that the old guy remained rooted to the corner, an observer and not yet a participant. There was something about him, but Carl was distracted when Kettil went flying by him. Ignoring the women—he'd get back to them later—he turned his full attention to coming to the aid of his friend.

It felt good to hit someone, Carl thought, as his beefy fist landed in a man's gut. This was someone he had worked with the last seven years, but right now, he was a convenient target for his rising anger. As the man crumpled, Carl grabbed Kettil and helped the gentle soul to his feet and they went towards the door, Gottfrid, his nose bleeding, right behind them.

The sun was long gone when the three men burst from the pub. They were angry and scared and uncertain what to do next. It was cold but none of them dared go back into the fight, especially with police sirens now audible in the distance. "I'm going to lose my car," Carl said, not for the first time. He was already a payment behind and the severance check was needed more for rent and food than the Volkswagen.

"You can't blame them, though," Kettil said. "No orders, no work."

Basic economic principals."

"Fuck the principals," Carl said. "I need a job!"

"We all do, Carl," Gottfrid said, staunching the blood with his sleeve. "And we're not going to find any in this shithole."

"*Det vet du,*" Kettil said agreeably. His get along nature had become increasingly irritating to Carl throughout the night. Carl was now very drink and very angry; he had been drinking through dinner, avoiding going home to face a worried wife, infant son, and a pile of bills. Simple as his life was, he had been spiraling for some time and this was going to send him right down the drain. The helplessness of it fueled the anger, aided by the beer.

"I need money. I need food. Most of all, I need someone to fuck."

"Don't look at me," Gottfrid said, hands held palms up. "What's wrong with your *wife?*"

"Wouldn't fuck you up the *arsle* if you paid me," Carl snared, ignoring the question. He then looked across the street and spotted the two women passing under a street lamp, hurrying away from the fight. He bought them two rounds and didn't even get any tongue for his efforts. "Bet Kirsten has a warm *muda.*"

"I wouldn't," Kettil began.

"I would," Carl said. "It's been too long." He started across the street, towards the oblivious women, both focused on a cellphone message. The other men followed silently, and Carl ignored them. He was drunk enough not to be thinking clearly and was letting his desires dictate his actions. And right now he desired to control his situation, live a little and the women, to his mind, were in the right place at the right time.

"Carl, don't," the fat man said. His voice carried and alerted the women, who looked up, smiling at first at seeing Carl, then their eyes widening with horror as they saw the expression on his face. Carl continued to stalk them and they hurried their pace, breaking into a run. So did he.

To an observer it had to be a comical sight, two women fleeing from a drunken lout followed by two other drunks. Their voices overlapped and could be heard for blocks given the late hour and quiet streets. Any hope of police interference was negligible so Carl felt emboldened. They were young and attractive and available. Willing was entirely beside the point right now.

Clara shrieked as he neared them, reaching with his ungloved hands. His left hand grabbed the blonde's scarf and she continued to run and shout. She lost a shoe and continued to move, now off kilter. All five rounded a corner as Kettil and Gottfrid came close to subduing their friend but Carl didn't want to be stopped. Not when he was this close.

He pushed himself and gained ground on the women, reaching once more, grabbing the red fabric of the brunette's coat. Kirsten shouted and stumbled, taking Clara down with her. They were suddenly a jumble of arms and legs, ready for the taking.

"One at a time," he said, breathing hard from the exertion. His frosted breath floated into the night air.

"Please...don't..." Kirsten cried.

"Please don't," came a new voice.

Carl paused to see who was speaking. Coming out of the shadows was the old man, the silly looking pointed hat and a large brim drooping in front of his face. He was using a walking stick of gnarled wood and wore black gloves. Carl judged him to be in his sixties and no real threat.

"Leave us be, *bögjävel*," Carl snarled.

"Is this how you act with women?" The man sounded incredulous but his tone also carried.

"What the fuck do you care? Get out of here!"

"And leave you to harm the women? I think not. Women are for loving and caressing, not attacking. You lose your jobs and all you can do is fight and brawl? Have you learned nothing?"

"I said: get out of here!" Carl shouted.

"Carl, let's just go," Kettil said.

"No, this guy thinks he can stop me," Carl said.

"Actually, I know I can."

As Carl began to reply, the staff swung up, striking his chin and knocking him back with enough force to send him to the sidewalk. Carl yelped and tried to get back on his feet but the tip of the walking stick was now pressing against his throat.

"Is this what the gods teach you? How to drink to excess?"

"The gods teach me shit," Carl said.

"Do you not worship the Aesir?"

"The fuck are the Aesir?"

"The Norse gods, you witless youth," the man said, a tinge of anger entering his voice.

"He doesn't worship anything," Gottfrid said, keeping his distance.

The two men were off to the man's left and the two women were finally getting to their feet. They were silent but their expressions indicated how frightened they were.

"A pity. A little worship might help his sorry lot in life. Why do you drink so much?"

Carl was rubbing a hand across his throat, which now was painful to the touch. "Lost my job. Got one?"

"Is that how you go about seeking employment? Drinking too much and attacking women? No wonder you're no longer working. You're a disgrace. Should you bother attending worship, you might find the guidance you so sorely need."

"A little divine intervention as it were," Kettil offered.

Carl sneered at him. "This old man knows nothing! He's just one of their faithful, bowing and scraping, hoping for Nirvana."

"It's Valhalla, actually," Kettil said.

"At least one of you is paying attention," the man said. "I am troubled by how few of the young attend. That is sure to anger the gods soon."

"Why would that be?" Gottfrid asked.

"The gods want one and all to worship them. They want everyone to embrace The Return and live a more pious life. You would all benefit from a little devotion. It might even help you find meaningful work."

"Paying work, old man? I have a wife and children," Carl said. He really, really didn't want to debate the stranger, but he was more fearful of being hit with the stick again.

He paused and bowed before the women, who remained, watching the exchange.

"Ladies, I apologize on behalf of this sot. Be free to depart."

Instead of running, they lingered so the man turned his attention to Carl who had felt the anger ebb from his body. The adrenaline rush flushed some of the drunken buzz from his system and all he was left with was anxiety and a sick stomach.

"Seriously, will a pious life get me a job?"

The man looked down at him and finally removed the stick from his throat. Carl rubbed it furiously, creating a soft burn at the point of impact.

"Try it and find out. All of you are missing the point. You have been called to worship and yet you worry more about your technology, your commerce, and yourselves, rather than the gods who are back to watch once more over their children. Your lives are adrift, aimless."

"And in exchange for all the bowing and scraping, what do we get, eh?" Gottfrid challenged.

"You get a life; a simpler, less complicated one, leaving you more time for one another and for the gods. It's not a bad tradeoff is it? Are the gods asking too much of man?"

Kettil began an answer when Carl finally rose unsteadily to his feet. He spat before the old man.

"That's my worship. You can worship them for all I care, but I have bigger worries today than making the gods happy. Fuck them. I'll make my own way."

The old man stood still, but Carl sensed his anger. He was clearly trying to control himself, which was good since that stick gave him a decided advantage. Kettil and Gottfrid stood at his sides, holding him steady. The two women continued to stand in place. There was utter silence for a long stretch until finally the old man turned away from them.

"Enough with you all! I've had my fill with selfishness and lack of self-control. Beat yourselves silly. I'm done tonight."

He continued back the way he came, moving further into the darkened street, his wooden stick making a rhythmic tattoo on the concrete sidewalk.

The three men watched him fade into the distance with Carl feeling both sick and utterly lost.

Seventeen Weeks After The Return

The last of the cars left the parking lot, leaving Rebeckah alone. It was a cold, gray day and she couldn't keep warm, even in the church. There was a pervasive sadness that engulfed everyone and while she could normally move on, today the mourning lingered. She knew two of the men and four of the children personally, had baptized two of them.

Rebeckah was still trying to make sense out of the senselessness, trying to comprehend how a minor fender bender turned into a riot. The police arrested a dozen people and many others had been hurt and hospitalized. And then there were the fatalities. A child crushed under the rioters, a man pushed through a plate glass window.

She was repeatedly asked why and she tried to explain life's great mysteries as best she could, but today even she was taxed to make it sound reasonable. It was time to go inside, shrug this off, and prepare for the morning's mass. Rebeckah had seen her flock dwindle in the months since the gods had returned. As with every other religious institution, the gods of myth made flesh rattled their beliefs and caused many to question their faith.

As she neared the church, she spotted an old man linger over the gray stone. Etched deep into the marker were runes and symbols, a stone that once rested at Helenelund and now greeted people when they arrived at Kummelby kyrka for worship.

Rebeckah never questioned her faith in God and continued to hold mass every Sunday although if people continue to abandon the church, she might have to reduce the number of masses to concentrate the parishioners, letting them draw strength from one another. As a result, seeing this stranger gladdened her heart for she wanted those who still had faith to feel welcome.

"Good afternoon," she said, extended a gloved towards the man. At first, he did not move but finally turned to his left, studied the hand and met it with a firm grip.

"Good morning," he returned, his voice oddly accented. He appeared to be in his sixties, thin and frail perhaps, but in good health.

"Were you here for the funeral?" She hadn't recognized him, but there was a huge crowd of mourners and she couldn't place more than a few people.

The question seemed to stump him and the man's gaze shot past her and he seemed to be wrestling with an answer. "What faith do you worship here?"

"Kummelby kyrka is a part of the Church of Sweden," she replied cautiously. Given how predominant the Church was, the basic question surprised her. With the accent, which she still couldn't place, she was uncertain where he hailed from.

"And you are Catholic?"

"Christian, actually. We are part of the Lutheran faith."

"You worship the one God, then. Not the Norse?"

She gestured toward him and said, "Let's walk, you and I. I see you as a man with many questions."

"True," he said with a surprisingly warm chuckle. "I have always devoured knowledge and that will never change."

"The return of the Norse is surprising," she said agreeably, leading him from the rune stone across the well-maintained lawn before the church itself. While a crisp morning, she liked taking a stroll to collect her thoughts before services began and welcomed the company. "I will admit to being taken aback by their presence but clearly they are not like you and I."

"Well, maybe not you," he said with a smile.

The comment made her laugh.

"One by one, the various pantheons of gods faded away and God remained and flourished," she said.

"But, I am given to understand that while here you worship God, there are those in Jerusalem who worship a different version of your God. And on the other continents, the people worship Buddha or other deities. In fact, you seem splintered over who to worship."

"I like to think of them as aspects of the one true Lord."

"A nice idea, but how do you reconcile that? And how do you explain the return of Zeus, Ukko, Teshup, and Hubak?"

"If I knew who they were, I might have a guess. Instead, I cannot explain them."

"Can your Pope?"

"The Church of Sweden is not aligned with the Vatican," she said. Odd he didn't know that. Is he facing mortality and just beginning to assess religion? It certainly wasn't unheard of for seniors to rediscover their faith.

"Huh," he muttered. "I am given to understand there are over nineteen major religions currently being practiced around the world. You are a Christian faith but there are over 34,000 separate Christian groups so which is the right one?"

She stared at him wide-eyed. "So many?"

"I've been doing a little studying on my travels," the man said.

"Where are you from?"

"I've been traveling and have decided to settle here, so am just trying to get acclimated to the country. A funeral you say?"

"Yes, for six people. They all died during the riot. Were you in town during that? What a horrible way to make a first impression."

"I've been this way before, but not for a long time," the man said. "And yes, I was present to see the madness. I could not believe how many people were just milling about, shopping and dining, and using their phones rather than engage with one another."

"We call that Saturdays," she said with a smile.

"I am not impressed. People have too much time to waste on frivolities," he said, contempt in his voice.

"As to your question, our Church would be classified as Lutheran, a form of Christianity based on the teachings of Martin Luther, from several hundred years ago."

"A young faith, then," the man said.

"Not as young as some, certainly older than many," she replied.

"A diplomatic answer," he said with approval.

"One learns to speak carefully in my role."

"Which is what here?"

"I am the priest assigned to this church," Rebeckah said.

The man studied her and she noticed for the first time that his broad-brimmed gray hat obscured the fact that he was missing an eye.

"A woman priest? Is that truly allowed?"

She grimaced at his expression, thinking such attitudes had gone with the previous generation. "It is in our Church. Has been for several decades, in fact. That's just one more way we differ from Pope Boniface."

"And how will you differ from the Norse? From Odin?"

Rebeckah wanted to begin speaking but bit her tongue and considered the answer. She had yet to truly delve into the pagan practices of the Norse, but knew that time had drawn near. If this man is asking, others will, too.

Just how did the Norse believers practice? She imagined ritual sacrifices of game and she knew them to be warriors but hoped their worship did not involve violence. They'd been back and walking among her flock for months now and she had not taken the time to study the,. Was she afraid they were real? Or something else?

"I honestly don't know. Let me tell you a little bit about our faith for starters. We follow the Bible, both Old and New Testaments. The words inscribed there guide our doctrine and practice. The Scriptures tell us how to behave, what needs to be done. Our Church is considered fairly liberal because we do not necessarily believe each word in the books is literal. Rather the unquestioned word of God, we use the Scriptures for guidance. How to behave toward one another, how to live a good life. We recognize they were written in less enlightened times."

"Admirable," the man replied, genuinely interested. "Most religious folk always strike me as overzealous, too protective of the Holy Words without really understanding who wrote them and for what reason."

"I really didn't know there were so many splinter religions, so many major ones, too. Each will struggle with the pantheons, which are numerous, too."

"And more are trying to establish a toehold, gain legitimacy. Your Shiites and Muslims fight for religious supremacy, wait until we see the pantheons vie for true supremacy."

"You make it sound like they all intend to cause a war," she said, now worried.

"I think each will be focused on gathering their people, their worshippers and consolidating their power. Maybe some border skirmishes, but all-out warfare? Someday, but not any time soon."

"You have some inside information?" She continued to walk, rather than let the cold creep through her coat. The movement would be good for her.

"As I said, I've been doing some studying and traveling. This is my impression"

"I really don't know much about the Norse but I can guess they will want to be worshipped. They summoned everyone home like the other beings…"

"Gods," he interrupted.

"As you will. I remain uncertain what they truly are and how they fit in the cosmos. I suppose they will honor nature such as the Odinists profess."

The man stopped walking, tightly gripping his walking stick. "What are Odinists?"

"I don't know much about them," she admitted. "They claim to honor Odin and the Norse ways. They are strong in Britain, where the Norse faith once stretched. There are pockets of believers here."

"Tell me more," he prompted with genuine interest.

"I can't without looking it up," she said.

"The Internet," he said.

"Yes. Presuming the Norse haven't shut it down overnight. So many gods are eliminating that which they do not understand." She began heading for the small one-story wooden structure that was both Church and rectory.

"Few are taking the time to learn," he said, more to himself than to Rebeckah.

He hesitated crossing the threshold but followed her to the right, away from the chapel and toward the small, cluttered warren of offices. This section of the building was unheated and she felt the chill in the air, despite her coat and gloves. She led him to her secretary's desk, with the desktop still humming away. Swiftly, she entered in the search term and a series of links came up. The man watched everything very carefully, not saying a word.

"See?" she prompted. Her finger ran down the numerous links to different organizations and websites describing the faith. At random, she clicked on a link and was taken to a stark black and white page describing what Odinism was all about.

"Well, I can't argue with a belief system that boils down to 'Faith, Folk, Family,'" she said.

"I agree. I find it fascinating this exists, that people have continued to follow Odin's way even though the other gods vanished from thought."

"I wouldn't put it that way," she countered. "We still study mythology in school. Didn't you?"

He shook his head.

"Interesting. Anyway, it says here that 'Odinists recognize man's spiritual kinship with Nature, that within himself are in essence all that is in the greater world, which perform within him the same functions as in the world.'"

"You can't argue with that either, can you?" He sounded downright amused.

"No, I can't. It's really not that far from some of our own beliefs and practices."

She clicked on a few more screens and rapidly scanned for additional information. As she scrolled, Rebeckah could feel the man inch closer to her, scanning along with her. On one screen, his rough-hewn hand shot forward, pointing to a specific site with enough force to move the monitor back several centimeters.

"What is this list?"

"It appears to be a series of Nine Charges that worshippers follow. Sounds like our Ten Commandments."

"But only nine. A more efficient system," he said. She heard some pride in the tone or was he just teasing her?

Together, they silently read the list:

To maintain candor and fidelity in love and devotions to the tried friend:

though he strike me I will do him no scathe.

Never to make a wrongsome oath: for great and grim is the reward for the breaking of plighted troth.

To deal not hardly with the humble and lowly.

To remember the respect that is due great age.

To suffer no evil to go unremedied and to fight against the enemies of family, nation, race and faith: my foes will I fight in the field nor be burnt in my house.

To succor the friendless but to put no faith in the pledged word of a stranger people.

If I hear the fool's word of a drunken man I will strive not: for many a grief and the very death groweth out of such things.

To give kind heed to dead men: straw-dead, sea-dead or sword-dead.

To abide by the enactments of lawful authority and to bear with courage and fortitude the decrees of the Norns.

"The Norns?" Rebeckah asked.

"They are the women who know the destiny of the gods themselves," the man said.

"Well, that's interesting, that even the gods have their fortunes foretold," the priest said. "Still, these are beliefs that are a little less universal than 'Thou Shalt not Kill.' But to be commanded to fight, that's a little harsh."

"It was the Viking way. The Norse way," he said. "These were rules written for those men, much as your Commandments were written for desert-dwellers."

"We've become very violent around the world, but I always thought Sweden would be immune. But of late, Scandinavia seems to be reverting to the time of the Vikings. There are so many more stories of fights and arrests. I pray for our citizens."

"These appear to be turbulent times, as people adjust from your god to the ancestral gods."

"I suppose that's one way to look at it," she said. "Will you be joining me for Mass in the morning?"

"It is not my way, but you speak well so yes, I shall linger and listen."

"I may make a believer out of you," she warned with a smile.

"You may try," he replied with a smile of his own. "But it is doubtful. I may sample your brand of faith and then go seek out others, including these Odinists."

He chuckled once more to himself and Rebeckah did not entirely see where the humor was.

Twenty Weeks After The Return

Franz looked up at the sky and shuddered. It was late fall and he expected the chill but now there were dark, rolling storm clouds filling the sky. Not quite cold enough for snow, so it was going to be a cold rain, ruining the festivities. The sharp air, though, let him savor the spices and baking coming from numerous homes. They made his mouth water and he began craving a fine dinner. With every step, people seemed gayer, preparing for the annual festival. Christkindlmarkt was one of his favorite places in all of Hamburg to visit during his favorite time of the year and this year everything seemed nice and opulent, despite the return of the Norse gods. It was if the German people were ignoring Odin and his ilk, at least for the holiday season.

Buildings, benches, and even trees were covered in bright, white lights that ensured the darkness of night was kept at bay. The square before the town's government was similarly lit with small shacks or buildings constructed atop paved and natural areas. Bathed in colorful lights, the town's central building was impressive, wide with a central tower. The upper level was lit in green, the rest in white and set against the darkening sky, was truly impressive. This city of Hamburg was bright, clean and filling rapidly with people as they seemed to abandon their work and came to be social.

The avenues were filled with people selling goods, much of it looked traditional, handcrafted, the way things should be. Artisans could be proud of their work compared with the mass produced goods that others sold in the stores. That was one sign of progress that would have to be addressed.

Each stall was lovingly decorated in bright colors and there were many servers dressed in garish motely, which people seemed to enjoy.

The first stall Franz paused at was a baker's and he studied the rectangular items mostly in brown, stacked high. Some had nuts embedded in them, others traced in some white sugar. There were others in tree shapes, also decorated in white. They smelled wonderful and he grew ravenous.

He reached into his pocket for his wallet only to be jostled by the man next to him. Instead of the usual "excuse me", the man shot Franz an accusatory stare. Franz stepped back and let the man pass.

Finally clutching a small bag of gingerbread cookies, he proceeded deeper into the market. Instead of the usual cheeriness, he couldn't help but notice the mood was different than previous years. People were suddenly complaining about the prices, vendors yelled at people, accusing them of shoplifting. The happy sounds of children at play were overwhelmed with shouts and arguments breaking out from every corner.

So much for peace on Earth and there certainly seemed to be a lack of goodwill towards anyone.

He rounded a corner, heading for his favorite beverage stall and its attractive owner. They flirted annually, ever since he was in college and she worked for her parents. Now she owned it and even though they saw each other this month every year, they felt warmly towards one another.

Hildy was as statuesque as ever, but her beautiful features had been twisted into a scowl as she berated a customer.

Franz hurried over to see if he could help, but she snarled at him, too. "About time you showed up! I wait every year and you're late!"

This could have sounded flirtatious but it was anything but. Franz had a sudden desire to be heading for home. Instead, he was pushed from behind and wound up tripping over a baby carriage and want face first into a wooden pole, holding up Hildy's stand.

"Watch it!" she shouted, rather than see if he was injured. This was most unlike her. In fact, he could see little cheer at all in this section of the market. Couples fought, an infant began to wail, and a dog growled at a passerby.

Just ahead, oblivious to it all, was an oddly familiar shape, tall and thin, with a pointed hat topping him like a very thin Christmas tree. He kept walking, ignoring the growing chaos behind him.

Franz rubbed the growing bump on his head, wishing Hildy would offer him some ice because he dared not ask her for any; not in the mood she was in.

Giving up on treating his injury, he also made up his mind this was not where he wanted to be and turned to leave.

That's when the fight started. He had no clue who started it. He had no desire to become a part of it. Instead, his eyes frantically looked left and right, seeking a safe escape route. There was, though, none to be had.

Patrons were grabbing goods off the various stalls to use as projectiles and weapons. Pocketbooks became shields and those wise enough to heed the clouds and carried umbrellas suddenly used them like cricket bats. The noise level grew to the point he could not hear any of the lovely holiday music that normally left him feeling serene.

He was elbowed in the side and shoved backward so one man could hurl himself at another. They wrapped their arms around one another, Greek wrestlers at the ready, and tumbled to the ground. A woman leapt over their prone forms to grab a nutcracker from the stall next to Hildy's and Franz watched in horror as it went flying into the back of a man's head, knocking him into a stall, his flailing arms smacking several others.

The human dominoes fell from one to another and Franz feared being trampled as his own anger rose. He now felt like he needed to lash out, and strike someone, anyone, just to feel a part of the action. Normally, he never fought, cheering his favorite rugby stars to do the fighting for him. Tonight was different.

A crack of thunder was heard overhead.

Franz jabbed an elbow into a man to free himself and it felt good. He craved doing it again but instead, he shoved two men aside, creating a path towards an exit. Ahead of him, though, men, women, and children were all in a tangle. This was a full-blown riot that he doubted even the police could easily quell.

Inch by inch, he clawed his way past bodies as he sought an exit, tamping down his own anger and fury. Up ahead he saw something that made his heart skip a beat. The fighting was still going on, but there was a little girl, separated from her parents and lost. She had a frightened look in her eyes and he knew she would be trampled if he did not intervene and get her to safety.

He reared back, planted his right foot for balance and then shoved mightily with his left, forcing one woman into a man into another man, and essentially clearing a path. As he stepped forward, a new figure blocked his way.

It was the man in the pointed hat. His one good eye smoldered and his brows were knit in the same anger everyone was feeling.

"Out of my way," Franz yelled.

"Something troubling you, friend," the man inquired.

"I am trying to get to that lost girl," Franz said, jerking his arm past the man. The other man turned his head, spotted the girl, who was now beginning to cry and nodded. He turned to approach her, Franz behind him.

The girl was maybe seven, in a red and green dress, her winter coat unbuttoned. She had red cheeks from the cold and tears ran over them.

"What is the problem, my child?" the man said to her.

She sniffled and then looked up at the man. Then she looked hard at him, taking in his tall figure. The long dark cloak, the walking stick, the pointed hat. Her crying stopped and she took in a deep breath. Her mouth formed an o-shape.

"Are you Father Christmas?" she asked in a squeaky voice.

The man glared down at her and there was a rumble of thunder in the distance.

"Do I look like Father Christmas?"

She shook her head up and down.

"Or maybe you're Knecht Rupprecht," she said.

The man shook his head from side to side.

Franz watched as the girl continued to study him, taking in his towering form. She did not seem frightened of him, and both seemed oblivious to the turmoil behind them. His own roiling emotions seemed held in abeyance.

"Are you Der Weihnachtsmann?"

Franz watched the man bend over and peer into the wide-open eyes of the small child. She stood maybe to his knee and was in a thick coat with a colorful blue scarf hiding some of her face.

"Do I look like him?" he asked, keeping his voice low.

"Yes," she said. "Except he has two eyes."

"You're very perceptive," Odin said to her. "And what is your name?"

"Ilsa," she replied.

"Are you parents about?"

"They're watching the singers. I got a Gluehwein for a snack." She showed him the dregs in a paper cup.

"I smell fruit," Odin said. "Tell me why you think I am Der Weihnachtsmann? Except for the eye, of course."

He crouched low, meeting her eye to eyes and she blinked unafraid.

"Well, you are tall and thin like he is. And you have the white beard."

"And what does this Der Weihnachtsmann do?"

"He brings presents, of course!" Her earnestness enchanted Franz and so, it seemed, the old man, whoever he was.

"Is that all? Why would he do this?"

"To reward good children," she said and then took a drink.

"Do children need to be given gifts to keep them good?"

"No," she said emphatically. "But it's a nice reward. That's what Mama says."

"No doubt it is," the man said.

As he considered this, the girl continued to stare at him, convinced she was speaking with the great gift-giver in the flesh.

"Where are your reindeer?"

He looked down at Ilsa. "My what?"

"Your reindeer. You ride eight of them to bring the gifts, don't you?"

"You are mistaken, my dear. I have no reindeer but a mighty steed named Sleipnir."

"What's a steed?"

"A horse. Mine is magical, with eight legs to carry me across the skies."

"Are you sure you don't have eight reindeer instead?"

"I think I know what I ride," the old man said with a laugh. "Behave and I may stop by your house and give you a ride to prove it to you."

"I know who you are," she said.

"Do you now?"

"You're Odin, aren't you?"

The man studied her for a beat then nodded. The girl's o-shaped mouth closed and she curtsied before him.

Franz was stunned. Odin. As in the Allfather, leader of the Aesir? Standing before him, letting the frenzy occur among those he expected to be his worshippers.

When the girl was done, Odin smiled at her.

The rumbling in the sky stopped.

"How do you know me, child?"

"Father Christmas has two eyes and a reindeer. You have only one eye."

"Quite right," he said. "And what do you know *about* me?"

"You're the god of war—but Mama says you're the god of poetry and music, too." She smiled up at him, the very picture of childlike awe and joy. "I like those much better."

The Allfather studied her quietly for a moment. Then his long face creased in a wide smile, and crinkled around his one eye. "You know what, little one?" he said softly, though the words carried easily to where Franz stood. "So do I."

"You're the father of Thor and rule in Asgard."

Odin continued to smile at her, eyes crinkling a bit. "Your mother has taught you well, I see. Will you come worship me?"

She solemnly nodded.

Just like that, Franz sensed the peace in the air. This was that golden period he recalled, as people were done with the harvest and began to celebrate, thanking for the gods for a good season. They would haul in the yule log for warmth and begin their celebration with much food and drink.

She squealed in delight, so much so that the fighting around them slowed to a stop as heads turned. Now many were gaping at the figure. Several seemed stunned or shocked, others broke into their own smiles while others whipped out their phones to grab an image of the god walking among them.

People dusted one another off, issuing embarrassed apologies. Couples hugged in forgiveness, still uncertain what sparked the arguments and fighting. Others helped vendors pick up their goods and straighten the stalls. Once more the loudspeakers could be heard, the gentle holiday music that sustained the feeling of peace.

Odin took the girl's hand, offering to help find her parents before he had to leave. "But you promised me a ride," she insisted. He laughed and nodded, and she smiled back, clearly certain he would not forget.

Franz hadn't known gods could laugh or how far their voices carried over the din. He wanted to consider all that happened but his face was feeling damp and was afraid he was bleeding. He raised a gloved hand to check for blood, but saw white flakes atop the brown leather.

The storm had passed and the threatening rain had turned to snow. The first of the season and it came down in beautiful, fat flakes. The thing Franz loved best about that first snow of the year is how it blanketed everything, a fresh coat of white promising new beginnings; a clean start for one and all.

A Medieval Knight in Vatican City

by *Scott Pearson*

The knight stumbled into an angry mob just as yelling and shoving turned into a brawl. Curses—plain from the tone although in languages he didn't understand—echoed in the narrow street between brick and stone buildings. A fist connected with his jaw, and instinct took over. With no clear allies in the crowd, he simply fought with anyone who got in his way. He punched, elbowed, kicked, and yelled without mercy. A man came at him with a broken bottle, but he knocked the bottle aside and smashed his fist into the man's face. The man fell flat on his back, unconscious. None were prepared for the wrath of a member of the Order of the Temple, and soon the people who remained standing scattered, allowing him a moment to catch his breath and take stock of his surroundings.

Étienne Joubert skirmished in the hard streets of a city he didn't recognize. The strange, unfamiliar clothing of the immobile bodies meant nothing to him. He didn't know where he was or how he had gotten there. Sharp, loud cracks filled the air along with unrecognizable roarings and metallic screechings. Sounds of breaking glass added a brittle edge to the mayhem. He looked up and down the now-deserted street. It was a mild day, and without the exertion of the fight it might have been slightly chill in the shadows between the buildings. The buildings themselves looked fairly conventional, but some of the designs and stonework were out of the ordinary. Most of the windows were shuttered, the residents hiding from the violence in the city.

He wandered down the brick-paved street, the sounds of fighting growing closer. He paused at a sign: Arlù Ristorante. Alongside the door of the restaurant was a handwritten menu of pasta dishes. Suddenly he was aware of being hungry but, on the other side of the clearest glass he'd ever seen, the restaurant was dark and empty. He turned away, thinking back to the angry cries of the mob he'd fought, and thought that perhaps some had indeed been speaking Italian. How did he come to be in Italy from . . . where had he been last? Paris? His memory was foggy. Joubert raised a hand to his head, searching for injuries as he continued down the street.

The sounds of fighting grew louder, and he wished for a weapon. Although he wore his red-crossed Templar tunic with a belt around his waist, no sword hung from the belt, and he had no chain mail beneath the tunic. Suddenly anxious to find others of his Order, he began to run down the street, toward the battle noise, his boots resounding against the bricks. The cross street he was approaching looked to be much wider than the one he was on. He saw two people race by at speed on some sort of small two-wheeled cart without a horse to draw it, and then several people ran past on foot. Apparently they were all being chased by what followed: a Minotaur. He was so astonished by this, he ran into the open without scouting his surroundings and was immediately knocked to the ground by another group of people fleeing in that same direction.

Joubert leaped to his feet just as a four-wheeled metal carriage, also moving without horses, screeched to a halt in the road. A young man in the rear seat waved something toward him through an open window. There was a loud retort and Joubert felt an intense searing pain along his left temple. He staggered back in surprise and raised a hand to his face, finding blood running freely from the wound. The man who had wielded this terrible weapon was still pointing it at him, but no more sound or projectile issued from it. With an angry curse the man dropped the weapon, swung open a door, and leaped from the carriage. The three other men in the vehicle also jumped out. Now Joubert saw they were all dressed much the same as he was, in long tunics, although out in the open they looked more like boys than men. He had fought beside soldiers like these in the Holy Land, yet here they had attacked him. Joubert hesitated, confused by everything that was happening around him.

He stood motionless as they reached back into the carriage and pulled out short swords, which they brandished in his direction with much more bravado than skill. The drawing of swords pushed his confusion aside. Joubert didn't understand why they chose to fight him—they did not appear to be Saracens—but he would oblige. They were clearly surprised when he stood his ground, but their superior numbers urged them on.

The one who had wounded Joubert charged forward. He clearly had no experience with the weapon, and Joubert dodged a clumsy swing before taking the sword from him and throwing him roughly to the ground. The three others looked nervous but rushed him as a group.

With a cry of *"Beau Séant!"* Joubert waded into them without further hesitation. His strong slashes of the sword knocked theirs from their hands, and the three quickly turned and fled, leaving their carriage in the road. Joubert turned to find his first foe coming up behind him, raising his magical hand weapon for another try. Joubert swung the sword, slicing open the young man's arm. With a pitiful cry, the man dropped the weapon and grabbed the bloody gash with his other hand as he fell to the street. This was accompanied by an excited chorus of shouts.

Spinning around, Joubert saw a group of people approaching, apparently celebrating his victory. Although he was ambivalent about defeating the young, inexperienced warriors, he was swept up by the strangers' reassuring enthusiasm. He picked up a second sword in his other hand, raised them both above his head, and gave a victory cry. The crowd responded in kind, cheering and clapping their hands, but their jubilance was cut short by a loud series of explosive sounds from the direction the warriors had come from. Most of the crowd immediately turned and ran in the opposite direction. A couple remained, gesturing for Joubert to follow. Since he had no idea where he was, following these people was not a difficult decision to make, especially as the violent sounds behind them got louder and closer. They ran down the street.

They passed more of the horseless vehicles, both two and four wheeled. Some were parked on the sides of the street, but others had been haphazardly abandoned, forcing them to dodge around the obstacles, although they would also provide cover if needed. One was burning, the dark, acrid smoke filling the street. Joubert froze at the smoke, a sense of doom almost overwhelming him for reasons he couldn't explain. His companions, coughing and waving the smoke from their faces, grabbed him and pulled him past. On the other side he saw the street ran through some narrow arches in an old city wall. The wall, at least thirty feet high, was a patchwork of differently sized bricks and stones, showing a long history of repair. The wall had a familiarity to it that Joubert found disturbing.

Several young men and women stood in front of the arches. They were sharing a bottle of wine, passing it from one person to the next. They shouted and shook their fists at Joubert as he neared, but backed away, more interested in drinking than fighting. Joubert let them be, following his new friends as they rushed through the arches, turned immediately to the right, and then swung to the left. A huge curving white structure came into view; it had no walls, just a forest of forty-foot columns holding up the massive roof. Joubert's companions led him straight toward the barricades that had been built between the columns. One had a gate held open and guarded by others that had been in his celebratory crowd. They ran through and the gate was slammed shut behind them. They emerged into a huge oval open space enclosed by two arms of the curving, columned structures. Two fountains and a central obelisk decorated the space.

Joubert found himself walking toward the obelisk, a strange feeling settling in his stomach. He noticed to his left that there had been a large gap between the two curved wings of columns, but a wall had been built across the opening. A large metal gate in the center was staffed by uniformed guards. Tucking his captured swords in his belt, Joubert stared at the obelisk as he approached. The familiar feeling the city wall had sparked returned, but more intense. Faint and dizzy, he wiped at the blood still running down his face from the wound at his temple. Then he finally recognized the obelisk. He'd seen it before, had stood right next to it as he did now, when visiting St. Peter's Basilica in Rome. But the obelisk was near the St. Andrea Chapel alongside St. Peter's . . . he spun around, staring wildly across the oval. St. Peter's was gone. Opposite the metal gate in the new wall, through another gap in the columned wings across an open square, there stood a giant church, topped with a dome stretching into the sky. Where had St. Peter's gone, and where had this come from? How could the landscape have changed so completely since he'd been here? He spun around again, as if another look might reveal the buildings he remembered, but the world remained transformed, and his vision blurred then darkened before he felt himself falling.

Joubert opened his eyes at the sound of voices. Golden sunlight streamed in through a window, making him squint. He was in a small but richly appointed room. The voices came from the other side of a door opposite the bed he was in. He slid quietly out of bed, noticing that the linens seemed smooth as silk, although they appeared to be regular cloth. He was ashamed to find himself undressed to nothing but his loincloth, but relieved that fresh clothes, like those worn by the people he'd seen earlier on the streets, were laid out for him on a nearby chair. He dressed as quickly as possible in the unusual clothing, which consisted of trousers of a blue material and a loose-fitting shirt. Looking out the window he could tell he was up a story from the ground. Through autumn trees, their leaves gone red and orange, were glimpses of the city beyond.

The voices continued—one male, older, sounding quite authoritarian, and a younger woman's voice—both speaking Italian, he thought. Moving to an alcove which had a water basin and a looking glass, Joubert saw the bandage on his left temple. He lifted the bandage and counted five sutures closing the wound. He put the bandage back in place, then ran a hand over his short hair, noticing the gray hairs among the black. Playing with the handles on the basin, Joubert discovered, to his surprise, that they produced hot and cold water. Soon there was a knock on the door. Whoever was out there must have finally heard him.

Shutting the water off, he walked over to open the door, but found that he was locked in. Then the knob started to turn. Apparently the person on the outside had just been warning him someone was about to enter. Joubert stepped back as the door swung open. His eyes widened when he saw the woman who stood there. She wore black trousers that were indecently tight and a bright red shirt that also accentuated her feminine curves. Her dark hair was cut short and openly displayed without cap or scarf, and she wore rectangular spectacles. Joubert had heard of them, but had never seen anyone wearing them. She was several inches shorter than his six feet, and looked up at him with an expression of nervous curiosity.

"Good day," she said in passable French, but with an odd accent. "May I come in?"

It seemed improper to have her enter the small bedroom with him. He tried to peek into the corridor to see the man he'd heard, but she moved to block the doorway, smirking as she did so. She was uncomfortably close to him. Joubert had had some indiscretions in his youth, but had faithfully honored his vow of chastity since entering the Order. With amusement he realized that he, who had survived brutal siege battles in the Holy Land, was discomfited by this enticing woman. Shaking his head, he also admitted he was too overwhelmed by his circumstances to stand on such formalities. Perhaps she had answers to his many questions about where he was and how he got there.

Retreating into the room, he said, "Yes, please." He turned and went to the bed, straightening the covers before glancing back at her.

She followed him in, closing the door behind her before looking at him for a time as though too excited to speak. He fidgeted awkwardly in the unfamiliar clothes he wore. Finally, she broke the silence. "What is your name, sir?"

"Étienne Joubert."

She pulled a small rectangular object from a pocket and tapped at it with her fingers. "Good, thank you." She stared at the shiny little thing for a while, a serious look on her face, then nodded. "Unbelievable." Looking back up at him as she returned the item to her pocket, she said, "Could I see the tunic of your Order?"

He tilted his head. He didn't really understand what was going on. "I don't know where it is."

"I'm sure it's in the wardrobe." She gestured toward it, on the far side of the bed.

Joubert walked over to the wardrobe, opened the doors, and found his tunic hanging inside. He drew it out and laid it on the bed. She stood and leaned over to take a closer look, running her hand across the fabric. It seemed rather familiar, as if she had put her hand on his chest. She looked up at him while still bent over the bed.

"This is incredible, truly." She stood up and walked around the bed toward him. "I've got a couple more questions for you, if you don't mind."

He forced himself not to step back as she neared him again. "No, but . . . who are you? What is happening?"

"Oh, I'm sorry." She held out her hand. "I'm Paola Sartini. I'm a professor of history at Sapienza University, and I've come to help you, shall we say, settle in."

When he took her hand, she gave him a firm shake then slowly let go. He'd heard of Sapienza on his visit to Rome, but a woman professor? Surely that couldn't be true. Nothing made sense here.

She noticed the look on his face. "Sorry. I know this must be very confusing for you, but it will all be clear soon, even though it's rather unbelievable. Why don't we sit?" Sartini sat in the chair and gestured at the bed. He shrugged and sat on the corner, again ignoring the impropriety. "Now, tell me, what year were you born?"

Joubert shook his head. "I don't understand. Why do you ask about my birth?"

She smiled sympathetically. "I'll explain everything, I promise, but I think this approach is the best way. Can you please tell me the year?"

"I was born in twelve-seventy-two. February ninth."

"And how old are you?"

"Thirty-eight." Even as he said it, something seemed strange about it, something significant.

"So . . . that makes your last memories of the year thirteen-ten?"

"Of course . . ." The strange feeling returned, similar to when he recognized the obelisk, as though some horrible truth were rising to the surface of a dark lake.

"What do you remember of thirteen-ten? What do you last remember before you were fighting in the streets?"

Joubert felt a tingling on his skin. He began to rub at his exposed arms, thinking, for some reason, of the smoke and flames from the burning carriage in the street. The tingling intensified, an echo of indescribable pain. He stood up straight but couldn't remain still as the tingling spread across his entire body. He clenched his eyes shut, but snapped them open immediately to avoid what he'd seen in his mind. Fire, fire rushing up, engulfing him. "Burning," he said through clenched teeth. He felt faint, but the pain kept him standing. Sartini was out of her chair, approaching him with a concerned look on her face. Whatever fortitude the pain had given him evaporated, and he swayed on his feet. "I'm burning!"

Sartini wrapped her arms around him, a moment of comfort that steadied him, then she guided him toward the chair. He allowed her to support him and tried to ignore the sensation of her body pressed close to his. She slid him down onto the chair and then left him there. He watched as she walked to the basin, took a glass from a small shelf, and filled it with water.

"There's no easy way to tell you this," she said as she walked back. She handed him the glass. "Take a drink." He did as she ordered. She sat on the edge of the bed. "The records are sparse and contradictory, but there is one extant account that names an Étienne of Vézelay among fifty-four knights of the Order who were burned as heretics in Paris on May twelfth, thirteen-ten. Are you from Vézelay? Do you remember being tried as a heretic?"

Joubert leaned back. He set down the glass on the small table beside the chair and gripped the arms of the chair with both hands. "I am from Vézelay. The Order was condemned by King Philip, but we were not heretics. We fought against the Saracens in the Holy Land. We were prepared to give our lives for our faith."

"I know."

"But what does this mean? I remember burning at the stake. Yet here I am." He lifted his arms and turned them back and forth. "And I am not burned."

She reached up and took his hands in hers. "I need to tell you one more thing, though it will be difficult for you to accept. It has been hundreds of years since then. This is the year twenty-eighteen."

Joubert pulled his hands away from her. "Are you mad?" He stood. "I want to speak to the man I heard talking to you. It was clear he was giving you orders. Who is he?"

Sartini stood as well. "He was not giving me orders." She took a breath and exhaled. "Well, he thought he was giving me orders, but—"

The door swung open and an elderly man in a white cassock, sash, and skullcap strode into the room. His hair was dark gray and he wore gold spectacles and a gold cross hung on his chest.

"Your Holiness," Sartini said, surprised at the sudden entrance.

Joubert's eyes widened—she'd addressed the man as the pope. He'd seen portraits of Pope Clement V, but this man was not Clement . . . just how long ago had that been? Sartini was telling him it had been more than seven hundred years. He didn't know what to believe. But he believed in God and the Roman Catholic Church, so he went down on one knee and kissed the Ring of the Fisherman as the pope extended his hand. His Holiness guided him back to his feet, giving him a piercing look. Joubert cast his eyes downward.

The pope and Sartini spoke rapidly in Italian. His Holiness seemed very certain about something at which Sartini shook her head. He waved a hand dismissively and spoke more sternly. With a sigh, Sartini turned toward Joubert.

"I'm going to show you something." She took the small rectangular object out of her pocket again. "We have many complicated machines that do things you wouldn't have imagined in your life. This little device can not only capture an image, a portrait, of you instantly, it can capture a series of portraits in a way that makes a moving portrait. Like a painting that can wave its arms within its frame. Do you understand?"

Joubert frowned. He glanced to His Holiness, who stood patiently smiling and nodding at him. "Show me."

She pointed the shiny little thing at him. "Say something."

"Why?"

She smiled and turned the thing around so he could see the side she'd been looking at. On its glass surface, he saw his own face which he thought was a mere reflection until he heard her voice from the object repeat, "Say something." He then saw his face move and heard his own voice say, "Why?"

Joubert pulled back from the tiny machine. "It talks back like an echo!"

Meanwhile, Sartini had turned the thing back toward her and was tapping on the machine. "Now watch this."

She turned the machine to face him. He saw the crowd in the street, that first crowd he'd fought with. It was like he was looking down at the crowd from a window on the upper floor of a building. Then the image moved sideways and he indeed saw a window frame and wall inside a room before the image centered on the crowd in the street. He could hear someone speaking Italian, but he couldn't hear the sounds of the crowd arguing. And then he saw himself appear on the image in the glass. He was just suddenly there in the street a few yards from the crowd. A limn of golden light surrounded him, then ran off like water before evaporating away in an instant. The image shook and he clearly heard the voice say, "Dio mio." On the screen he stumbled forward into the crowd as they started fighting, and he watched himself wade into the brawl just as he remembered. He pushed the magical device away.

"I don't understand. Is this real? What does it mean?"

The pope took a step forward and took Joubert's face in his hands. Joubert froze in place, overwhelmed by the contact with His Holiness. In halting French and a nearly impenetrable accent, the pope said, "You are the miracle I have been praying for, a soldier of God to turn the tide." His Holiness raised a hand to the bandage on Joubert's temple. "You have already sealed the covenant of your service to the Church with blood."

In that moment, all Joubert's confusion seemed inconsequential. His Holiness had prayed for a miracle, and God had obviously sent Joubert back with a purpose.

Joubert nodded his head within the cradle of His Holiness's hands and said, "Where are my swords?"

Hidden within a small group of pilgrims, Joubert watched with disdain the Templar knights training in St. Peter's Square on a sunny late-October day.

It had been just over two weeks since he'd returned to life and His Holiness had yet to give back his swords, but these so-called knights were allowed to fumble around with their blades while wearing red-crossed tunics. Meanwhile, Joubert, eager to begin a new Crusade against the followers of the pantheon who surrounded Vatican City, could only stalk back and forth in the Vatican gardens. His Holiness believed Joubert needed more time to adjust to his new surroundings. Sartini visited him daily to instruct him on how the world had changed, both since Joubert's time and lately since the gods returned. A French student from her university, Denis Royer, had some knowledge of Old French and was helping teach Joubert English. Pope Boniface X, who also spoke English, said it would make it easier for Joubert to communicate with the other members of the Order. Such as they were. They claimed a hidden lineage through the centuries back to Joubert's own, but he was uncertain. Sartini had taught him the full scope of Philip's revenge on the Templar, and in Joubert's thoughts, often dark and lonely, he despaired of any secret link between then and now. But his reverie was interrupted by the painful clatter of a sword dropped to the bricks of the square.

He could stand it no longer. These men needed to be able to wield a sword properly because modern weapons often didn't function within the realm of the pantheon. Stepping out from the pilgrims, Joubert unfolded his tunic, which he'd smuggled out of his room under his shirt. Pope Boniface had made it clear that Joubert was supposed to keep to himself. His Holiness wanted to treat Joubert like some sort of secret weapon. As much as Joubert felt obliged to follow the pope's wishes, he also felt the calling to serve the Order, a duty he took upon himself hundreds of years before Boniface was even born. Joubert shrugged into his tunic over his new daily clothes. One of the pilgrims, an elderly man, well-dressed for a tourist—gray pants and jacket, a shirt and tie, and carrying a gray hat with a black hatband—seemed to recognize him. Ignoring the man, Joubert stomped over to the Templars.

"No, no, no," he growled. They looked like they were rehearsing a sword fight for a play. They turned as one to face him, and he could tell that they all realized who he was. He grabbed a long sword from the closest of them and swung it over his head. The pilgrims yelled with excitement as the other knights took defensive stances. Joubert plowed forward, barely pulling his swings. The clash of swords rang out and the pilgrims cheered as if watching a competition. In moments, three Templar were on the ground, two disarmed, one holding a broken nose gushing blood. Joubert handed the sword back to its owner and patted the bleeding knight apologetically on the shoulder. They did not seem angry, but instead swarmed him with questions that he couldn't follow. Joubert's smile did not fade until two of the Swiss Guard were suddenly at his side to escort him back to his room. Royer was with them. His modern French accent was much more pronounced than Sartini's, but they understood each other well enough.

"His Holiness doesn't want you out in public like this."

"A sword must see the outside of its scabbard in training if not in combat." He could sense the Templar gathering at his back in support. "If I'm not allowed to fight, at least let me help train these men."

"I'm only the translator. Arguing with me doesn't do you any good." One of the Swiss Guards said something to Royer in Italian. Royer nodded and said, "His Holiness wants you to go back to your room right away."

Joubert shook his head. "Listen to me. These are supposed to be Knights of the Order. They need to learn how to swing a sword without lopping off their own feet."

"Excuse me," said someone behind Joubert. Joubert spun at the interruption, which had been spoken clearly in his own French. It was the old pilgrim, who now stood close by. He was a few inches shorter than Joubert, but seemed comfortable with interrupting an angry soldier.

"Might I suggest that you don't discourage them. Few have the faith to serve the Order these days. The Templar are spread thin."

Joubert was too annoyed by the criticism to wonder about the man's linguistic abilities. "I do not question their faith, just their swordsmanship. When we battle the pagans—"

"Is that what you want to do? Lead these men into battle?"

"Of course, I am a Soldier of Christ." Joubert placed one hand over the red cross on his tunic, patting his chest.

Royer stepped in between them. "His Holiness also wanted me to remind you that he doesn't want you wearing your tunic."

Joubert glared at Royer, then reminded himself that Royer was just the messenger and had nothing to do with Boniface's elusive plans for the Templar. With a resigned shrug, Joubert stepped away from the crowd of trainees. The knights all looked disappointed, but the old man looked back at Joubert with concern. Joubert allowed himself to be escorted away, but he did not take off his tunic in front of the knights and pilgrims. Before they got too far, he looked over his shoulder for the old man. The old man was still watching Joubert.

On a cold and rainy November day, Joubert walked alone through the gardens of Vatican City. It was nearly a month since his incident with the Templar, and still His Holiness would not allow him to do anything. Beleaguered Christians, struggling to hold on to their faith in the presence of demanding pagan gods, continued visiting the Vatican despite occasional flare-ups of violence. Joubert had arrived in Rome on Meditrinalia, a Roman festival celebrating the new wine vintage. Pagan youth had enthusiastically embraced the ancient holiday, turning it into an orgy of drunken violence. It was no war of the pantheon, just malcontents and bullies going after those who were afraid, the easy targets. The skirmishes had triggered anti-Christian riots that were still flaring up around the very walls of Vatican City over a month later.

Joubert hunched his shoulders and kept plodding along the soggy grass and around the trees, his wet hair clinging to his face and neck. He had not cut it since returning to life, and it was getting long. Just that morning when Sartini had stopped by, always a high point of his monotonous days, she had suddenly run her hand through his hair. He had felt the same pleasant discomfort he often did in her presence, and he shook his head slightly when her hand lingered on his shoulder.

"I should bring scissors the next time I come and take care of that mop for you." She smiled. "But only because you fidget with it. I think it suits you."

The thought of the intimate contact, her hands in his hair, her body close behind him, made him step away and look out the window. She made no comment on his reaction. Instead she apologized for not being able to stay, and explained she was helping out a sick colleague by taking his class for him. She had to leave right away.

As she left the room, she said, "Remember, next time . . ." and made a scissoring motion with the first two fingers of her right hand.

Now Joubert slicked his wet hair back off his forehead and found himself thinking about letting her cut it. He pushed the thought away and vowed to shear himself. His life was confusing enough already. Royer had come by after the midday meal, but Joubert had given the young man the slip in order to wander alone in the gray overcast gardens, wondering why God had returned him to this incomprehensible world.

"You can be a most difficult man to find."

Joubert turned around so quickly, he spun water off his soaked clothes and hair like a shaking dog. The old man who spoke Old French stood a few feet behind him holding a large black umbrella and smirking.

Pushing his hair back off his face, Joubert tried to strike as dignified a pose as he could in his soggy clothes. "Where did you learn to speak French so well?" Not even Paola was this good; her Old French was a bit stilted. She'd studied the changes in the language, but current French still influenced her pronunciation and grammar.

The old man smiled. "Before I retired, I was a professor of French literature in New York, and had an interest in the time period. When I heard rumors of you, I simply had to meet you."

Joubert recognized the city as one across the ocean in a land unknown in his time. "You traveled all this way to meet me?" Joubert was astonished. Of course, travel in this day and age was much easier, at least when all the gods allowed it.

"Yes. I know something of the Templar, and I have acquaintances in the Order. Through them I heard the truth behind the video that spread over the internet." The old man had lapsed into some English for the modern words, but Joubert had learned those terms. The video of his appearance had "gone viral," Sartini had explained. She had told him that in the days before the return of the gods he might have become famous from that video, but technology behaved erratically now and didn't have the reach it used to. Because Pope Boniface had endeavored to keep Joubert a secret, many around the world thought the video a hoax, just a "special effect" added to a typical street fight. But the modern Templar Knights knew of Joubert's miracle.

Joubert stepped a little closer, and the old man shifted his umbrella to provide Joubert some protection from the steady rain. "You didn't seem all that pleased to see me."

"I'll admit you were not entirely what I expected."

"And what exactly did you expect?"

"Let's just say you weren't completely different from what I thought I would find. You were very inspiring for the others." With a frown, the old man added, "Perhaps too inspiring."

Joubert frowned back. "What do you mean?"

"They have been very . . . enthusiastic in your absence."

"His Holiness has kept me close at hand since that day in the square. My training style was both too public and too dangerous for his liking." He shrugged. "But what do you mean? What have they been doing?"

"They train often, and they train hard. Injuries are not uncommon. And they have taken to going on patrols."

"Does His Holiness know?"

"I get the impression that he does." The old man glanced back over his shoulder in the direction of the basilica. "Officially, the church has done nothing to endorse or discourage them."

"What exactly do they do on these patrols?"

"This is why I've been trying to find you, so you could see for yourself. Follow me."

The old man walked briskly toward the nearest wall. Joubert followed closely to stay under the umbrella. He was starting to shiver after standing still while they spoke.

"They don't go far," the old man said. "Just around the perimeter of the walls. But they still find enough to do."

"What do you mean?" Joubert had to step out from under the umbrella as they navigated through a stand of trees. They emerged from the trees onto the heliport. Joubert had not seen one of the metal hovering bugs in person; few people trusted flying over pantheon territory. Pilgrims came to Italy by ship, or flew in further away from Rome to avoid the risk of angering Uranus, god of the sky, and then traveled the roads into Rome.

"You'll see soon enough, if I timed this right. They always follow the same route." They walked across the wet grass to the nearest arrowslit. The old man peered through the hole down onto the street below, Viale Vaticano.

Just then Joubert heard an odd, pained bellow from behind them, slightly muffled, as if in the distance. Joubert turned and hurried across the grass and then the hard surface of the heliport in the direction of the sound. He could hear the footsteps of the old man following behind him. The muted roar came again, deep and angry, yet somehow desperate. Changing course toward the animal-like sound, Joubert rushed to another arrowslit and looked for the source of the noise.

Across the street Joubert saw a half-dozen knights in tunics circling around a Minotaur. The knights had their swords out, but the Minotaur was unarmed. He breathed raggedly and exhaled threatening sounds at the men harassing him.

"What is this?" Joubert said, mostly to himself, but the old man leaned in behind him and replied.

"They were inspired by your enthusiasm for the fight. They patrol outside the walls and confront the pagans as they can."

As Joubert watched, the circle of knights closed in on the Minotaur. With a growl, the cornered pagan monster lashed out. Even from across the street, Joubert could hear the snapping of bones in a knight's arm. But then the swords of the other knights swung down on the beast. The Minotaur, bruised, bleeding, broken, fell to its knees with a howl that echoed off the Vatican walls. It was a ruthless and pointless victory, and Joubert felt ashamed that his passion had led the men to such behavior. But it wasn't over.

Before Joubert realized what was happening, too quickly for him to cry out to stop it, two of the knights raised their swords on either side of the Minotaur and swung down with brutal efficiency, severing the bull's head from its human body. The head tumbled forward to the ground as the body fell to the side with a wash of red down the sidewalk. Two of the other knights grabbed the head by the horns and lifted the gruesome trophy in the air.

"What in God's name are you doing?" shouted Joubert.

The men looked around, confused, unable to discern where the voice had come from. Joubert waved a hand through the arrowslit until he caught their attention, then put his face as far into the opening as possible. "Stop this at once." In English, he added "No, no!"

One of the men stepped forward, sheathed his sword, and cupped his hands around his mouth. He shouted back at Joubert, but Joubert couldn't understand him. He looked over his shoulder at the old man, who began translating. "He asks if it's you, and he doesn't understand why you seem angry. They've taken the fight to the pagans, just as you did in the Crusades."

Joubert shook his head at the old man. "We are not in the Crusades. That was a different world. What they've done out there was just a slaughter that will most likely bring retribution on innocent pilgrims like yourself."

"I don't really think of myself as a pilgrim or an innocent, but I understand what you mean." He tossed his umbrella on the ground. Joubert hadn't even noticed it had stopped raining. "What shall I tell them? They are waiting for your orders."

"Tell them to bury the poor beast they've killed and then get back within the walls before any more blood is spilled."

The old man held Joubert's gaze for a long while, then nodded. Joubert walked away even as he heard the old man yelling his orders down to the Templar. He stalked across the heliport toward the trees. Behind him came the hurried steps of the old man catching up to him. Joubert left the path and cut back through the trees.

"Now what?" the old man said.

"I don't know. There must be another way. We tried the merciless approach in my time and it gained us nothing more than temporary victories, followed by crushing defeat. These devout fools are ready to simply try it all over again."

"What do you think Boniface wants?"

"The day of my return, he told me I was a soldier of God sent to him to turn the tide. Since then he has had me learning history and English, but has forbidden me to take any real action. I don't know what he wants." Joubert stopped abruptly and took hold of the old man's arm. "What do think? You spend time with the other knights, you move around the grounds as if you are known here."

The old man laughed. "I do not have the ear of His Holiness, if that's what you're implying. My connections are strictly a one-way street. As far as my being on the grounds, the Swiss Guards pay little attention to an old man wandering through the trees." He patted Joubert's arm with his free hand. "If you want my advice, I would suggest that the question you should be pondering, the long-term concern, is not what Boniface wants or what you want . . . it's what will happen if what you two want are different things." He nodded at Joubert, turned, and strolled off, using his closed umbrella like a cane. He glanced back over his shoulder and added, "The Templar will follow your lead. At least, as much as they are allowed to."

Joubert just stood and watched the old man walk away, finally disappearing around the Tower of St. John. He still had no idea who the old man was and had forgotten to ask for the retired professor's name in all the excitement. As Joubert tried to make sense of the situation, the rain returned. With a shiver, he headed back to his room.

Joubert stood in the Basilica at the monument to Pope Alexander VII waiting for Sartini. He was astonished at the craftsmanship of the piece, its lifelike figures pale against the soft mounds of cloth captured in carven stone. The gold skeletal angel of death emerging from beneath the red jasper folds fascinated him, probably, he supposed, because he must have seen the angel of death in person, though he didn't remember it. In the months since he had returned to life, he had yet to remember anything between his death on the fire and his appearance on the streets of Rome. Surely God Himself had looked upon Joubert before returning him to continue the fight of the Order against the pagans, but he didn't remember.

He shook his head. The difficult last several years of his previous life were also largely a blur to him. From the bloody battles and brutal siege at Ruad—where he barely escaped the treachery of the Mamluks with his life—to his slow, wandering return to Paris and his arrest and trial, he had only indiscernible glimpses and whispers of what he had gone through. Just the previous week, His Holiness said that it was a blessing to not remember such terrible defeats and the unjust trial of the Templars. Royer had been there as interpreter. Joubert's beginning English, although improving, was not up to deep spiritual discussions. His Holiness spoke some modern French, but any exchanges beyond the most basic were problematic.

Of Joubert's experiences after death and before his return, His Holiness had said, "The mind of no living soul could truly encompass the sight of the face of God. You had to give this up for the opportunity to serve Him again in the mortal world."

"The opportunity?" Joubert had not considered this. "I had assumed that this was commanded upon me by God. Do you think it's possible I chose this fate for myself?"

"I cannot know the will of God, but I believe you would have made such a sacrifice. Imagine, turning away from your eternal reward in heaven so that you could once again fight for the true God in this vale of tears. Such sacrifice indicates a profound faith, my son."

"Then let me act upon that faith. The pagans surround us and prey upon the pilgrims. It grows steadily worse. Let me guide the Templar and protect the faithful." He didn't explicitly state that he thought the Templar were contributing to the hostilities and needed to be reined in, but His Holiness seemed to understand the implication.

Boniface frowned. "The Order has long found its way without you, and these young men are coming into their own." His expression softened, and he placed a hand on Joubert's shoulder. "These are ever days of strife. But it is not yet the time to reveal you."

"I'm sorry, I don't understand." It pained Joubert how frequently he had to say that.

"The spreading rumors of your existence are more powerful among the pagans than my acknowledgment of you would ever be. Let them worry about a resurrected warrior of God while you train and the Order grows. By keeping you hidden, the faithful soldiers come to Rome for a chance to glimpse you. There will come a time to fully reveal yourself. I expect a sign from God to show us the way. And when all is ready, when the ranks are full and hungry for battle, and you know this world as you did your own, I will unleash the Order like the Crusades of old." He lifted his arms to heaven and bowed his head.

Joubert knelt at the feet of His Holiness, but was troubled. He turned his face so that Royer would not see. It was a conversation that had repeated over the months, but the sign from God did not come, nor was their any great influx of volunteers for the Order. The small contingent of Templar within Vatican City grew increasingly volatile as His Holiness enflamed their spiritual passions while Joubert, during his fleeting moments with them, tried to keep them from violent provocations of the pagans who surrounded them. To what end was the pope stoking this rage? There would be no winning back Rome from the pantheon, much less the Holy Land from the gods of Egypt, not while God—the one true God Joubert had been raised to follow—remained aloof and only delivered miracles as ambiguous as the return of a lone knight.

As much as it pained Joubert to even consider the idea, he felt that His Holiness was making a mistake by counting on prayers that, if they hadn't been answered in centuries, were not suddenly going to be answered now. Because of this, going to mass no longer brought Joubert much comfort. Instead, he relied on his time with Sartini for peace of mind, though it shamed him that his own prayers did not bring him such calm. In fact, what he had been most grateful for recently had originated with the pagans. After two months of anti-Christian riots, an unspoken truce had descended as the pagans celebrated the solstice and Saturnalia.

The faithful had gratefully flocked to the Basilica for Christmas, and the gates of the square had been thrown open. Joubert had been hopeful of a long-term détente, but by mid-January fighting was again breaking out in the streets. The gates were closed, and visitors carried letters from their priests to help gain entrance. Those few brave enough to risk the potential wrath of the pagans walked nervously through the enormous Basilica, peeking around columns as if expecting to be ambushed even within Vatican City. Joubert had watched the ragtag Templar struggle to provide safe passage, but, far from discouraging confrontation, the legacy of their brutal patrols made their mere presence outside the walls a provocation.

Of course His Holiness wouldn't allow Joubert himself to go outside. Since the incident in the square not long after his return, Joubert hadn't worn his tunic once, instead blending into the thinning crowds wearing clothes like everyone else, while his Templar brethren—still struggling with their swords and undependable modern equipment—fought and fell in the streets of Rome.

In English, someone said, "Excuse me."

Joubert turned toward the familiar voice. The old professor stood there, not facing Joubert but instead gazing at the monument like a tourist on his first visit. Joubert had seen him a handful of times since the rainy day in the gardens three and half months before. He'd learned the professor's first name was Stephen, but the mysterious old man was not very forthcoming on other subjects. Joubert asked the Templar about Stephen, but none of them knew any more than he did. Still, they all somehow had the sense that Stephen was someone to be trusted, like an elder statesmen. That wasn't so difficult to understand given Stephen's thoughtful character and supportive behavior; the strange thing was that the Templar also kept him as a secret among themselves. They would never refer to him in the company of faithful civilians or clergy. Joubert assumed it was an example of the tradition of paranoia the Templar had borne since going underground after the treachery of King Philip and the complicity of Pope Clement.

"Just who are you?" Joubert said in French. He was tired of all the mysteries that surrounded him, of never understanding why people did what they did.

"I've told you before, I'm a retired professor from New York." Stephen glanced at Joubert, then turned his attention back to the sculpture.

Joubert shook his head. "And you can just travel all the way to Vatican City and live here for months so that you can occasionally whisper your wisdom into my ear?"

Stephen laughed. "Something like that." Then he turned serious. "I did not come here to presume to tell you what to do. I'm here to provide what support I can."

"But why? What is your connection to the Templar? Were you in the Order in your youth?"

After a moment's hesitation, he shrugged. "Not exactly. Let's say we had shared interests."

Joubert waited, but Stephen volunteered no further details. "And what of His Holiness? Your comments often imply a deeper knowledge of him, as well."

Stephen shrugged again. "A trifle. I met him once or twice in his youth, decades ago. It was by chance, I doubt he would even remember me." He peered closely at Joubert. "It was before I resigned from the clergy."

"You were a priest?" Joubert tilted his head in disbelief. "And then a professor of French literature? When did you find time to join the Order?"

"As I said, I was never officially in the Order. I've just led a complicated life. Now, when in this interrogation are you going to ask why I've come to see you?"

With a frown and a sigh, Joubert gave up on prying anything more out of Stephen for now. "I wasn't planning on asking, since you never seem reluctant to tell me what you think."

"Fair point. What I think is that events are coming to a head. The cities, both Rome and the Vatican, are on edge."

Joubert didn't need Stephen to arrive at that assessment. Lately the street fights were growing more frequent and violent as the Ides of March approached. Springtime in Rome should have been beautiful and relaxing, but the month of March belonged to the god of war, and the pagans were celebrating with drunken feasts and banging swords on shields, and the atmosphere in the city led to an escalation of hostilities. The pagans weren't just striking random targets of opportunity. They had staked out the entrances to harass anyone coming or going, and they sometimes stopped and looted supply trucks. It was slowly becoming a siege.

"The question is," Stephen continued, "what role will the Order play? Tinder or match?"

"I don't believe those are the only two options."

"Then what?"

"I think the Order could douse that fire, or at least control it. Since the killing of the Minotaur, I've thought about the roots of the Order. It started simply to protect the pilgrims. That should be the core philosophy.

I tried to tell His Holiness, but he still has visions of past glories. As for me, I don't believe the Order should be in the business of wars, invasions, or conquering. That helps no one in this world. The Order should be a wall between the faiths."

"Then impart that idea to the knights."

"I'm in no position to do so. I cannot appear to speak against His Holiness to the Order. You said yourself that they can only follow me as far as they are allowed to."

"I think you underestimate your ability to find a third option."

Before Joubert could reply, Sartini rushed up. "Sorry I'm late." They still usually spoke in French when they weren't with Royer or His Holiness. Although Joubert's English was improving nicely, he preferred the comforting easiness of talking with Sartini in French. "It's worse out there today." She meant crossing into Vatican City. "As good as it is to get you out of here now and then, I'm wondering if we shouldn't go." She then looked at Stephen. She had not met him, and Joubert, following the knights' lead, hadn't told her about him. She obviously hadn't noticed the men talking as she approached, and she apologized in Italian, only to be as shocked as Joubert had been when the response came in Old French.

"I speak better French than Italian, truth be told."

"What a surprise!" Paola looked back and forth between them. "Maybe you should just stay here and visit with Mr. . . .?" She looked at the man expectantly.

"Oh, just Stephen, please."

"Then call me Paola. And you've already met Étienne, obviously."

"I've seen him around," Stephen said, looking back and forth between them. "But don't let me change your plans. We'll talk some other time. And don't worry too much, when I came in from the south, I didn't have any problems. But it won't be that way later this week."

"He's right," Paola said. "We go today or wait until after the Ides. Come on, there's a place I've been meaning to show you for months. It's a tourist spot, so I'm sure it's fine. It's getting there that makes me a little nervous."

Joubert shrugged at Stephen. "Until we meet again."

With a nod, Stephen said, "We will have much to discuss."

"What would you have to discuss?" Sartini asked. They strolled side by side up a sidewalk as they approached one of Rome's many obelisks. To their right was a beautiful view of the city. The ground rose enough here that looking to the west you were at rooftop level and could look across the sprawl of ancient buildings.

"He probably wants to ask me religious or historical questions. Much like you do." Joubert felt bad misleading her, but he was unsure how much he wanted to share with her. Not that he didn't trust her, but he didn't know how much His Holiness questioned her about his activities. He didn't want her to get caught in the middle of the situation.

She hadn't brought it up on the short drive here from the Vatican. He hated cars and kept his eyes closed as Sartini tore through the tiny streets at dangerous speeds. Although he'd been vigilant as they first left Vatican City, in case they were set upon by pagans, there had been only a small group of protestors by the gate as they turned left onto Via di Porta Cavalleggeri and entered the nearby tunnel. After a turbulent morning, the day seemed calm.

Sartini waved her arm at the church on their left, apparently putting Stephen out of her mind. "This used to be a vineyard in the fifteenth century. The church was built under French patronage. There are a lot of French connections around here. Come on." She grabbed his hand and led him to the right, onto a stairway curving down and around where the obelisk stood. It brought them to the top of a broad stairway down to a landing, with stairways on either side of that leading down to yet another broad stairway that finally reached street level. "These are the Spanish Steps, but they were funded by a French diplomat."

Sartini continued her history lesson, although she was talking about a film now, clearly enjoying herself. Joubert wasn't listening. There were lots of people enjoying the steps and the view, and he felt exposed and surrounded. Although Sartini trusted the anonymity of wandering the crowded streets of Rome, he was uneasy. It was true that most violence happened in the immediate environs of the Vatican where pagans and Christians had the most open confrontations, but the mood in the city was increasingly hostile, just as Stephen had said. Joubert looked around, trying to appear like an interested tourist and not a man surrounded by enemies. He both resented not being allowed to wear his tunic and having to admit a lone Templar would not be safe in the city. Most likely these were all pagans, followers of the pantheon. He felt at least some people in the crowd were looking back at him suspiciously. Could they have seen the pictures of him? He didn't think the pagans were supposed to use such machines, but the rules were hard to discern in this world. He glanced sideways at Sartini, but she was either oblivious to the situation or ignoring it. It was true that there seemed to be an understanding that certain spots should remain open to everyone regardless of their gods, but Joubert didn't trust the whims of the pagans.

"I think we should go," Joubert said quietly.

"No, we haven't gotten gelato yet." She accelerated down the steps. She still held his hand, and he stumbled forward until he matched her speed. "And you must see the fountain."

Joubert could already see a fountain in the square at the bottom of the steps. "It looks lovely, but I really think—" He stopped talking as a young man came toward them quickly, walking along on a landing on the lower steps. Joubert noticed the man's angry stare seemed focused on Sartini, not him; he hadn't expected that. He'd often seen men looking at her, but always with something else clearly on their mind, never with anger. Joubert stepped in between Sartini and the man, putting his left arm out and back to stop her behind him.

Sartini made a surprised sound as she bumped into his arm. The man stopped abruptly when he took notice of Joubert for the first time. He looked Joubert up and down, then peered around at Sartini. In an instant the stranger and Sartini were in a loud argument, their Italian too fast for Joubert to follow at all. He had to adjust his arm to keep Sartini behind him as he watched other people on the stairs attracted to the sound of the argument. A few of them came closer, nodding their heads in agreement. Joubert did not like his position on the stairs or the number of potential combatants. He needed to stop this.

Stepping forward, Joubert said, firmly but not shouting, "*Non.*" At the same time he poked the man in the breastbone with the first two fingers of his right hand. Joubert had strong hands, and he could hear a solid *thump* as the man coughed and gasped. Grabbing Sartini's hand, Joubert led her briskly down the remaining steps before a curious crowd could gather. He hurried past the gelato and flower stands and didn't spare the boat-shaped fountain a glance as he hurried them out of the square.

"Where can we get back to the car?"

Sartini didn't answer immediately, clearly shaken by whatever the argument had been about. Finally, she shook her head and pointed ahead. "On the right. Past the trees."

They kept walking quickly. Joubert glanced behind to make sure no one pursued them, and it appeared safe. "What was that man talking about?"

"He recognized me from university. He called me a traitor to my people."

"I don't understand."

"I'm Italian, but I don't follow the pantheon."

"Of course not, you're Christian."

Sartini rolled her eyes. "No, I'm not."

"But you work for His Holiness."

"I keep telling you—I don't! You know, before The Return, Sapienza students protested visits by the popes. I was kind of surprised when he came to me for help, but I do have specialized knowledge of your time. I was willing to work *with*—not *for*—him because of personal interest. What historian wouldn't want to meet someone like you?"

Joubert stopped in the shade of a tall palm tree. He looked around again, but no one seemed to pay them any attention. "I still don't understand. Who do you worship?"

She laughed. "No one. I'm an atheist."

Joubert laughed at her joke . . . until he realized she wasn't joking. He squinted at her, more confused than ever. He felt a little lightheaded.

"I never told you outright because I knew it would be difficult for you. And as we became friends, it just . . ." She shrugged. "I didn't want anything to come between us." She touched him gently on the arm.

The brush of her fingertips caused the same little jolt as always, but he was too distracted already to think about it. "How does an atheist live in a world full of gods?"

"It's a philosophy, not a science. It's not meant to correspond directly to reality. Some people call us abstainers, but I think that sounds too passive, so I still prefer atheist. Obviously, I acknowledge the gods, but I choose my own path. Maybe I should be called a nouveau atheist."

As she continued her explanation, her words faded from his hearing. He felt as though the ground began to tilt and spin. She stopped talking, a look of concern on her face. She reached a hand to his cheek. He felt her soft touch, but his vision darkened like it had before the obelisk in St. Peter's Square.

Joubert staggered across the grounds of Villeneuve du Temple under the light of a gibbous moon. It was a chill October, and he could see puffs of his breath as he made his way to the Church of St. Mary. He had a blanket from the dormitory wrapped around him, but the damp Parisian air seemed to slice through to his bones, bringing a shiver to his very soul. It was his soul that had finally driven him from his sleepless bed, a soul he feared he was losing. He could not sleep, and he could not wait any longer to unburden himself.

He had returned to Paris earlier that week after wandering slowly through Europe on the way back from the Holy Land. That summer Joubert had visited St. Peter's Basilica, hoping to find inspiration, something to justify all of the Saracen blood he had on his hands, but there had been no answers forthcoming; Pope Clement V lived in Avignon, and Rome seemed leaderless, with powerful families competing for dominance.

Joubert pulled the blanket tighter around his shoulders. He wore only his tunic and loin cloth beneath the blanket, his arms and legs were bare. The tall turrets of the dungeon loomed over him, and he heard somewhere in the night the snuffling and stamping of horses. He hurried across the wet grass, his bare feet cold, past the cemetery to the church, and flung the doors open.

"Father! Father Paquet!" Joubert's call echoed around the empty church. He wasn't sure if the young priest would be in the church this early, but as the echoes died down the glow of a single candle appeared in the rotunda. Joubert dropped the blanket to the floor and wiped his feet before padding across the cold stones to meet the priest.

Paquet looked wide awake, his dark hair, as black as his cassock, neatly combed. His dark eyes glittered in the candlelight. "Étienne?" He held the candle further away from his own eyes to better light his pre-dawn visitor. "What is it?"

Joubert, who'd been gone for years, was surprised the priest knew his name. He had met the priest briefly just days ago for the first time. "I cannot keep my doubts to myself any more. I have seen and done terrible things."

"Come." Paquet led him to a nearby pew, where they both sat, facing each other. "What you have done in the Holy Land you did in service of God."

"So we are told." Joubert looked down in his lap, where his hands rested palms up. They looked like foreign objects, something he did not place there of his own will. "Why would God require these things of us?"

Paquet set the candle down on the pew between them and folded his hands. "Only out of necessity. The Saracens—"

"Have their own God and claims," Joubert interrupted. "I'm sorry, Father, but I see no end to this. The Order has been pushed out of the Holy Land, but for how long? Surely we will return in greater numbers and kill more pagans. As blood runs deep in the name of God, we tell ourselves that heaven is full of those who can wield a sword without mercy or doubt."

"I would never say you should be untroubled by the necessity of the sword. Doubt is a part of faith, is it not? Do we not prove our true faith in God by believing in spite of uncertainty, in spite of questions that can not be answered in this life? We must take our leaps of faith over very real chasms of doubt. This is how God tests us."

"Then I am failing the test. Or perhaps I am refusing to take it anymore." Joubert stood and held his arms out. "These arms are grown strong on the necks of men I do not know, who only try to kill me because they also believe they are doing the will of God. Is this really what God wills, that I should not use these arms to love a woman, but only to kill the men of another land?"

Paquet also stood. His face was calm, unreadable, but his voice sharp. "You took the oath of the Order willingly. You could have stayed in Vézelay, tending the vineyards, overcharging the pilgrims and Crusaders, and loving all the farm girls you wished. But you became a knight of the Order of the Temple, knowing full well what that entailed. And vows or not, you knights occasionally fall into the embrace of a woman, don't pretend otherwise."

Joubert was so surprised by the priest's frank response that, before he could censor himself, he blurted back, "And priests have their housekeepers who wear suspect smiles for living with a celibate." Even as he finished speaking, he felt himself flush with shame. He dropped to his knees, but before he could beg forgiveness, Paquet laughed, a full-throated, head-thrown-back guffaw that reverberated throughout the rotunda.

"You are as quick and pointed with words as you are with sword, honorable knight," Paquet said as he sat back down. "Now get up, don't torture your knees on that stone. Sit with me."

Uncertain, Joubert remained kneeling. "But, Father. I have lost my faith. All that killing in the Holy Land . . . what god would want that? The belief that used to fill my heart has bled out on the battlefield, leaving me pale and empty of hope for this world." He bowed his head and waited to be rebuked.

Silence stretched out in the church. Outside there were the sounds of horses and men calling to one another. Joubert lifted his head and glanced toward the door before daring to look back at Paquet. The priest smiled understandingly. "There are more than two paths through life. To leave the path you have traveled so far does not mean you must now take the path to hell. It does not mean you are lost. Perhaps you have found your true path. Not everyone needs god to be righteous."

Joubert felt his expression must have been an exact counterpoint to Paquet's—while the priest looked self-assured and wise, Joubert felt nothing but confusion and doubt. Before he could gather his thoughts enough to speak, the doors of the church burst open loudly. Both he and Paquet leaped to their feet.

Three soldiers of King Philip IV marched in, their boots clacking loudly on the stone floor. Paquet stepped forward. "What are you doing? How dare you storm into the house of God in such a manner."

"How dare I?" The lead soldier said with a sneer. "How dare you, Father, to allow men such as these into this house. Now you will stand aside or be treated as one with these false knights."

Paquet did not move, but the two other soldiers stepped around him and grabbed Joubert by the arms. Joubert was still too shocked by everything that had happened to resist. He simply stood there as the head soldier intoned, "In the name of King Philip, you are under arrest for heresy."

As Joubert was led from the church, he looked back over his shoulder at the priest. Paquet stood there, his face still unreadable but somehow comforting. He nodded at Joubert with a grim smile. Joubert returned the nod, then walked proudly between the soldiers as they brought him to the Templars' own dungeon.

Joubert paced back and forth in his small apartment as he waited for Pope Boniface. It was the day after the memories of his arrest had come back—along with his feelings about his faith. After experiencing the events of that long-ago morning as if in a vision, he'd become aware of Sartini's beautiful face near his own, looking at him in concern. She ran a gentle hand across his forehead and through his hair. "Are you back with me?" she said.

He nodded. "I think so." Glancing around, Joubert saw that he was sitting beneath a palm tree. They were still in the Piazza di Spagna. Passersby looked down at him as if he was a public drunkard. Sartini helped him to his feet and they turned right onto Via di San Sebastianello and hurried up the street in the shadows between buildings. At the end of the block was a wide flight of stairs that got them back to Piazza della Trinità dei Monti at the top of the Spanish Steps.

The ride back to Vatican City was quiet. Joubert had huddled in his seat as he always did, but even Sartini was silent, obviously thinking about what had happened. Joubert had not shared the details of his vision, and she had not asked. After Sartini walked him to his room, however, she had broken the silence.

"You remembered something, didn't you?" Again she touched him lightly on his forearm. He had to pull away from her it was so overwhelming. She let him walk away and folded her arms across her chest. "Please tell me this isn't about what I said. That whatever's troubling you is from your past."

He didn't respond. Since turning up in this world, his faith had seemed to be his foundation. Now he knew his faith here in Rome had been an echo of something he lost centuries ago. Yet here we was in Vatican City, a favorite of the pope, who wanted him to fight a new Crusade, a pointless, wasteful war. His only remaining source of comfort was the woman who stood in the room with him, who was in danger from her own countrymen because of gods and the people who followed them. And because of him.

He was not ready to share what had happened to him that morning in St. Mary's, not yet. But he knew one thing. "You should stay here tonight."

The flurry of emotions that crossed her face made him realize the implications of his wording. He couldn't think of all that. "On the grounds, I mean. To be safe from the pantheon. There are other rooms . . ." He trailed off, embarrassed, thinking again what he had thought when they had first met, that she unnerved him more than a charge of Saracens. Lost from his faith, he was released from his vows. Everything was different.

"Oh, of course," she said, a complexity of expressions still haunting her face. He almost unburdened himself of the vision, but then her expression cooled. "But the university grounds are secure. I'll be fine there."

"But he was from your university."

"So he would have had many chances to approach me there, but he didn't. He was emboldened off campus. Most people on campus are open-minded. We're open to all faiths, and haven't had any problems. At least no more than you'd expect from any large group of twenty-year-olds living on their own." She paused, realizing that wasn't helping. "Don't worry, I'll go straight to my apartment and lock the door. I'll report him to the campus police."

They stood staring at each other. He did not want her to go, but felt out of his depth. Joubert knew she would do what she wanted regardless of any demands on his part. The interaction between men and women in this age was radically different, and his relationship with her was unprecedented and complicated. He also knew that the revelations of his memories had left him shaken, and he needed time alone. If she stayed, she would continue to press him for details. He slumped into his chair, feeling weary, as if he had lived through all the hundreds of years since his birth.

"I don't know," he said.

Her brow furrowed. "You don't know what?"

"Anything."

Her expression softened. "I'll be okay. Everything will be okay. I'll come see you tomorrow." She had briefly held his hand before leaving. Then she called when she got to her apartment to let him know she was safely locked in and to say good night. It was the first time he experienced feeling close to someone over the telephone, another machine he disliked. He wanted to talk to Stephen, but none of the Templar knew where to contact him. Joubert had slept poorly, and the clatter of weapons and echoes of shouts filled the night. The telephone awakened him from a light, troubled sleep. It was Sartini.

"I don't want to leave my apartment. It's really bad out there today. The campus police have even issued a warning."

"I wish you had stayed here."

"Me too."

They were quiet for a moment. He was aware that neither of them had qualified their previous comments, as they had last night. She knew something had changed even though he hadn't explained it to her.

"Yesterday I remembered my arrest. I remembered that I had essentially renounced my faith just before the soldiers arrived to take me to the dungeon."

"Oh, Étienne." There was true pain and concern in her voice. Joubert was surprised how much emotion could come through the wires of machines. "I wish I were there. Do you feel the same way now?" She paused again, and again he said nothing. He knew she understood better than anyone what an untenable position he was in. She broke the silence. "What are you going to do? Are you even ready to decide what comes next?"

"I don't know. I tossed and turned all night, thinking and dreaming about it. I guess I will finish the discussion I started with my confessor all those centuries ago. But now I confess to His Holiness."

"I'll come over as soon as I can." Before he could protest, she added, "I'll beg a ride from one of the campus police. I'll be fine. See you soon."

He'd been pacing in his room ever since. He'd gotten in touch with Royer, who luckily had spent the night on the grounds. Joubert didn't want to have to rely on his beginning English for this discussion. Royer had arranged an audience. His Holiness always came to Joubert's room, part of keeping Joubert a secret until receiving a sign from God to do otherwise. Joubert was just about to call Sartini to find out if she was on her way yet when there was a knock at his door. It was His Holiness and Royer, so Joubert would have to worry about Sartini during his audience with the pope. His Holiness would not wait on the threshold while Joubert made a telephone call.

Joubert sighed as the men walked in. "I'm sorry, Your Holiness, but I have something troubling to discuss with you."

"March is always a difficult month with the pantheon," Boniface said, assuming that was what Joubert wanted to talk about. "Do not let it worry you. They will be fasting soon, and the fighting will settle down. We must bide our time."

"You mean bide our time until we start the fighting all over again."

"The path of the righteous is not an easy one. It is good that you do not like war, Étienne, as long as you remain ready to answer God's call to arms. That time is nigh, I feel."

Joubert turned away, looking out his window. The trees of the Vatican Gardens were rich with spring-green leaves. He'd been admiring this view for five months, through fall and winter and into spring. It was considered a small room in these days, but it was a palace compared to the dormitories of Villeneuve du Temple, far beyond what his vows to the Order would normally allow, certainly rich beyond belief to one used to battlefield tents at best while fighting in the Holy Land.

"I lost my faith on the battlefields of God, Your Holiness. My empty heart was hidden by the fog of years behind me, but now I remember. I could not resolve God and war, and since war was so clearly true, I found

God to be false. Such is what I was confessing the very morning I was arrested for heresy."

A deep silence filled the room. Royer looked uncomfortable as he translated. His Holiness appeared stunned, even angry. "But the miracle of your return must prove to you that God exists. Even the false gods prove His existence as we see their pagan displays of power beyond the natural. The supernatural fills the world, and you transcended the fire of your death through the supernatural intervention of God Himself."

"Yes, of course. I no longer deny God, but I also no longer feel the calling to fight in His name. What do all these gods need of war?"

"That is not our question to ask! God has given us all we need to know in scripture, and we must follow him in faith, trusting to His wisdom."

"Father Paquet told me not everyone needs god to be righteous."

"Then this Paquet was an apostate. God is righteousness, and to fight for God is a righteous path. This cannot be questioned by men of faith."

"But how does this end before both sides stand deep in the blood of their faithful soldiers? This is a new world, and we must find new ways."

The pope turned and opened the door. "I will debate this no longer. I am going to pray to God for guidance, and I hope, for the sake of your eternal soul, that you do the same." Boniface walked rapidly out of the room.

Joubert hurried after the pontiff, leaving a confused Royer behind in his room. "Your Holiness!" Joubert called in English. Boniface continued up the corridor. Two young priests, one tall, one short, were coming down the hall toward Boniface. Joubert knew the pope would not want any of this discussion to take place in public, but he no longer cared so much what His Holiness wanted. Joubert needed some resolution to this discussion and was increasingly on edge with worry about Sartini. He had hoped she would have arrived by now to help him through this. With brisk strides of his long legs, he caught up to His Holiness just as the priests were passing. Joubert noticed a nervous glance from both young men as he stepped between them and the pope, and thought that they must have noticed him raising his voice to His Holiness, a scandalous transgression.

Joubert was turning his back toward them to try to catch the pope's eye when a peripheral glimpse of motion drew his attention back. He turned his head just in time to see them drawing short swords from behind their backs. With a shout Joubert pushed His Holiness toward a nearby door into a room off the hallway and dove toward the armed men. Behind him he heard a thump as Boniface hit the door, which luckily wasn't shut all the way. As Joubert plowed into the men, the door slammed open and the pope fell into the room, giving him some cover.

Joubert grabbed the sword arm of the tall man as they hit the wall of the corridor, but was only grasping at the other man with his left hand. The tall man grabbed Joubert's throat with his free hand, but Joubert ignored that for a moment. The short man was scrambling away, cursing Joubert in the name of various gods as he tried to bring his sword to bear without hitting his compatriot. Joubert spun to his left, swinging the sword arm of the tall man down to parry the short man's attack. The swords clashed together, driving the short man's sword down. Then Joubert swung the tall man's arm quickly back up, catching the short man in the jaw with the flat of the blade.

The short man, his jaw slammed shut in midcurse, cried out with a spray of blood after biting his tongue. Now Joubert shoved the tall man back against the wall. He let go of the tall man's sword arm, and swept his right arm across his body and down, breaking the tall man's grip on his throat. He smashed the palm of his left hand into the tall man's forehead, driving the man's head into the wall. Joubert then jumped back to get some maneuvering room, expecting to feel the point of the short man's sword at any second.

The short man was indeed just starting to run at him with his sword arm extended, but he was now rushing toward the spot where Joubert was no longer standing. Joubert grabbed the short man's sword arm and guided the sword into the thigh of the tall man, using the short man's own inertia to drive the point deep into the flesh. The short man froze for a second as the tall man screamed. Joubert punched the short man solidly in the nose, and he staggered back, leaving his sword in his compatriot's thigh. The tall man dropped his sword as he clasped at the one protruding from his leg. He slumped to the floor.

Joubert retrieved the fallen sword and spun toward the short man. The short man stared back at him for just a second, blood streaming from nose and mouth, before fleeing back up the corridor. Joubert turned to check on Boniface, but His Holiness was already up and standing in the doorway looking stunned at the bloody mess Joubert had made of the two men.

"Are you injured, Your Holiness?' Joubert said in English.

"No, I'm fine. A bruised shoulder, perhaps." He stepped into the corridor and looked down at the failed assassin on the floor. The pagan was pale and trembling, mumbling to Zeus for strength as he tried to staunch his bleeding. Boniface turned away from the pagan. "You saved my life, Étienne. Tell me that you don't feel the strength of the Holy Spirit as you must have in the Holy Land."

Joubert looked between the pope and the pagan. "There is nothing holy about it. I see two people, both wanting to kill the other for god." He slipped back into French. "I walk the path of righteousness by stopping it."

"Étienne!" Royer ran up to them, cell phone in hand. He went pale at the scene before him.

"What is it?" Joubert grabbed Royer's shoulder to give him strength.

"There's rioting at Sapienza. Followers of the pantheon have stormed the campus."

Joubert felt sick to his stomach. "You will drive me there." Joubert turned to the fallen pagan. "I regret doing this, but I have great need." He grabbed the sword by the hilt and, as gently as possible, drew it from the wound. The man writhed on the floor in renewed pain. Joubert, now with a sword in both hands, nodded at Royer. "Let's go." Royer took off running for his car.

Boniface grabbed Joubert's arm. "You cannot leave me unguarded!"

"You can call for help from my room, Your Holiness, for both you and this injured man. You have all the other Templar to protect you. I must leave." He shrugged out of Boniface's grip, and ran after Royer.

Royer's driving made Sartini's seem safe, but Joubert did not begrudge the careening drive eastward across the Tiber and through the winding streets to the campus apartments where Sartini lived. Royer had almost run down a small group of people who tried to block the road as they came out of Vatican City. After his moment of fear seeing the bloodied assassin, the young man had risen to the occasion, a grim look on his face as he accelerated the car, scattering the youths in tunics out of their way. He had not let up since, aggressively passing every chance he got in the midmorning traffic. During the drive, Joubert took Royer's telephone and called Sartini, struggling to punch in the numbers as he was slammed back and forth in his seat. There was no answer.

As they neared campus, young men and women streamed away from the university on foot, many with bloodied noses or blackened eyes, limping along or cradling an injured arm. The campus police were out in full force, and the worst of the riot seemed over. Finally they were racing into the foyer of Sartini's building, then up the stairs, Royer leading the way. Joubert had never visited her apartment, a fact that now pained him. They raced to the second floor, down a hallway, and around a corner. A body lay outside an open apartment door. It was Stephen. His eyes were closed, one of them swollen shut. He held his right arm tight to his body, but Joubert couldn't tell if he was protecting the arm or his stomach. Joubert thought he was dead, but, as they approached, Stephen turned his head at the sound of their footsteps. He struggled to get up, failed, but still tried to stretch his left arm across the open doorway to block them from entering.

Joubert said, "What are you doing here?"

"Oh, it's you. Good." Stephen's voice was faint and hard to understand, his lips torn and bloody. He slumped back down to the side of the door, his left arm now limp at his side. "I'm sorry. I fought them as best as I could."

"But—"

"Don't bother with me," Stephen said forcefully, which made him cough, a deep rattling sound. "You need to go to Paola . . . now."

Joubert stared into the apartment. He felt as though he couldn't blink. Furniture was overturned, glass shelves smashed. There was blood. He forgot about Stephen and entered the apartment. "Paola?" There was no response at first, the only sound the crunching of broken glass beneath his boots. "Where are you?"

He heard something, a sigh, a whimper. Hurrying around a corner he first saw a bare foot, her leg, a pool of blood. Joubert rushed to her side, taking her right hand in his. Her eyes were closed. A trickle of blood ran from the corner of her mouth down a pale cheek. Her left hand held a stab wound in her stomach. A visceral battlefield smell froze his heart. "Paola?"

Her eyes fluttered open. They looked blank, unseeing, for a moment, but then she turned toward him, and they brightened. "Étienne." Then tears ran from her eyes. "You found me."

"Yes." He ran a hand through her hair. "Nothing could have stopped me."

"I know." She smiled and squeezed his hand. "I'll miss you."

"No," he said roughly. "I'll be right here."

"I know. But I'll be going soon."

"Paola—" he started to say, but she was already gone.

Joubert never clearly remembered the next several days. The car ride back to Vatican City was a blank. He could only acknowledge that, logically, it must have happened. But then there were a series of sharp memories: Returning to his room and throwing the two short swords on his bed before slipping on his tunic. Seeing His Holiness somewhere in a hall, but with one look the pontiff stepped into a room and closed the door as Joubert stalked past. Striding though St. Peter's Square, rallying the Templar to his side, a fire in their eyes he had never seen before, a reflection of the rage that burned within himself.

After that, there were blurry glimpses of the streets of Rome as though wrapped in fog, a chill silence covering the city, broken only by the clash of metal on metal, the begging of the wounded, the lamentations of the dying. He heard himself shouting, "Bring me the ones who killed her!" followed by days and nights of blood and screams falling on the city like a cold spring rain.

Joubert became aware of knocking on his door. He sat in his chair looking out across the gardens, lush and green in the afternoon sun. April had come to Rome peaceful and quiet after the Battle of the Ides of March. Christians and pantheon alike celebrated spring. The Spanish Steps were full of flowers, and the Vatican was preparing for Easter, which came late this year. The knocking continued. He heard Royer call his name. He didn't respond.

It was all the things they hadn't talked about. When she hadn't been asking questions about himself and his time, she'd been telling him about her time, not about herself. By the time the siege was broken and the fighting done and he was back to his senses, she was buried and he didn't know where. He didn't know her family or her friends. Royer must have known, but Joubert didn't ask and Royer didn't offer, apparently unsure how to broach the subject. It was just as well.

After a short break there was more knocking on the door. Joubert sighed and stood up. He had asked Royer about Stephen, but no one seemed to know what had happened to him. Was he dead and buried in Rome? Returned to America? Royer said he had told them to go, that help was on its way, but he hadn't looked good. Joubert remembered none of that. Perhaps that was just as well too. Stephen had fought bravely to protect Paola, and Joubert had just left him there on the floor bleeding.

Joubert opened the door. Royer stood there looking sympathetic. His Holiness stood behind him, a stern look on his face. Boniface walked through the door, sweeping past the other men. Joubert exchanged looks with Royer, who shrugged before stepping in and closing the door.

Boniface glanced around the room. Joubert had not been much for housekeeping lately. His Holiness shook his head. "I think this has gone on long enough," His Holiness said in English.

Joubert said nothing.

"The Order needs you. What you did . . . it inspired all of them. The pagans respect and fear them now. There's been no violence in over two weeks. We expect the square to be full for Easter, with no worry of what will happen to the faithful as they gather."

Joubert spoke as much in English as possible, lapsing into French when necessary, relying on Royer to help him get his point across. "But at what cost, Your Holiness? All I did was bloody my hands. How many of these children—and children they were—had ever lifted a sword before? They rallied around the worst of their own because they knew no better. I do know better."

His Holiness waved his hand as if brushing away Joubert's concerns. "The sins of war will be forgiven by God, and the blood of heathens cannot stain the hands of the faithful. It is time to assert ourselves in this world of false gods. The news of our victory has rallied the faithful around the world. The Order has gotten more volunteers in the last two weeks than in the last two years. This is the sign I have been waiting for. God expects his flock to fight for their faith, and you shall lead them."

Joubert was not surprised by the vehemence of His Holiness; the pope spoke with the fervor unique to those who call for war without having fought in it. "Maybe God already gave you a message that you didn't hear. He sent me, an apostate, back in the tunic of the Order, but unarmed and unarmored. Maybe that was a sign in itself."

Boniface frowned. He said nothing.

Joubert sighed. "I'm not saying we can avoid fighting in this world, that is a sad and obvious truth. But perhaps the Templar shouldn't be leading a holy war, but instead serving as a holy defense. Perhaps we can lead the faithful by standing strong for our faith but not killing for it."

"After the victory you have won, you want to stop? To not advance, but to merely hold your ground?" The pope's face reddened as his voice rose. "No, you are a knight of the Crusades, and you will return the Order to its original prominence, a force for the church against the pagans."

"I will lead the Order, but in a new direction, and they will gladly follow. We will become a reborn Templar, the Nouveau Templar. We will fight for the faithful when necessary, but we will not oppress the other faiths, just as we would not have them oppress us."

His Holiness stared grimly at Joubert. Joubert did not blink. The two stood quietly for a minute while Royer fidgeted uncomfortably.

Finally the pope seemed to relax. "Perhaps you make a point. We must still show mercy to our enemies." He turned his back on Joubert and Royer to look out the window. "Of course, we need to think beyond Rome, to the position the Templar and the Church should have in the world." He turned back toward Joubert. "The pagan gods have carved up Manhattan among themselves while faithful Christians have become an oppressed minority. This presents the perfect home base for these new Templars. You will establish a strong Christian presence in New York, a counterpart to the Holy See in Italy."

Joubert didn't know what to say. He had not expected His Holiness to actually give him what he asked for. He couldn't help but wonder if there was something else going on, if something had happened while he'd been fighting or mourning that influenced the pope in this direction. Regardless, the important thing was that he was finally getting a chance to do something constructive. And maybe this would be a good change for him in other ways, to leave Rome and its memories behind him. A fresh start for both himself and the Order.

He knelt to kiss the Ring of the Fisherman. "Yes, Your Holiness."

Joubert stood at the window looking at the sun shining on the trees. The gardens looked more beautiful than ever, now that it felt less like a view from a prison cell. His Holiness was finally letting him free in the world. He had little to do until he left for Manhattan. He didn't know how to travel in this day and age, those details would be handled by someone else. Would he fly in an airplane? He shuddered. He would prefer to sail across the ocean. As his gaze followed a flock of birds out of the sky and down to the ground, he saw Stephen standing beneath the trees looking up at him.

He leaned forward, face pressed against the glass. It was definitely the old professor. Joubert ran from his room, almost falling down the stairs, then rushed outside. Stephen was still there, standing in the shade waiting for him. Stephen stepped into the sun to firmly shake Joubert's hand, a wide smile on his face. He looked exactly as he had when Joubert saw him in the Basilica, with no traces of his wounds.

Joubert was shaking his head in disbelief. "I am glad to see you, but how did you survive? You look like you were never injured."

"I'm a fast healer." He smirked as he said it. "How are you?"

"I'm better. I'm going to New York City to lead the Templars."

"Are you?" Stephen looked skeptical.

"I just spoke with His Holiness earlier today. It's settled. I'm going to transform the Order into the Nouveau Templar. No Crusades. We will protect the faithful without oppressing the pagans."

"And you believe the pope is simply going to hand over his army to you? Let you change it to a peacekeeping force?"

Joubert was a bit taken aback at the edge in Stephen's voice. "It's what he told me just hours ago."

Stephen frowned. "That morning we spoke in the Basilica. The morning before—"

"Is this important?" Joubert did not want to speak of that time.

"Yes. The Swiss Guards saw me speaking with you and Paola. They told Boniface that they had seen me talking with you before. They told him that, now that they thought about it, they had seen me around frequently."

"How do you know this?"

"I tried to contact you that afternoon, to find out what had happened while you were out. I'd heard rumors of a disturbance. But the Swiss Guards intercepted me. I was not allowed into Vatican City."

"I tried to find you through the Templar."

"The guards found me before I was able to contact anyone. It was getting too dangerous to just wait outside the city walls to try to get a message to you or the Order. I went back to my hotel and then the next morning I was able to track down Paola. She seemed the easiest way to get a message to you. The trouble was I didn't know if she was connected to the church or not. We were both suspicious of the other. But we soon figured out we were on the same side. Then, before we could call you, they broke into her apartment. I cannot tell you how sorry I am I was not able to save her."

Joubert closed his eyes. "I thank you for what you did. Without you we may not have had our last words." But he did not want to think about those terrible final minutes, not now. Instead he focused on Stephen's comment about His Holiness and the Order. "Why do you doubt that Pope Boniface is giving me command of the Order?"

"He wanted you as a figurehead to rally the faithful. You're the miracle soldier. He may be the pope, but he's just an old man elected by other old men. You are a soldier of God returned. And now he's seen, beyond a doubt, how effectively you can command the Templar. But you want to lead them in a different direction. You would confuse the faithful. Has he ever seemed to support your ideas before this morning?"

Joubert felt his stomach turn. "No."

"No." Stephen paused to look around, to make sure they weren't being watched. "I was recovering from my wounds during the days of battle. But once the smoke had cleared—"

"I still can't believe you survived. Your wounds seemed—"

"I'll get to that in a moment," Stephen said. "Once it seemed safe to walk the streets, I tried to reach you again. The Swiss Guards were still watching for me. But this time they took me straight to Boniface. He pelted me with questions about my relationship to the Templar, how I knew you, if I had known Paola, what the knights thought now that they had been through such a bloody battle under your command. He didn't sit me down and tell me his plans, but the nature of his questions made his point of view just as clear.

"I'm certain the Order will not become your Nouveau Templar. He's getting rid of you. The Nouveau Templar will be a splinter of the Order, relegated to the strange mess of gods that is Manhattan. The true Order, if you will, will remain in his pocket."

Joubert was stunned. Everything Stephen said rang true. How had Joubert believed he'd changed the pope's mind so quickly? He became angry with himself and His Holiness. "I don't need the Order, then. I will learn this New World and its language. I will do what I can with those willing to follow my path."

Stephen nodded. "You are not lost if you're willing to make your own path. Not everyone needs god to be righteous."

Joubert felt like the ground lurched dizzily beneath his feet. "What did you say?" It had been just under six months—or a little over seven hundred years—since Joubert had heard Father Paquet say that very phrase.

"Unlike you, I've kept my faith. I just don't think it's that important for everyone. Aren't the results of a person's ethics more important than the source of their ethics? God or logic, I don't care how you decide to be a good person. Before The Return, I always preferred nice unbelievers than mean-spirited believers. Now, with gods everywhere, I feel the same way. I don't care who you follow, or if you are indifferent to all these immortals. Just be a good person."

Joubert stared closely at Stephen, remembering all his cryptic comments, rethinking them, fitting them back together. Finally, he imagined away the wrinkles and gray hair. "Father Paquet?"

"I have not gone by that name for centuries. Now I'm Stephen Hugh Wilkins, retired professor and"—he straightened his jacket—"occasional valet when I find the right person with the right cause." Stephen smiled. "Let me be your guide in New York, sir."

"But how can this be?"

With a pat on Joubert's shoulder, Wilkins said, "You're not the only miracle in the world. You just took a shortcut while I walked the long road. But here we are, reunited, and both headed for Manhattan."

Joubert pondered this revelation until he found his voice again. He focused on one minor detail, perhaps to stave off thinking about everything else. "So when you said you had met Boniface in his youth—"

"Yes, his youth, not mine. I looked exactly as I do now. When they took me before him I was worried what would happen if he recognized me. In fact, I fear that he did. There was a look in his eye late in the interview . . . but there's no way to know without asking him. What I do know is that soon after that the interview was over and the Swiss Guard hurried me from the room. Perhaps, even subconsciously, that motivated him to get rid of me. And, by association, you. Funny how serendipitous the universe can be, isn't it?"

For a moment Joubert just stood there, then, for the first time in weeks, he began to laugh.

Sestercentennial Day

by William Leisner

For most of the residents of Vientiane, Laos, the twentieth day of the fifth month in the Year of the Horse started out as just another day. It had rained through most of the night, but the clouds had broken by daybreak. The sky now glowed red and orange as the sun peaked over the horizon, promising another typically hot and humid summer day. Even if the Western calendar hadn't fallen out of common usage here and throughout Asia over the past decade, they still wouldn't have considered this day as anything special. Most would have of course recognized the Gregorian calendar date—the fourth day of July—as Independence Day in the United States, but this meant no more to them than the Lao New Year would have in Denver or Dallas or Des Moines.

The date definitely meant something to Chris Vang. She quietly climbed out of bed before the first ray of the dawn's early light had breached the windows of her family's apartment, and dressed quickly and quietly in the dark so as not to wake her sister. She pulled on a pair of white cotton shorts, and her old Minnesota Twins baseball jersey, one of the last pieces of clothing she had left to remind her of home. Then she reached into the very back of the bottom drawer of her bureau, and grabbed hold of a tightly folded, bedsheet sized piece of fabric she had hidden there. She shoved the triangular bundle under her arm and padded barefoot to the front door.

"This is not a wise idea," the family's household spirit whispered to her from the miniature shrine set on a pedestal by the entryway. As usual, Chris ignored it as she slipped her feet into the pair of sandals left by the door, then left the apartment.

She took the stairs down rather than calling for the rickety elevator.

She emerged from the stairwell, and paused to scan the building's old and empty lobby. Once she was sure there was no one else around, she made her way to the front doors, past the long-disused security check-in desk and through the non-functional metal detector. Up until fourteen years ago, this building had been the United States Embassy to the Lao People's Democratic Republic. The latter nation had ceased to exist following The Return—the Marxist contention that religion was the opiate of the masses did not go over well with the Jade Emperor and the other newly-returned gods of the Asian world, and the ruling Communist Party of Laos was disbanded.

As for the United States, the government in Washington had also been thrown into turmoil, and their ambassador in Vientiane completely cut off from her superiors in the State Department. She had allowed her non-essential embassy staff to go home, but vowed to remain at her posting until given clear orders to do otherwise. In those weeks following The Return, the embassy received more than four hundred American citizens of Asian ancestry, mostly Hmong who had been drawn to their homeland by the call of the gods, but who had no homes or surviving family to return to in this foreign land.

Chris paused as she reached the glass doors, one hand resting on the crash bar, and looked out across the compound's courtyard toward the main gates. She saw there were already signs of life out in the street beyond. A coffee and pastry cart was in place across the road and already serving to a short line of patrons, and delivery bikes zipped back and forth. Once she walked out these doors and was spotted with the object under her arm, she would be committed to this course, no turning back. Not that she had any intentions of turning back…but…until now, it was an open option. The household spirit was right—what she was planning was not wise, and would probably end up being dangerous.

Chris took a deep breath, pushed the door open, and stepped out into the already muggy morning. Moving quickly down the concrete steps, she made a straight line to the flagpole that stood at the center of the courtyard. It had been unadorned since the *Naga* of the Black Stupa, newly arisen along with all the other gods of the world, finally convinced the ambassador to leave. The flag had been lowered in a formal, though slightly rushed, ceremony witnessed by the expatriated Americans who had by then established residences in the abandoned staff quarters and offices of the American Embassy compound.

With little ceremony now, Chris Vang unwound the line from the double-pronged cleat, unfolded the bundle in her arms, and hooked the brass eye at the upper corner at the edge of the blue, star-dappled field through the first of the two fasteners tied to the rope. She did the same for the bottom eye, being careful not to let the large striped cloth touch the ground as she fumbled with it, just as she was taught back in Girl Scouts. She tried not to rush, but at the same time, she knew this could all be for naught if she dawdled for too long.

At last, the flag secured, she began to pull hand over hand on the rope. The rusted pulley at the top of the pole initially squealed in protest, then began to turn freely, and within seconds, the flag reached the top of the pole. The morning air was dead still, but the red, white and blue banner could not have been any more conspicuous if there had been a gale-force wind pulling at it. The foot and bicycle traffic on the opposite side of the embassy compound walls had stopped, and a small crowd began to gather just outside the open gate. Another pair of early risers exiting the building after her had stopped short just outside the door, staring in shock.

Chris tied off the cord and took three paces backwards, keeping her eyes upraised. From the corner of her eye, she saw a few scattered faces starting to appear in the windows of the old embassy building. She willed herself to ignore them, focusing on the banner she had just raised, and placed her right hand over her heart.

"*Oh*—" she started to sing, then immediately stopped, mortified by the decidedly unmelodious sound that had just come out of her mouth. She cleared her throat, and tried again. "*O-oh, say, can you see, by the dawn's early light...*" It was quite a different thing, Chris realized, to be one voice amongst thousands singing all together at a baseball stadium, and another thing entirely to perform one of the more challenging musical compositions ever written solo, a cappella, and without practice. Not that she could have practiced; no one had dared sing this song aloud here in over a decade. "*...at the twilight's last gleaming...*"

This is not a wise idea, the household spirit's voice repeated in her mind. She found it harder to ignore now that its words were now proving true. "*Whose bright stars and...bright stars...*" she continued, fumbling the lyrics but refusing to stop now. When she had first dreamt this idea up, she had envisioned her fellow Americans in exile cheering and joining in this show of patriotic pride. Many of them were first-generation Americans, just as she was. Chris's grandfather had been a refugee from Laos during the civil war here in the 1970s, and his son, her father, had been born in one of the squalid refugee camps across the river in Thailand. All through her childhood, they had impressed upon her how very fortunate they were to be living in the free world.

Chris was aware of the growing crowd of curious onlookers at the edges of her peripheral vision. There were at least a hundred now, with more flowing in from the streets into the courtyard. But all they did was stare, as if they had never seen the Stars and Stripes or heard the National Anthem before in their lives.

As if they had all completely forgotten.

"And the rockets' red glare, the bombs bursting in air..." Her voice sounded, in her own ears, like a small animal was being tortured. But she refused to waver, and forged on. *"Gave proof through the night that our flag was still there…"*

"O—" It was just one other voice, soft and extremely tentative sounding, but clearly coming from one of the many spectators clustered by the front door of the old embassy building. The other singer realized she had anticipated Chris, and stopped herself after that single note. But Chris followed her lead, welcoming the addition of her voice. *"—say, does that star-spangled banner yet wa-a-ave..."*

"O'er the land of the free..." Chris's voice cracked again, this time from emotion, as more and more of the crowd joined in. *"...and the home of the brave?"* The final line echoed off the compounded perimeter walls, and was followed by a thunderous round of applause. Someone in the mob started up the chant, "U-S-A! U-S-A!" At that moment, the slightest of breezes kicked up, and the flag slowly unfurled as the wind got caught in its loose folds. Chris kept her head upraised, in part to keep the tears welling in her eyes from falling.

It was then that the *xiezhi* leapt over the tops of the compound walls and began their attack.

Lieutenant Akamu Thammavong was fully aware that this day was the Fourth of July, and what that meant. As the senior officer of the Vientiane Police Force charged with enforcing the peace in the section of the city where so many expatriated Americans had resettled, he made it his business to know such things. All the better so as to be able to anticipate trouble from that segment of the population.

So he was not at all surprised when, early that morning, a small *xiezhi* burst through the door to the station, gouging a large groove into the wood with the horn on the top of its head. "Lawmen!" the goat-sized, dragon-like creature said, its nostrils flaring. "You must come!"

Thammavong's partner, Officer Kale Silosoth, looked at the beast with an annoyed expression. "What? At this time of the morning?" he asked, a spray of pastry crumbs from his morning *pah thawng ko* flying from his lips.

Thammavong, though, was immediately up out of his seat. The *xiezhi*, legendary arbiters of justice, had served the Vientiane Police Force very well in the years since their reappearance, and were extremely effectual in dealing with the run-of-the-mill problems such as pickpocketing and domestic disputes that made up ninety-five percent of law enforcement duties in the prefecture. If they were asking for assistance from their mortal human counterparts, there was something very out of the ordinary going on. "What is it?" he asked.

"A mass disturbance at the American Compound!" the *xiezhi* answered in a high, excited voice.

"Ah-ha!" Thammavong turned to Silosoth with a wide grin of vindication. "I warned you it would be something today!" said as he retrieved his service pistol and its holster from his top desk drawer.

"Yeah, yeah," Silosoth said, rolling his eyes as he also stood. "You've been saying the same thing this time every year; you were bound to be right eventually."

Thammavong swallowed the sarcastic reply he was tempted to spit back at Silosoth as they followed the *xiezhi* out the door, and climbed into the SAIC patrol car parked out front. The younger man had only been stationed to this district two years earlier; he hadn't been here that first Independence Day, the year after the *Naga* emerged from beneath *Thart Dam* and drove the whites from their embassy. After that hard crackdown, the turmoil surrounding the date in subsequent years had been minor. But this year, Thammavong had warned Silosoth, would be different. This year—A.D. 2026 on the Western calendar—marked the 250th anniversary of the founding of the United States of America, and that meant they could expect some of the worst demonstrations and riots since The Return. Silosoth had simply scoffed then. Now Thammavong, unfortunately, would have the last laugh.

Signs in Lao script gave way to ones written in English as they drove toward the heart of Americatown, and the stately beauty of the city's

French Colonial architecture turned perceptibly dingier. Thammavong had lived and worked in this part of Vientiane for nearly twenty years, and every time he came here, he felt a terrible sadness for what had become of the neighborhood. What had once been a very good pho noodle restaurant on Lan Xang Boulevard now had a neon sign in its front window boasting "REAL HAMBURGERS!" in garish red letters, and constantly reeked of cooked water buffalo. Next door, a pawn broker displayed a plasma television screen playing a never-ending loop of flashy old Hollywood superhero movies. Hip-hop music played from the open windows of buildings that had been taken over and turned into overcrowded immigrant housing.

After another turn, the nineteenth century structures gave way to the drabber styles of the twentieth, and the first signs of trouble became evident. Angry voices hurled insults at them in both English and Hmong as they rolled up to the graffiti-scrawled wall that surrounded the American Compound. Thammavong pulled the car up directly in front of the gates, as a pack of *xiezhi* held a crowd of agitated Hmong at bay on the opposite side of the street. Silosoth opened his door, got out of the car, and suddenly stopped. "Son of a bitch," he whispered as he stared up over the wall. Thammavong followed his gaze, and saw what had prompted his reaction: an American flag waving lazily in the morning breeze. Thammavong turned back to his partner with a withering glare. At least now he understood they were dealing with more than a few illegal fireworks being shot off.

Inside the compound, a larger crowd was being held back against the inside walls, and against the sides of the buildings within the compound. There were more angry shouts hurled the policemen's way, but the loudest ones were rewarded with a sharp poke in the midsection from their *xiezhi* guards. At the center of the open courtyard, just a few meters from the base of the flagpole, a figure lay prostrate on the grass, one of the larger *xiezhi* pinning her down with its front paws. The beast growled menacingly at an older man who had approached too close, who was shaking his head in worry at the detained young woman. Thammavong marched in that direction, putting himself between the girl and the man he took as her father. "I assume this *meka* here is responsible for *that*," he said to the *xiezhi*, jerking his head up toward the top of the flagpole.

The *xiezhi* nodded its head, while the young woman tried to twist her head and look up at him. "You say *meka* like you think it's an insult," she snarled at him.

"Christine," said the father, in a weary, overindulgent tone. American parents, in Thammavong's experience, were far too permissive with their children, their daughters in particular. Little wonder this girl had taken up such rebellious habits.

"Let her up," Thammavong told the beast. "And haul that damned thing down," he added to Silosoth, gesturing again to the flag.

His partner moved to untie the line, and the *xiezhi* moved off the Hmong girl while still keeping a warning eye on the father. But the girl remained on the ground, making no move to get back up. For a split second, Thammavong worried that the beast had injured her, but he quickly decided instead that it was more likely she was feigning injury, trying to put him off his guard. "Get up," he ordered, and when she still refused to move, he stepped over to where she lay, at the same time easing his gun from its holster.

"Christine, do as he says," the father pleaded, ineffectually. The girl still didn't move a muscle, and kept her arms circled over the top of her head, in the same protective posture he assumed she'd taken when she was first knocked down.

The policeman raised his gun hand as he stepped close enough to prod her thigh with the hard toe of his leather shoe. "I said up," he said, and then prodded her again, with more force. "I mean now, you stupid *meka* piece of—"

"Stop that now!"

Thammavong assumed at first it was the father who had spoken, but the voice had come from another direction, further away. Then he caught the movement from the corner of his eye, and spun that way, training his gun on the elderly white-haired man who had stepped forward from the crowd in front of the nearby building. At the same time, the large *xiezhi* that had pinned the girl charged him. It took the policeman an extra second to realize he recognized the man who had dared to interfere with the process of justice as Song Shangkun. He cursed to himself silently, unable to do anything else as he watched the righteous beast bear down on the most powerful man in Vientiane.

Song just fixed his hard, dark eyes on the approaching beast, and said, in a sharp tone, "This is not just."

The *xiezhi* halted suddenly, ripping deep furrows in the grass lawn as its legs stopped in mid-stride. A look of confusion crossed its broad flat face as Song told it, in his cultured Beijing accent, "An armed man kicking a young, unthreatening woman is not a righteous act, and speaking out against it cannot be an unrighteous one."

The beast appeared genuinely perplexed by this turn of events. Malefactors in this place commonly declared actions the police ordered taken against them were unjust, or in violation of their "rights." But the moral authority this human exuded, and the logic of his assertions, were enough to stall the beast into inaction.

Song stepped confidently past the confused *xiezhi*, and over to where the young Hmong-American woman still lay on the grass. Switching from Mandarin to English, he asked, "Are you injured, young lady?" with the unflawed Oxford accent of a BBC announcer.

"No," Chris Vang answered, accepting the hand he offered and getting to her feet. "No, I'm okay."

Song nodded once. "Go with your father," he said as he released her hand, then turned to the policeman. "Lieutenant Thammavong, surely there is a better way to deal with this current situation."

"What are you doing here, Mister Song?" Thammavong asked as he holstered his weapon. "How are you involved in all this?"

"I'm here on an unrelated business matter," he answered. In his life before The Return, Song Shangkun had been a senior executive of China Yangtze Power. At present, he was serving the will of the Jade Emperor by overseeing the modernization and expansion of the hydroelectric power network throughout the Mekong River Valley. Because Americatown consumed more electricity than all the rest of Vientiane, he spent a significant amount of his time dealing with issues here. "I'm afraid I'm uncertain what exactly you're referring to as 'all this', however."

"This!" Thammavong shouted back, gesturing his arms to take in the flag that now flew at half-staff, and the crowd of cowed onlookers.

Song gave the younger man a tight, condescending smile. "Do you think if I had anything to do with raising a flag over this compound, it would be that one?" he asked with a humorless chuckle. A few others, including Officer Silosoth, chuckled at that as well. It was well known that Song was the proud grandson of one of the heroes of the great Mao Zedong's revolution, and had also been one of the directors of the 2008 Beijing Olympics, responsible for turning his home city and country into a showcase for the world during the last-ever summer games.

Thammavong scowled, but quickly redirected his disrespectful expression from Song to the Hmong woman. "What is your name?"

"Christine Amanda Vang."

"Well, Christine Amanda," Thammavong said, spitting the Western names out like they were fish scales on his tongue, "who put you up to this?"

"No one."

"No one," Thammavong repeated flatly.

"No one," she insisted. "No one else. Just me."

Thammavong fixed her with a venomous glare and moved in closer. "So, you decided all by yourself, on a whim, to incite a riot?"

"It was a peaceful commemoration," Vang argued, ignoring the efforts of her father to quiet her. "At least it was, until your damned dragon-dogs attacked!"

Thammavong grunted in the smug Hmong woman's face. He'd never had this kind of trouble with white Americans back when he first joined the police force. Granted, he'd had very little contact with the diplomats and staffers of the United States Embassy, and on those occasions when the Vientiane Police had to deal with American tourists, those matters were usually handed over to the Ministry of Foreign Affairs, so as to avoid any international incidents. But back then, the Taliban attacks on New York and Washington were still fresh memories, and the U.S. was still neck-deep in their wars with Afghanistan and Iraq. Even at their most arrogant, those white Americans understood that the world beyond their borders did not necessarily care much for them, and there was no guarantee of their safety this far from their shores.

But these *hmong mekas*—American-born Hmong—were an entirely different matter. The gods themselves had called them here, "home" to a land where they had never lived before. And even though it wasn't the home they knew, with all its decadent comforts and mockery of any kind of morality, they had the nerve to demand all these things here. Like this arrogant American whore, in her man's shirt and bare legs, talking back to him as if she were his equal.

"I'd have to agree with the young lady's account." Thammavong blinked in surprise, and turned to face Song with an openly shocked expression. "I witnessed nothing in their commemoration that would have justified the intercession by the *xiezhi*," the elder gentleman continued.

"The commemoration itself was reason enough," Thammavong said, trying with only limited success to keep any betrayal of his irritation from his voice.

"Why?" Song asked. "There's no law against this gathering, is there?"

Thammavong said nothing, because in truth, Song was correct. Technically, the only laws left were those that had been in place during the dissolution of the People's Democratic Republic, and had not explicitly been declared null and void by the *Naga* and the Jade Emperor. But they'd always allowed Thammavong wide latitude in keeping peace within the city, and even here in Americatown, his authority was not questioned openly. Until right now.

"Mister Song, with respect," Thammavong said carefully, "this is a police matter. It is not your concern."

Song approached the policeman, put a hand on his shoulder, and gently turned him away from the Vangs, toward the open center of the courtyard. "It doesn't need to be a police matter, though, does it?" he said in a low, confidential tone. "Give the girl's father the chance to save face, and let him deal with his daughter himself."

"Why would I do that?" Thammavong asked.

"I would be happy to explain, Lieutenant," Song said with gentle smile. "Let's you and I sit and talk."

Thammavong considered the elder man for a long moment, before turning back to Silosoth, still standing beside the flagpole with the line in his hands. "Get that thing off of there," Thammavong called to him, "and get back to the stationhouse." Then he turned to the girl's father. "I am going to let this matter drop. I hope neither of you give me cause to regret that decision. Because if you cannot be responsible for keeping your daughter under control, that responsibility falls to me. Am I understood?" he asked.

"Yes, Lieutenant," Chris's father said, while Chris silently stared daggers at the Lao policeman.

Thammavong met her glare directly. "You are not in America anymore," he informed her. "You would be wise to remember that."

"As if I could forget," Chris muttered at Thammavong's backside, as the lieutenant stalked off with Song and Silosoth.

Her father grabbed hold of her elbow and jerked her around, turning both of their bodies away from the retreating policemen. "Good gods, Christine, what were you thinking?" he asked in a low, rushed voice.

"Let's not do this here, okay, Dad?" she answered, looking around the mob still lining the perimeter of the courtyard. The pack of *xiezhi* had retreated from their defensive positions, and either followed the policemen out of the compound gates, or leapt over the tops of the walls to continue their regular patrols of the city. Once they were gone, a collective murmur of relief rose into the air, and the gathered crowd began to disperse back into the buildings that made up the embassy compound or into the streets of Americatown.

Chris's father, still grasping her arm, led her back into their building and rode up the elevator with her in silence. Once they reached the door of their converted apartment, he pulled her inside, shut the door behind them, and then let his temper loose. "What in the world were you thinking, pulling something like that?!"

"Is she all right?" called Chris's mother as she appeared from the master bedroom, with Chris's sister, Mary, peering out from the doorway. "I saw that *xiezhi* knock her down and pin her to the ground…"

"I'm fine, I'm fine," Chris said, trying to pull herself loose from her father's grip.

He was not letting go, though. "What possessed you to do such a stupid thing?" he demanded.

"Because it's the Fourth of July," Chris said. "Just because we're not in America anymore, that doesn't mean we have to stop being Americans."

"We raised you to be smarter than that!" her mother told her. "Did you think the *xiezhi* and the police wouldn't just let a stunt like that go unnoticed?"

"It was a risk I was willing to take," Chris told her.

"It was that Kou Thao who put you up to this, wasn't it?" her mother asked.

Chris sighed, as she always did whenever her mother decided to bring up her acquaintance with Thao. "No, it wasn't."

"Then why?" he father demanded. "Why would you do such a stupid thing?"

"Jesus, dad, I'm a grown woman. Stop treating me like I'm a child."

"You're still my daughter…"

"Right," Chris said. "And so you need to control me, like Thammavong said."

Her father winced at that accusation. "I'm not interested in controlling you," he told her.

"You know your father isn't like that," her mother added in Father's defense.

"No. I know you're not, Dad," Chris said, softening slightly. "But still, it's not like I have any control over my own life. Here I am, twenty-eight years old and still living with my parents in converted office building, sharing a bedroom with my kid sister, stuck here because there's no space left in Americatown, and no one in the rest of the city will rent to an unmarried woman because that means I'm either a whore or a lesbian. All that on top of being treated like a second-class citizen because I'm *meka*, with no rights, no future, nothing!"

Chris hadn't realized she had been shouting until she stopped, and a long silence filled the apartment. "I'm sorry," Chris finally said in a tiny voice, her chin lowered to her chest.

"You know this isn't the life your mother and I had hoped for for either of you," Father said softly, addressing both Chris and Mary.

"I know," she said. "And I know it's not your fault we're here."

Again, the apartment fell silent. No one was willing to say aloud what they all knew to be the fact: none of them would be in this place now, if not for Grandfather. When the gods returned, and the boundaries fell between the spirit world and the world of the living, they had all felt the draw back to their ancestral homeland, a powerful yearning that seemed to come from every gene in every cell of their bodies. But it was Chris's grandfather, who had been born here in Laos, and who had spent years fighting to defend his family and home here, who made the decision to act on that drive. He was the one who insisted on giving up the lives they had built in the United States, and to reclaim this land from the oppressors who had driven him out almost a half-century before.

So the Vang family sold all they owned and booked passage to the far side of the globe. Eight months after their arrival in Laos, Grandfather was dead. In the interim, the Jade Emperor had established communities of worshippers in Manhattan's Chinatown and other heavily Asian areas around the United States. But by then, there was no returning. Chris and her family were stuck here, permanently.

"Chris…" her mother said gently, "I wish things were different. I really do. I wish we were still back home and that you could have the same opportunities in life that your father and I had."

"But wishing isn't enough, Mom, Dad. Don't you see that?" Her parents just looked to one another, neither having a good answer to that.

Just then, a dull thudding came from the apartment's front door. The family exchanged nervous glances, and when no one else made a move to answer, Chris went to the door and put her eye to the peephole. Standing out in the corridor, a large orange and black tiger glared straight back at her through the lens. "Mister Thao wishes to see you."

Chris winced as the voice of the spirit animal sounded inside her mind, and then turned back to her parents. "I'm going out," she told them, quickly opening the door and closing it behind her before they could even raise a protest.

The century-old colonial riverside villa where Song Shangkun had taken up residence had been built for a French rubber magnate to oversee his company's operations in Indochina. During the Japanese occupation of the city during the Second World War, it had been used as a military command post, and in more recent years, it had housed ranking members of the Lao People's Revolutionary Party. The gods had destroyed the nearby Presidential Palace shortly after The Return, as a demonstration of their newly reclaimed power, but this less-assuming edifice still stood, and had retained its role as a seat of hidden power here in this capital city.

Balconies encircled the mansion's upper floors, affording a commanding view of the Mekong River. However, Song Shangkun and Akamu Thammavong sat on the opposite side of the building, looking out over the city, toward the *Thart Dam* and Americatown. "Lieutenant," Song said, as he waved away his Lao serving girl, and poured tea from the silver service she had just brought out for them, "you know what day this is on the Western calendar, I assume."

"Of course I do," Thammavong said. "4 July 2026."

Song nodded indulgently. "And you know, of course, the particular significance of this day for your expatriated American citizens: the Sestercentennial of the Declaration of Independence from Great Britain by her North American colonies."

Thammavong nodded, though he was only assuming, by inference, that the Latin-sounding word meant the two hundred and fiftieth anniversary. "Which is why I had anticipated something like what happened at the American Compound this morning."

Song smiled tightly at the Lao officer as he sipped at his tea. "Were you aware that the resolution by the Continental Congress to break away from their mother country had actually come two days earlier, on the second day of July? And that the fourth is merely the day the declaration was made public?"

"I wasn't aware of that, no," Thammavong admitted.

"Well, there's no reason you should; few Americans are ever taught that bit of history, either." Song took a long sip of tea. "Of course, the British Crown wasn't particularly impressed at the time. The war with their rebellious colonies carried on for five years after that, and another two years passed before the Treaty of Paris was finally signed in 1783."

"I'm afraid, sir, I don't understand the point of this history lesson," Thammavong said.

"It's an interesting thing about history," Song said, putting his cup aside, "that we chose certain dates and give them great significance, which they may not, in fact, deserve. American Independence arose from a long series of events stretching back over years and years. Likewise, what occurred at the American Compound this morning had relatively little to do with the coincidence of today's calendar date."

"Oh?"

"Here's some history you're probably more familiar with," Song said. "About sixty years ago, the United States began secretly and illegally arming Hmong tribesmen here in Laos to serve as a guerilla army against the Pathet Lao. Then, when the Americans ended their war in Vietnam just over fifty years ago, they abandoned the Hmong, who were then persecuted by the new Lao government for having sided against them."

"'Persecuted' is a pejorative way of describing what happened," Thammavong interrupted. "They were the enemy, and—"

"Semantics aside," Song cut him off brusquely, "millions of Hmong who had called this land home for generations—just as you and your ancestors have—were forced to flee. Ironically, many of them relocated to the United States, where they started new lives and new families, but in their hearts, this was always their home. Then, fourteen years ago, those refugees were invited back to this home by the gods, and thousands of them from America answered that call."

"Hundreds of thousands," Thammavong said.

"No, Lieutenant," Song said, raising his index finger as if to mark an important point. "I'm talking only about those veterans of the CIA's war, the ones who called Laos home. They are the ones who welcomed the gods invitation to return here as a blessing. The younger generations, the ones born and raised in America, see their lives here as a curse."

"It's hardly a secret that most of these *hmong mekas* don't want to be here," Thammavong said. "You need only take a short walk through Americatown to see that."

"But they are here, and they aren't going anywhere," Song said. "What's more, Lieutenant, is the elder generation who brought them here are rapidly dying off. And once their tempering influence is gone, you are going to see more and more young people like Miss Vang from this morning acting out. Unless, changes are made to the way you react to such events."

"Changes?" Thammavong asked doubtfully.

"You cannot make these young people deny or forget their American backgrounds. You need to relax your constraints on them..."

"Relax them?" Thammavong asked, in disbelief. "Mister Song, it's been all we can do to keep Americatown as contained as it is around the old embassy, and to prevent their influence from spreading any further through the city."

"I know you have, Lieutenant," Song said. "And in doing so, you've created a powder keg. If you continue to deny these people any way to express themselves—even in the smallest, most limited ways like this morning's ceremony—do not be surprised when Americatown explodes."

Thammavong shook his head as he stood up from his chair. "I appreciate your concern, Mister Song. But as long as I'm in charge of keeping the peace in this city, I don't intend to let that happen."

"I'm sure you don't," Song said and he picked up his teacup again, not bothering to see Thammavong out, or to even look up at him. "Keep just one more thing in mind, Lieutenant Thammavong," he added just before the policeman disappeared back into the house to be on his way. "Rebellion lies at the very heart of the Americans' heritage."

One of the most infamous spots in all of Vientiane was a dank little bar called Rick's Café Américain. All but hidden at the far end of a dark and narrow alley just a block away from the Black Stupa, Rick's had the reputation, like that of its classic movie namesake, of being a haven for some of the shadier characters of expatriate community, including gamblers, smugglers, and black marketeers.

When Chris Vang was escorted into Rick's, those disreputable patrons all stopped in mid-conversation to turn and stare at her, and watched in silence as she walked straight to the back office, and swung the door open without knocking. "You wanted to see me?"

The man behind the desk lifted his head and glared hard at her. "Just what the fuck was it that you thought you were doing this morning?" Rick Thao demanded. His actual name was Kou, but he had adopted the name of Bogart's *Casablanca* character once he had established his bar. "Seriously, Vang, what the motherfucking fuck?" Unfortunately, he didn't have anywhere near the charm or the class of a Humphrey Bogart, and came across instead as an Asian Joe Pesci, only slightly shorter and balder.

"I was doing what no one else, including you, had the balls to do," Vang told him.

There were very few people in Americatown who dared to talk to Thao in such a way. There were fewer still who could do so, and have Thao simply laugh it off. "You got balls, Chrissy," he said. "Big brass ones." The two had first met years ago on the ship that had brought their families from San Francisco to Ho Chi Minh City. He was eight years older than her, and even though they had little in common beyond their Hmong heritage, they'd established a sort-of friendship in those first uncertain days at what was then still called the American Embassy.

All expression of friendliness dropped from Thao's face now. "Thing is, there's a big difference between balls and brains. What do you think you accomplished with that little show of yours, huh? Other than getting yourself on that prick Thammavong's radar screen?"

"Were you even there, Kou? Did you see what happened?"

"I heard," Thao said.

"You should have been there," Vang said, smiling. "There were, like, over a hundred people there, cheering and chanting, 'U-S-A! U-S-A!'"

"A hundred people," Thao snorted. "Whoop-de-fucking-doo. I can get two hundred people lined up here by announcing that I have a shipment of Budweiser coming in on the next boat."

"Oh, come on," Vang said. "This is a lot bigger than selling a few cases of bootlegged beer, and you know it."

He shook his head at her. "You should have run it by me first."

"Why?" she asked. "So you could shoot me down?"

"So I could tell you why it was a bad idea," Thao said. "Seriously, Vang, do you really think you're going to start a revolution with a hundred people?"

"We need to start somewhere," Vang countered, and started pacing the small office. "We need to do more than sit on our asses, passing a joint around and talking about the things we could do to get back our rights, but never doing any of them."

"Oh, and you think Thammavong is going to give you your rights now, do you?"

"No," Vang answered, "I know no one's going to give us anything, Kou. We're going to have to work, and to fight. Together," she added pointedly.

"Don't you talk to me about fighting, Chrissy," Thao said. "Where I grew up in California, we had Hmong gangs and black gangs and Latino gangs going at each other all the time. I know fighting, and I know that you don't go out to start a fight until you're ready to win it."

Vang rolled her eyes. Kou liked to talk up his gang experience a lot, though she seriously questioned how much of it was real, and how much was just macho posturing. Either way, she had never been impressed, and definitely wasn't now. "Do you think I don't see what this is really about, Kou?"

Thao narrowed his eyes at her. "What do you mean, what this is really about?"

Vang stopped her pacing, pivoted in place to look directly at Thao, and then banged her heel twice on the floor. The hollow sound of the trap door leading down to the hidden storage space beneath the bar echoed back into the room. "I mean, you have a pretty good thing going here, with this bar and with your 'specialty import' business," she told Thao. "You've found a way to make the status quo work for you, and what you're worried about is what you might lose if things change. You hold yourself up as a big man to us *mekas*, but don't actually give a shit about anyone but yourself."

"All right, Chrissy," Thao said, pushing himself up from his seat and stepped out from behind his desk. "You do whatever the fuck you want. Fight the power, stick it to da man, whatever you want to do." He moved slowly but menacingly toward Vang, unsubtly forcing her away from the hidden trap. "But if any of it brings Thammavong down on me, I will fucking end you. Got me?"

Chris Vang nodded, and said nothing. For the first time since they'd known each other, Thao actually managed to frighten her. But as she turned and left his office, she took solace in knowing that she'd done the same to him.

As the day wore on, the temperatures climbed up toward forty degrees. Fans and air conditioning units running at full blast throughout

Americatown strained the power grid, causing brownouts and blackouts all across the city. The heat and the humidity and the frustrations all fed into the general sense of unease that had been triggered by the crackdown that morning. Word of what had happened at the American Compound spread as if carried by monsoon winds to every corner of Vientiane, from the riverside docks to the jungle's edge. Whether the discomfort and anxiety of the city's mortal residents caused agitation within the spirit world, or whether the opposite was the case, was a matter for philosophers and buddhas.

Chris Vang stood in front of her open bedroom window, sweating through her baseball jersey and fanning herself with a flimsy rice-paper fan. Alone with only her own thoughts for company, she stared down into the eerily empty courtyard below, and at the still naked flagpole standing like an abandoned relic at its center. Raising her eyes over the compound walls, the dark spire of the Black Stupa stood in sharp relief against the cloudless blue sky.

Chris had hated this place from the moment they arrived almost fourteen years earlier. In actuality, her dislike had begun long before The Return, back when her grandfather would tell her his stories about growing up in his tiny little mountain village. Though he spoke fondly of his innocent youth before joining the war, to the small girl who had never known want, the life he described sounded beyond intolerable.

The city of Vientiane was not quite the third-world shithole she had feared it would be when it was announced that the whole family would be moving here. It was no Minneapolis of course, but it did have electricity and indoor plumbing, contrary to her worst fears about the place. Beyond that, though, there was little to recommend it, especially in those early days. As more Americans moved in, expanded outward from the embassy, and started to reshape the surrounding neighborhood into what was now called Americatown, it grew slightly more bearable. But there was no escaping the fact that they would never truly belong here.

"You do belong here."

Chris jumped, as she always did when the spirit of the household intruded on her thoughts that way. "Dammit, stay out of my head," she muttered just under her breath.

"This land is a part of you," the spirit continued without acknowledging her protest. "That other mortals drove your clan away does not change this. The land and the people are one. In your heart, you know this is so."

And the worst part was, the spirit was right. She did feel the connection—spiritual, genetic, whatever it was. Still, she argued with disembodied voice, telling it, "No. I can't just accept that I was meant to till rice paddies and make babies for whatever guy my parents decided to marry me off to. I was born an American. I was supposed to do better things with my life."

"A computer animator."

"Yeah," Chris said, surprised. The household spirit always spoke to her in an archaic voice; just to hear it a mention a modern concept like computer animation was enough of a shock that it took an extra second for her to wonder how it would have even known about the teenage ambition she'd been forced to give up when she moved here.

"This land is part of you, but it is not the only part of you," the spirit said. "You are Hmong, and you are *meka*. You cannot deny either."

"But that's exactly what I have to do," Chris countered through angrily clenched teeth, "as long as I'm living in this damned backwater."

"Mortals have made this world as it is; other mortals will make it as it will be. You can do differently than your ancestors. You can shape the world that is yours, Little Paj."

Chris's breath caught. Paj—Hmong for "flower"—had been the name of her grandmother, and when she was little, grandfather would call Chris his little flower. He'd stopped calling her that after grandmother died, when Chris was four, apparently because he found it too painful to remind himself of his loss. "What...?" Chris managed to whisper. But there was no further response.

For half her life now, spirits and gods had just been part of the everyday normalcy of life. But now, for the first time since she was a child, she felt the prickling of goose bumps all over her. She knew—as much as anyone knew such things—that it was the spirits of ones ancestors who acted as the protectors of the household. But she never considered the idea of the spirit that was sheltered in their shrine as having any connection to any once-living relative of hers. She wasn't sure she wanted to consider it now, the idea of her grandfather's soul caught in a tiny shrine...No. She definitely didn't want to think too much about it.

And yet...just the thought that she still had his support and encouragement was enough to make her pull herself up a little straighter. She could continue to bemoan her fate in this world she had found herself in, or she could have the courage to try to change it, no matter what Rick said, or the police did. Her grandfather had risked his life a hundred times over by the time he was her age, first fighting in the war, then fighting to bring his family to the free world. She could hardly shy away from doing the same.

With new resolve, she headed back out the door and into the streets. It was still the Fourth of July, and there were going to be fireworks.

The annual Fourth of July party was already in full swing at Rick's. It was never actually called the Fourth of July party, and anyone who referred to it as such was sternly disinvited from ever setting foot in the café again. But those in attendance fully understood the significance of the event, and even though the frankfurters had been produced in New Zealand, the barbequed beef ribs in Japan, and the beer in Australia, it was thoroughly and unquestionably an American affair.

The crowd was noticeably smaller than in years past, though, and the mood markedly subdued. The events of the morning had put a lot of people on edge, and as Rick Thao worked the crowd, playing the part of the gregarious host, he overheard more than a few people talking about Chris Vang's prank in less than complimentary ways.

A part of Thao could sympathize with her, he supposed. They all missed lots of stuff from their old lives back in the States—the big houses and big cars, and being able to buy anything you wanted over the internet and have it shipped to your house the next day. And of course, Thao was more than happy to provide his customers with whatever small creature comforts he could, if they were willing to shell out the kip for them.

But most of the expats here had managed to adjust to life in Vientiane and to accept the world as it was now—a world where there wasn't much of the United States left to properly celebrate anymore, what with a Red Indian buffalo Manitou living in the White House, and the ancient pantheons fighting over a patchwork collection of territories across of North America just like the colonial powers once had here in Asia. Vang, though, just couldn't seem to let go of the past. She was the worst kind of troublemaker: a true believer. He just hoped that, after their little chat earlier that afternoon, she'd cool it with her patriotic fervor. If not...well, Thao didn't want to think about what he might have to do.

Unfortunately, those thoughts were pushed to the forefront of his mind when the alley door was flung open, and Lieutenant Akamu Thammavong burst into the bar. His hard unpleasant eyes surveyed the room, and he brought his fingers to his lips to blow a loud, ear-piercing whistle. Every head in the place whipped in his direction, and once he saw he had the room's attention, he announced, "This section of the city has been put under an emergency police curfew. Everybody is to leave this establishment immediately, and be in your homes and off the streets before sundown."

"What?" Thao bulldozed his way through the crowd of stunned patrons to where Thammavong was standing. "Sunset is hours away still, Lieutenant. You can't do this."

"I don't think you want to test me on what I can and cannot do, Mister Rick," the Laotian policeman told him, thrusting a finger into the smaller man's chest.

Thao would have liked to grab hold of that finger and snap it backwards. Instead, he took a single step back, and slipped his right hand behind his back. "I don't want no trouble here, Lieutenant," he told the bigger man as his fingers brushed reassuringly against the bulge underneath his sports coat, where he had his Glock pistol tucked into his belt. "I just want to be able to run my business here in peace."

"And if you want to continue doing…business here, Mister Thao," Thammavong said, making it plain that he was not referring merely to the café, "then you will do as you are instructed."

Thao hesitated a moment, studying the policeman's eyes. Then he turned to the rest of the café. "Sorry, folks. Looks like we're going to have to wrap things up a little early tonight." The volume of unhappy murmuring that started when Thammavong issued his order rose sharply in response. It chaffed him to be seen as caving in to the cops, but like he had explained to Chrissy Vang earlier, he was too smart to engage in a fight he wasn't ready to win. By cooperating with Thammavong now on this one small thing, he'd be in better position later, should things in Americatown start getting worse.

Then, they got worse. "I'm not too late, am I?"

From the look on Thammavong's face, he instantly recognized Vang's voice, and spun toward the door where she stood, still in her worn old Twins baseball jersey. "You," he snapped. "I thought I warned you about making any further trouble, Miss Vang." Thao was slightly amused to realize that Thammavong was just as unhappy to see Vang again as he was.

"What trouble?" she asked. "I'm just here for the party."

"The party is over," Thammavong told her curtly. "I would advise you to turn around and leave this place right now, before something regrettable happens. That applies to all of you," he added, addressing the rest of the crowd, who had been watching this exchange in rapt attention.

"Why?" Vang asked, giving no indication that she was about to leave, or that she would move aside from where she stood directly in front of the door for anyone else to comply with the policeman's order.

Before Thammavong had a chance to make any response to her brazenness, Thao lunged across the room, and grabbed her roughly by the arm. "Dammit, girl, what did I tell you?" he growled at her.

"If you won't fight until you know you'll win," she answered him, "then what's the point?" Then she looked past Thao to Thammavong. "You can't persecute the Americans in this city like this anymore. We have our rights."

"No, Miss Vang," the Laotian sneered. "As I reminded you this morning, this is not America. The only rights you have," he said, addressing the entire café, "are the ones I say you do."

A tense silence filled the café, broken only by the drone of the air conditioning. Thao looked from Thammavong to his customers, and realized that they were all looking expectantly in the direction of himself and Vang. Thao, having no idea what they were expecting of either of them, turned to Vang as well. She, in turn, looked defiantly to Thammavong, drew a deep breath, and then opened her mouth:

"O-oh, say, can you see, by the dawn's early light..."

In contrast to her performance earlier that morning, Chris Vang's voice rang out strong, steady, and pitch perfect. Thammavong appeared to be at a loss to understand this behavior, and was further shocked when, all around him, other patrons started to join in: "What so proudly we hailed at the twilight's last gleaming..." Thao found himself smiling in spite of himself, and wondered if the girl was purposely recreating one of the most famous scenes from the film that had inspired his bar's name.

Thammavong, rather than countering with his own rendition of the Laotian National Anthem, pulled out his sidearm and fired two shots into the ceiling. That ended the sing-along, and sent the café's crowd stampeding toward the door, knocking Vang backwards into the alleyway, where she was unwittingly kicked and stomped upon until she managed to drag herself out of the path of the panicked mass, and curl herself up into a protective ball.

As the last of them surged out of the narrow passageway and into the boulevard, Thammavong stepped out to consider the prone and injured woman. "I'll call for an ambulance," said Thao, and started to turn back inside to go for the phone.

"Don't," Thammavong said, stopping Thao with the single word. The policeman leered down at the girl as she let the arms she had wrapped around her head and face fall away. The policeman waited for her to lift her head and make eye contact with him, then said, with a crooked smile, "Now perhaps, when you are told to keep yourself out of trouble, you'll take the advice more seriously, eh, *meka?*"

Chris Vang fixed him with an unwavering glare, and drew a deep breath through bleeding nostrils. "*Gave proof through the night that our flag was still there!*" she belted out defiantly.

Thammavong, his gun still in his hand, raised and pointed it at Vang. "Whoa!" said Thao. "Lieutenant, hold on…"

"*O, say, does that star-spangled banner yet wave…*" Vang continued, even as she was afforded, in the dying light of the day, a view straight down the pistol barrel.

"Be quiet, *meka* whore," Thammavong said. His voice was calm, emotionless, and chilling. Without thinking, Thao reached again for his own weapon. He hadn't wanted to start this fight, but now that it had been begun, he was going to defend his side.

"*O'er the land of the free, and the home—*"

As Thao wrapped his fingers around the grip of his gun, Thammavong's pistol discharged with a muffled bang. The muffling of the shot was due to one of the pack of *xiezhi* that appeared in the alley, having sensed the escalating altercation, charging Thammavong and clamping its jaws over the policeman's wrist, hand, and weapon just before the bullet cleared its muzzle.

The policeman screamed as he was knocked into the alleyway wall by the creature. Another of the *xiezhi* snapped at Thao, startling him and causing him to accidentally squeeze his gun's trigger before pulling it free from his belt. He screamed as well as the bullet hit at the back of his leg and he collapsed to the floor.

"Let go of me!" Thammavong shrieked the *xiezhi* biting down on his arm, and pulled the trigger of his gun twice more. The creature gave no indication that it felt a thing, and instead of letting go, whipped its head wildly back and forth, throwing the lieutenant off of his feet. With another powerful jerk of its neck, the animal tossed the man backwards in an arching curve, and atop its muscular scaled back. A second *xiezhi* prodded at Vang with its horned forehead until she pushed herself up onto her hands and knees, then slung herself over the top of its back also.

Thao watched as the two were carried out of the alley and disappeared around the corner, then started dragging himself across the floor to call for help. "Big brass ones on that girl," he muttered to himself, not so much in annoyance as in admiration.

Thart Dam—the Black Stupa—had stood in the heart of the Kingdom of Vientiane for centuries. Legend had long held that it was home to the seven-headed *Naga* who protected the city and its people, and its dark exterior had once been decorated by a layer of gold. One hundred and ninety-nine years earlier, that gold had been stripped away by the invading Siamese Army, after they overthrew King Anouvong and burnt Vientiane to the ground. The *Naga* did not lift a single one of its heads as the people of the city were forced to flee into the jungles or up the Mekong River Valley.

Vientiane remained all but abandoned for generations, and the Black Stupa was nearly swallowed into the encroaching jungle. What had once been a magnificent monument took on the appearance of a forgotten ruin, weeds sprouting from the network of cracks formed by years of rain, wind and neglect. Eventually, when the French came to lay their claim to this part of Indochina, the capital was rebuilt and many of its grander temples restored, but the Black Stupa was left as it was in its dilapidated state. Vientiane changed hands several more times after, falling to Imperial Japan during the Second World War, then briefly retaken by the French before the Laotians were granted their independence. Decades of civil war followed, culminating in the genocidal rule of the Communist Pathet Lao. Through all of this, the supposed protector of Vientiane remained slumbering beneath its stupa.

Now, the great river spirit stood before its monument, its seven heads swaying in sinuous synchronicity above and around the Lao man and Hmong woman the *xiezhi* had brought before it. "What is this?" the center head hissed. "What have these two mortals done, that we needed to be disturbed?"

The larger of the two *xiezhi* paused to spit out Thammavong's service pistol and three spent bullets, then looked up to the *Naga*. "The male tried to murder the female," the *xiezhi* explained in a clear and respectful tone, "because she acted against his will."

"All mortals have murder in their hearts," said another of the *Naga's* heads.

"And all mortals also, at some time, displease their mates," added a third.

"I am *not* his mate!" Chris Vang blurted, earning her a sharp poke in the backside from the smaller *xiezhi*.

In a motion like a cracking whip, one of the *Naga's* long serpentine neck doubled onto itself, and suddenly, a head the size of a medium-sized car was directly in front of Vang. Featureless black eyes held her fast, as slit-like nostrils drew in her scent, then blew a blast of hot, damp air back out at her. Chris fought every instinct in her body in order to keep herself standing still and steady during the monster's inspection.

Finally, the head rose away again. "You've stopped this murder, though," the *Naga* addressed the *xiezhi* again. "We repeat our question: why have we been disturbed?"

"This male is a police officer," the large *xiezhi* explained, sounding apologetic. "His word is the law in the city, but the female's actions were harmless. Because he acts as protector of your city, we bring this question of justice to you."

All seven of the *Naga's* heads sighed. Then, it brought one of the heads down again, mere feet above the ground, and considered the male. "Well," it said, "what say you?"

Thammavong swallowed hard, then squared his shoulders back and said, "The girl's actions were not harmless. She has been trying to sow discontent and incite revolt against the established order here in this— your—city. I admit, I may have let my emotions get the better of me earlier, but I'm not a murderer..."

"Of course you are, human," the *Naga* interrupted. "All of your kind are murderers at heart." It was for precisely that reason that the *Naga* came to regret the vow it had made to protect the mortals of this village long, long ago.

"...but it was only to prevent her from doing any true, lasting harm," Thammavong continued, "and to protect the rest of the people of Vientiane, the ones who belong here."

"I belong here," Vang snapped. "My family is as much part of this land anyone else's. And the land is a part of me."

The head that had been fixed on the male now pivoted to the female, and sniffed at her again. "You are of this land," it said, "but you've come here from outside." The scent of this female was similar to the one that once emanated from the nearby walled compound, the one that had been ruled by a woman who called herself "Ambassador" who claimed it as sovereign territory of a foreign nation.

"My clan was driven away years ago, and I was born in a land called America. But now my clan has returned to our home."

The mortals who lived in this village centuries ago, when the *Naga* still involved itself in their affairs, would also drive their undesirables out into the surrounding jungle, where they would inevitably fall prey to the tigers or other predators. Then the villagers would congratulate themselves for not having taken those humans' lives themselves. That evidently had not changed, but the fact that mortals had found a way to survive their banishment was new. "America," the *Naga* repeated, recalling that was the name the Ambassador used for her nation.

The female nodded. "They took my grandparents and parents in after they were forced to leave Laos. I was the first of my clan born as an American, but I am still Hmong, and I still belong here."

The *Naga* found this contradiction curious, and decided it would need to learn more about this "America." But that was for a later time. "The male accuses you of being a danger to the others of this land," the *Naga* said to her.

"I'm not the danger," Vang said. "He thinks my ideas are dangerous—American ideas, like all men are created equal, with the right to life, liberty, and the pursuit of happiness…"

"Happiness is all you decadent capitalists care about!" Thammavong fired back. "You've taken over more and more of this city to feed your excessive appetites and avoid the slightest discomfort…"

All seven of the *Naga*'s heads opened their maws, and let out a chorus of earthshaking roars. Both Vang and Thammavong were knocked backwards onto the ground, and the head that remained closest to ground level now hovered directly over both of them. It shifted focus from the two mortals to the *xiezhi*. "This conflict is one of *ideas?*" the head asked.

The beasts quavered slightly. "Ideas are neither just or unjust," the larger *xiezhi* said. "It's only when mortals act on their thoughts that we can intervene."

"Then suppressing ideas cannot be just, either," the *Naga* said. "If these 'American' ideas do lead to revolt, you can judge at that time which side is just in their actions."

"That will be too late!" Thammavong cried out. He pushed himself up on his elbows, and scrabbled along the ground to get out from underneath the large, scaly jaw that hung less than two meters over him. "You need to understand the threat these people pose to our way of life! You need—"

Whatever else the male mortal thought the *Naga* needed to know was lost when a long, thick forked tongue flicked out from the dipped head's mouth, wrapped itself around the human's middle, and then pulled him down its gullet. The *Naga* lifted its head up high, so that its neck stretched straight up and down, and so Vang could see the small lump travel all the way down its long throat.

"Is that all?" one of the other heads asked the *xiezhi*. They indicated silently that is was, and then the ground opened up underneath the *Naga* as it descended back into its subterranean den. The *xiezhi* dispersed, leaving Chris Vang alone in the shadow cast by the Black Stupa against the setting sun. She lay there for several long minutes, trying to process all that just happened. The sky above darkened and the stars started to come out, forming into the same familiar constellations here as they did back home.

Kale Silosoth paced slowly around the hospital bed where Kou Thao lay in a drug induced sleep, recovering from the surgery done to his leg. The doctor had warned him that it would be a long wait for the patient to come out from the anesthesia, but he needed to make sure he was here as soon as he awoke. There were far too many questions he needed answers to.

Silosoth had already been on his way to Rick's Café, directly behind the ambulance responding to the report of a gunshot injury, when the *Naga* made one of its rare appearances. The policeman detoured to the Black Stupa, where the girl from the American Compound was lying alone on the grass, dazed. She told Silosoth that it was Thammavong who had been responsible for the shooting at Rick's, which unfortunately did not surprise him—the lieutenant had come back from his meeting with Song Shangkun with a strengthened resolve to crack down on America-town, and that den of criminality would have been the logical place for him to start.

Her story was called into doubt when Silosoth finally reached the nearby bar, where Rick Thao told him and the emergency medics that, while Thammavong had been there earlier, the café owner had in fact shot himself accidentally. However, the details of Thao's story turned confusing and disjointed as the effects of heavy blood loss and painkillers kicked in. At one point, when Silosoth had tried questioning him about the Vang girl's role in the night's events, Thao only laughed, and then started singing "La Marseillaise," of all things.

The door at the end of the recovery ward opened. Silosoth turned, expecting to see the doctor returning. Instead, it was Song Shangkun who entered. "Officer Silosoth," he greeted him with a small dip of his head. "How is he?"

"The doctor isn't sure if he'll be able to keep his leg," he said, resisting the urge to ask why the foreign businessman should take an interest in Thao. "They're talking about flying him a better hospital in Hanoi."

"'Better' being a relative term in this case." Song shook his head. "I've heard what happened to Lieutenant Thammavong."

Silosoth raised one eyebrow skeptically. "I wouldn't believe what that American girl says so readily."

"Oh, I would," Song said earnestly. "With respect, your colleague's irrational prejudice against the *hmong mekas* in Americatown most certainly constituted a danger to the welfare of this city. I don't doubt the *Naga* came to the same determination."

Silosoth tilted his head and frowned. "A danger? How do you mean?"

"Mind you, I have no more love for the United States than you Lao do," Song said. "However, there is no denying that the Americans were the primary driving force of human progress throughout most of the last two hundred and fifty years. They rose from their status as an exploited European colony to become, before The Return, the last superpower on Earth. In contrast, once we here in the East shook off our colonial oppressors, we expended far too much time and energy trying to hold progress back, in the name of tradition." He gestured to Thao, still unconscious in the bed between them. "There's no reason, in the year 2026, there should not be a fully modern medical facility in this capital city, one capable of treating this man's injury as well as any other in the Western world."

"And you think these Americans will be able to bring that about?" Silosoth asked, glancing doubtfully at the man in the hospital bed.

"I'm not saying that they'll perform miracles," Song said. "But step out of their way, and I believe you'll be surprised at what they'll prove themselves capable of. People like Miss Vang and Mister Thao here not only come from a world that has long embraced progress, but they bring that ambition which drives that progress, and the willingness to push back against whatever forces hold that progress back."

"We call that the American spirit," Rick Thao said, surprising both of the other men in the room.

"How long have you been awake?" Silosoth asked.

"Long enough to hear Mister Song's lovely testimonial to the good ol' U. S. of A.," Thao answered as he slowly cracked his eyes open, and turned to the police officer. "Of course, the one thing he didn't mention is that progress will also take a lot of cheaply available electricity. And in turn, that progress will create a greater demand for even more electricity."

"That's somewhat tangential to the subject at hand," Song said, shooting a sharp annoyed glare at Thao.

"So, that's what this is all about?" Silosoth asked Song. "That's why you were defending the girl at the compound this morning? For your own business interests?"

"I can't deny that my business would stand to benefit," Song said. "But that is not the only reason I spoke in Miss Vang's defense."

"With respect, sir," Silosoth said, "what other reason would you have to do so?"

Song sighed softly. "I suppose you're too young to remember the incident at Tiananmen Square?" he asked.

"What incident?" Silosoth replied.

"What's Tiananmen Square?" Thao added.

The older man just shook his head. "It's no matter," he said, pushing the memory of that distant June day, and of the final argument he had with his son the morning before, back down into the dark recesses of his memory. "Suffice to say that sometimes, protest is the only way to affect change in a society, and that a little rebellion now and then can be a good thing."

"That sounds like something an American would say," Silosoth said.

"Yes. One of their Founding Fathers, Thomas Jefferson," Song told him as he turned to take his leave. "As I've said before, the Americans do have their good qualities...."

Root for the Undergods

by Phil Giunta

The core message of all motivational speakers can be boiled down to one simple concept—take control of your life and fulfill your potential. There had been a time when Orlando Start, superstar of the inspirational circuit, raked in seven figures annually simply for preaching that message.

Yet now, a decade into this new age where the destiny of the human race had been torn from its collective grasp by callous deities, how could one fulfill one's potential when mere *survival* was questionable? How could people hope to be motivated to better themselves when their will has been stripped and their lives shattered?

Orlando Start no longer had the answers. He couldn't even save himself.

In the years since The Return, the tours had been cancelled, the Blu-ray sales had bottomed out, and Orlando's clients, family and friends had immigrated to the lands of their ancestors as commanded by the gods of their fathers.

Battles raged between domestic and foreign pantheons as the Native American gods fought to keep people from fleeing their territories. Still, millions had managed to escape across the globe, hoping to evade death and start anew on foreign soil. Orlando's wife had been one of them.

Intractable as usual, and despite the odds against him, Orlando had refused to leave the United States or swear fealty to Kishelemukong, the Native American god of the Lenape that ruled over the area. For a time, Orlando's disobedience went unnoticed in the chaos. He had even managed to live well and quietly off his savings.

Until six months ago, when the gods had finally caught up with him.

Yet rather than kill Orlando outright, the state government had merely blacklisted him from society. All of his debts had become immediately due and his bank accounts frozen. He'd been unable to seek legal counsel or find a job. He couldn't even buy food at the local grocery store, when it actually had anything in stock. As far as the world was concerned, Orlando Start had ceased to exist.

Here and now, the thirty-eight year old was alone, bankrupt, and days away from living on the streets.

It was 7:30 a.m. on a serene Monday morning as Orlando reclined in the driver's seat of the Range Rover. In his closed garage, the hum of the engine provided a rhythmic bass to the soft blues sax on the radio. Together, they brought an odd sense of comfort, soothing Orlando's misery. A few more breaths and it would all be over. *I'll die on the streets anyway. May as well get it over with now. To hell with the house, to hell with the gods, to hell with this life.* Orlando closed his eyes and inhaled deeply...

An instant later, a jarring mechanical whine shook him awake. He peered up through the sunroof and watched the panels of the garage door glide by overhead.

"Son of a bitch." Orlando sat up and squinted against the morning sunlight reflected in the rearview mirror. He climbed out of the car and massaged his throbbing head before running a hand down the side of his stubbled face.

A shadow moved across the floor of the garage and as his vision cleared, Orlando found himself staring at what looked like a reject from a Renaissance Faire. Long brown hair and an unkempt beard framed the craggy face of a man in his mid-50s. He stood well over six feet tall, a head above Orlando, but it was the maroon chainmail tunic and leather body armor that were most striking. Black leather gauntlets, studded in gold, covered his wrists and forearms. Black pants ended at gray fur boots.

The man looked him up and down before speaking in a low, gravely voice. "You are Orlando Start?"

Suddenly self-conscious, Orlando tried in vain to smooth the wrinkles in his grimy polo shirt. He felt the beer stain from the night before and decided instead to cross his arms over his chest. He squared his slumped shoulders in a feeble attempt to preserve what little decorum he had left. "That depends on who's asking."

The man bowed his head solemnly."I am Taranis, god of thunder."

Orlando paused. "You mean like Zeus or Thor?"

Taranis forced a thin smile. "Yes."

"Never heard of you."

"Few have in this age, which is the reason why I'm calling upon you."

"Come again?"

"I wish to hire you."

Orlando blinked. "To do what?"

"You are a motivational speaker, are you not?"

"Well…yes." *At least, I was…*

"Then we wish to engage your services."

"We?"

"My pantheon requires motivation."

"And what pantheon is that?"

"We are Gallic."

Orlando shrugged.

"Perhaps you're familiar with the ancient Empire of Gaul in Western Europe."

"OK, yeah, sure. Sorry, I slept through parts of my Western Civ class in college. Well, actually most of it."

Taranis raised an eyebrow.

"But I remember Gaul. Though I didn't know they had gods of their own."

"That appears to be the popular misconception," Taranis said, "one that we hope you can help us correct. You see, upon our return, we were dismayed to find that so few historical references about us had survived the ages. We were once a distinct pantheon, but many of our legends have been assimilated into Celtic or Roman lore.

"As a result, we have no followers, no believers, no army to defend against the Romans. They constantly plunder and divide our lands amongst themselves with no regard for the suffering they inflict on the mortals. Our pantheon has been all but forgotten."

"How many of you are there?"

"At present, we are merely five. However, I suspect there may be others in hiding throughout Europe, awaiting the day when we can unite and reclaim what belongs to us. We hope you will help us accomplish this."

"Let me see if I understand you. I'm supposed to motivate you and your, uh, colleagues to stand up to the other pantheons so you can take back your lands and reinstate yourselves as respectable, powerful deities who will then engender the love and worship of the people."

Taranis smiled and spread his arms. "A brilliant summation. Despite appearances, you're very astute."

Well, hot damn this is a new one. It could also be the first step to getting my life back. I wonder how far I can press this turn of luck?

"My fee isn't cheap."

"Money is of no concern to us. If we are successful, you will have more than you ever dreamed."

"I dream high."

Taranis smirked. "Yet you have fallen so low."

"Says the god who comes to me for help. Look, I can offer support, ideas, and perhaps a different way of looking at a world that has changed dramatically during your absence, but in the end, we all fight our battles alone."

The god of thunder nodded solemnly. "No truer words have ever been spoken. I take it that you accept the offer?"

Do I have a choice? Orlando Start, motivational speaker, shook hands with the god of thunder.

"So how do we get to your place?"

Taranis nodded toward the Range Rover. "This chariot will be suitable."

Orlando let out a chuckle. "We're going to drive to Europe? You realize we're in Philadelphia, in the United States."

Taranis opened the back door and climbed in. "Of course. Trust me, young man."

Shaking his head at the absurdity of it, Orlando climbed into the driver's seat and turned off the radio. "I just have one last question. How did you even find me?"

"One of my brethren happened across a few of your videos in a rubbish pile. Curious, we viewed your presentations and found them rather inspiring, so we followed the advice on the packaging."

"Let me guess—"

"Call Orlando right away and Start changing your life today!" the two sang in unison.

Orlando closed his eyes. *I hate that goddamn jingle.* He looked at Taranis in the rearview mirror. "So, where to?"

"Bring us out into the road."

"Which direction?"

"It matters not."

A moment later, the Range Rover was in the middle of the street. Taranis leaned forward. "I shall take it from here."

"What?"

The vehicle began moving, slowly at first, then suddenly accelerating at an impossible rate. Panicked, Orlando stepped on the brake pedal to no avail.

"Stop! What the hell are you doing?" Orlando pointed to the upcoming intersection. "The light's red!"

"Yes, a most cheerful color it is."

Orlando cringed as the Range Rover blasted across the intersection. Angry horns and screeching tires faded into the distance as the car raced toward the expressway. Orlando cussed, threatened, pleaded and finally begged Taranis to stop, but the god merely laughed.

Orlando could do nothing but scream as the speedometer topped off at 220 mph on their way toward morning rush hour.

Then there was lightning.

Less than a minute later, the Range Rover came to a dead stop. Bolts of electricity faded, replaced by a mid-afternoon sun high in a cloudless sky.

Orlando was still screaming when a hand slapped the back of his head. He drew in a sharp breath. "Ow! Dammit, I hate backseat drivers. You almost got us killed!"

Taranis grinned as he opened the car door. "Fear not. There is a reason I am also known as the wheel god. Come, the others are eager to meet you, Orlando Start."

Orlando leaned forward and gazed through the windshield at the stone block archway and raised iron gate. A concrete path, relatively new compared to the ancient stone walls on either side, led beyond a tower to a distant courtyard. "Where are we?"

"Vianden Castle, Luxembourg. Magnificent, is it not?"

"Fantastic. You have a men's room? I need to take a leak."

Taranis sighed. "Mortals."

"Hey, I've been holding it the whole trip."

"Why did you not go before we left?"

Taranis had done better than a men's room. He'd escorted Orlando to his "quarters," a modern four-room suite complete with a master bedroom, private bath, spacious living room, and a fully stocked kitchen with dining nook.

Back in the high life. Orlando tossed his duffel onto the king-sized bed and stripped down. His clothes reeked of booze and cigarettes. Years ago, he had learned the value of keeping an overnight bag in the trunk of his car. At the peak of his career, there had been more than a few last-minute seminars, parties, one-night stands and spontaneous escapes to exotic locales.

Never before had he been as grateful for a shower, shave, and change of clothes. Twenty minutes later, he was a new man. The waistline of his jeans bunched up slightly as he tightened his belt. He'd been too stressed-out to eat much over the past month as he watched his life disintegrate.

Dry, hazel eyes stared back at him from the bathroom mirror as he combed and gelled back his thick chestnut hair. If Lacey were here, she'd say it was in desperate need of a trimming. Fleetingly, he wondered where she was right now. No sooner had his career dried up than their marriage soon followed. What The Return hadn't taken from him, she had picked clean.

Forget that gold-diggin' bitch. You can do better. This is your chance to get back on top, to redefine yourself in this new age.

Orlando checked his look in the mirror. *Not quite your old self, but it's a start.* He rolled his eyes at the unintended pun and took a deep breath.

It was time to meet his divine clients.

"This is an amazing place," Orlando said in a reverent tone as he walked beside Taranis through the Arms Hall with its vaulted ceilings and warm amber lighting. On their right, entire suits of armor and mannequins in chainmail stood in glass display cases along with swords, shields and halberds. In one corner, at least a dozen medieval cannon balls lay scattered on the floor beneath a window while a section of wall was decorated with a rack of halberds spread out in a fan formation.

"Was this yours at one time?"

"No." Taranis shook his head. "Vianden was constructed in what by your calendar is the eleventh century. We last walked among you a thousand years before that. This castle apparently fell into ruin in its lifetime and underwent significant restoration over thirty years ago. It is kept in pristine repair by the State as a national monument of Luxembourg. We negotiated with the Grand Duke for its use as our home."

"Negotiated? You couldn't have just taken it by force?"

"That is not our preferred method."

Orlando filed that away as they entered the Knight's Hall. The vaulted ceilings and amber lighting continued, but the stained glass windows and blazing hearth at the far end lent the room a more hallowed atmosphere.

That, and the three gods milling about.

Almost in unison, they turned to study Orlando. Instantly, he measured up the intrigued, the dubious, and the hostile. His thoughts were finally seized by the enormity of what he'd agreed to. *This should be interesting...*

A tall, muscular god broke away from the others and approached. His was the only bald pate among them and he narrowed deep set eyes of crystal blue at Orlando. He met them in the center of the room, clad entirely in black from turtleneck to cargo pants to military boots. Ramrod-straight posture completed his menacing appearance.

"It's about time, Taranis," he snarled. "I thought Mars would march his army halfway across France before you returned."

The god of thunder ignored the other's bluster. "Orlando Start, this Segomo. He is what you might call our—"

"God of War." Orlando extended a hand.

With an expression of disdain, Segomo accepted it. Orlando clenched his jaw as he felt his fingers squeezed in an iron grip.

"Very astute for a mortal although somewhat impetuous to interrupt a god when he is speaking."

Taranis held up a hand. "Calm yourself, Segomo. We called him here, if you remember."

Segomo grunted. "*You* called him here."

"Actually," a genteel, crisp voice called from behind Segomo, "Abellio and I are quite intrigued to see what this mortal brings to the table."

"Of course you are, Grannus." Segomo rolled his eyes and muttered, "God of spas and thermal springs." He widened his eyes and trembled in mock fear before stepping aside, allowing Taranis and Orlando to pass.

If age could be applied to a god, Grannus would qualify as the eldest of the lot. His short silver hair was combed forward and his beard neatly trimmed. He wore an untucked blue oxford shirt over khaki pants and black sandals. He reminded Orlando of a kindly old doctor that his mother had taken him to as a kid.

Grannus smiled and waved him over to the hearth. He raised a hand toward the gaunt, barefoot teenager standing on the other side of the fireplace. "This is Abellio."

Orlando could scarcely believe that this ginger-haired boy in a Superman t-shirt and black jeans was a god.

"Cool shirt," Orlando said. "And what is your specialty?"

"Apples."

Orlando raised an eyebrow. "Beg pardon?"

Grannus chuckled. "Abellio is the god of apple trees."

"I see."

Abellio crossed his arms. "Don't judge me."

"No, no." Orlando held up his hands. He turned, pointing to each god in turn. "Thunder, war, thermal springs, apple trees. I thought there was one more?"

"Vasio," Taranis said. "He is unlikely to join us."

"And why is that?"

"He spends a great deal of time in solitude, I'm afraid," Grannus replied.

"He's depressed," Abellio added, taking a bite from an apple that materialized in his hand. He held it up. "Would you like one?"

"Uh, maybe later." Orlando scratched his head as he wrapped his mind around all of this. "What is Vasio's area of expertise?"

The four gods looked at one another. Finally, Taranis shrugged. "No one recalls."

"That's why he's depressed," Abellio said. "Hasn't said a word since The Return."

Orlando was incredulous. "It's been ten years! Not one of you can remember what his abilities are?"

"And he refuses to remind us," Taranis said.

Orlando thought for a moment. "Maybe I should speak to him one-on-one later."

"Good luck," Segomo grumbled, something he seemed to do well and often. "He's useless as far as I'm concerned."

Abellio snickered. "Says the war god with no army."

"And what would you do against the enemy, apple boy? Hurl rotten fruit?"

"That's enough," Taranis barked in vain.

"I think you're overcompensating, Segomo," Grannus said. "When the Romans first conquered Gaul, your legacy, your very essence, was stolen by Mars. You were left forgotten just like the rest of us and now you want revenge."

"And I shall have it."

"At what cost, Segomo? Let us say that you do manage to raise an army against Mars, which I doubt, how many mortals will you sacrifice to regain your status?"

"As in days of old, as many as it takes."

"OK!" Orlando raised a hand. "Hello, mortal over here. Not too comfortable with that idea—"

"Not all wars must be fought with weapons. Not all wars require bloodshed."

Segomo waved a dismissive hand at Grannus. "Spare us hot air from the god of hot water!"

Taranis clapped his hands. Thunder rumbled through the skies. The floor trembled. The gods fell silent.

He looked at Orlando. "Forgive my sometimes churlish brethren."

"Just thinking out loud here. It would be helpful to know exactly what you want to accomplish, what your goals are." Orlando's doubtful thoughts raced to keep up with his confident mouth. "I think I can work with you to find a way to achieve them together as a team."

Taranis nodded. "That sounds reasonable. Perhaps we can discuss it as civilized beings over a meal. Shall we proceed to the dining hall?"

As they made their way, Abellio fell in beside Orlando. "Make sure you save room for my apple pie. It has graham cracker crust."

"Really? I love graham crackers."

Segomo shook his head. "Oh, for the love of Gaul!"

It was a feast fit for, well, a god—chicken, ham, beef, various vegetables and breads, beer and wine. As they ate, Taranis called everyone's attention to a 90-inch LED television screen mounted on the side wall of the dining room. It displayed a map of what appeared to be Western Europe, with very different national borders and unfamiliar names.

"Gaul," the god of thunder began. "This is a fairly accurate map provided by Wikipedia. This is the first century, before it fell to Julius Caesar. Our empire encompassed all of present-day France, Luxembourg, Belgium, parts of Switzerland, Germany, Italy, the Netherlands and the British Isles.

"You asked us what our goal is, Orlando Start. In short, we want France back and that is all. It was the single largest territory in Gaul. The Romans are content to ignore a nation as small as Luxembourg. The

Tuatha dé Danann have no designs this far south. The Norse have their hands full with Switzerland, Belgium, Germany and elsewhere and we have no quarrel with them, but I'll be damned if I allow the Romans to retain control of France."

"Since The Return," Segomo spoke up in a civil tone—it seemed the booze had had a calming effect, thankfully. "Mars has slaughtered all who opposed Roman rule. Millions have lost their lives. Those his armies have not murdered, Jupiter has seen fit to starve by burning crops and poisoning water supplies until the people acquiesce."

"France is in turmoil," Grannus said. "If we could regain control, we would ensure peace and prosperity."

Taranis nodded in agreement. "Most of France is bereft of internet access and mobile phone communications. Many areas decimated by the Romans have been without electrical power for months at a time."

Orlando sat back in his chair and nodded thoughtfully. *What the hell am I supposed to do here?* Finally, he let out a long sigh. "What efforts have you made so far to help them?"

His question was answered by uncomfortable shifting and downcast eyes.

"For the past ten years, you haven't even *tried?*" Orlando leaned forward. "You hide within the four walls of this castle, worrying, arguing, making idle threats—and living very well might I add—while your lands are divided up and your people left to die! Does that about sum it up?"

Not one of the gods would meet Orlando's burning glare, not even Segomo.

He took a deep breath before plunging ahead. "You tell me you want followers, believers. You tell me you want to build an army against the Romans. To do that, you need to win the people away from them. The Romans' power is based on the very same things that keep you cowering inside these walls."

"And what is that?" Taranis asked in a low, seething voice. "Choose your words wisely, Orlando Start."

Orlando was getting to him now. *Excellent. Move in for the kill now and hope you're still standing when the dust settles.* "Fear and intimidation. Let me ask you something. What do the four of you have to offer that's different from that?"

The gods shrugged as they glanced at one another, at the floor, the walls.

"You're gods!" The words echoed through the vast hall. "Figure it out! You brought me here to motivate you, but I can only help those who are willing to help themselves. If you can't even do that…"

Orlando paused for effect, looking at each one in turn.

"…then what's the point of you?"

He rose from his seat and turned his back on them to leave. "We'll pick this up again in the morn—"

The burst of sizzling heat would have scorched the side of his face had the lightning bolt been just a few inches closer. Orlando spun away and ducked as it blasted one of the oak doors from its hinges.

Pushing himself to his feet, Orlando stared at the smoking hole in the door that now lay across the corridor. When the echoes of the blast had finally faded, Orlando turned to face Taranis.

The god of thunder slowly lowered his arm. The other gods gaped at him. "I brought you here to help us, not insult us, mortal."

Orlando merely smiled. "Now, that's what I'm talking about. If you can do that here," he pointed to the map on the screen, "you can do it out there. Have a good night."

Orlando massaged his temples as he paced the entire length of his suite. *What the hell have I gotten myself into? I don't know a damn thing about these beings. I can't help them, but if I don't, they'll kill me. I should have refused the offer and let the carbon monoxide do its thing.*

"What manner of thought is this for such a spirited orator?"

Orlando spun to find Grannus and Abellio sitting in the living room.

"Apologies," Grannus continued. "I suppose we should have knocked. We're not accustomed to having guests. If you are concerned about suffering the wrath of Taranis, have no fear. He has calmed himself and now all is well. You simply struck a nerve, Orlando Start, because you were correct."

"Then the question becomes what are you going to about it?" Orlando asked. "How will you proceed to attain your goal, to capture the hearts of the French people and restore peace and prosperity?"

"We're hoping you can inspire us to find a way," Abellio said.

"Gods are only as powerful as the faith placed in them by mortals," Grannus added. "Even the people of Luxembourg, largely Roman Catholic, ignore us. We have all become feeble shadows of our former selves."

Orlando shrugged. "Well, then, tomorrow we will discuss ways to win back the faithful. Hopefully, I can convince Vasio to make an appearance."

"Doubtful."

"Then can you take me to him tonight? I'd like to meet him."

Grannus looked at Abellio. "Would you mind escorting him to Vasio's quarters? I'm going to call maintenance about the door in the dining hall. If the Grand Duke hears of this, he'll evict us for sure."

"I warn you. Vasio is eccentric. Don't expect much."

Abellio slowly opened the door and led Orlando into the dimly lit quarters. The room was sparsely furnished, its only illumination provided by various candles placed atop tables and scattered about the floor.

As they moved further into the room, Orlando froze at the sight of a pale, emaciated young man with long auburn hair sitting nude in a lotus position, surrounded by candles. His eyes were closed and his breathing shallow. Most remarkably, he was levitating nearly two feet off the floor.

"It appears Vasio is meditating," Abellio whispered.

"Maybe we should come back later."

Stay, Orlando Start. I am nearly finished. We have much to discuss.

Orlando looked at Abellio. "What?"

"I said nothing, but I think I should rejoin the others. I suppose you're welcome to wait here."

"Well—"

With that, Abellio departed, leaving Orlando alone with the naked, floating god.

Does this ease your discomfort? The voice forced itself into Orlando's mind.

He turned to face Vasio, but he was gone. "Uh, hello?"

By the open window.

Orlando looked to his right. There, staring out into the starlit sky stood Vasio, fully clothed in white pants and a loose-fitting tunic.

I always enjoy the view of the River Our under the stars. It's lovely, wouldn't you agree?

"Yes, indeed it is. So...we missed you at dinner."

There is little point in small talk, Orlando Start. Earlier you asked the others what my abilities are. None could answer you because none can remember.

"Yeah, they said you were depressed because history has forgotten you most of all."

And well they should have, but that is not the entire truth. My abilities are different from those of the others. Wherever I am present, violence, fear, intimidation all cease to exist. Since The Return, I have protected Luxembourg, preventing the Romans and other pantheons from invading simply by making their mortal military leaders disinterested, apathetic towards the idea of invasion.

"Taranis said that the Romans ignore Luxembourg because they consider it insignificant."

That is partially true. The Romans have eyes for France, which makes my efforts even more of a challenge since my abilities work only on mortals. Mars and Jupiter can still inflict sufficient damage even without their armies. That is why I hope your efforts with the others are successful. I will need them.

"So what do you call yourself then, the god of—"

I have no need of useless honorifics. Results are all that matter to me.

"If I understand you correctly, you could stop most of the violence in France simply by going there and walking around?"

In limited areas, yes, but doing so would leave Luxembourg vulnerable.

"But you're a god. Can't you protect both countries?"

When I last walked among you, I was worshipped in a small town known today as Vaison-la-Romaine in southern France. I was able to protect the villagers against Roman attack for a time. Eventually, Caesar's armies were victorious, but the people managed to retain their authority of the town and were never fully Romanized.

"So in the end, you successfully prevented loss of life."

But only in that village. However, since our return, I've grown stronger. Through extended meditation, my abilities allow me to protect this country and I am attempting to push my influence farther into France. Understand that I am not trying to force apathy on everyone in their daily lives, merely suppressing a tendency toward violence. This is why so much of my time is spent in seclusion.

Orlando was stunned. Four gods bicker and sulk for a decade while this one quietly does all the work, but no one knows it.

It is not important that they know at this time. They are my brethren, but their incessant arguing and blustering distracts me. Thus, I remain silent and apart for the sake of my meditations.

"I understand. I won't say a word about this, I promise."

In the light of the moon, Vasio smiled for the first time. *Your words seem to have deeply affected Taranis. I applaud your courage and your veracity.*

It will be interesting to see how our relationship develops. I suspect it will be mutually beneficial.

Orlando shook his head. "I can't see how. I'm so far out of my element here, I have no idea what to do next."

You will know when the time comes. Do not for a moment think that you were not meant to be here, Orlando Start.

Orlando spent the rest of the night in his quarters staring at the ceiling or out the window, pacing and fretting and generally not sleeping.

I don't know if I have what it takes to do this. What the hell am I supposed to say to motivate gods?

For the sixth time, he walked to the window and peered down at the River Our far below. Its lazy current glistened as it reflected the lights from the village along its banks and the full moon suspended high in the night sky.

Orlando imagined himself standing here a thousand years ago. Would he have been able to see the river at all or would it have offered a perfect mirror of the heavens unhindered by modern lighting?

Gently, he pushed open the window and reached out, placing a hand on the cool stone exterior of the castle wall. He closed his eyes as he pondered the life of this wondrous place. *What stories these walls could tell—* walls that had once fallen into ruin before being restored fairly recently in the eyes of history. Vianden had been given new purpose, redefined in an age unimaginable by its builders.

It came to him then. Orlando opened his eyes and smiled.

He knew exactly how to motivate the gods.

"Change." Orlando stood in the Knight's Hall addressing an audience of four deities seated at a thickly glazed hornbeam table. "Change is a force unstoppable by man or god. Some embrace it, others fear it. Change can bring frustration, confusion, even anger, but even the four of you with all of your wondrous abilities, must adapt. And in some ways you have. "Yesterday, Taranis showed us a map of Gaul from Wikipedia. Most of you have updated your wardrobe to more or less contemporary style. Hell, Abellio's wearing superhero t-shirts."

"I find comic books entertaining," the god of apple trees chimed in.

Segomo shook his head.

"Don't judge me."

"And therefore," Orlando continued, "in your own small way, you've adapted to modern times. But none of that will bring you closer to your goal of being counted among the mighty pantheons of the world. Change forces us out of the cocoon of comfort we all wrap around ourselves when we become used to the old ways.

"The walls of this castle have been your cocoon for ten years. If you stay here, you will be left behind, forgotten as gods. Eventually, you might even be reviled by the people as freeloaders. I don't believe you want that to happen."

"What would you have us do?" Grannus asked.

"Among us mere mortals, we have certain public figures we call celebrities. Many of these famous people attract a massive following of supporters, but fame is fleeting and some of these celebrities disappear from the public eye for various reasons. There are a few cases, though, when they regroup and find the motivation to redefine themselves. They change not only their physical appearance, but they find something inside." Orlando tapped his chest. "Whether you call it heart, or courage, or sheer willpower, they each take the risk to step back out onto the world stage a different, stronger person."

Orlando held out his hands. "If mortals can do it, what's holding back the gods?"

"We have been who we are for eons. How do we *redefine* ourselves?" Taranis asked.

"Take risks. Put yourselves out there and do whatever it takes to win the belief and faith of the people by offering them something different— something better—than the suffering being inflicted upon them by the Romans."

Orlando paused. "Gentlemen, it's high time *you* made a comeback."

"If you're suggesting we go to France," Segomo said. "May I remind you that we would be severely outnumbered by Mars and his army. Should we encounter them, they will likely kill us all."

More excuses. Orlando felt his temper simmering. "Then that is a risk you'll need to take, god of war. Either that, or continue to wallow in self-pity and excuses behind these walls. For that matter, you might as well pack it in and return to the obscurity from whence you came."

Taranis slowly rose from his seat. Orlando tensed in anticipation of another lightning bolt. Instead, the god of thunder stepped forward and stood before him.

"You have a brave tongue, mortal, but I wonder if you have the temerity to act upon your words, to join us in France."

Orlando met the god's intimidating gaze. "This isn't my fight, but if that's what it takes to motivate you, count me in."

Orlando Start. Vasio's summons touched his mind, causing a mild surge of pressure above his eyes. Orlando winced as a feeling of profound distress overcame him. Vasio was troubled. *Turn on the screen to your right.*

"Are you ill, Orlando?" Grannus asked.

"No, but I think there's something you need to see." He turned to his right to find a wall-mounted television that had not been there a moment ago. He backed away from Taranis and turned it on.

A Luxembourg news correspondent was in the middle of imparting the details of an attack by the Roman army on Gers in the Midi-Pyrénées region of southern France. Hundreds had been killed and over one million hectares of crops and orchards set ablaze in a vicious strike led by Jupiter, Roman god of thunder, and Mars, god of war.

Grannus shook his head, his eyes beginning to glisten. Abellio's shoulders slumped. Segomo's hands clenched into fists and his jaw muscles twitched. As gods, they were a pathetic lot.

"If there was ever a chance to make a comeback," Orlando said quietly. "This is it."

Taranis sighed. "But we cannot leave Luxembourg unprotected."

"Trust me, Luxembourg *will* be protected."

"How do you know this?"

"I can't tell you right now, but I have a feeling you'll find out soon enough." He held up his car keys. "Now, if the wheel god is ready, my chariot awaits."

This time, Orlando made a conscious effort to calm himself and enjoy the ride, marveling at the veins of lightning that streaked and flashed all around them. Finally, the spectacle faded and the Range Rover screeched to a halt on a section of rural highway that led through vast farmland, or what was left of it. Every field in sight was in flames—a conflagration straight to the horizon. In the middle of the road, people and animals lay dead or close to it while others wailed over them. Children cried—those that had survived.

As soon as he stepped out of the car, Orlando fought back the urge to vomit. The air was thick with smoke and redolent of scorched flesh.

He leaned against the Range Rover and took several deep breaths before regaining his composure. *It'll take days to put this out.* He turned to the gods. "What can you do about—"

Taranis was already in the air, soaring skyward. Within a minute, roiling storm clouds formed from nothing and spread out in all directions. Explosions of thunder startled the people into nervous silence. Frightened eyes turned toward the heavens. Then the rain came, a torrential downpour over the fields, and *only* the fields. Not one drop fell on the road.

"Grannus, what can you do for these people?" Orlando asked. "Can you help them?"

The elder god hesitated.

"You're a god of healing."

"Using thermal springs…spas."

Orlando looked around at the nearby fields where the fires were already extinguished. Several depressions in the steaming ground were rapidly filling with water, creating pools. He pointed to the closest ones. "What about them? Can you work your mojo in there?"

Grannus nodded. "I think so, yes."

With help from the gods of war and apple trees, Orlando and Grannus worked with the victims to move their dead and wounded into the pools. Grannus moved from one to the next, dipping his hand into the water.

Orlando felt the sudden warmth through his clothes as he carried a girl no more than ten years old into the pool. He splashed her burned face and arms with water before briefly dunking her as if performing a baptism. As he looked on in awe, scorched flesh peeled away and dissolved in the water, leaving healthy, unblemished skin. He lifted her up and she threw her arms around him.

"Merci, monsieur."

"You're welcome, sweetheart."

He let her go and she ran off to another pool where her dead parents had been brought back to life. Orlando stepped out of the water to make room for other victims. He found Abellio in a field across the highway.

"Abellio, what else can you do besides apple trees?"

The teenage god shrugged. "I've often thought about trying my hand at citrus fruit."

"What else?"

"What are you asking of me, Orlando?"

"What…else…can…you…*do*?"

"I don't know."

Orlando grabbed him and spun him around to face the ruined crops. "Don't push me! I'm a god!"

"Then fix this. Restore these fields."

Abellio took in the extent of the damage and shook his head. "I only do apples…"

Orlando moved in front of him. "Abellio. Redefine yourself now, today."

Abellio held his gaze for a moment. Finally, with a deep breath, the skinny ginger god in a Green Lantern t-shirt, torn jeans and bare feet started off across the field.

And in his wake, crops began to grow.

Orlando Start, gather Taranis and Segomo.

"Vasio?" Orlando muttered. "What's wrong?"

Mars and Jupiter are moving against the Palace of Versailles.

"Why?"

They've discovered that it secretly houses the largest concentration of French resistance fighters. The Romans will destroy it.

"How do you expect Taranis and Segomo to prevent that?"

I simply need them to provide a distraction, to stall the attack, but they need to move immediately.

"OK, I'll do my best. Although I don't know what good it will do."

Trust me, Orlando Start.

He found the gods waiting for him by the Range Rover.

"We have decided to seek out Mars and Jupiter," Segomo said. "To avenge the pain they inflicted upon these people."

"Are you sure that's a good idea?"

"Did you not advise us to take risks?" Taranis retorted.

With a sigh, Orlando nodded. "In that case, you'll find them preparing to attack the Palace of Versailles."

Segomo frowned. "How do you know this?"

"I listen to the voices in my head. Look, I promise I'll explain later. We need to go now."

"We should take Grannus in the event of casualties," Taranis ordered. "Abellio's talents are best employed here. As for you, Orlando Start, it may also be wise for you to remain out of harm's way. Segomo and I are more than sufficiently motivated to take action. You have our gratitude."

"Uh, wait a second," Orlando said. "I've come this far. I'm not about to sit on the sidelines now."

"If there should be a battle in Paris, you could be killed," Segomo said.

"If you want to continue using my *chariot*, then I'm staying in the game."

"We could take it by force."

"Last I heard, that was not your 'preferred method'."

The Range Rover rolled to a stop on the Place d'Armes just beyond the courtyard of the Palace—and directly in front of the Roman contingent. Mere inches from the front bumper, two men turned to face the vehicle. Correction: two gods.

And one of them bore a passing resemblance to Taranis, right down to the chainmail tunic and iron breastplate covering his torso. *Jupiter.* Which meant the lean one in the military fatigues, combat vest, and sunglasses was probably Mars. *Seems some of the gods have indeed redefined themselves.*

"Shit," Orlando blurted from the backseat.

"Remain here," Taranis ordered as he and Segomo exited the vehicle. Orlando did not argue, though he did lower the rear passenger window.

Grannus sighed. "I had better get out there in case they all start killing each other." With that, he stepped out of the car, but kept his distance from the others.

"So, the gods of Gaul dare venture out of hiding from their insignificant corner of Europe," Jupiter taunted. "Forgotten throwbacks from a bygone age that have no place in this one. Did you really think you would escape my notice in the farmlands?"

Taranis shrugged. "Your notice was of little concern. However, I am surprised by you, Mars. The god of war *and* agriculture burning crops? You always had a reputation as a protector of the Roman people, not an aggressor."

"And when these people learn to accept Roman rule, they will have the benefit of my protection."

Segomo stepped forward to within inches of Mars. "We will stop you from decimating any more of this land."

Mars smirked. "You and what army?"

As if on cue, gunfire erupted in the courtyard followed by shouting and a blur of motion from all sides. Hundreds of armed men and women stormed the plaza, most wearing military fatigues. Others were covered completely in black and still more were in street clothes.

The resistance! Shit, this is getting tense.

The Romans leveled their weapons on the newcomers.

"Just like old times, Taranis. I suggest we let the mortals kill one another," Jupiter brought his fists up, sparking and pulsing with energy, "while we take our contest to a higher level."

With that, the Roman god of thunder propelled himself to the clouds. Taranis turned to Segomo who had not relented in his staring match with Mars.

"Go," Segomo said. "I shall deal with this one myself."

Taranis flew out of sight.

"You are but a pallid reflection of me," Mars said. "We conquered you before and will do so again. You should have remained cowering in your castle."

Mars backed away and joined the front line of his army. He fixed his eyes on the militia that had formed a perimeter around the plaza. "I will ask only once for your unconditional surrender! Throw down your weapons."

No one complied.

"As I expected." He faced his men. "Open fire!"

Orlando ducked and squeezed himself between the front and rear seats as both sides released a barrage of automatic weapons fire. Above his head, every window in the Range Rover shattered. Shards of glass fell over him as a spray of bullets pierced the seat backs. Orlando covered his ears against the din both on the streets and in the sky.

"Stop shooting holes in my car!"

After a few moments, no further bullets entered the vehicle and Orlando risked a glance through the gaping hole that had been the windshield. Outside, Segomo stood, his fist swirling in the air above his head. Surrounding his forearm, a whirlwind of bullets grew thicker and denser as every shot fired from nearby Roman guns was sucked in. In one fluid motion, the war god drew back his arm then thrust it forward. Bullets fanned out, spraying in every direction. Roman soldiers fell amid screams and blood. The resistance fighters cheered as they continued firing.

In a fit of rage, Mars reached down and lifted the Range Rover by its front bumper. The floor dropped away beneath Orlando as he tumbled into the cargo space. His head and shoulder blade cracked against the rear window, knocking the wind out of him. Although the world stopped spinning after a few seconds, the vehicle lurched and slid on its roof until it collided with a concrete wall at the edge of the plaza.

Wincing against the pain, Orlando lay motionless, unable to turn his head or move his right arm. Above him, explosions of thunder and the crackle of lightning blended with the shouts and gunfire all around him. Orlando let out a chuckle at the irony of it. *Back where I started. Gonna die in my car.*

The cacophony of death and destruction abruptly ceased. Even the heavens fell silent. Orlando frowned. With what little mobility he could muster, he contorted his body until his feet pressed against the rear window. On the second kick, the cracked glass relented and he crawled out onto the pavement. To his right, combatants from both sides had simply stopped and lowered their weapons. Even Mars and Segomo stood shoulder-to-shoulder, staring in confusion at their respective mortal troops. All heads were turned in the same direction as if gazing at a fixed point that Orlando could not see until the throng of bodies parted—

—and Vasio emerged.

He did not stop, but continued past the crowd toward the Range Rover and knelt down beside Orlando.

Can you hear me, Orlando Start?'

"Yeah. I could really use some of Grannus's miracle water."

He is tending to wounded across the plaza. I have summoned him.

"How did you get here?"

I made a breakthrough in my meditation, one that has allowed me to increase my influence across a larger distance. I am still physically in Luxembourg. What you see before you is merely a projection, but have no fear. There will be no more violence today.

Orlando laid his head down onto the coarse concrete. "Oh, thank God."

You are welcome.

Mars roared at his men. "Fools! Open fire, I command you!"

No one raised their weapons, not even the resistance fighters. Instead, shoulders shrugged, feet shuffled and mortal faces held an expression of apathy.

The Roman god whirled on Segomo. "Who was he that strolled through here, one from your laughable pantheon? What have you done to my men?"

Segomo shot a sidelong glance at Vasio across the plaza. "I'm...not entirely certain."

Mars crossed the distance between them in two steps, placing his face within an inch of Segomo's. "You can be certain of this. I will find out what power this is and how to defeat it, and then I will be back! Mark my words."

The gods of war held each other's gazes for a moment longer before Mars barked at his troops. "Fall in!" His men lazily gathered in formation and spirited away, along with their commanding officer.

Segomo exhaled as the French cheered.

Just then, Taranis descended from the heavens, looking a bit the worse for wear as he touched down beside Segomo. Yet again, there were cheers. He spoke quietly to his fellow god. "In the beginning, Jupiter definitely had the better of me, but when I heard the cries of victory from our people, I suddenly felt rejuvenated. I found myself able to hold my own against him. As the mortals would say, I gave as good as I got. Eventually, Jupiter simply departed."

Segomo grinned. "As did Mars, though he was rather perturbed. I think we should have a talk with Vasio, but for now we have won the day!"

"Indeed." Taranis turned toward Orlando. Grannus was at his side now. "But not without some motivation."

Two days had passed since the incident in Versailles. After a dip in a tub of Grannus's healing water at the palace, Orlando had been sent back to Luxembourg in the wreck that was his only remaining earthly possession. Since then, he'd spent the time wandering the halls of Vianden Castle, regrouping and contemplating his future.

Here and now, he sat alone with his thoughts in the dining hall, pushing bits of potato pancake around his plate and flipping through news channels on the wall-mounted television. Most reports were in German or French, others in English, but all told the same story more or less accurately.

After Vasio had quelled the confrontation with the Romans and mysteriously vanished, Taranis had restored electricity to the entire country. He'd quickly become known as the God of Power. Orlando looked forward to the responses from the established religious groups.

Segomo had wasted no time in announcing his intention to reform the French military, placing himself in charge, of course. On the screen, he stood surrounded by cheering resistance fighters while the caption read: "Segomo—God of Defense and Protection."

Well, you grumpy old bastard, you finally got your army.

A French news anchor reported that Abellio was continuing to restore crops in the rural farm lands and was being hailed as the God of the Harvest. He'd even encountered a Gaulish fertility goddess named Onuava who joined him on his mission.

I'll be damned. Taranis was right. There were other gods in hiding.

As for Grannus, he had pledged to continue healing the sick and wounded and resurrecting the recently deceased with his miracle water. *I should bottle that and sell it.* According to the German reporter on the scene, another Gaulish goddess of healing, Sirona, had already been traveling from town to town discreetly working with the victims of Roman attacks, but had been hard-pressed to keep up. Now, she and Grannus were a team, known as the God and Goddess of Life.

Yet nowhere in the media was there mention of Vasio.

Orlando sighed. "Forgotten again, buddy."

I have no need of notoriety, Orlando Start.

With a jolt, Orlando dropped his fork. "Christ, I don't think I'll ever get used to that."

"Then perhaps this method of communication would be less jarring to you."

Orlando looked up and gaped as Vasio sauntered into the dining hall and took a seat opposite him. He reached for the pitcher of orange juice and poured himself a glass.

"Yes, I can speak," Vasio said. "I simply choose not to most of the time."

"Yeah, well, you know, no offense, but you could really stand to eat a few of these potato pancakes, or an omelet, maybe a loaf of bread."

Vasio smiled and sipped his juice. "The meditation takes more out of you than you realize. Even for a god, it is all-consuming."

"Look, I know you said you don't care for publicity or a catchy title, but," Orlando raised his glass, "to Vasio, God of...*Peace*. You realize, of course, that despite ducking the media, you've revealed yourself to the world."

Vasio shrugged. "So be it. Perhaps the time was right. Results are all that interest me, and what peace we have achieved could just as well be credited to you, Orlando Start. Your words of encouragement, and dare I say your faith, provided my brethren and me the motivation to come out of isolation and present ourselves anew to the people. You are indeed a paragon of inspiration. The question is, where does Orlando Start go from here?"

Orlando sat back in his seat and sighed. "Honestly, I thought I could stick around and help, with the gods' consent, of course. The way I see it, the French could use a little motivation right now. They've seen terrible violence at the hands of supreme beings. It might take some convincing, possibly even some counseling, for them to heal and move forward to accept a new, unfamiliar pantheon. I'd like to spread the word that the new gods in town are beneficent and that the people no longer need to live in fear."

Vasio nodded in approval. "So, the motivational speaker has redefined *himself* as well?"

"Yeah, you could say that. It feels good to make a comeback."

Axel's Flight

by Steven H. Wilson

"We're going to Sweden because why?" Axel Sage had asked upon his mentor's announcement that they were boarding a longboat bound for Stockholm. A flying longboat, thank you very much, which was the property of Frey, god of the sun and the rain.

"An open boat at altitude?" was the next question. "I'll freeze my ass off!"

"Don't be irreverent, Axel," Bragi had chided; but he'd also smiled. All through the years they'd spent together, as the god of poetry had taught Axel the craft of the bard, he'd smiled at behavior that had always infuriated Axel's parents, his teachers, and, when he'd had time for them, his friends. Bragi found Axel's attitude of challenge refreshing. It reminded him of the elves, who were, after all, great fun to be around when they weren't scheming.

"I thought the point of going to Europe—"

Bragi had held up a hand and had not smiled. "'Tis Scandanavia. Do not call it…" the word had come out as though involuntarily, as if it were vomit. "Europe."

"Scandanavia, okay. But I thought you guys—"

"We guys?"

"You gods then. I thought you all wanted us to return to our ancestral homelands. Mine's the Netherlands, and maybe Wales, not Sweden."

"Being from the Netherlands," Bragi had said, "is a bit like being from this land you once called 'The United States.' It means you're a mix of breeds. There were Galls in your land, and Gypsies, and even Arabs; but most important to you, Axel, there were Vikings. Your Viking blood is what called out to the Aesir and brought us to you."

"My blood looks like everyone else's and you might remember that the first god it called to me was Loki. Not a plus."

Loki had caused quite a bit of trouble for Axel when he'd first encountered the gods in New York.

"Ultimately, though, it brought us together. And you are one of the most worthy of my pupils." His eyes had crinkled. "Even if you are a bit rough around the edges!" His eyes were surprisingly bright for one with snow white hair and a habit of speaking in verse; but Bragi was a god. Age, for him, was nothing but a matter of preference. The rules didn't apply. Nor did they apply for Axel Sage, at least, not the way they used to, the way they'd applied to humanity during the entire time the gods had been away. Now Axel had the gift of youth, the gift of the Apples of Idunn. Idunn was Bragi's wife, and she was the keeper of magical Apples which, when bitten into, allowed an aging person to become young again.

When Axel's beard had started to become thicker and his face began to fill out a little more than it ever had, when his jeans had become tight around his belly, Idunn had brought out a small antique chest made of Ash wood, opened it, and handed Axel an apple.

He'd bitten into it, and, within a half hour, suddenly noticed that he was hiking up jeans sagging at the waist. When next he'd looked in the mirror, was his face, perhaps, a little more angular, a little less rounded? The apple worked as advertised, unlike the imitations which had cropped up on the black market since Idunn had returned with her Aesir brethren. Axel had access to something which humankind had sought at least since Ponce de Leon.

Every few months after that, Idunn had brought out the same apple. There was no flaw in its perfect, ruby skin. The bite he'd taken had healed as magically as his extra pounds had gone away. Nearly thirty years old, he still had the lean form of a teenager just crossed into manhood. An immortal, after all, could maintain any apparent age he liked. Bragi thought that an eternal post-adolescent would be most appealing to music fans, and he seemed to be right. Axel played to sold out crowds all over the sections of North America to which Bragi could get him access. He'd even performed on Broadway several times, and played Carnegie Hall. His personal fortune, in gold, stored in a hall owned by Odin, was more than his parents had earned in a lifetime of work. This return of the gods business wasn't such a bad deal after all.

But if the apples of youth made him continue to feel like a teen, the flight to Sweden had made him feel like a scared little boy about to piss his pants. They'd boarded the boat in New York Harbor. It was, as promised, a Viking longboat, carved wooden prow in the shape of a beautiful woman and all. It was large for such an ancient design, over two-hundred feet long.

Bragi had stopped before it on the pier and gestured, gazed at it wonderingly, and proclaimed, "Skidbladnir. Based on the Skei, grandest of the designs of your ancestors, Axel."

Hoisting his guitar case and traveling bag on his shoulder, Axel had said, "Seriously? You can't make me believe we're flying that all the way to Sweden."

With a twinkle in his eye, Bragi had shoved Axel onto the gangplank. "We are."

When the ship had cleared the Verrazano Narrows Bridge, Bragi given a signal, and the dozens of men and women seated on thirty benches lifted their oars toward the sky, as a bird spreads its wings. Skidbladnir had lurched from the water and soared, like that selfsame bird, into the sky over Jamaica Bay.

Axel had screamed, run to the stern, made the mistake of looking down, and vomited.

Bragi and the dozens of men and women had laughed their asses off.

This was air travel in the age of The Return. No longer was humankind permitted to fly among the clouds, or venture into space. That was the province of the gods. If humans were to fly, it would be a privilege granted them as a reward. At first, Axel could have done without this particular privilege. Once he had recovered, however, resting in a small shelter constructed on the deck for those precious souls who couldn't face the biting wind in their face and the clean, bracing air above the clouds, he'd gingerly ventured back to the prow. Now he'd found he actually could stand the sensation of being in an open boat high in the sky. In fact, it was fun.

Now, back on solid ground, he stepped up his pace to keep up with Bragi, who was making a bee line for the entrance to Globen, a structure which had carried the name The Ericsson Dome until the gods had declared that multinationals had placed their names on quite enough signs throughout the world, and that it should be the names of the gods on men and women's lips, not the names of the providers of cell phones.

"Dude, you booked me at Globen?"

Bragi turned, and his merry eyes were not so merry. "I have asked you, Axel, not to call me 'Dude.' And yes, I supposed I have 'booked you.' Tonight you play for an esteemed company. Odin has redirected this grand hall for purposes more fitting than tournaments of Ice Hockey. This is now the hall of warriors, where the Vikings train for battle."

With the return of Odin, the Swedish Army, one of the oldest standing armies in the world, had been transitioned from a body which served under government bureaucrats to a group which was at the disposal of Odin and the other Aesir gods. The one-handed war god Tyr had taken over the offices of the Inspectors General of the Army and Navy, the Supreme Commander and the Minister for Defence. He had then canceled a program of recruitment intended to transition the armed forces away from conscription, a concept the Aesir found repulsive, for what was the point of sending men to battle who didn't want to go? In place of contract labor and recruitment drives, Tyr had introduced a series of contests, open to all and held before an audience with no admission charged, by which the Viking Warriors selected the mortals most fit to join their ranks.

A P.R. firm had gotten involved and convinced the Allfather and Tyr that they could be of assistance. The result was that *Who Wants to be a Viking?* became the most popular entertainment in all of Scandinavia, once Odin had deigned to have it broadcast over the television device he otherwise so disliked. There were some complaints (unexpected by the Aesir, but which Axel could have told them would come) about women not being eligible. These were quashed quickly by the introduction of a program for female contestants. *Who Wants to be a Valkyrie?* was an equivalent ratings success, and was even more popular in non-Scandinavian countries where television was allowed. The Aesir quickly became the most popular leaders Northern Europe had known since, well, the Aesir. Sweden, Norway, and Denmark` had re-united under Odin's banner. By godly decree, the European Union was no more.

"I'm playing for the Vikings? Sort of like a U.S.O. show?"

"I know not the U.S.O.," said Bragi.

"My parents told me about them. Entertainers who would visit the troops during the war and...entertain them. Boost their morale. Mom and Dad had some run-ins with them when they protested the Viet Nam War."

"Why did they protest a war?" asked Bragi.

"Um...because they didn't see any reason for us to be in it?"

"Did your enemy attack you?"

"No."

"Did they steal from you?"

"No."

"Did they rape your women?"

"Uh uh."

"And still you went to war?"

"Apparently. I didn't. I wasn't born."

Bragi shook his head. "Then I'd say 'tis a good thing we've returned. Without us, you didn't know when to go to war and when not to. But 'tis true, warriors must have inspiration. That is why you've come. The new Children of Odin must hear from the leading bard of our people." He clapped Axel on the shoulder. "And that is you."

"Axel Sage, warriors!"

The crowd erupted in a cacophony of applause and table-pounding. Not bad for a matinee show, thought Axel, especially a matinee show where the audience was made up of burly men in the peaked helmets and leather armor of the ancient Vikings. This made even some of the clubs in the Village seem like tame crowds.

"Come back out here, Axel!" said the emcee, one of those slick TV stars who'd found a way to survive the almost-death of his medium. Axel didn't really want to go back out. He'd already done a full set and an encore, and he was...boat-lagged? Whatever. The guy kept beckoning to him urgently, however, so Axel sauntered out from behind the pipe and drape, smiling and giving the audience a jaunty wave.

As Axel crossed to him, the earpiece, coupled to his wireless mic, buzzed and the director said, "Down Center, Axel." Axel obeyed, going back to wave to the audience, who began a renewed burst of applause. Axel quickly realized the ovation was only partially his, for others were taking the stage behind him. He knew better than to look back, so he continued to make eye contact with his audience, picking out one at a time at whom to make faces, give a thumbs up, or practice funny gestures. He was miming that he admired one Viking's helmet when a slab of concrete landed on his shoulder. Casting his glance to the side, he corrected himself. It was not a slab of concrete, it was a very large hand, and it belonged to Odin, Allfather of the Aesir gods.

A minute ago, Odin had been at the head of the hall, on a raised dais opposite the stage. Now, suddenly, he was beside Axel, clad, not in the garb of a Wall Street banker, as he would be in New York, but in the ceremonial garb of the old Norse warrior god. On his shoulders perched two huge, black birds, the ravens Huginn and Muninn. Odin was flanked by others, who came to stand around Axel in a loose semi-circle. The "horseshoe of death," his choreographer back on Broadway called it. It was terrible stage blocking, but who was he to correct the gods? Of course, his choreographer had been an actual Muse.

On Odin's right was a god with one hand. His right arm terminated at the wrist and was covered by a gleaming cap, which matched his polished helm and armor. It was Tyr, Axel knew from seeing his portrait outside the arena. On the left was a woman so beautiful that Axel's breath caught. She was so lovely she almost glowed. Or perhaps she did glow. Clearly, she was a goddess.

The announcer called out, "The Lords and Lady of the games, ladies and gentlemen! Allfather Odin, Tyr, god of war, and Freyja, Mistress of the warrior's paradise, Fólkvangr!"

The crowd gave a renewed roar.

"Axel Sage," Odin pronounced in a deep, rich baritone. The crowd hushed suddenly. "I have watched you, these past years, as you have studied under our brother Bragi. You have become truly a worthy bard. In all the history of your race, I can think of few to call your equal."

Axel smiled and nodded gratefully. He hated being praised in public. He never knew how to react.

"It is fitting, then, that you should be included in a noble company." Odin gestured behind him, beckoning to someone who wasn't on stage. From behind the pipe and drape emerged two men about his own age, both in ceremonial Viking garb. They came to stand before Axel. Odin pointed to one and said, "This is Johan."

Johan nodded to Axel. He was a beefy young man, not stocky, but muscular. A slightly doltish farmboy smile split his face under his helmet, highlighting dimples and a prominent chin. His blue eyes were wide and a bit wild. He looked like nothing more than a dumb jock fratboy in costume for a party.

Odin nodded to the emcee, and the polished, over-driven voice rang out across the hall. No doubt it did likewise on televisions everywhere. "Johan. Winner of nineteen rounds of our competition. Picked by the gods as the best of the new Vikings, a winner in the warrior's tradition. Can you imagine the feeling—"

Odin held up a hand, and the announcer stopped.

"Johan will lead our new Vikings in battle." He gestured to the other man, thin and intense looking, with no helmet and his face framed by straight, long hair. His pose suggested self-assurance. His flinty eyes showed intelligence, and perhaps arrogance. He was a serious type. Axel imagined he didn't smile easily. "This is Ragnar."

"Ragnar, star of the Learning Channel's hit show, *Explorers*," said the emcee. This time he stopped and waited for Odin.

"Ragnar builds our warcraft in the Viking tradition. As Johan is brave, he is inventive." The Allfather leveled his eyes on Axel. "As you are inspirational, Axel Sage. These are our leaders among men. We invite you to stay here and be one of them."

The crowd erupted in applause again, and the announcer barked, "What an honor this is for Axel Sage. Few mortals are asked to join the gods here in the Hall of Odin permanently, and Axel—Wait, the Allfather has more to say."

In fact, the Allfather nodded to Johan, who stepped forward, a short sword held flat in both his hands, as if in offering.

"The Allfather has said 'Don't leave your weapons lying about behind your back in a field; you never know when you may need all of sudden your spear.'" Johan spoke the words carefully, but with gravity and import. He was almost pompous, with that fake sincerity that only the insincere can manage when they've finally tricked themselves into believing something.

"That means never to go about unarmed," Johan continued, as if his previous words were in some foreign language. "Without weapons," he added.

Johan extended the sword, bright and shiny, but still looking like something out of a museum showcase. He held it by the blade and presented it to Axel.

"This is yours, in recognition of our invitation to you, to be a Viking."

Axel reached for the sword, not really sure what to do with it. He was afraid he'd slice Johan's hand if he took it. Beside him, Ragnar stepped up and held out his hands, miming that he wanted Axel to do likewise, and asking silent permission to take hold of Axel's fingers and position them correctly. Ragnar guided him in the ceremonial acceptance of the sword. He held it up, brandishing it for the audience, who seemed to approve.

"In our traditions," Odin called out, "'tis not enough to merely build or conquer. A man's soul must be fulfilled, as must the soul of a god. Your music, Axel, is fulfilling to us. We ask you to be Bard to the company of the Aesir and the New Vikings. Sing to us of what we will accomplish. Put the fire in our hearts. You will be given the finest hall in which to live, and will have your choice of a wife. What say you?"

Axel reeled. Live here? Move to Stockholm? Play for the same audience forever? Choice of a wife? He glared stupidly at the elder god.

Odin, seeing his confusion, apparently decided that the show had to go on.

"What is Axel's answer?" shouted the emcee into his mic. "We'll bring that to you in just a moment!"

As the program apparently cut to a commercial, Odin turned to consult in whispers with Tyr, and Ragnar stepped in and tentatively nudged Axel's elbow.

"They caught you by surprise, didn't they?" he asked. His English was perfect, but there was an accent Axel couldn't place. He was from some Northen European country, obviously.

"Yeah, kinda," said Axel.

Ragnar gave a slight roll of his eyes. "They love their pageantry. They think everyone just can't wait to play their games."

Axel just nodded, aware of the scrutiny of the gods.

"Man," said Ragnar, studying his face. "You're out on your feet!"

"It's been a long trip," agreed Axel, leaning in and whispering as Ragnar did.

"Let me get you the hell out of here," said the Viking conspiratorially.

Ragnar stepped forward toward Odin and waited to be recognized.

"Cunning Ragnar," said Odin.

Ragnar gave a slight bow. "Allfather, our guest is tired and hungry. May I offer him the hospitality of our hall?"

Odin smiled. "Indeed. Rest, Axel Sage. The television audience is accustomed to waiting for an answer. Your brother Vikings will take you to refresh yourself."

Ragnar guided Axel by the elbow, heading backstage, but Johan, on the other side, collected him in a one-armed bearhug, dragged him downstage toward the audience, and then seized Axel and Ragnar's hands together in his and held them up in a three-handed victory salute.

The crowd went wild.

When Johan had absorbed enough adulation, and Axel had nearly gagged on his cologne, he ushered them backstage. Once out of sight, he took off his helmet, revealing shaggy blonde hair, and clapped Axel on the back too hard.

"Awesome show! You joining us is gonna rock!"

Axel shook his head, confused. "I'm not sure—"

"Let the man breathe, Jim Bob," said Ragnar.

Johan looked annoyed. "Okay," he said to Axel. "Get some rest. But your answer to Odin is going to be a huge moment. Smart, playing the suspense that way."

"I wasn't playing," said Axel.

"Whatever. Anyway, you don't have to give him an answer tonight, because we're going dark for a couple hours while they turn the arena. Set it up for battle."

Axel had caught a few minutes of *Who Wants to Be a Viking?* The central arena of Globen would indeed have to be cleared of the chairs that had been added to the field to accommodate his enormous audience. They'd filled the stands and then some.

"Come back when the games are over, around nine," said Johan. "That's the feast. All the mead you can drink. Get some sleep now, though, 'cause after the feast, you ain't goin' home alone. The girls are gonna line up for you, and Axel Junior's gonna be busy all night!" Johan nodded to indicate exactly what part of the body he meant by, "Axel Junior."

Axel winced. He decided he really did not like Johan.

Fortunately, the gregarious Viking announced, "Gotta run, man. Things to do. See you at nine, and great show! Seriously robust!"

Robust? wondered Axel as Johan jogged away.

Ragnar shook his head. "Asshole, right?"

"Pretty much," agreed Axel. "Why did you call him Jim Bob?"

Ragnar almost smiled. "That's really his name. He's American, like you."

"He may be American, but he's nothing like me. How did you get hooked up with him?"

"I'm not, really. Odin likes to pair us because we're the two mortals he's promoted to be leaders. Like he wants to promote you. Johan swings an axe and is working on fathering a new Viking race. I build ships."

"Flying ones, like Skidbladnir?"

"No. Not yet, anyway. Come to the shipyards at Skeppsgarden one day while you're here. I'll show you what we're doing." He gestured toward a pair of steel double doors leading out of the cinderblock maze of the backstage area. "For now, let's get you settled."

"Where is this hall Odin was talking about? What is it, some kind of Viking hunting lodge?"

Ragnar actually grinned. "Maybe in the old days. Now it's the Hilton around the corner."

Two hours later, Axel, having slept not at all, wandered into the bar of his hotel. He dropped into a booth in the corner, annoyed, wanting no company. How could he have been scared to the point of puking his guts out, traveled an ocean in an open boat, performed a concert...and then not be able to sleep? Sometimes the human body was frustrating in its mysteries.

He asked the waitress for a recommendation on beer and ordered her top pick. He knew nothing about Sweden and less about beer. He wasn't much of a drinker, even with Bragi's best encouragement. Axel scanned the bar. It was a typical lobby bar, open, facing the registration desk, with a fireplace as its focal point and blond wood on every surface that wasn't brushed steel.

The bar wasn't crowded. Axel noticed one man staring at him from the corner: young, dark, immaculately dressed. He did not respond when Axel caught his eye, but he did not look away. Probably a fan who couldn't think how to introduce himself.

Axel wasn't in the mood.

His beer arrived, and the waitress held out a slip. It was as quickly snatched from her hand before Axel could take it.

"This one's on me."

A girl slid onto the bench opposite him, handing a the waitress a coin. (Odin distrusted paper money.)

"Hi, Axel. I'm Anika."

She was pretty...probably the prettiest girl he'd ever met, and he'd met goddesses by the score. She was young, about his age, or the age he appeared to be. Hair the color of sunshine enlivened a face that didn't need makeup, and her smile shut down any protest he might utter that he wanted to be alone. And she knew his name.

He held up the beer and said, "Thanks."

"I saw your show," she grinned. "I haven't seen a decent concert since I was twelve. Mom and Dad brought us here after The Return, and the music's not what it used to be, back home."

"Home?"

"Minnesota. St. Paul. I've heard of you, of course. Who hasn't, after you trounced Loki back in the day? But with the recording industry as dead as Scientology, I've never had any way to hear your music."

It was true that live performance was a musician's only outlet these days, except for a small, lively trade in vinyl, which kept the classics and a few independents alive in New York.

"So my music doesn't suck?" Axel noted the young man in the corner was still staring. He shifted so as not to see him.

"Bragi wouldn't sponsor a fraud. You've got a unique style. Your songs all tell a story, but it's not a story so locked down that the listener can't put herself into it. I listened and closed my eyes, and I could just feel like I was..." She stopped and noticed his baffled smile. While talking, she'd pantomimed her words and had closed her eyes. "I'm sorry, I'm rambling."

He laughed. "Kinda."

She grabbed his free hand and squeezed it. An electric shock ran from his hand to his spine and lit up every nerve in his body. "I know, I do that, especially when I meet someone I admire, and...well, dammit, Axel, you put dreams in people's heads!"

Axel reflected that he didn't at all mind the idea of putting a dream in this young lady's head. He left her hand in his, sipped his beer and realized it was better than any he'd ever had. He'd stopped feeling tired.

"Bragi said I'm here to inspire the...troops."

"Troops is a good word," she agreed. "That's what they are. Troops with broadswords and axes instead of AK-47s, and longboats instead of tanks, but troops."

"You'd think the arrival of the gods would bring peace," said Axel.

Anika's eyes narrowed. "You'd think, but then you'd be amazed how many of the returned gods are war gods. Though they did end a lot of wars."

"So, I guess your parents follow the Aesir?"

"Oh yeah. Dad's big into Odin. Mom actually studied the loom under Frigga. They're here now, for the games."

"You too? You like the games?"

"Actually, I work here," she said, and her last syllable was accompanied by the blast of what sounded like the blowing of a horn. It was muffled, but couldn't be missed by anyone within a hundred yards. It came from the small bag which lay on the bench at Anika's side. She pulled out a cell phone, silenced it, and smiled apologetically. "And that's actually my cue."

He nodded at the device. "There's no cell service here, is there?"

"There is, but only for Odin's chosen. I think it's more magic than tech. Well, gotta run." She scooted sideways and stood, squeezing his hand once before releasing it. "It was nice meeting you, Axel. I'll catch you at the Feast, right?"

"Uh...right." He'd forgotten about Johan's dinner invitation. "What exactly do you do at Globen?"

She smiled radiantly, tossed her hair and said, "You'll see."

He watched her walk away, smiling, noting the perfection of every part of her body in motion. His smile faded, however, as he realized that the young man in the corner was still staring. His desire to avoid all contact magically erased by Anika's sudden appearance, he jumped up and crossed to his observer.

"Uh, 'scuse me," he said pleasantly, "I don't mean to embarrass you, but did you want to ask for an autograph or something?"

He wondered if the poor guy would be too tongue-tied for words, but he seemed not at all intimidated. He raked his green eyes over Axel and smirked for a moment. "Hardly." The eyes continued to glare, to hold Axel's. Fiery green eyes, filled with contempt.

Only once before had he seen eyes that brilliant shade of green.

"You!" whispered Axel, realizing he sounded like some cliché cartoon character.

"Me," acknowledged the other, satisfied with himself.

"Loki, what are you doing here?"

"I wouldn't be anywhere else. The Allfather is training new followers!"

"But what are you doing here," pressed Axel, "watching me from the corner like some kind of pervy stalker?"

Loki chuckled. "I'm just waiting for the fun to begin."

Axel raised a finger and stabbed it at the trickster god. "I've stayed out of your way! I haven't done anything to you since—"

"—Since you cheated me on a bet," finished Loki. "I don't like to be cheated, Axel."

"That was years ago!"

"Years are nothing to the Aesir."

"And Bragi said Odin said the whole thing was your fault!"

The disguised Loki shrugged. "Fine. Odin says you were right and I was wrong. I have no claim on you."

"All right then," said Axel, starting to leave.

Loki called after him, "But I've been known to disagree with Odin a time or two. Watch your back, Axel Sage."

Axel arrived at Globen nearly an hour before the Feast was scheduled to begin, a combination of restlessness and excitement having taken hold of him. The restlessness was partly a result of being in a strange city and a different time zone, and partly the result of meeting up with Loki again after all these years. The excitement, well, that was all about Anika.

He couldn't get her out of his thoughts. The girl got to him. Since puberty, Axel had been considered cold and unapproachable by others, despite the passion he channeled into his music. Conversely, he considered himself supremely, even inconveniently emotional. He just cared most about developing his talent. It didn't occur to him to focus his efforts on sexual conquests, as so many young men did. Well...there had been a few. Quick, shallow encounters. Not satisfying. And relationships were messy. People were complicated and usually high-maintenance. He hadn't met anyone who, in his mind, managed to come anywhere near that secret, sacred place where music lived.

Anika was...different. Something in her smile, her frantic chatter, her blue eyes...something hit him over the head like a baseball bat. Something...magic. He had no say in the matter. He couldn't wait to see her again. He'd heard of love at first sight before, but he'd always considered it just a poetic contrivance. How could you possibly be in love with someone you'd just met? Silly.

But...wow. How could anyone not be in love with Anika, having met her?

Rainbow hues bathed the enormous dome of the Globe as Axel arrived. It was Winter in Sweden, and the sun had set (unreasonably, Axel thought) before 3 PM today. The Swedes suffered through hellishly short days in the Winter months, with three hours less daylight than Axel was accustomed to on a December day in Phoenix or even New York. Globen, lit up as though it were Christmas, almost justified the extended night, dwarfing the surrounding buildings and catching the light as though the Moon had fallen to earth, reached out and sucked up the day and all its light and color.

As he made his way to the entrance, Axel caught sight of a familiar figure, tall, lanky, neck craned toward the sky, facing the globe.

"Ragnar!" he called out as he approached. "Hey, man, thanks again for bailing me out earlier." He extended his hand in greeting, but Ragnar was looking up again.

Axel came and stood beside him. "What are we looking at?"

Ragnar pointed to a spot near the pinnacle of the enormous sphere, where, at about 11 o'clock from Axel's perspective, a spotlight picked out a small splash of red protruding from the surface. It was blocky, pointed at the top, and looked to Axel as though Snoopy might have landed his doghouse cum Sopwith Camel on the top of the globe.

"What is that?"

"The Moonhouse," Ragnar responded bitterly.

"Moonhouse? Never heard of it."

Ragnar was silent for a moment, and Axel felt that, just maybe, his immortal soul was being judged. "I suppose there's no reason why you would have heard of it...not anymore."

"Is there even any way to get up there?"

"See the tracks?" Ragnar pointed to lines which bisected the globe on two sides. "That was the the Stockholm Skyview, a tram ride to the top of the Globe. It closed in 2012."

"Oh." With The Return, many large-scale engineering projects had stopped in their tracks.

"That's a traditional Swedish cottage," explained Ragnar. "It was placed there as a prototype. The designer planned an identical cottage on the Moon, placed by robots. It would have been the first permanent structure built by humankind on another world."

"Lemme guess—"

"The gods forbade it."

"Did you have something to do with the project?"

Ragnar shook his head. "Only in that it inspired me. Since I was a small boy, all I wanted was to go into space. The idea of artists and engineers, building a house, extending our reach to another world in a manner both concrete and familiar...it gave me hope. Humanity...humanity was made to explore...to go forth...to put our feet on alien ground...to say, in no uncertain terms, 'I was here.'"

Axel wanted to apologize. He didn't know why, exactly, but he felt this man deserved to be told that someone was sorry.

"I guess...that's not going to happen anymore, huh?"

"No," said Ragnar quietly. "I guess not. Now humanity...like the Vikings...are warriors for the gods. We fight their battles, and they take care of us."

"Wow. Ragnar, y'know...when the gods first returned, my career was sidelined for a while. I thought there was no hope for me. I guess I found out differently."

"Because of the gods?"

"Bragi has helped me a lot, but I don't like to look at it that way. My own gifts saw me through. Now I'm doing what I always dreamed of doing."

Ragnar's eyes bore into him. "Are you? Entertaining the troops? Is that what you dreamed of, Axel?"

Axel didn't answer. Not out loud.

No. It wasn't what he'd dreamed of.

"Forgive me," Ragnar said at Axel's silence. "I didn't mean to bring you down. I am not happy when I am here. I am anxious to return to the seaside, to my boats. I only came to get approval on my designs. I will be going back in the morning."

"Will you be attending the Feast?"

"No," replied Ragnar. "No, I have seen the Feasts. But you have not. I suppose I should let you go. Everyone's...in there." He inclined his head toward the entrance to Globen.

The words "in there" sounded like a curse.

Despite Bragi's coaching, Axel was unprepared for the spectacle of the games, an immense, instense panorama of action directed from a raised dais by the one-handed Tyr. It was not the gods who were the spectacle, it was the controlled chaos of the games themselves, if games they could be called. Literally thousands of men swarmed the field on the stadium's floor, jumping, charging, slashing at each other with swords and axes, jabbing with spears. The din of their weapons clashing and of their screams drowned out the cries and applause of the audience.

An usher appeared almost instantaneously at Axel's elbow, smiled, and guided him quickly forward among the rows of seats. "This way, Mr. Sage," she said excitedly. "We have a V.I.P. seat for you."

Following, Axel looked up to identify a blur of motion which had caught his eye. It looked like...it was...a horse...a flying horse. He shouldn't have been surprised, only he'd always assumed that these mythological creatures (no longer mythological) would have wings. This animal looked no different from the horses back home. It just happened to be about a hundred feet in the air. On its back was a woman in chain mail. She guided her mount in an arc over the audience, then into a dive toward the field of battle. The field of play? Axel didn't know the appropriate terminology. As she came close, just over the heads of the contestants, she hovered and reached out. It looked like she touched one of the men on his shoulder.

"The Valkyrior," said a voice beside him. He turned to see Bragi, who took him by the arm and guided him to a seat. As he took it, a woman's voice sang out over the crowd in a musical cry of triumph.

"Right," said Axel. "I recognized them, but..."

"But you've never seen a horse fly."

"Only in the movies," said Axel. "And not even there, lately."

The gods had curtailed a good deal of Hollywood's output over the last decade, offended by the CGI special effects which made their miraculous powers seem commonplace. Only swift action by a consortium of gods of arts from various pantheons had prevented the outright destruction of the likes of Harry Potter and Lord of the Rings, and such films were rarely seen now by mere mortals.

"Each Valkyrie monitors the conflict. As a contest between two or three warriors becomes close, she chooses the winner and the loser. You saw that one tap her chosen one."

"He wins?" said Axel.

"No. The touch of the Valkyrie tells the warrior his battle is coming to an end. He makes a final gallant surge against the foe, and then he is carried away by the warrior maidens of Odin."

"So the battle is rigged, like professional wrestling?"

"Certainly not! The warriors stand or fall on their merits. The Valkyrie merely indicates the decisions of the fates."

"So they're not, like, the referees? What happens if a player commits a foul?"

"What is a foul?" asked Bragi.

"You know...breaks the rules?"

"Rules? Axel, this is a battle. There are no rules. Cowardice is forbidden. If a man runs in fear, he will be disciplined. Otherwise, Odin has sworn an oath, on behalf of all the Aesir, never to interfere. War is sacred to us. It must measure the true mettle of a man. If we interfere, it is meaningless."

"But if things get out of hand—?"

"Look," said Bragi, "there is the young man who presented you your sword."

Axel had forgotten the weapon, though, out of respect, he'd strapped it to his hip as Bragi had shown him before leaving his hotel room. He followed Bragi's gesture and saw Johan, enshrouded in armor, surrounded by four other Vikings, rearing back with an axe in his hand, ready to strike. Axel recognized only his large, credulous blue eyes under the shadow of his helm. He looked unsteady on his feet, however.

As if to confirm Axel's observation, a horse swooped down toward the young Viking and its rider, a girl so heavily clad in her ceremonial trappings that she might have been Axel's own mother and he'd not have recognized her, tapped Johan on his shoulder.

"Guess he's out," said Axel to Bragi. He waited expectantly, curious to see exactly how a young woman was to lift a bulky guy like Johan off the field of play.

True to Bragi's prediction, the touch of the Valkyrie spurred Johan to action. He brought his sword back at waist level, screamed a scream so gutteral it surely blew his vocal chords, and charged blindly forward toward his opponents. He leapt, leaving his feet, his body going airborne as he struck, missing entirely, but colliding with the arcing blade of one of his targets. Johan landed ignominiously on his shoulder and hip, his body coming to rest a few feet away from his head.

His head. Axel gaped, his eyes locking on the open eyes of Johan as they stared, unseeing, up at the audience. His head...no longer a part of his body...his dead body.

Axel didn't hear Bragi calling his name, didn't feel the steps of the arena beneath his feet as he bolted for the exit, didn't register that he had tripped in his flight. The world shifted out of phase, and he saw without seeing, heard without hearing. His gut wrenched and he vomited all over the cold, hard surface before him. Everything that had been in his stomach came up, and then he continued to heave, gagging.

He didn't know how long he stayed there, helpless, tears leaking from his eyes, his mouth foul and rancid. He couldn't bring himself to move. In his mind, he still saw those staring blue eyes, looking up at him, dead and empty.

After an eternity, a hand clasped his shoulder. Another took his opposite elbow, and he felt himself lifted to his feet. A man and a woman, one carrying a mop and bucket, the other holding a pressure sprayer, were moving in to where he'd just puked all over the step. They smiled sympathetically, apparently neither surprised nor annoyed by the disgusting mess he'd created.

He allowed himself to be led upward, out of the arena. Numbly he registered that Bragi must have come to his aid. He turned to speak, but, dammit, all he saw were those sightless, blue eyes, dumb and stupidly vacant, still staring at him.

"Dude, you okay?"

Holy gods, they were real! It wasn't his imagination. Those eyes really were right in front of him, looking at him, still stupid and vacant, but...alive. They were in a skull miraculously once again attached to a very living body.

"Johan?" croaked Axel, his throat raw. He sounded like a frog after a week in the desert.

His eyes must be deceiving him. The dumb jock either had a twin brother, or else Axel had hallucinated the entire thing.

But Johan said, "Yup. That's me. Alive and well...again."

Axel shook his head frantically. "But...your head! They cut off your..."

Johan grabbed both his ears and pulled upward. Axel frantically back-pedaled, expecting, in defiance of reason, that the head would lift off its perch and reveal the bloody stump he had seen just moments before. At the memory, Axel's stomach cramped again.

"It's back on, see?" said Johan. "Not going anywhere." He gave his ears several experimental tugs.

"Okay, please stop doing that," said Axel, taking another moment to will his stomach to calm its gyrations, he asked, "What did I just see?"

Johan shrugged. "You saw me die. Don't worry, it was so fast it didn't hurt. I don't remember it, really. Except, y'know that thing they say, about how the eyes can still see for a second after the head is cut off? I'm pretty sure it's true. I think I remember seeing the floor of the stadium after my head hit, and it was upside down." He spread his arms. "But I'm back now, see? And no worse for wear."

"That's not possible," said Axel.

Johan looked at him for a moment as though he were the stupidest creature alive. "Seriously? Have you never seen the show?"

"I've seen it," said Axel, feeling like he was back in school and hadn't done his homework. "I guess I just...didn't watch enough."

Indeed, *Who Wants to be a Viking?* bored him silly. Annoyed him, even. He'd never made it through an episode.

"Then I guess nobody told you how things work here," said Johan.

"I was beginning to," said Bragi, who'd come up behind them. Axel realized that the audience had begun to file out around them. The games were apparently over for the evening.

"See, the battles are for real," Johan explained, "with real wounds and real death. But there are these amazing women who can heal any wound and even raise the dead."

"The Valkyrie," supplied Bragi.

"Right," said Johan. "So, when a bro's about to go down, the Valks swoop in and tap his shoulder, to let him know. That's his cue to try and take out as many other guys as he can before he dies. And then he, well, dies. The Valk carries his body away on her flying horse."

"He is restored to life again," finished Bragi. "Long ago, the Valkyries brought the slain to the halls of Valhalla, or to Folkvangr, depending on whether the dead warrior was more favored of Odin or Freyja, goddess of beauty and love. In those heavenly halls they battle eternally by day, then feast and drink together into the wee hours. If they are slain or dismembered, their wounds are healed as the feast begins. No injury is permanent. Only life is eternal for them."

"So...Valhalla is...Stockholm?"

"No. Valhalla is another realm, as is Folkvangr. Odin...despite the protests of some...has brought the custom of battle and restoration here to Midgard so that the new Vikings, lacking centuries of tradition to gird them, may have a taste of what it is to be a true warrior."

"But...the gods allow all this...suffering?" asked Axel.

"I told you, Axel, that we are sworn not to interfere. That is a sacred oath. Men must learn to fight their own battles."

"Yeah, I'm pretty sure we knew how to do that before you all came back."

Behind him, there were footsteps, and Johan smiled in recognition of the new arrival. "And here's the pretty lady who brought me back." He pointed, indicating for Axel to look behind him.

Axel turned and saw her, still clad in the armor of the Valkyrie, face flushed from battle, hair like sunshine over eyes like the crystal heart of an icy fjord.

"Anika!"

She grinned and reached out to take Axel's hand. "I brought him back after I picked his sorry ass for death. He was way off his game today." Her eyes sparkled and she whispered to Axel, "Told you I worked here!"

"I am merely saying, Allfather, that it is a misuse of the divine gift of regeneration, letting the dead come back to life on Midgard as they did in Valhalla. As the mortals say, why should our boys buy the cow, if you're giving away the milk for free?"

Axel was trying to not hear Loki's whining drone. He sat several seats away, but his voice wormed its way to Axel's ears no matter how loudly those closer to him talked, sang, or laughed like idiots.

Odin did not seem troubled by the Trickster. He smiled patiently and said, "'Tis my milk to give, blood brother. The sacred traditions of the Viking warriors were lost over the centuries before the return. We can't wait for them to re-evolve naturally, with our enemies virtually massing at the gates of Asgard."

The playing field at Globen was now a mass of long tables. The turn had been made quickly, and, from Axel's perspective, invisibly. Of course, the staff had had the time during which he threw up to pull it all together. He hadn't been sure he'd be able to eat again any time soon, but Anika had laid one finger on his breast bone, traced it down to his navel, and, suddenly, the nausea was gone. "The gift of Eir, which is healing, can do more than just raise the dead," she had told him.

A hand struck Axel between the shoulder blades, causing him to sprawl forward and have to catch himself on the oaken table with his hands, lest his face plant itself in the remnants of roast boar on his plate. He looked up and smiled patiently at Johan, standing unsteadily behind him, cradling a rough-hewn goblet of mead.

"Dude! This meal is robust!"

Removing Johan's meaty hand from his neck, he said, "You keep using that word. I don't think it means what you think it means."

"I don't know what it means! I just like it! 'Robust!' I figure it's gotta be about boobs!"

Beside him, Bragi laughed with silent force. "I do love mortals."

Odin was reminding Loki that he was not a jealous patriarch. It was Zeus of the Olympians who punished the god who gave gifts to humankind. He made Prometheus an outcast.

"I feel his pain," said Loki. "I feel like an outcast among our people these days."

"That is because you wish to keep all the gifts for yourself," said Odin.

"There's my girl!" sang Johan. Anika had appeared, carrying a flagon of mead in each hand. All the Valkyries were working circuits among the tables with mead. "Gimme a kiss!" Johan seized her by the waist, nearly spilling all her mead, and tried to force his mouth over hers.

She pushed his face away by the cheek, laughing. "Ew! Not here! And brush your teeth!"

Johan nibbled at her ear. "Aw, baby, why ya gotta be like that?"

"Because you're drunk, and you're doing that to every Valkyrie that's here," Anika said cheerfully.

"Only the hot ones," protested Johan.

"Apparently, that's all of us," sighed Anika. "And especially the Hoff-statter Twins."

"Well, I mean they're twins, baby. They're like, identical! Don't be jealous! I'm a big guy. There's enough of me to go around!"

She stage whispered to Johan, "The twins were just talking about that, in fact. They were speculating on whether or not you're big enough to share."

Johan contemplated this, then said, "'Scuse me. I gotta use the little Vikings' room." He disappeared, Axel presumed, in the direction of the Hoffstatter Twins.

"Subtle," Anika observed, shaking her head. She leaned in to Axel, holding out a flagon. "More mead, Axel?"

He placed his hand over his goblet. "I'll get drunk."

She leaned in closer, whispering, "No, please don't do that. I have something to show you later."

Axel screamed and pulled his arms tighter around Anika's waist. Beneath the hooves of her horse there was nothing but air, cool, crisp Winter air. And far below it were the icy peaks of the Fells, the Scandinavian Moun-tains, peaks which dropped sharply into the blackness of the sea below.

"You're not going to throw up are you?" Anika called out over the wind which sang in his ears.

"No." He felt some embarrassment that, in addition to being present for his reaction to Johan's death, she must have heard of his misadventures aboard Skidbladnir. Looking up into the perfect, unmarred midnight blue of the Northern Sky, however, where the stars glittered like flecks of ice, it was hard to feel anything but wonder.

"Where are we?" he asked, blowing a cloud of frosted breath into her hair.

"Over Norway. That's the Norwegian Sea below us."

The black waves lapped at the feet of the mountains, highlighted by iridescent splashes of light from what had to be the brightest moon that had ever shone. The sensation of falling as Anika's horse plummeted suddenly downward was not distressing to him. Wind ruffled his hair and blew sweet-smelling locks of hers into his face. The snow-blanketed ground sped upward toward them, and, like a feather from a pillow, settling to rest, the horse touched down on a plateau overlooking the sea.

Anika dismounted, her feet settling almost knee-deep into the snow, and pulled Axel down with her.

"Why did you bring me here?" he asked.

"Because every Norseman needs to see this. To look out over this much of creation this way, to see the drama of earth and sea coming together, and the sheer scale of the world we live in...you can see it here better than anywhere on earth. This is what it is, Axel, to be one of us, and understand what an amazing place this world really is."

She turned to him and pulled him close, burying her head in his shoulder. "Besides," she whispered, "I wanted to get you alone." She looked up, used her fingers, curled in his hair, to guide his head down, and kissed him. Her lips and tongue were crisp and cold like cider.

"Uh..." he stammered. "I thought you had something going on with Johan."

She rolled her eyes. "Lots of girls have something going on with Johan. I mean, look at him! As long as he keeps his stupid mouth shut, he's like the perfect Viking icon. But he doesn't own me, Axel." She kissed him again. He did not resist. Her hands crept up his chest, one snaking its way into the collar of his coat and finding the bare skin of his neck beneath. He almost flinched, expecting a shock of icy frigidity, but her touch was not cold at all.

Indeed, with her against him, he was not cold at all. He did not object when she removed the fur parka she'd loaned him and let it fall to the ground, spreading out like a blanket, onto which he landed as she pushed him backwards and fell in top of him.

● ● ●

Later, as she lay cradled in his arms under the midnight sky, he asked, "Why did you pick me?"

She laughed and bit his nose. "Because I like you?"

"No, seriously—"

"I'm just a star-struck young girl who'd do anything to sleep with a rock star?"

"You are not! You're...you're a freakin' Valkyrie! You ride a flying horse! You raise the dead!"

"And I fly over the field of battle and choose the bravest and the noblest men to live in paradise. I don't have time for interviews, or dates. There's no courtship. I look at a bunch of guys, point, sing out and say, 'that one.'"

"And then they die horribly."

"I lured you to your doom, didn't I?" She tickled the exposed flesh at the base of his spine, making him giggle despite himself.

"If that was doom, I died happy." He sat up suddenly. "Say, am I dead? What did you do to me?"

"What do you mean?"

"How can we be out here, like this," he gestured to indicate their mutual lack of clothing, "and not be frozen to death? It's gotta be below zero out here." He scratched the back of his head. "I've got ice caked in my hair."

"You wouldn't believe where I've got ice caked," she laughed.

"But—"

"It's a side-benefit of the divine powers Odin gave all of us. I can raise the dead, heal the sick, ease the mind of the traumatized...and I can prevent you from ever being affected by things that would injure you or kill you."

"So, I'm invulnerable now?"

"Only when you're with me."

"It's unbelievable."

"Says the thirty-year-old with the body of a teenager."

"How do you know how old I am?"

"*Teen Beat.*"

"Oh my god."

"You're five nine, you weighed a 145 pounds ten years ago—"

"Still do, thanks to Idunn's apples."

"—and you have a goldfish named Marbles."

"I never had a goldfish named Marbles. *Teen Beat?* Really?"

"Hey, I was only twelve when you played Carnegie Hall. Cradle-robber!"

"Creepy stalker chick," he retorted. "Wasn't it a come-down to meet a teen idol and have him puke all over the steps first thing?"

"I'm used to it. Most of the boys lose it in one way or another their first few times here. Johan peed his pants."

"No."

"Oh yes. But the healing touch gets you past those initial jitters."

"Oh, so now I'm ready to ride into battle?"

"Are you?"

"Hell no."

"Good. I don't like warriors. Couldn't stand jocks in high school. To arrogant. Too brash. Too dumb."

"But Johan—"

"All of the above. Cute blue eyes—"

"Don't remind me," muttered Axel. "I couldn't get his eyes out of my head after...it happened. So I guess your healing touch fixed that too, or there's no way I could do...what we just did...after seeing someone's head cut off."

"Nope. That's evolution, my dear."

"Huh?"

"Witnessing violent death promotes your instinct to perpetuate the species."

"That's sick."

"Take it up with Darwin."

"I figured Darwin's ideas were gone forever, now that all the creation myths have come to life at once."

"No. Now everyone has to face the fact that all the creation stories can't be true at once, at least not literally, and so we have to be broad-minded. Open to the idea of metaphor and symbolism. Scientists can still define how the universe works. It's just that now there are beings among us who can bend or break the rules."

"You're changing the subject, and I need to know. Am I cuddled up on the mountain-top with Johan's girl?"

"I'm not anyone's girl. Not yet."

"Johan seems to think otherwise."

"Johan shouldn't think. It doesn't suit him. And he only follows me around making puppy-dog eyes since my sister died."

"Your— I'm sorry."

"Thanks. She was my twin, actually. Not identical. She was the cheer-leader, the prom queen. She dated most of the football team. When we came here, and the games were established, she applied for the Valkyrior. Flying around watching boys fight was right up her alley. She dragged me to the tryouts, and they told me Father Odin wanted me to join. I was just sitting on the sidelines. I said no, but...You've met Odin. If you can say no to him, let me know how. It's like refusing a favor to Santa Claus. So we became Valkyries."

"What...happened to your sister? I mean, you have all this power. You can raise the dead..."

For a moment, a profound sadness swept over her face. She tucked her head into the crook of his neck, and he thought she was going to cry. For that moment, Axel felt the cold of the air around him and the snow beneath him. He started to shiver. Anika looked up again, and the cold went away.

"A god or a god-protected mortal, can die forever. Through direct attack by a god of equal or greater power—"

"Your sister was murdered by a god?"

"Not murdered. It was an accident. One of the gods slipped with a spear."

"Which god?"

"I don't know. Odin took the memory out of my mind, so that I wouldn't suffer."

"Oh." Neat trick, Axel thought, but it didn't seem appropriate to say it out loud.

"Anyway...because it was a god-inflicted wound, I...we couldn't... raise her."

He gently stroked her back and kissed her hair, the way Mom used to do for him when he was upset. He'd never had to do that for anyone before. No one had ever come to him when they were hurting. Maybe because he didn't notice people hurting? "Don't talk about it anymore."

"No, it's okay. She's...wherever mortals go when they die, and I'm here, honoring her memory."

Nearby, Anika's horse pawed the snow and made that snuffling sound horses make. He must have been getting hungry.

"Did she like it?" he asked. "You sister, I mean. Did she like being a Valkyrie?"

"Having hundreds of hot, sweaty, testosterone-injected Vikings at her mercy? Are you kidding?"

"Do you like it?"

She brought up her hand and stroked his cheek. "It has its perks."

"Yeah, I guess. It's just...it's dangerous. There are a lot of gods hovering around down there. I know they've promised not to interfere, but..."

"After...my sister," said Anika, "Odin really clamped down on the gods about their oath. Up till then, some of them would get caught up in the action and charge in. The Aesir are laid back gods, the nicest gods on Earth, I think; but they do love them a battle. Sometimes they just can't help joining in the fun."

"Fun," echoed Axel dubiously.

"You don't approve of the games, do you?"

"It's just...I can help thinking...Humanity spent all these years longing for peace. My parents' generation staged all those protests. There were still wars, but the world also moved more and more toward diplomatic solutions. I mean, The Berlin Wall fell peacefully, and nuclear weapons went unused for, like sixty years—"

"Before the gods eliminated them," supplied Anika.

"Yeah. But why did they take away our weapons of mass destruction only to encourage us to cut off each others' heads with swords? Is this divine intervention? Pointless violence?"

She considered it. "Odin says we have to be ready for battle. The different pantheons don't agree on a lot of things—control of land, control of worshipers, use of technology—"

"Sounds an awful lot like the same mess we were in before they got here. Only now none of us have a say."

"Did we ever have a say? Did many Americans get to decide that A-bombs be invented? Did the millions in the Arab nations vote to have the Twin Towers fall?"

"Maybe not. But at least it was humans that were in charge."

"You mean we let our lives be controlled by people with no more power than we have. That's one of the reasons some of the gods think we'll never be fit to lead ourselves. We'll never grow up."

"I don't know, Anika...I just don't know if I can get behind the idea of singing for the troops, inspiring my brothers to go into battle, when it's really someone else's battle."

"It may be someone else's battle, but it's the only game in town. And life was never safe...or permanent." She rolled until she was comfortably settled on top of him, her eyes only inches from his. "On the other hand, there's a lot to be said for eternal youth, now isn't there?"

She kissed him with such intensity that he found he couldn't breathe.

"And besides youth, you've got incredible luck. I mean, dude, you scored a Valkyrie."

Johan accosted Axel the next morning at the Hotel. He and Anika had just finished breakfast, and she had gone to the ladies' room.

"Pulled an all-nighter?" The blond jock stood over him, sneering. "Teaching her to strum your guitar?" He nodded in the direction of the restrooms, indicating that he knew Anika was with Axel.

Axel took a sip of his coffee and breathed, forcing himself to be polite. "How are the Twins?" he asked pointedly.

Johan was not amused. "It doesn't matter. They're just a couple of chicks. I got an image to maintain. Doesn't mean you get to spend the night with my girl." He leaned in close. "Now where were you?"

"Where we were is none of your business. And if she's your girl, you shouldn't sleep around on her."

Was it his imagination, or did Johan's chest puff out?

"Who's gonna stop me?"

Axel raised his eyebrows. "Seriously?"

"Did you sleep with her?"

Axel stood. He couldn't take this slab of beef, but enough was enough. "I said it was none of your business."

Johan stepped forward, his sternum in line with Axel's nose. "It's my business, rock star. She's my girl."

"I don't think she sees it that way."

"Well I see it that way," pressed Johan. He stabbed Axel's shoulder with a finger. It was like being jabbed with a nightstick. "If you want her, you'll have to fight me for her."

"What?"

"Tonight." Johan jabbed him again.

"What is this, Medieval Times?"

"It's the rules, Sage. You want a Valkyrie to be your girl, fine. But if you're challenged for her, you have to fight. They're not just any bitches off the street, and they don't go to cowards. You fight, or she's mine. Odin's rules."

"And she has no say in this?" demanded Axel.

As if the question deserved no answer, Johan said only, "I'll see you tonight at the Feast." He laughed. "I'm gonna enjoy this."

When Anika returned only moments later, asking about Axel's obvious state of unrest, he told her what had happened. He had to admit he looked forward to her reaction. It should be good, he thought. She'd go tell Johan that she was no man's property. She'd ask him what ever made him think he rated a girl like her. She'd question his intellect, his parentage, his ability to feed himself. She—

She just looked at Axel, silent.

"Anika?"

She looked up, suddenly seeming tired. "Those are the rules, Axel. Like you said, I picked you. It's kind of expected that Vikings and Valkyries will pair up. As soon as Odin invited you to stay, I knew I wanted us to be together. But if someone challenges you, you have to fight."

Axel didn't know what to address first: the fact that she could be okay with such a barbaric concept as men fighting for possession of her, or that she had so calculatingly "picked" him. He had fallen hard, but her decision seemed a little...creepy. Was he being played?

He looked in her eyes. No. No, this was real. This was magic.

"Is this what you want?" he asked.

"Of course not, Axel! It's just...it's the way things are. Now. For me. And you. Odin will give me to the man he thinks deserves me. If two men want me, they fight and the winner receives Odin's blessing. If one of them refuses to fight, then he doesn't deserve me."

"The hell with Odin's blessing!"

Anika's eyes flashed in anger. "That's blasphemy," she said coldly.

"Are you serious? You'd let yourself be given to the winner of a fight? To him?"

"Won't you fight for me?" she asked quietly.

"Him?" Axel repeated. "He's twice my size, and how long has he been training?" He reached out and took her hand. "I...I like you, Anika. I've never met a girl like you, but...There's no way I can win in a fight with that beast. I don't know how a woman in the 21st Century can even be part of something like this."

She swallowed. "If you want to be with me, you have to live in my world. Even if you want...someone else...if you're going to be one of us, these are the rules."

He looked away from her, not knowing what to say. His gaze caught Johan out in the lobby. He was talking to another man, probably bragging about his challenge. His compatriot confirmed this by casting his eyes and his mirthful smirk in Axel's direction. The eyes were familiar: a telltale green.

The shipyards at Skeppsgården were old, though perhaps not as old as the Vikings. According to signs placed around the edge of the water for tourists, they'd been active in the 1600s, when the great warship Vasa had been built there over the course of two years, and then sunk on her maiden voyage after traveling less than a nautical mile. Signs also advertised the chance to visit the wreck, which had been raised in 1961. Axel made a mental note to see it. Perhaps it would inspire him to write a song, something on the order of a Gordon Lightfoot piece, but with humorous jabs at failed government projects.

Yes, making fun of war preparations in this land seemed appropriate just now.

But Axel had come here to get his mind off Vikings, taking up Ragnar's invitation to see the building of the longboats, and hear about plans for exploration, a pastime more interesting to him than cutting off heads and then seeing them reattached.

Across the harbor—smaller than he'd expected, not seeming as grand as New York's or San Francisco's, or even Baltimore's—he recognized Ragnar. The tall, gaunt Viking also spotted him and held up a hand.

Ragnar was not what one would call effusive. In fact, Axel would label him downright grim. He didn't smile automatically upon seeing an acquaintance, as most people did. Of course, for most people, it was probably not a sincere smile. It was a reflex, something drilled into their heads as a method of scoring points and being liked. Axel got the impression that Ragnar could smile, he just didn't give away his smiles unearned. After the emotional chaos of his confrontation with Johan, restraint was refreshing.

Ragnar had a huge crew, all Scandanavian, of course. One or two of his men and women had the dark coloring of other ethnic derivations: Spanish, Indian, even African. All had some Viking ancestry, however, and had apparently heeded Odin's call to return to the lands controlled by the Aesir.

A half-dozen ships were underway, a couple almost finished.

"That one," Ragnar said, pointing, "is ready to be taken to the armory, to have weapons installed." He said it with mild contempt. "Odin is experimenting with cannons, even though gunpowder didn't make it here until at least a hundred years after Christianity was institutionalized."

"Damn new technology," muttered Axel.

Ragnar did smile at that, though coldly.

"Any of these boats going to fly?" asked Axel.

"I doubt it. These are built for mortal use." He jerked his head toward an enclosed boathouse at the far end of the row of slips. "But let me show you something."

Ragnar used a rough key to open a large padlock. In Axel's childhood, even the smallest private facility doing this kind of work would have had a keypad or RFID reader. Now, most people were back to padlocks. He followed the shipbuilder into the dim, dank interior of the place, blinking his eyes as Ragnar flipped on bright worklights.

"Wow," breathed Axel as the light revealed, floating in the black water under the open floor a partially submerged marvel. She looked like Nemo's *Nautilus* as conceived by Disney, but she had the lines of the longboats outside.

"The gods may be getting rid of satellites," said Ragnar, "but even before they came, there probably wasn't an inch of the earth's landmass humanity hadn't mapped."

"I miss Google Earth," said Axel.

"Vikings are supposed to be explorers too, not just warriors. Their boats used to carry them over water to lands no human—or at least no Viking—had ever seen. But there's nothing left to discover on land. We've seen it all. Going across the sea is old news. To explore, we either have to go up...or down."

"I didn't think submarines were allowed anymore."

"There are a few," said Ragnar. "Mostly controlled by worshippers of sea gods. Neptune's cult has a whole fleet in the Mediterranean. Odin gave permission to build this one. Well, actually Thor approved the project. He's the explorer. He said he'd work out deals with the sea gods." He looked admiringly at his work. "I hope to test her soon." He waved his hand, indicating a gangplank which ran to the small conning tower of the vessel. "Come aboard."

Axel disliked submarines. He'd never felt anything akin to

claustrophobia until he'd toured one a few years ago. Being inside something so small and cramped, knowing that all around you there was no air, and being completely unable to see out, was not a feeling he relished.

Ragnar's sub, however, had an amazing view of the water around it. The hull was almost entirely transparent. Lights mounted on the outer shell lit up the surroundings for quite a few feet on every side.

"It's largely formed Lexan," Ragnar explained. "It's been a challenge, calculating to allow for the amount of pressure I want it to be able to survive. I want to take her deep, you see."

"It...she's amazing," said Axel quietly. Ragnar seemed to want to say more, so he prompted. "I guess you keep her under lock and key so no one tries to take a joy ride?"

"I have to be careful," Ragnar replied. He seemed to consider Axel for a moment, weighing his fitness to hear more. "You see, I can't let too many people know what I'm laying the groundwork for."

Axel got the distinct sense he'd been approved for a top security clearance.

"Other than exploring the bottom of the sea?"

Ragnar nodded. "As I said, there are two ways to go to find the undiscovered: down...or up."

"Flight?" asked Axel, then, realizing, "Space?"

"Yes. Space."

"They've forbidden it."

"Yes. But one day, Axel, we're going to need options for getting off this rock. You've seen what they're up to. The Aesir are probably the most reasonable of the gods, and yet what have they led us to? A TV show where people get killed and resurrected? We invented reality TV without them. We launched devastating wars without them. Wasn't the return of the gods supposed to put us on the right path?"

"So they said."

"Look around you, Axel. Don't you think, just maybe, what the return has done is show us what the true origin of our problems is?"

"The gods?" asked Axel.

"Not the gods themselves, but what they represent: our blind need to follow, to be told what to believe, to have our minds stuffed with thoughts and fancies of someone else's creation. To fill the void of uncertainty in our souls with some kind of certainty, even if it's a false one. Even if we live...and die...for nothing."

"Why are you telling me this? If you need to be careful? You've known me for, like, five minutes."

"No," said Ragnar. "You've known me for five minutes. I've known you for many years." He hesitated, then added, "At least, I've known your music."

Axel couldn't help but roll his eyes. Was everyone in this town a fan? "Not the same thing," he responded.

"But enough that I've got a good idea where you stand on humanity and gods. Axel, you were among the first to actively stand up and challenge one of them! Everyone in Scandinavia knows of your bet with Loki all those years ago, how you proved that you could succeed as a performer without godly influence. You...you're an inspiration to those of us who are not content to simply follow."

"Even though I've spent the last ten years living off the favor of the gods?" asked Axel.

"And what favor you have, you won." Ragnar stretched out his hand. "I believe I can trust you, Axel. I believe you should know my secret. I...I choose to believe in you."

Axel took the hand, clasped it, but said quietly, "Be careful, Ragnar. With someone like Loki around, things aren't always what they seem. We should watch what we say, and to whom we say it."

"Methinks you flirt with blasphemy, young Bard."

"Huh?" Axel spun at the familiar voice. Bragi sat on a bench looking out on the water.

"What do you mean, 'blasphemy?'" asked Axel, not wanting to give away anything Bragi didn't know.

Bragi stood and began to walk away from the harbor, hands clasped easily behind his back. Axel followed him.

"You question the justice of our wars," said Bragi. "You wonder if our divine guidance is not for the good of humanity."

Axel inwardly sighed with relief. He had thought Bragi was talking about Ragnar's confessed plans. Still..."How did you know?"

"Your young Valkyrie came to see me. She was hoping I might counsel you on her behalf."

Axel stopped and leaned on a railing, staring at the ground. This conversation was overdue. He'd wanted to talk to Bragi about everything... Odin's offer, the girl...but then things had just spun out of control. "I don't know what to do, Bragi. Anika's the most amazing girl I've ever met. I might be in love with her, but..."

"But you question her life's path. You are not sure you wish to share it."

"Yeah."

"What if I told you that this is what Odin wants for both of you?"

"That's part of my problem, Bragi. I just met Anika. She seems completely decided that she wants me, now and forever. I guess she wants to get married."

"She does."

"And I'm head over heels in love with her. How often does that happen?"

"More often than you think."

"How often does that happen," asked Axel, "without the gods playing tricks with someone's mind." When Bragi didn't answer, Axel asked, "Am I under a spell? Are my feelings for Anika just...magic?"

"Is not all love magical?"

"Yeah. That's what I've been thinking. But there's magic and there's magic. Bragi, I don't even know if my feelings are real, and now I'm being asked to go let Johan carve me up like a turkey! If that's what Odin wants—"

"What if it were?"

"I...I don't know if it's what I want for me." He looked up into his mentor's kind, blue eyes. "Is that blasphemy?"

"Do you know the story of Adam and Eve?" asked Bragi suddenly, as if they'd been speaking of nothing in particular.

"Yes. They disobeyed God and lost paradise."

Bragi stopped and turned. "Tell me...do you think Jehovah expected Adam and Eve to obey, or did he realize that they would ignore his rules? Don't children have to test the boundaries, make mistakes, and break the rules, in order to grow?"

"Are we still talking about my thing with Anika? Or is this about—"

Bragi held up his hand. "Do not speak to me of the secrets of others, Axel."

So. Bragi did at least know Ragnar had a secret. He didn't want to admit it or be responsible for it.

"Your heart is true, Axel Sage. I know it well. If what your heart wants seems to go against the gods, perhaps your heart has wisdom you have not yet mastered. Discover your heart's wisdom, Axel. Do not be deterred by cries of blasphemy."

"But you're the one who—"

Bragi smiled. "But know that the cries will come. Be prepared for them."

"Dammit, Bragi, why do you have to be so mysterious? I just need some advice, you know?"

Bragi nodded. "When the Aesir need advice, we speak to Mimir."

"Mimir? The guy who got one of Odin's eyes?" Axel had sung ballads about Mimir. He thought they were largely allegories.

Bragi smiled. "If you seek counsel, go to the Stockholm Public Library. Tell them you want to speak to the Head of Counseling. Tell them I sent you."

It was growing dark as Axel entered the Library building, an overwhelming, cylinder-crowned orange structure built into a hillside. It reminded him of something he'd have built out of colorful wooden blocks as a child. The great open lending hall was circular, making him feel a bit like a gladiator in the Coliseum. He stopped at the information desk and passed Bragi's message, that he was to see the Head of Counseling. He was relieved that the young man behind the desk spoke perfect English as he informed him that "it" was on the third level, and pointed to a door above them.

Axel took to the indicated stairway, thinking, It?

The door he'd been directed to was labeled clearly but unimpressively, "Head of Counseling," and it was not locked. It opened to a dark-paneled anteroom, lit only by the fading light from a single window. There was no receptionist. In fact, the room appeared empty.

"Hello?" he called, taking a tentative step inside. If this was a counselor's office, he didn't wish to violate anyone's privacy.

"Come in," said a rich voice, edged in a faint crackle of age. It seemed to come from a wing chair arranged at a small table, facing the window.

Deciding the counselor occupied the chair, Axel circled round to face him; but the chair was empty. Before it, on the table, sat a rather bizarre sculpture of an old man's head, mounted on a polished, hardwood base, and enshrouded in a silver wig. Weird decoration.

"Uh, I'm here to see the Head of Counseling."

"You're seeing it," said the head, its eyes suddenly snapping open and training on Axel.

Axel jumped backwards, colliding with a metal cart. "Holy shit!" he squeaked.

The head laughed, a wheezing sound, and nodded towards the chair.

It occurred to Axel that nodding was a risky activity for a disembodied head to attempt.

"Take a seat," said the head. "The chair is for my visitors. I have no need of it."

Axel edged carefully around the table, never taking his eyes from the apparition at its center, and sat slowly.

"You weren't prepared for my appearance, were you, Axel?"

"No," he admitted. "Bragi just told me to see the...Head...of Counseling." He twisted up his mouth. "Cute."

"Bragi always had a dry sense of humor. I am Mimir."

"I know. You took one of Odin's eyes."

"In exchange for a drink from my well of wisdom. I became the Allfather's advisor, but his enemies beheaded me. He embalmed my head and enchanted it, so I could advise him for all time."

"I...think I'd heard that," said Axel uncomfortably. Then he muttered, "This is the creepiest damn thing I've ever seen."

"But not the creepiest thing you ever will see," laughed Mimir.

"You can see the future?"

"I can. You have a great future before you."

"So what's the—"

The head inclined sharply. Had Mimir a hand to hold up, Axel inferred he might have done so. "Be warned," said the ancient relic, "there are limits to my power to help you. You may ask one question per visit, and you may visit only once daily, and only when I am available. Occasionally, Odin still carries me with him on his journeys. Consider your question carefully."

He took a moment. He knew what he wanted to ask. Framing it correctly was the key. Who he wanted to ask about, what he wanted to know...what should he do? "Do I...Do I have a future with Anika?" He felt silly as he completed the question. Did Mimir even know who Anika was?

"No," said the head. "You and the Valkyrie have no future together at all."

Okay, so he knew who she was. The abruptness his statement, the reality of it, stung Axel. He'd wanted an answer. He knew, suddenly, he hadn't wanted this answer, even as he knew it was the answer.

He almost asked "why?" He didn't.

Mimir spoke anyway. "This afternoon, at the games, Loki's tricks may cause her death."

Was it an answer to his unspoken question? Axel would never know, for he was out the door and on the run before the disembodied prophet head's words had finished echoing off the walls of the anteroom.

Axel ran.

He'd gone nearly a mile when it occurred to him that there must be a five mile separation between the Library and Globen, and he wasn't sure of the route. He'd ridden the subway to get there. He couldn't wait for a train now. He had to find Anika, warn her. He'd jumped into a Taxi, not even bothering to read the fare posted on the window of the car.

Mimir's sad prediction, that he and Anika had no future, lashed at his mind. The lash cut deeper with the realization that they might have no future because she was going to die, here today. And why? Mimir said it would be Loki's doing. Why would Loki want to kill Anika? Because Axel was paying attention to her? Was he that vindictive, after all these years, that he'd kill an innocent girl because he wanted to get back at Axel? The lash cut deeper still. Was she to die only because Axel came here, on a mission in which he had no interest?

At the entrance, he was stopped by a staffer in a royal blue golf shirt embroidered on one side with the óss, the rune symbolizing Odin. It was now part of the official logo of the Vikings, establishing their brand identity on t-shirts, coffee cups and knit beanies.

"Mr. Sage! They're expecting you inside. I was told to escort you as soon as you came."

He followed the young man into the great hall. As soon as he emerged into the stands, a figure in gold noticed him and pointed. It was Heimdall, ever sharp-eyed. No doubt, he'd watched Axel run here all the way from the library. Heimdall nudged Odin, who called out, "Come forward, Axel Sage."

He called it out without a microphone of any kind. His voice still rung out above the crowd, over the entire expanse of the arena.

Axel descended and approached the table of the Allfather. Johan stood a few feet away, expectantly. Music suddenly swelled, and the crowd applauded. Axel felt like the bride at a very bizarre wedding ceremony.

"Allfather," Axel began, "I have come here—"

Johan stepped forward, arms crossed, and barked out, "He has come here to answer my challenge."

Not looking at him, Axel said, "No, actually, I haven't. I've come here because the head of Mimir told me—"

"Allfather!" called out an all-too-familiar voice.

Axel winced and said "Oh, shit," quietly to himself.

Loki emerged from the crowd of Vikings milling about Odin's table.

"My blood brother," Odin recognized him carefully, his single eye narrowed with suspicion.

Loki strutted forward, no longer in disguise as he had been. His red locks spiked out proudly in all directions, as though his head were aflame, and he wore the traditional tunic and leggings of an Aesir.

"My protege," he gestured to Johan, "is in love with the Valkyrie Anika, and has been for some time. She has, sadly, surrendered her virtue to this..." he glanced disparagingly at Axel, "musician."

"By our laws, then," said Odin, "the girl belongs to Axel Sage."

"She doesn't belong to anyone!" snapped Axel.

"Silence, mortal!" Loki's voice was like thunder, ringing off the great dome.

"Oh, Loki, please don't be tiresome," sighed Odin. He looked at Axel. "You shouldn't speak unless spoken to, young man. There are protocols."

"Sorry, Allfather," said Axel. "But—"

Loki cut him off. "It is inappropriate for a Valkyrie to give herself to a coward. A Valkyrie's hand is intended only for a true hero."

"You're calling me a coward?" asked Axel in disbelief. "Seriously, you?"

"The boy has the courage to speak up before the gods," observed Odin.

"But he did not accept Johan's challenge to combat!" said Loki. "Who, other than a coward, would bed a good woman, and then refuse to fight for her honor?"

Odin looked gravely at Axel. "Did Johan challenge you?"

"Yes, but—"

"Then you must fight him or relinquish your claim. Loki is correct, a Valkyrie must wed a true hero. She cannot be paired with one who is cowardly or meek. Did you come here to fight?"

"No," said Axel, impatient.

He started to say more, but Johan called out, "Coward!"

"I didn't come here to fight because I don't see Anika as property," said Axel, addressing only Odin. "I know you gods ruled a long time ago, but the human race has changed. I think we've changed for the better. We don't see women as things for men to fight over." He looked around to see if Anika was even here. He hadn't seen her when he came in. Overhead, he spotted a line of flying horses, hovering, Valkyries astride them. He assumed she was among them.

"A man and a woman choose each other now," he explained to Odin. "If Anika wants Johan, I guess she can have him."

Odin shook his head. "T'is not that simple, Axel. You are our chosen bard of the Aesir. You cannot simply shirk a challenge. T'would brand you a coward, as Loki says."

Axel shrugged. "If I know I'm not a coward, I don't know why I should care what Loki says. Or anyone else. But Allfather, you need to know—"

He was about to share Mimir's warning with Odin when a commotion erupted behind him. Preparatory to the games, banquet tables were laid out around the perimeter of the arena. They held refreshments to keep up the strength of the contestants as they prepared for battle. Around one of them, a scuffle had developed. There was the telltale sound of metal clashing against metal, there were screams of rage and pain. A circle of combatants grew as Vikings charged in to see what was wrong.

"I did not call for the games to begin," muttered Odin.

Valkyries, seeing battle begin, swooped down on their horses to attend to the victims. One girl—it was not Anika, Axel saw—came in close to the throng of pushing bodies and raised weapons. A muscled arm reached up from the center of the mob to seize the leg of her mount. With a sickening scream from the horse, it and its rider were pulled from the air. The outer circle of the mob expanded as people backed up. Seconds later, the horse took flight again, arcing up toward the pinnacle of the arena, mounted by a one-handed rider.

"Tyr," said Axel. "What's he doing?"

The war god threw back his head and shrieked.

"He's in the rage," said Odin. "The rage of the beserker."

"Where he doesn't know what he's doing, and just kills everything within reach?"

The Allfather nodded, he rose from his throne, stepped down to the field and strode briskly toward the nearest table. Axel followed, curious. Odin scanned the table and grabbed a metal bowl containing sliced mushrooms. Picking one up, he sniffed at it, touched it briefly with his tongue, then replaced it in the bowl. He shouted for assistance, and a blue-shirted staff member appeared.

"Collect all of these," said the Allfather, shoving the bowl briskly at the girl's chest. She took it, fear in her eyes at the god's urgency. "All the mushrooms. Dispose of them immediately!"

"Are they poisoned or something?" wondered Axel.

Odin shook his head. For a moment, Axel thought he was about to hit something. He took a careful step backward. The one-eyed old man could easily have broken him in half with a blow, and he knew it.

"In ancient times, warriors ate these mushrooms, which you would call hallucinogenic, to bring on the berserker rage."

Axel looked at the tables, where frantic staff members dumped the contents of silver bowls into garbage bags. "So I guess those mushrooms didn't come from Wegman's?"

"No. From the steppes of Asgard. T'is the only place they grow. We have not allowed their use here, for, if a god were to eat them, any mortal in his path could be killed with no hope of revival."

"How did they get here, then?" asked Axel.

Odin took a deep breath and closed his eyes. "Someone's idea of a joke."

Axel, sickened, turned and looked back to where Loki still stood. The trickster was grinning.

"Wait," said Axel, "have they all eaten them?"

Odin nodded.

Around them, the screams built. The ringing peals of sword on sword sounded louder and faster. Every man on the floor plunged into a mass of arms and legs, writhing and striking out, as Valkyries buzzed like bees about their heads.

The Vikings were, to a man, insane with rage.

"Isn't it glorious?" laughed Loki. "I made sure the cameras are on." He looked up at the stands and clucked his tongue. "Pity the audience is so sparse, but those here will have a tale to tell their grandchildren."

"What have you done?" demanded Odin.

"I've raised the stakes, Blood-brother. These little games where we raised the dead every night were all well and good as entertainment; but our warriors were becoming complacent, careless. They knew there was actually nothing to lose. They weren't afraid. What is a battle, after all, without a tang of fear?"

"I did not approve this, Loki," said Odin.

Loki spread his hands in supplication. "Call me an innovator. A rogue genius. I've brought the excitement back." He craned his neck and looked at the ceiling. "And oh, look, Axel. Here's a stake in the game that might even set your coward's heart beating."

One of the Valkyrie was flying, not toward the battle, but up and around the dome. Bearing down on her was Tyr, on his own flying mount. Even from here, Axel could see the feral grin on his face and read the madness in his eyes. His quarry kicked her mount and dropped, heading toward an exit from the field. Tyr urged his horse into a dive and caught up with her. Swooping by, he seized her sword arm. Girl and god struggled. Her helm flew off and crashed to the ground below. Hair spilled out, long and loose.

Hair the color of sunshine.

"Anika!" shouted Axel.

Tyr had pulled her half out of her saddle. She struggled for balance as he drove his mount upward, carrying her and her horse along with him.

"If she falls..." said Axel in horror.

"There will be no saving her," finished Odin, "if she falls while in direct combat with a god."

Loki leaned in to Axel, leering. "You wouldn't fight for her. Now, will you stand by and see her die?"

"I came here to keep her from dying," Axel hissed. "At your hands."

Johan, his face ashen, looked out on the chaos before them. His comrades, his friends and teammates, were hacking at each other, shaking and shrieking like rabid animals. Axel could read in his face that this was too much violence even for him. Johan silently mouthed the girl's name... for the first time, Axel believed the dumb jock might actually care about somebody.

"We've got to do something," Johan said pitifully. He was near tears.

"Stop this, Loki," said Axel. It was not a plea. It was an order. He stepped toward the trickster, lifting up on his toes in a vain attempt to look him in the eye. "You can stop this, I know you can. Save her. This is just another of your attempts to get at me—"

Loki merely smiled.

"Is everything all about you?" said Johan from behind him. He grabbed Axel's shoulder and spun him around. "You think the whole world revolves around you and your music and your stupid guitar?" He pointed frantically at the girl struggling above. "We're the only ones who can save her!"

"We're being played." Axel looked to Odin. "The gods put us into these situations, where we have no choice but to play by their rules. We're forced to fight, forced to die. Why?" He pulled his arm out of Johan's grasp and approached the eldest god. "Why, Allfather?"

Odin's voice was cold. "I am good to mortals," he said with dignity, "but I do not answer to them."

Axel hesitated. If he pissed off Odin, all really was lost. "But you don't want her to die. You didn't want this. Can't you stop it?"

"I cannot," said Odin sadly. "We all took a sacred vow not to interfere in the battles, so that the training could be real. The space is blessed. Things must play out as they do. Tyr is not in his right mind, but none of us who are can interfere. We would become powerless."

"It has to be us, Axel," Johan pled. "Help me."

Axel looked again at Tyr, whose one good hand was now grasping at Anika's throat. Both her arms were engaged, her hands about his wrist, trying to pull his hand free of her.

"How do we stop that?" wondered Axel.

"You goddamned coward." Johan struck out with the flats of his hands, catching Axel's shoulders and knocking him off his feet. He fell on his ass.

The young Viking turned and ran toward the field. Axel called after him, but was ignored. Sickening dread crept over him. Johan was right. There was no one to save Anika but the two of them. Johan was well-trained, but stupid. Axel wasn't trained at all. Could the two of them manage to get Anika away from Tyr? And then what? What about his next mortal victim?

Johan made for a Valkyrie who had landed her horse and was watching the battle from the sidelines, having given up trying to make any sense of the living and the dying. As he approached, the girl said something Axel couldn't hear, a protest of some sort. Johan shoved her aside and mounted her horse, taking to the air.

It was, after all, the only way to get to Anika. Axel had ridden only once, and with Anika's help. If he was going to get up there, he'd need an experienced rider with him. He rushed forward. "Johan, wait! I'll go with you!"

But the Viking was beyond hearing. Rider and horse shot up like a missile on course for Tyr. Drawing his short sword, Johan gauged his distance, calculated his opening, reared up and leapt off his mount and onto Tyr's back. With his left hand, he clawed for a purchase, finally tangling his fingers into the god's hair. Tyr swatted at him with his handless arm, as if he were a gnat. With his right hand, Johan held up his short sword. Axel expected an immediate attack, but, instead, Johan just held it there and gazed at Tyr. It was as if he expected the sight of the blade to hypnotize the mad god.

"What are you doing?" Axel muttered.

Continuing to flail at the nuisance on his back, Tyr wrapped his good arm around Anika's head and pulled. She was slipping off her horse. Johan, apparently frustrated that whatever he was expecting did not happen, began to strike at Tyr's helmeted head with the flat of the sword, peppering him with clanging blows. Tyr was at least annoyed, for now he released Anika, who was able to right herself in her saddle. While she tried to pull away, vainly, because Tyr still had his leg entangled in the horse's reins, Tyr made a fist of his single hand, reared back, and punched Johan full in the face.

It was a damaging blow. Johan had not bothered to don a helmet. He reeled from the impact. His left hand let go of the hunk of Tyr's hair that was all that held him in place. He fell from the god's back and plummeted.

"No!" shouted Axel. Oblivious to the carnage before him, he ran to the field where Johan lay twisted and broken on the straw-laden earth. He knelt beside the Viking, whose face was already covered in blood. Clearly, Tyr had broken his nose and several bones with the force of his blow. Blood trickled also from his mouth, and Axel knew internal organs had been ruptured.

Johan reached up to him, but hadn't the strength to raise his hand even a few inches.

"Stay still," said Axel, his voice hoarse with tears of shock. "I'll—"

Johan tried again to grab Axel's hand. The light was going out in his eyes. "Sword..." he rasped.

Axel looked at the discarded short sword, which had fallen a few feet away.

"What about the sword, Johan?" he asked. It seemed silly. Johan was dying. This was no time for trivialities, and yet he had seemed to be expecting something from that sword.

"M-magic," breathed Johan. "Loki...Loki said...would save her.

C-cure...Tyr..." Tears streaked down his face, making tracks in the blood. "Loki...lied," Johan managed. "Said Anika...wouldn't be hurt." He took a deep, racking breath. Axel wanted to tell him to be quiet for his own sake, but he also needed to hear the rest of the confession. "If I fought you, A-Anika'd...hate me...This way...she'd see you were...coward...I'd...win..." Suddenly he gave a small shudder, not even a gasp. Axel realized the eyes, still focused on him, were blank.

Johan was dead. Behind him, Axel heard Loki's cackling laugh.

Axel continued to look at the eyes, the dead blue eyes, of the man who was supposed to be his enemy. Those eyes had looked to him in supplication, seeking some sort of comfort for their owner, who realized he'd been tricked to his own death.

Axel's own eyes saw nothing else. Even as he jumped to his feet, even as drew the sword from the scabbard at his hip, all he saw were dead blue eyes in a field of red. He charged at Loki, the sword extended. He had no idea even how to hold a sword, but that would not stop him from driving it into the trickster's heart.

"Bastard!" he shrieked as he ran forward blindly.

Something appeared in front of him, and he collided with a body. He fell backward, unable to balance. The shock snapped him out of his killing rage, and he looked up into the face of Odin. The Allfather had stepped between him and Loki.

"Axel," said Odin softly, looking down at his sprawled form, "you must control your temper with Loki. He is a god, and you are mortal. If he cripples or kills you, I cannot undo the damage."

"You are interfering!" snarled Loki.

"Around me is ever neutral space, Loki," Odin reminded him. "And neither Axel nor you are sworn participants in combat."

Axel ignored their bickering. He was again looking up. Anika was once again in Tyr's grasp, kicking her feet as he lifted her bodily from her horse. She hung in midair, suspended by her own hands only as they dug into Tyr's wrist.

Mimir had said they had no future together...but he couldn't let her die.

The sickening thought struck him again that perhaps the only reason they weren't to share a future was that she was about to die. Either way, even if he were flying in the face of destiny and he were about to lose, he had to do something. If he was going to survive the next few minutes, he needed to be able, after they were over, to live with himself.

The horse Johan had ridden into battle had gently touched down, called by its original rider. Axel charged forward, startling the Valkyrie who was about to take its reins.

"Sorry," he said briskly. "Need your ride."

Then he stopped. How the hell was he supposed to get on this thing? He'd never ridden a horse. This was insane! He couldn't—

Above him, Anika screamed, a strangling cry.

He remembered seeing her mount the horse, remembered her coaching him in doing it himself. He dug his fingers into the beast's mane, hooked a foot in the stirrup, grabbed the pommel as Anika had, and hoisted his leg over. He was on a horse. Now what?

He'd heard that horses knew when they'd been mounted by an inexperienced rider. What did they do? Did they go easy, because they didn't want the rider hurt? Or did they buck and throw the rider, because they didn't want to have an incompetent leading them?

This horse trotted forward and took suddenly to the air.

Oh yeah…it depended on the horse.

Axel was circling the arena, the horse in a holding pattern, as though the field below were a busy runway at the airport.

Below him, Odin called out, "The reins, Axel! Use the reins!"

Right. He gathered the reins in both hands, tightened them, pulled the horse's head up and yanked so it had to look at Tyr. Then, remembering how Anika had urged her mount up over the mountain peaks, he dug his knees into its flanks.

Axel flew. Fast.

Within seconds, they'd made their target. Anika's eyes were wide with amazement as he came level with her. Tyr turned, eyes still burning with madness. This close, Axel could see that there was no shred of a reasoning intellect behind them. This was not the strategist who'd assumed command of a great national army, this was a brute, a rabid animal.

Never taking his eyes from the girl's Axel reached in with one hand, holding the reins in the other to calm his mount, and tried to pry Tyr's fingers from her throat. Stark fear lit Anika's face as she looked downward, and Axel realized prying her free would only let her fall to her death. He'd have to catch her, and, at the same time, make Tyr let go. He—

Something hit the side of his head, and Axel's vision left him, overtaken by bursts of light. "Seeing stars." He'd heard the expression. He'd never been hit hard enough to experience it. His horse had automatically retreated as its master was attacked. He looked a few feet away to see Tyr wildly swinging his metal-capped arm. He'd used it as a bludgeon. Axel resolved to stay the hell away from that.

He yanked down onto the reins, putting the horse into a dive so that they were directly below Tyr. Then he urged the animal upward, reared back, lashed out with his sword, and frantically chopped at Tyr's good arm.

The war god roared and kicked at Axel's head. He managed to dodge the blows, mostly. He focused on causing Tyr as much discomfort as he could.

It worked. With a scream, Anika began to drop. Axel let the sword fall to the earth, grabbed the reins with his right hand, and shot out his left to grab her. He aimed for the waist. He caught her under the shoulder. His arm damn near popped out of its socket, and he found himself rotated forty degrees in the saddle. They were both about to go down.

Fortunately, Anika was better at this than he was. The pressure on his shoulder lightened as she found her own handholds and levered herself upwards, settling into place behind him. She enfolded his chest with her arms and laid her head against his shoulder. "You did it, Axel," she whispered into his ear. "You saved me."

A bellow from above and to the left reminded Axel that this was but a reprieve, not a full pardon. If he could make the ground, and side of the field where Odin stood, that was neutral space. They'd be safe.

He brought his mount down and away from Tyr, hoping he could outfly the god. He was doing it! He was actually saving the girl!

Anika was saying something. Giving advice? No, it sounded like..."I'm sorry, Axel."

Huh?

Then he felt the tap on his shoulder, and he knew. The Valkyrie couldn't shirk her duties, even if the chosen was her rescuer.

This was it. What could he do?

What the Vikings all did. He could finish what he'd started, before the end.

Tyr had circled below, anticipating that Axel would try to get to Odin, and safety. He couldn't go down. With a cry, the war god lifted his blade and gouged the rear, left leg of Axel's mount. The horse shrieked in pain and began to fly wildly for the ceiling of the dome. Axel tried to soothe it, even as he looked upward. He saw the suspension of the dome's arch, the service catwalks. Yes, if he got Anika there, she could get to safety. Tyr had the raw strength to simply tear the catwalks asunder, but, if Axel could make himself a target, distract Tyr from Anika's escape long enough, it just might work.

Axel assaulted the horse's flanks with his knees.

His enemy screamed and flew at them again. Axel's horse, already in pain, being driven on a collision course with the dome, spooked by the screaming warrior, bucked. The sudden gesture caught Axel by surprise, throwing him off balance. The reins slipped from his hands like water flowing through outstretched fingers. He clawed for the mane, but he couldn't get any purchase, and the weight of his legs, pulled from the stirrups, drew him downward.

Axel fell.

Sunlight danced somewhere above his eyes. The light was soft and warm. Very, very warm. It gathered around his body and swirled him in comfort. The light played with his hair and whispered in his ear.

Heaven, Axel concluded. I made it. He was in Heaven, and he was warm and safe. The light itself caressed him and loved him. This would not be a bad way to spend eternity, then. They'd made it sound so stagnant and boring in Sunday School, but this was fine.

"Wake up, sleepyhead!"

Anika came to light beside him on the bed.

He shook his head to clear it. "Is this...Valhalla?" he asked.

She giggled. "This is my apartment, doofus. You've been here for three days."

He sat up, rubbing the back of his head. It didn't hurt, but rubbing it seemed like the thing to do.

"I fell," he said dumbly.

Anika nodded.

"Did I hit my head?"

"You fell on your head," she said bluntly. "Pretty much shattering all the vertebrae from here to here." She illustrated by pulling his head forward and touch spots on his neck and bare spine.

"But no one could survive.... Oh," he said, realization dawning. "I...I died."

She nodded. "I brought you back."

"How could you? I was killed by a god! Tyr—"

Two gentle fingers stilled his lips. "Tyr just scared your horse. You fell off, ya klutz! He never touched you, so you were salvageable."

"How did you get away? What did they do with Tyr?"

"Oh, once he'd seen you fall and I was beyond reach, Tyr left the field of battle. Once he was outside the ring, Odin could act to contain him until the mushrooms wore off. Then we just had to wait for the Vikings to fight it out and heal their wounds."

"Except for Johan," Axel remembered.

"Yes," she said gravely. "His wounds were god-inflicted."

"I'm sorry," said Axel. "I thought he was a jerk, but I know you liked him."

"I never liked him, Axel. I mean, I'm sorry he's dead. I would have married him, but not because I loved him. I only...there are rules. When I marry, it has to be a hero fit for a Valkyrie. And I must agree to be with a man who's willing to fight for me."

"That just seems barbaric." He brushed her hair with his fingertips. "You're too good a person, too smart, too capable...to let yourself be treated like property."

She shrugged. "In the end, it worked out, right?"

"Huh?"

"If a man claims me, and he fights for me and proves his bravery, I am his." She took his hand, brought it to her lips, kissed it, and held it captive in both her own. "You were brave, Axel. You fought for me. You died for me."

"I didn't mean to," he protested.

"No, you meant to save me, though. And you did. After you...fell...I got to the catwalk."

"That's what I'd planned," he said quietly.

"Well, it worked. I was able to climb down to safety pretty quick. Tyr was too mad to figure out how to squeeze in there. It was a good plan, Axel. A really good plan."

"Yeah, well..."

"And you took to riding so quickly, with barely any training! Axel, you're good at this!"

He looked down, not wanting to meet her eyes. "Can we...not talk about that...right now?"

"Sure," she agreed. Her voice became playful again quickly. "Can we talk about something else you're good at?"

She fell into his arms and kissed him. Axel decided that, yes, this subject didn't disturb him.

But they didn't talk.

● ● ●

Loki's trial was the day after Axel finally awoke. Axel was the star witness. There was no need to await prolonged recovery, for the magical healing of the Valkyries had accomplished its work of restoring the body whole in three days. No physical therapy, no MRIs, no follow-up exams.

The Aesir had gathered as a council to judge their brother. Axel had never seen so many gods in one place, despite having been to sessions of the United Pantheons on occasion. Bragi was there, and Axel recognized what had to be Thor. The Valkyries lined up, forming part of a circle about Odin's throne with the Vikings and the other Aesir. Axel also spotted Tyr, now recovered. The war god smiled apologetically, but with dignity, and inclined his head at his former opponent in respect.

The circle broke, and Odin strode in toward the throne, Loki following him. The Allfather sat, and Loki stood, facing him, his expression belligerent.

"Loki, my blood brother," said Odin, "you have transgressed against your brother gods, and against our mortal charges."

"You play games for mortals' amusement," said Loki evenly. "It ill-befits gods."

"I will decide what befits gods, Loki, at least what befits the Aesir gods. And you are not here to criticize. You are here to answer simply, did you feed the mushrooms of rage to our brother Tyr?"

"I did."

"You shall be punished for that, then." Odin looked to Axel. "As our prime witness, Axel Sage, do you have other charges to bring?"

Axel stepped forward from the circle at Odin's beckoning and faced Loki. "You also tricked all the Vikings. You fed them the mushrooms—"

"Inadmissible!" cried Loki. "What I do to mortals is of no consequence."

"You piece of shit," muttered Axel.

There was an answering gasp from the circle.

"Axel, even a god on trial must be treated with courtesy," warned Odin.

"Courtesy," said Axel bitterly, "right. He drove a couple hundred men insane and made them hack each other to pieces—"

"Temporarily," said Loki. "Both the insanity and the hacking to pieces. They're no worse for wear now."

"The Vikings have sworn an oath, Axel," explained Odin. "They know they may be wounded, and they know there may be deception, illusion—"

"They're pawns of the gods," finished Axel.

Odin hesitated. "I wouldn't put it that way."

"Better to be pawns of the gods," said Loki, "than pawns of the television networks, as they were before we came back. How many football players, Olympic athletes, actors and singers were used, abused and deceived by your old system, I wonder?"

"I'm sorry, Axel," said Odin, "but the charge does not apply."

"And I suppose killing Johan is all right?" asked Axel.

"No," said Odin. "That is a serious charge. The boy Johan was in our care. Tell all the Aesir, Axel, what Johan told you ere he died."

Axel looked around at the expectant faces of gods, Valkyries and Vikings. "He said Loki briefed him on the whole plan with the mushrooms. It was supposed to be a setup so that Anika would be in danger, and I'd be too scared to help her." He looked to Tyr. "Why did you attack Anika?"

"Loki," said Tyr, pronouncing the name with contempt, "stole a bit of fabric from the girl's cloak and used it to enchant the mushrooms. The scent, combined with the madness induced, made her my target. In my rage, I sought only her death."

Axel rounded on Loki. "And then you told poor, stupid Johan that his sword was enchanted, that its mere touch would snap Tyr out of his rage."

Loki rolled his eyes. "Not my cleverest trick, but the boy, as you said, was dim."

Axel stabbed a finger at Loki, wishing it were that same sword. "So dim that he died playing out your joke!" He looked back at Odin, swept his hand to encompass the assembled onlookers. He had no idea how courtrooms worked in real life, much less in Asgard, but he knew what Alan Shore would do. He milked the moment for all it was worth.

"After months," said Axel, "of being convinced of his own invulnerability, of having hands, feet and even his head cut off, and then recovering, you sent him into battle with a mad god of war, the greatest and bravest fighter among the Aesir, believing he had a secret weapon. Johan was decieved, and Johan was stupid. He never stood a chance." Axel stepped up to Loki and looked him in his emerald eyes. "You murdered him."

"He died with honor!" Loki shouted to the assembly.

"No," said Axel. "He died for nothing. For your amusement. And you would have let Anika die too, as long as it humiliated me."

"So? We have other stupid Vikings."

"Enough," snapped Odin. "Axel, you have given your testimony, and it has been heard. Loki has betrayed his brethren and he has killed a mortal in our care. Both are grievous crimes. I ask my fellow gods what shall be the punishment."

"Cut off his hand," said Tyr quietly.

Loki looked momentarily frightened, then said, "I'll roll you dice for it, Tyr. One of my hands...against your only one."

Tyr, who knew better than to play Loki in any game, shook his head and whispered, "Go to Hel."

Loki bristled. "Don't take my daughter's name in vain, Tyr."

"Silence," barked Odin. "Any other punishments to suggest?"

"Exile," said Bragi. He stepped forward and came to place a hand on Axel's shoulder, drawing him carefully away from Loki. "As god of bards and singers, I know well how important an audience is to a performer. And Loki is a comedian." His gaze swept over Loki for emphasis. "A very dangerous, wicked comedian, but a comedian all the same, a performer. He must have an audience. Deprive him of it. Send him away. Send him off by himself."

The other gods nodded approval.

"It is done," said Odin. "Loki, you will go from this realm to the nether world, to be spoken to, seen or heard by no creature, mortal or god, for a period of ten earth years."

"Ten years!" protested Axel.

"It's not your place to speak," said Bragi quietly.

"Ten years," affirmed Odin. He looked at Axel, not unkindly, "we have a great deal of experience dealing with Loki's misbehavior. Ten years will be enough to teach him."

Odin nodded, and two gods Axel didn't know came forward, took Loki by the arms, and led him from the circle. The Allfather watched him go, then looked back to Axel. "You showed great bravery, Axel, both in fighting Tyr and in your words here today. It's clear you still need to learn decorum, but, overall, you are a credit to our number. And..." he beckoned someone at the edge of the crowd with his hand.

Anika stepped forward and came to stand beside Axel. Smiling, she snaked her hand into his.

"You have won the hand of a Valkyrie," Odin went on. "She has chosen well. I'd say tonight's shall be a wedding feast. What say you, Axel Sage?"

Axel turned and looked into eyes as deep and blue as the North Sea, brushed hair the color of sunshine and bathed in a smile so radiant it could melt the fjords.

And he gave Odin his answer.

A cold north wind had swept in over the Stockholm Harbor this morning, bringing a chill uncharacteristic even for this Northern Land on a day this late in the year. It was June, and the sun was high, warming Axel's face as he stood on the deck and let the breeze sweep over him.

About him, his shipmates busied themselves. Today was the maiden voyage, a day of celebration for the crew, the builders and the designers, but for no one else. The TV cameras would not come. The news photographers would not swarm on the dock. They were at Globen, today, for a contest which would determine the champion who would lead the Viking warriors at the side of Tyr. That this effort, too, was a mission given by Odin did not matter.

No, the *Aegir's Glory* had only a teenaged sketch artist, one of the crew, a nineteen-year-old redhead. She was wiry and small, with an elfin face that watched Axel now and grinned at him under a mop of curls. She chewed her pencil momentarily before touching it to her sketchbook again. He wondered if she was drawing him. She'd done several renderings of him playing for the crew by firelight in the evening, these past few weeks.

None would make the papers, of course, and no one in Northern Europe had access to Flickr or DeviantArt. Better that way, thought Axel. He preferred to think that, for a while at least, Anika would be spared his image in the news.

"Why?" she'd sobbed, clutching the folds of his jacket as they stood in a corridor beneath the stands at Globen that day. "I thought you loved me."

Axel had almost cried himself, but he was too caught up in the anger he felt.

"I'm sorry," he'd said gently. "But it's just...this life isn't for me, Anika. Using us is what the gods do. It doesn't matter that some are good like Odin, and some are evil like Loki. It matters that they use us. I know we'd made a mess of the world before, but..." he waved his hand to indicate the whole sphere above their heads. "This isn't any better."

"But you fought for me!"

"I fought for you because I couldn't let you die, because it wasn't your fault that you got caught up between Loki and me."

"We were good together," Anika moaned. "You could stay. You don't have to fight! You can play your music while—"

He shook his head, and her weeping increased. "I'm sorry, Anika," he said again. "You're amazing. You're beautiful and loving and... you're amazing. But I can't forget that you would have given yourself to Johan."

"But it's different with you! Johan would have been duty! I want you!"

"But you'd put duty to the gods ahead of what you wanted."

"Isn't that what we're supposed to do?"

"It's not what I'm supposed to do," said Axel. "I don't know what the rules are. I don't know what a human's place is in the age of gods, but I know this: I won't let anyone force me to live my life on their terms. I'll live on mine."

"I wish I could do that," Anika whispered.

"You can."

She shook her head. "I made a promise, Axel. I promised my sister I'd stay here and honor her memory."

"Then I guess you have to stay," he said sadly. "But I can't."

"Where will you go?"

The questioned echoed, staying in his mind even now, months later. "Where will you go?" she had asked.

Where indeed.

At first, when he'd given Odin his answer, the Allfather's eyes had smoldered, and Axel thought it possible he would be struck dead on the spot. There had been silence in the hall, the king of the Norse gods and rebellious bard staring each other down. Then Bragi had spoken.

"Father Odin, you have offered my student a great honor. Strength, courage and victory in battle are qualities of our mortal worshippers which bards have sung and historians told down through the ages, even while we were gone from Midgard. And yet...there is a greater heritage to which our people are heir."

"And that would be, Bragi?" asked Odin, not taking his angry eyes off Axel.

Bragi came around and clapped a hand warmly on Axel's shoulder. "Exploration, Father. Above all, the Vikings are remembered as explorers. Their sons are remembered as the first to cross the seas and set foot on alien lands. Are these not also proud accomplishments?"

"I never said they were not."

"Then might I propose," said Bragi, smiling, "that we make Axel a counter-offer?"

And Odin had smiled as well.

"Prepare to make sail!" Ragnar's voice rang out above the wind, over the soft, white ripples in the deep blue of the harbor.

Axel looked up at his friend, smiling down from where he stood on the tower. The wind caught his long, pale hair and it streamed outward. He, too, was a Viking, but not a warrior. He was the son of centuries of Viking tradition, an explorer, the captain of an intrepid ship, going to find new worlds as had Erik the Red and Leif the Lucky. They would plant their flag in new ground and taste the sweet, new wine of foreign lands.

So what if those lands were under miles of water? They were still unseen by human eyes, untouched by human hands. They waited for their visit from the greatest explorers their world had ever known.

Axel placed his hands in his pockets against the chill, and his knuckled struck the mass of Bragi's parting gift to him. It was one of Idunn's apples, carefully contained in a hand-embroidered bag. With it was a note on parchment, written in Bragi's hand, with, gods help him, a quill pen. It said "Do not share unless you mean it! And come home to see us sometimes. B."

As the anchor was drawn up and the lines released from the moorings, as *Aegir's Glory* slid gracefully out of her berth, her birthplace, the crew prepared to vacate the deck and take their places inside. Soon they would slip beneath the waves and begin exploring the world that would be their home for months to come.

One ceremonial gesture was left. At Ragnar's signal, each quietly touched the glittering brass mission pin on his or her jacket, a salute to their shared goal, their secret pact. As fingers brushed three gold stars which stood out before silver spiral galaxy, they meditated on the words the pin represented, the words they lived by but could never speak aloud, lest the gods should hear the whisper.

Tomorrow the stars.

Dia de los Muertos

by Steve Lyons

"Senorita Velez, you must believe me, I did not kill her."

The interview room was long and narrow. Pale yellow brick walls. There were no windows. A desk fan sat in one corner of the floor, but wasn't working.

"Look," said Ruby Velez, "I have to be—"

"How...how could they even think I would—?"

"I have to be honest with you, Senor Sandoval."

"Maria is...She *was* the one true love of my life."

"I don't think there's much I can do for you, Senor Sandoval. I've been looking at the police reports, and the evidence is—"

Her client lunged across the worm-eaten table between them. His clammy hands had Ruby by the wrists before she could pull away from him. The desperate look in Nicholas Sandoval's swollen eyes was all too familiar to her.

"I could never have hurt her!" he swore. "Not her. Not my Maria. I would sooner have torn out my own beating heart than..."

He seemed to realize what he was doing, then. He slumped back into his chair with a defeated moan. Ruby let out the breath she had caught. She cast her gaze downward at the jumble of papers in her lap. She shuffled through them, half-heartedly, as if to sort them into some kind of order.

"According to the reports..." she mumbled, awkwardly.

"Yes, I know what the reports say: that Maria and I were alone in her apartment when she...when we..."

"The best advice I can give you, Senor Sandoval—"

"But you must have a copy of my statement there too?"

"Yes. Yes, I have your statement." It was in the pile somewhere.

"I did not kill her, Senorita Velez. But I know who did."

"The best advice I can give you is to plead guilty to the charge."

Sandoval shook his head, his nostrils flaring. "You sound like all the others."

"I really think—" began Ruby.

"You know a guilty plea will not affect the sentence."

"I know, but…" Ruby swallowed. "It might at least allow you to make your peace with the gods…I mean, before…"

She stared down at the papers again. She had only been handed them—had them thrust into her arms, more like—a few hours ago. Could she have missed something in her speed-reading of them? Something vital?

It was highly unlikely, she thought. She *had* read Sandoval's statement.

"Maria and I," said Sandoval, "we were not alone in that room. She was there too. My wife; rather, I should say, my ex-wife."

Ruby flipped through her papers for more details. "Valeria Medina de Sandoval," she read aloud. "Born October 14th 1987."

"She was jealous of my love for Maria, you see. Always so jealous."

"Died April 23rd 2029, at the age of forty-one," continued Ruby.

"It was she who…who put her hands around Maria's throat and…"

"And that's your story," said Ruby. "Your defense. That's what you want me to tell the court two days from now."

"Is it so impossible to imagine?" pleaded Sandoval. "At this time of the year, of all times, when the spirits move among us?"

"But you're asking me to believe—"

"I was there, Senorita Velez," insisted Sandoval. "I know what happened. Maria—my gentle, beautiful Maria—she was strangled by Valeria, my ex-wife. She was murdered in cold blood by the vengeful ghost of a dead woman!"

"There isn't a lot I can tell you, Senorita…"

The mustached detective glanced at Ruby's business card and corrected himself: "Pardon me, *Senora* Martinez."

He brushed a stack of files and a scattering of sandwich crumbs off his desk in a corner of the police station's open-plan front office. He dropped into a sprung chair behind it, motioning to his visitor to take a seat opposite.

Ruby didn't react to the cop's slip. Her card announced her, after all, as *Lic. Ruby Velez de Martinez*, although that wasn't the name she chose to go by.

"You were the investigating officer in the Maria Flores case?" she asked.

The cop nodded, his small, dark eyes not meeting hers. He hadn't introduced himself as he had shaken her hand brusquely, but Ruby's notes identified him as a Lieutenant Alameda. She had re-read those notes twice, waiting for him to spare her a moment.

"If you had telephoned ahead..." he grumbled.

"I was only assigned the case this morning," explained Ruby, "and the trial—"

"—begins the day after tomorrow," Alameda concluded, impatiently.

"My client requested a change of lawyer, because he felt—"

"The last one told him he didn't believe his crazy story."

"I know you must be busy, Lieutenant, but if you could just—"

"I hardly need to tell you, do I?" Alameda picked up a coffee mug, eyed its murky contents mistrustfully, set it down again. "It must be the same for you too, in your profession. Every year, as soon as the festival rolls around—"

"I suppose so."

"If only half our cases could be as straightforward as this one."

"You have no niggling doubts, then?" asked Ruby.

"That Nicholas Sandoval strangled his mistress? None at all."

"She wasn't his mistress, Lieutenant. My client's ex-wife is—"

"—three years dead. Yes. He's not the first, you know, to try something like this. I don't expect he'll be the last. The 'spook defense', we call it around here."

Ruby nodded. "Yes. I know."

"Every road traffic accident, the driver swears he was swerving to avoid a spirit in his headlights. Every petty thief was only stealing to feed his dead grandmother."

"Yes," said Ruby again. "I know."

She had just been a kid at the time of The Return. But she remembered her father telling her that the world had changed forever.

Ruby's heart had been set on practicing law, since the time she had led her first classroom debate and won. There was no point now, according to Papa. There would be no crime by the time she was grown up, because the gods would always be there, watching—and who would be brave enough to risk their wrath?

Things hadn't worked out that way.

The jails were more crowded than ever, hence Sandoval's still being held in police custody. Partly, that could be blamed on the soaring population. Many Mexicans were poverty-stricken and desperate enough to break the law, whatever the consequences.

And these days, of course, there were so many new laws to break.

"We have dogs going wild for no reason," said Alameda, "radio frequencies jamming—and do you have any idea how many suicides I'm called out to, this time of the year? On top of that, you have the nuts who hear voices in their heads, the ones who think they're settling old scores for dead friends or family members."

"OK," said Ruby, "So, what—and please, bear with me a moment here—what exactly do you find so 'crazy' in my client's sworn statement?"

A muscle twitched in Alameda's cheek. His mustache bristled. At length, he answered: "Sandoval was alone in that apartment with the victim."

"And one other, he says."

"We found no evidence to support that claim."

"But none to disprove it either. Your forensic team found...well, obviously, they found that Senor Sandoval was a frequent visitor to Maria Flores' home, which he doesn't deny, but otherwise—"

"He didn't leave a set of fingerprints on the young woman's neck, if that's what you mean," said Alameda, "but all the same—"

"And there were no witnesses to the incident."

"The neighbors heard—"

"They heard shouting—muffled shouting—and a scream," said Ruby, hoping that she hadn't missed anything in the papers, "which was then choked off. All of which is entirely consistent with my client's statement. No one actually saw—"

"And for that matter, nor did he," Alameda interrupted. "Your client didn't actually see a thing either."

"He saw Maria Flores choking to death," persisted Ruby, "although no one had laid a finger on her. And he claims to have sensed—"

"—an evil spirit in the room." Alameda snorted derisively.

"Isn't that how it works? Isn't that what...?" Ruby stopped herself before she could say, *Isn't that what most people believe?*

That the spirits of the dead are invisible to mortal eyes, but that their presence can be felt by those to whom they were closest in life?

"But the spirits are…" Alameda spread his arms wide in frustration. "They're just the spirits. They don't…"

"They can't affect the real world? Is that what the gods say?"

"Now, listen, Senora Martinez, I know you're young and probably keen to—"

"That's Velez, if you don't mind. Licenciado Velez."

"Sandoval had every motive for murder, you know. Friends of the victim say she was seeing someone else, and that they quarreled over money. They—"

"How many more, Lieutenant?"

Alameda broke off from what he was saying. He looked at Ruby blankly.

"How many have tried the 'spook defense' as you call it? Oh, I don't mean the voices and the glimpses out of the corner of the eye. How many suspects claim to have experienced direct physical intervention by a…an incorporeal force?"

Alameda shrugged. "A few. Most drop it long before it gets to court."

"Perhaps they wouldn't," said Ruby, "if only someone would listen to them."

Alameda sat back, and for the first time a smile tugged at his thin lips. "Take it from me," he said quietly, "put a spook defense in front of a Supreme Justice and he'll tear you to shreds. I've seen it happen."

"I have a duty to my client," said Ruby, "whose instructions are—"

"One week from now," Alameda interrupted, "Nicholas Sandoval will be dead and buried. That is, of course, barring the 'intervention' of the gods themselves. Are you sure you want to put your career on the line for a lost cause, *Licenciado* Velez?"

It was a humid summer's evening in Mexico City.

Ruby unchained her bicycle from the rack outside the police station. She was glad to be out of that stuffy building, but feeling pensive. She wasn't quite sure why.

She stowed her papers in her saddlebag, fished her pager from the inside pocket of her tailored suit jacket. She checked there were no messages from the office.

She hadn't meant half the things she had said to Alameda. He'd annoyed her by keeping her waiting for so long, and she had known how to needle him in return. The truth was that Sandoval's ghost story had sounded crazy to her too.

Hadn't there been at least some veracity to her arguments, though?

Ruby wheeled her bike out onto the road and mounted it. She didn't have much traffic to contend with. The Aztec deities that ruled her country—along with the whole of South and Central America—had not banned motor vehicles from their lands as some pantheons had; fuel, however, was prohibitively expensive.

The sidewalks, on the other hand, were thronged with people out celebrating the ongoing festival. Some were blind drunk already, liable to spill out into Ruby's path without warning. She was forced to keep her wits about her.

Many of the revelers were clad in traditional costumes and had painted their faces to resemble leering skulls, or wore masks to achieve the same effect.

Ruby cycled by shop windows filled with papier-mâché skeletons, arranged in wry or humorous poses. Confectioners and bakers displayed their wares of decorated sugar skulls and cookies, while even public buildings were festooned with party lights and tissue garlands in the shapes of cavorting cadavers.

The sweet smell of copal incense permeated the evening air.

In Ruby's childhood, the Day of the Dead had fallen at the beginning of November. The gods had restored it to its rightful, pre-Columbian place in the calendar, and so now it was celebrated throughout the month of August.

As Ruby skirted the historic Centro district, she couldn't resist a glance up at the New Great Pyramid of Tenochtitlan. Seventy meters tall, it filled the huge plaza once known as the Zócalo, towering over the buildings around it.

As usual, there was plenty of activity on the pyramid's steps. Ruby saw no sign of the Lady of the Dead, however. Often, Mictecacihuatl would emerge from the temple area at the pyramid's apex, to overlook the festivities from her grand, elevated throne.

On the corner just ahead, a scuffle flared up in a queue outside a dingy-looking, subterranean nightclub. It was sorted out, before Ruby had to worry, by the doorman: a skin walker in the shape of a sleek black leopard.

Another reminder, she thought, of how much humanity had had to adjust to in the past two decades; how much that, previously, would have been thought impossible but was now a part of everyday life.

Ruby knew what she was supposed to do about Nicholas Sandoval. She was supposed to talk him into changing his plea; failing that, to palm him off onto another representative. As a last resort, she could present his case as he instructed, but in such a perfunctory manner as to signal to the court that she didn't believe a word of it.

The alternative had been stated bluntly enough by Alameda. Ruby—at least, her professional reputation—would be "torn to shreds," and Sandoval would be just as dead. *Barring*, he had said, *the intervention of the gods themselves...*

He might have spoken more truly than he had known.

Home for Ruby Velez was a loft apartment in the city's main business area, with hardwood floors and chrome and glass furnishings. The real estate agent had used words like "minimalist" and "spacious" in describing it to her.

It had never been intended that she should be here alone.

Hello, honey, she wanted to say but didn't, *I'm home!*

She had set up the *ofrenda* in its usual place on the dining table, which she had pushed up against an inside wall. Its single candle had burned almost down to the holder, but nothing else had been disturbed. It never was.

Only once had Ruby knelt before that makeshift altar and talked to the person to whom it was dedicated. She hadn't said much, even then. She had felt too self-conscious, declaring her private feelings to thin air.

And the apartment had felt no less cold and empty for her halting efforts.

The ofrenda had been new, back then. Ruby had rebuilt it in each of the three years since, only really out of religious obligation. She piled it high with flowers and fruits and photographs of the deceased, as was the custom.

She had filled a bowl with his favorite chocolates. She had laid out his favorite books and CDs and the keys to his beloved sports car, although she had thought a lot more than twice about that. His golf bag, she had stood against the table with his cap and visor balanced on the protruding clubs.

She wished she *could* talk to him again. She wished she could tell him about the crazy thoughts whirling about in her head and ask for his advice. Even though she would probably have disregarded it and done her own thing, as usual.

Ruby turned on the radio. Not that she especially enjoyed its gods-approved programming; she just wanted some sound to fill the silence. She selected an unexciting meal-for-one from the freezer and tossed it into the microwave.

Ruby had loved the Day of the Dead, once. She remembered, as a kid, dressing up in a Batgirl costume, making decorations, playing party games.

Superhero costumes were banned these days, of course. The same went for vampires, Jedi, wizards and anything else that the gods considered idolatrous; any ideas from abroad that had crept in to pollute their sacred traditions.

It didn't matter to most people. They loved the annual festival still. And they *believed* in it, in its promise of a fleeting reunion with the loved and lost.

They believed in it so wholeheartedly that, every August, a good number of them took their own lives, though the gods forbade this too. As Alameda had reminded Ruby earlier. They chose to rejoin their loved ones for all time.

Ruby almost envied those people. She wondered, sometimes, what it would be like to such have such absolute faith in anything.

She sat at the chrome and glass coffee table with her overheated dinner. She let the voices and the music on the radio wash over her. Every now and again, she cast a glance across the room at the ofrenda, at the offerings to her late husband.

And felt nothing.

"Yes, yes, I sense a presence at your shoulder."

The woman called herself Xiuhtonal, though Ruby doubted that this was her birth name. She described herself in her print advert as a "shaman-priestess"; twenty years ago, she would probably have said "medium" or "fortune-teller".

She wore flowing, colorful robes and an elaborate headdress, and her skin was like cracked leather.

"I…I didn't really come here to—" began Ruby.

"Oh, it's clear that you miss him very much," said the shaman-priestess.

"Yes," said Ruby. "Yes, I do, but—"

"And he misses you too. He is unhappy, so terribly unhappy."

It was not what she had expected to hear.

Ruby wondered if this had been a mistake. She had rung around several shaman-priests and priestesses this morning, and Xiuhtonal was the only one who could offer her a sitting today. The festival was a busy time for her profession too.

Ruby had come here with questions, but they died in her throat.

"Your loved one has a message of the utmost importance to impart to you. He shouts it at the top of his voice, but cannot seem to make you hear him."

"What...what message?" Ruby found herself asking in a choked voice.

Xiuhtonal's eyes darkened. "I cannot say. The words are for your ears alone."

Yeah, thought Ruby, *that figures!*

She shook herself, made an effort to sit up straight and focus. The copal haze that filled the cluttered booth was making her feel light-headed.

"Listen," she said, clearing her throat. "I need to ask you—"

"How long has your loved one been gone?" asked the shaman-priestess.

"I...He...Three years. It was three years ago in May."

She nodded as if the answer didn't surprise her. "He knows how difficult you are finding it to move on. But please understand that it is difficult for him too. His love for you is a chain that binds him to this mortal realm."

"I've tried," insisted Ruby. "I really have tried to...If he's with me as you say he is, then why can't he—?"

"He has sent you signs of his presence," the shaman-priestess declared, "many signs, but you refuse to see them."

"But couldn't he...?" Ruby pulled herself together again, reminded herself what she was doing here. "I've heard the spirits can affect the... the mortal realm. If they choose to. Is that...? I mean, have you ever come across—?"

"Ever since The Return," said Xiuhtonal, "the spirits have become more..."

"Tangible?" prompted Ruby.

"Most people can feel their presence among us now. We feel the love they still hold for us in their hearts, whereas once that gift was given only to a chosen few."

"But isn't that…? I mean, pardon me, but couldn't that just be because we believe in the spirits more strongly? Because I don't think the gods have ever said—"

"Or perhaps…" the priestess-shaman interrupted Ruby, sharply.

Ruby waited for her to continue.

"The Return may have opened a door between the realms," Xiuh-tonal suggested. "A door that, before, may only have been ajar, but now has been torn from its hinges."

"Yes," said Ruby. "Yes, I like that. But the thing is, I need—"

Xiuhtonal put a hand to her head. "I see them in my dreams," she intoned in a manner that was suddenly quite theatrical. "Poor wretches they are, that make the long journey here to find themselves unwanted or forgotten."

Ruby was stung by the shaman-priestess's tone, although she had made no accusations. "I make the necessary offerings," she maintained. "I always have!"

"But has your heart ever truly been in those offerings," Xiuhtonal asked, "or have you merely been going through the rituals?"

Somehow, she had brought the conversation back to this.

"This is the fourth festival since Luis's passing," she said in a deathly undertone. "His four-year voyage across the Land of the Dead is almost done."

Ruby frowned. "You know his name. You said Luis's name. I never told you…"

She leaned across the round table that stood between them. She almost grabbed Xiuhtonal by the wrists, as Sandoval had done to her yesterday, but she stopped herself. "Ask him to, I don't know, do something. Move something. I'll put my pen on the table. Ask Luis to move it, make it roll, or just flutter the tablecloth or…"

"I am sorry," said the shaman-priestess, flatly. "I can't do that."

Ruby sighed. "Of course you can't." She returned to an earlier thought. "The gods have never actually said, have they, that the spirits have a physical presence?"

Xiuhtonal protested, "Oh, but they can move mountains, if we believe—"

Ruby shook her head. "Sorry. I need more than that. Something more than just…than feelings."

The shaman-priestess's demeanor changed again. She glanced around furtively, as if someone might have snuck into the booth behind her and be listening in.

"I did hear…" she began, hesitantly. "A regular client of mine was out walking one afternoon, when she was…*kept* from turning down a particular street. A moment later, a car crashed into the shop that she had intended to visit. Her brother had passed on only weeks earlier; my client swears it was his hands she felt on her shoulders."

"Uh-huh," said Ruby. "What else?"

"Another client, a personal friend of mine, was engaged in a boundary dispute with his neighbors. He needed an old photograph, of his grandfather outside the family home, which showed the original position of the fence. He searched the house from top to bottom, but couldn't find it. The next morning, it was lying at the foot of his bed, as if the grandfather himself had placed it there."

"Hmm," said Ruby.

"And I did hear of a woman who…Her husband had been a violent man, by all accounts. She lit a candle for him during the festival all the same, but placed it beside one lit for her mother, whom he detested. The husband's spirit, I heard, overturned the ofrenda and snuffed out the mother's candle."

"Does this woman have a name?" asked Ruby. "Can she be contacted?"

Xiuhtonal shook her head. "But you will hear such tales told everywhere, if only you stop to ask and are prepared to hear the answer. I…"

She became hesitant again. "I had my own…encounter with an angry spirit. It was several years ago. I was still…I was sitting with a young man. He wanted desperately to know if his late mother approved of his new relationship. I could sense that she…in fact, she disapproved most strongly, but I…"

"What happened?" Ruby prompted.

"I felt the spirit was being…She wished to cling on to her son, even if it denied him a chance of happiness. You must understand, I…I had never dared anything like this before and never since, but I resolved to tell the young man what I thought he needed to hear. How foolish I was, and how impertinent! I opened my mouth to utter the lie, and I felt a…a pressure around my throat that stopped my breath."

She put a hand to her collar, reflexively, shuddering at the memory.

Ruby eased a pen and notebook out of her jacket pocket.

"OK," she said, "I'm going to need you to take me through this from the beginning, please, one step at a time. And I need to ask one more thing of you, if I may."

The shaman-priestess's eyes grew dark again, uncertain, as they focused back on the here and now, and on her visitor.

"Would you be prepared to repeat this story," Ruby asked her, "in a court of law?"

She spent the afternoon in the José Vasconcelos Library.

She claimed a reading table, between half-empty shelves that had been inexorably denuded of one "blasphemous" text after another. She ordered up two bound volumes of each of the major newspapers, and ate a tuna sandwich as she waited for them.

She missed the Internet. But even the library's computerized catalog was in the process of being transferred back to a card index system.

The newspapers arrived, set down on Ruby's table in a cloud of dust and echoes. She started with *El Universal*. The volume for the second quarter of this year.

The murder of Maria Flores was well covered, with a front-page headline, several follow-up articles and a brief obituary. Ruby read them all carefully, seeking any minor detail that hadn't made it into the police reports.

She hadn't realized, before, just how young Maria had been: barely half the age of her alleged killer. She also hadn't known that Maria had formerly been employed as a maid by the Sandoval family.

Little new light was shed, however, on the circumstances of the crime itself. There was a photograph of Nicholas Sandoval being bundled into a police van, bewildered quotes from three of the victim's neighbors and no mention of malevolent spirits.

Nor did that week's other papers yield much useful information.

Ruby turned her attention to the other volumes she had requested, instead. The ones from three years ago. She wanted to find out more about the second suspect in her case—and the best way to start, she thought, was by reading her obituaries too.

This time, she found far more than she had expected.

The demise of Valeria Medina de Sandoval had also made it onto the front pages. In fact, now Ruby half-remembered being aware of the story at the time.

There were photographs of fire trucks outside the Sandovals' home. Nicholas Sandoval was pictured again, a little younger, more hair on his head, but unmistakably him. He was wrapped in a heavy blanket, being conveyed to an ambulance by a pair of paramedics. He looked deathly pale.

One paper had a shot of the funeral, and he was in that too. As he stood by the graveside, he was comforted by a younger woman. It took Ruby a moment to recognize Maria Flores behind a black, netted veil.

They were holding hands.

Ruby sat, staring at that picture for a long time, as the library slowly emptied and its lights began to be shut off in sections around her. It was still fairly early, but opening hours for most public services were reduced during the festival.

There was one more thing she had to do, before she gave in and let herself be ushered out of the building. She didn't want to, but couldn't help herself.

She knew exactly where to find it in each paper. The editions for May 13th of that year. Page five, bottom left hand corner in the first; page seven, top right in the next.

In contrast to Nicholas Sandoval's two lovers, Luis merited only a few column inches to mark his passing. Ruby knew the words by heart, but read them anyway.

He was described, almost invariably, as a "young professional." A "promising young barrister," only one reporter expounded. His recent marriage—two days before his death—was usually cited, although Ruby's name was only mentioned once.

She ran her fingers across the newsprint until they were black. Like worrying at a fresh wound, or just needing to convince herself that it was real.

Even after all this time…

No other vehicle had been involved in the crash. Nor was there any suggestion that the driver had been under any undue influence. A police spokesman suggested that Luis had swerved to avoid a wild dog or other animal in the road and lost control of his brand new sports car. Just one of those things.

Perhaps he saw a spirit in his headlights too, thought Ruby, darkly.

That evening, after she had digested her microwave meal and recycled its cardboard container, Ruby Velez turned off the radio and talked to her dead husband.

She didn't feel right, kneeling in front of the ofrenda, so she pulled a dining chair up to it instead and sat with her elbows on her knees, her head stooped.

"Well, Luis," she said, "I went and did it. I…"

Her words died away into the silence. She braced herself and tried again.

"I called in at the office before it closed. I filled out the forms."

"This is the fourth festival since Luis's passing," Xiuhtonal had reminded Ruby. *"His four-year voyage across the Land of the Dead is almost done."*

He wouldn't be able to visit her again next year.

"I didn't tell the senior partners," she said. "Two of them had already left for the golf course and the third is on leave. I guess they'll hear all about it soon enough. I half-expected to be struck down by a bolt of lightning as soon as…"

She gave a nervous half-laugh. "Well, as you can see, it didn't happen. There'll be plenty more lightning bolts to come, though, I don't doubt it.

"This time next week, I could be a national celebrity. Or a national joke. Ruby Velez: the woman who dragged a god into court."

She hesitated. "I ought to explain. About the name. It isn't that…I would have been very happy to be Senora Martinez, your wife, you know I would. I just can't bear to be Senora Martinez, the…the widow. I don't want that to be how I'm defined. It isn't fair. We had no time at all. We…"

Ruby took a deep, shuddering breath.

"What the hell am I doing?" she whispered.

The ofrenda hadn't been disturbed since she had set it up on August 1st. The books and CDs were slowly gathering dust. Not a one of the chocolates had even been unwrapped. That wasn't how the spirits worked, of course. Purportedly, they absorbed the vital essence of the offerings without ever touching them.

How very convenient for them! Ruby thought.

"I don't expect them to do it," she confessed. "I don't expect a clerk of the court to go skipping up the steps of the Great Pyramid to serve a subpoena on the Lady of the Dead. Not straight away. I expect to be tied up in legal wrangling over this one for a long time to come: months, maybe even years.

"No bad thing for my client if I am. They want to execute him on the last day of the festival. If I can delay a guilty verdict until after then…

"I can buy Nicholas Sandoval another year of life, at least. A year to build my case for an appeal. I'll go public. I can find more people like the shaman-priestess, scores of people, who will testify to physical encounters with the spirits. It won't be...It won't prove that a spirit strangled Maria Flores. But then, I don't need proof, do I? I only need a reasonable doubt."

Ruby stood and began to pace the apartment. Her thoughts were running away with themselves, finding new possibilities that in turn charged her with a nervous energy. It had been a long time since she had felt like this, and she had missed it.

It had been a long time since she had been able to think about the future.

"I'd have public opinion on my side," she considered. "People believe in the spirits, in their power. And the gods, they certainly *want* us to believe. A case like this, it could make international headlines. I'd be making legal history!"

She caught a glimpse her reflection in a wall mirror, saw something in her own eyes. A flicker of self-doubt? She peered more closely. "But what happens if I do?" she asked. "What then? If I take the 'spook defense' to court and it works...

"No one could be convicted of any crime again. Not during the month of August. Any suspect could blame the spirits for anything, everything. And no one could prove otherwise, because dead men don't tell tales. They certainly can't be cross-examined on a witness stand. The Day of the Dead would become...It'd be a free-for-all!"

She shook her head, tore her gaze away from the mirror, resumed her pacing.

"It wouldn't be my fault. I didn't bring the spirits here. The gods did that—so, why shouldn't they be held to account for it? Why shouldn't they be made to...at least explain to us what the rules are?"

Ruby turned back to the ofrenda, as its guttering candle died.

"That's all I really want," she concluded with a plaintive sigh. "Just to know what the rules are. Because this...it's about more than just one man, isn't it? I don't know if I believe that Nicholas Sandoval is even innocent. But he could be, that's the point. And I can't...I won't bury my head in the sand any longer.

"I can't choose to believe in a...a lie, however comforting. You understand that, Luis, don't you? Please, tell me you understand."

She was talking to herself.

No matter how much she wished it, Ruby couldn't hear his voice.

She couldn't feel the touch of his fingers on her hand or his breath on her neck. She couldn't smell that dreadful shaving gel that he always insisted on using. He wasn't there.

Before she went to bed, she lit a fresh candle for him.

She stood with the spent match smoldering between her fingers and stared into the mesmerizing, dancing flame. As if it might somehow twist and curl itself into a shape that Ruby recognized. It was hopeless, of course.

"I'm sorry," she whispered to no one in particular as she turned and walked out of the room. "I tried my best."

Ruby's sleep, that night, was unsettled.

She lay awake in the bed that she had never shared with Luis, mentally editing and reediting the content of her opening statement for tomorrow. Even when she managed to sink into a light doze, she was haunted by anxious dreams.

Ruby was in court, but still wearing her silk nightdress. She resolved to ignore the tittering at her back. She would show them all soon enough, she thought.

She drew breath to call her first witness. Before she could, there was a flash of light beside her, and she turned and came face to face with a goddess.

The Lady of the Dead was somehow larger and brighter than life. She occupied the witness box as if she weren't quite a part of the world but only touching it.

Her head was a skull, but smooth and white like fine bone china. Long, jet black hair flowed from beneath a golden headdress, which was garlanded with owl feathers. One moment, the goddess's eye sockets appeared empty; the next, they gleamed with a fierce intelligence...and a hint of amusement?

She nodded to confirm that her name was Mictecacihuatl. She wasn't asked to swear an oath; to whom would she have sworn it, anyway?

And now, at last, Ruby's moment had arrived. Her time to prove herself.

Only...she couldn't remember what she was supposed to say. Standing there, transfixed by that hollow-eyed gaze, she had no voice. And the titters behind her grew louder and more scornful, until everyone in the courtroom was booing and jeering at Ruby, crying shame on her for her wickedness, her lack of faith.

It was then that Ruby realized her dreadful error. She had mistaken the Lady of the Dead for a witness in the case—when, in fact, she was the judge.

She knelt in fear as the goddess rose from her seat and kept rising. She loomed higher and higher above the trembling Ruby until she filled the entire courtroom, until she was much *bigger* than the courtroom. She pointed a skeletal finger at Ruby's forehead and, in booming, sepulchral tones, she pronounced her verdict:

Guilty! Guilty! Guilty!

Ruby still couldn't find her voice. *I only wanted to know the truth*, she wanted to cry out loud but didn't. *What did I do that was so wrong?*

Court officials seized her by the arms, hauled her back to her feet. As if in answer to her unvoiced pleas, they dragged Ruby to an ornate door that hadn't been there a moment earlier and yanked it open.

Outside, night had fallen early. Still, the Day of the Dead festivities continued unabated. Skeletons danced on the moonlit streets of Mexico City. In contrast to the revelers of the day, however, there were no face paints or masks in evidence.

These cadavers were genuine: spirits of the recently-dead exulting in the gifts showered upon them by the still-living. They showed off their new clothes and gadgets, ate their favorite foods, enjoyed the latest songs by their favorite artistes.

Ruby was looking through a doorway into another world. A world that was somehow overlaid upon her own. Or perhaps, she thought, it was vice versa.

It was a joyous world, even beautiful in its own macabre way.

But then, the spirits parted—as, impossibly, did the streets and buildings around them. Bones and brickwork alike went spinning, reeling out of Ruby's field of vision, until she could see all the way across the city.

All the way to the wrought-iron gates of the Panteón de Dolores.

And there, still held fast, unable to turn her head even, she was forced to bear witness to an altogether more sobering scene.

More spirits came shuffling through the cemetery gates, in procession. They were draped in filthy, moldering rags and dragging heavy chains behind them. Their backs were stooped and their skull heads bowed in misery. Their teeth were chattering with the graveyard cold and they were weak and dizzy with hunger.

There was no joy in this beautiful world for them. No brand new clothes or gadgets or food or song. These emaciated wretches were, as the shaman-priestess had described them, the unwanted. Trudging back to their untended graves alone.

Ruby knew, before she saw him, that he had to be somewhere among them.

She knew him at first glance, although there was no flesh on his face. She recognized him instinctively by the shape of his head and his slight stature. She recognized the scraps of his favorite golf sweater, and his familiar cap and visor.

She wanted to run to him, but her captors held her back. She tried to call his name, but couldn't. Her pleading, desperate gaze met Luis's eyes—his eye sockets—and for a moment she almost fooled herself into believing he could see her too.

He let out a plaintive howl and turned to leave the world forever. He dragged his chains along the cemetery path away from Ruby. And she saw that Luis's shoulders were trembling violently, as if he were weeping to himself.

If only, she thought numbly, the dead were blessed with tears to shed.

It didn't help that the police kept her waiting again.

Ruby sat in the front office of the stuffy police station. She tapped her foot and sighed heavily, but no one seemed to take the hint. She shuffled through her papers, but couldn't focus to read them properly.

She couldn't get the dream out of her mind.

She checked her watch. She had arrived at the stroke of nine o'clock. That had been forty minutes ago. Perhaps the cops had been told to keep her here, she thought. The senior partners at Ruby's firm could have heard about the subpoena and be trying to contact her. She had left her pager at home, in case they did.

She wiped a sleeve across her tearing eyes, stifling a yawn. She was startled by a fragment of the dream behind her eyelids. A flash-frame image of a weeping cadaver.

She leapt to her feet, involuntarily.

She caught sight of a familiar face. The corporal on the front desk was dealing with an inquiry, so Ruby rushed past him before he could think to stop her.

Lieutenant Alameda's mouth was full of a breakfast bagel. "Nicholas

Sandoval," she harangued him while he couldn't interrupt her. "His trial begins today, remember? I need to plan his defense with him, and yes, I know it's still the festival, but I've been waiting here all morning and I'm busy too, Lieutenant, and—"

"Lieutenant?" The desk corporal had caught up with Ruby. "I'm sorry, I—"

Alameda finally managed to swallow. More in gestures than in words, he sent the corporal to find out what had happened to Ruby's client and invited her to sit down in the meantime. Ruby thanked him, a little stiffly, and accepted the offer.

Alameda sat across his desk from her, as before. He laced his hands behind his head, leaned back in his chair. "You couldn't talk him round, then?" he asked, mildly, his dark eyes hooded. "Sandoval. He's still going with the spook defense?"

Ruby nodded. As an afterthought, she added, "Damn right he is!"

Alameda raised an eyebrow.

"Radio interference," said Ruby. Alameda looked none the wiser. She reminded him, "Two days ago. You said that, during the festival, you have trouble with your radios. You implied it was due to the spirits."

"What of it?"

"So, even you, Lieutenant, even you and your fellow police officers, evidently you believe that the spirits are strong enough to—"

"Now, hold on a minute!"

"Either they can affect the mortal…the physical world or they can't. It must be one way or the other. You can't blame the spirits for your troubles, but then dismiss my client out of hand when he says the same. So, which is it?"

"I don't…I can't answer that for you," Alameda confessed.

"You'll have to answer it," Ruby promised him, "in the witness box."

Alameda seemed to think about that. He sat up, rested his elbows on the desk, chewed on his bottom lip. "You're serious about this, aren't you?" he said quietly. "You really intend to go ahead with—?"

"Any reason I shouldn't be?" asked Ruby.

"I think…I think maybe you should get to know your client a bit better, before you lay yourself out on the sacrificial stone for his sake."

"I'm not doing this for him," said Ruby. Alameda's eyebrows twitched again and she corrected herself, "Not just for him."

"You must know about the wife by now," said Alameda.

Ruby squirmed. "I…Were you involved in that case too?" She remembered the newspaper reports she had read in the library. Photographs of fire trucks outside the Sandovals' home.

Alameda shook his head. "I heard about it."

"The inquest said—"

"Senora Sandoval had drunk herself into a stupor. She probably never woke up as her bedroom burned around her. The fire was started by a cigarette. Nobody's fault but the victim's own. A tragic accident. Her husband—"

"—was asleep on the couch downstairs," concluded Ruby.

"They had argued that afternoon."

"So, what are you saying, exactly?"

"We found no evidence to dispute the coroner's findings." Alameda shrugged. "I don't know. If the maid hadn't chosen that day to go out of town…She might have shed some light on what the row was about, at least."

"The maid," said Ruby. "Maria Flores?"

Alameda didn't answer that question. He didn't need to. There were skeletons marching through Ruby's head again. They were howling and wailing and rattling their chains in torment.

She shook herself to drive the image away. "OK," she said. "So, let's assume that what you're trying to imply is—"

Alameda jumped in: "I'm not implying anything. Not a thing."

"Let's say that…that Sandoval was having an affair with his maid, and his wife found out. It could certainly explain why Valeria drank so heavily that night and was so careless. But surely that—?"

"It would also mean," Alameda chipped in, "that Senor Sandoval was facing a crippling divorce settlement. The house was in Senora Sandoval's name, did you know that? It was left to her by her parents."

"Either way," said Ruby doggedly, "that only gives Valeria, her spirit, a stronger motive for strangling the mistress, doesn't it? And for doing it in such a way that her husband, her former husband would be likely to take the rap."

Alameda sat back again. "Perhaps," he conceded. "Or perhaps, Licenciado Velez, you are staking a great deal on the word of an unrepentant killer."

At that moment, the corporal from the front desk reappeared. He took his senior officer to one side and they talked in hushed, urgent tones for what seemed like a long time, glancing over at Ruby more than once. By the time they were done, she was in no doubt that it was bad news. She stood up to face Alameda as he returned.

His expression was grim. "I'm sorry you have been kept—"

"What's happened?" she demanded to know. "It's Sandoval, isn't it?"

"Nicholas Sandoval…" Alameda paused, taking a deep breath. "He attempted to take his own life this morning. As it happens, it wasn't a particularly good attempt. The prisoner cut his left wrist with a plastic knife. He was found when an officer went to collect him from his cell for your meeting. He—"

"Where is he? *How* is he?"

"With a doctor, and evidently he'll be fine. Well enough, so I'm told, to stand trial this afternoon."

"I want to see him," said Ruby.

"I'm afraid that won't be possible," said Alameda.

"I'm his lawyer," she insisted. "He has a right to—"

The cop cleared his throat, uncomfortably. "That's just it, I'm afraid. I have been asked to inform you that Nicholas Sandoval no longer requires your services. He has elected to represent himself in court."

"But that's ridiculous! I have to talk to him. He probably thinks—"

"I can't force a prisoner to see you if he doesn't want to," said Alameda.

"But he probably thinks I don't believe him, like the others. He doesn't know how much work I've put into this case since—"

"He has also asked to change his statement."

The words were like a slap to Ruby's face. She could hardly begin to process what she was hearing, let alone formulate a considered response to it. She just gaped at the messenger, until she realized that her mouth was hanging open and closed it.

To his credit, Alameda betrayed no pleasure in her disappointment. "Nicholas Sandoval," he stated, "now wishes to confess to—"

"No," protested Ruby, voicelessly.

"—to the crime of first-degree homicide against his partner, Maria Flores, and to enter a plea of guilty to said charge in the Aztec Supreme Court. Try to look at it this way, Licenciado Velez. Is it not far better to learn the truth now, than later? Far better for us all, I think. We can leave the whole matter in the hands of the gods now. Let them see to it that justice is done."

● ● ●

It was the last night of the festival, and the carnival was in full swing.

On the city's teeming streets, alive with music and laughter and dance and drunken abandon, Ruby Velez felt alone. At every turn, she was confronted by leering effigies of the joyful dead. She must have been the only person not dressed up for the occasion. She felt as if she were drifting through that other world from her dream. A world that had no place for her. She was the unwanted spirit here.

She had woken up this morning with Nicholas Sandoval's fate on her mind.

Now, at last, the sun was setting on the Day of the Dead for another year. As it sank behind the Great Pyramid, a deathly hush settled over the world like a blanket.

The dancers wound down as their music petered out; chattering tongues were stilled and laughter stifled. And, one by one, about ten million heads were turned and raised towards the pyramid's apex. Ruby followed the gazes of ten million pairs of eyes, although she dreaded what she knew she would see.

The Lady of the Dead had appeared outside the temple area.

Ruby hadn't seen her since the dream. She hadn't dared look for her. The sight of the goddess, even so far away, brought back memories of waking in a cold, nervous sweat, her heart pounding. Nor was that the worst of it.

Ruby's eyes scanned lower down the pyramid, as low as she could see over the intervening buildings. She found a cluster of a dozen or so people, wearing light tan prison uniforms, being driven up the steps by guards with rifles. She tried to pick out her former client among them, but failed to do so.

Perhaps that was for the best, she thought.

She had witnessed this ritual many times before. She had steeled herself to witness it again. She had felt that, in a way, it was her duty. She couldn't do it.

She couldn't watch as each prisoner in turn was strapped down to the stone slab in front of the temple. She couldn't watch as a priest gouged twelve hearts out of their cavities and presented them to the looming, cadaverous figure of the goddess.

An offering to ensure that she would continue to watch over the blessed dead, and return to preside over the festival that was held in their honor again.

Ruby turned away from the grisly scene. She pushed and weaved her way through the spellbound crowd, on her way back home.

She had done the best she could.

She had written a note to Sandoval, and extracted a promise from Lieutenant Alameda to deliver it personally. She had asked him to call her. He hadn't. Alameda had told Ruby, off the record, that Sandoval had had a disturbed night, before the trial. He had had to be sedated after waking up screaming in terror.

What nightmares had tormented him, she wondered? What had frightened him more than the prospect of death itself?

Across the street from her apartment, lights blazed inside an electrical store. Ruby found her eyes drawn to the window display.

A male dummy was seated in front of a television, with a microwave meal on his lap. Surrounding him were the ubiquitous papier-mâché skeletons. Two skeleton children played hide and seek around the chair. Grandmother craned forward to see the television screen. Mother Skeleton perched on the chair arm, with a bony hand laid tenderly on the dummy's shoulder.

The moral of the tableau was spelled out in stenciled letters across the window glass: They Are Always With Us.

It seemed that Ruby had been hearing that message a lot. In one form or another.

She had withdrawn the subpoena, of course, though not before the senior partners at her firm had learned about it. She had a meeting booked in for next week to explain herself to them. She hadn't worked out yet what she was going to say.

Perhaps it was nothing more than a guilty conscience, she thought, that had pricked Nicholas Sandoval into confessing. Guilt over the crime with which he had been charged and for which he had been condemned? Or over something else entirely?

The end result was the same, either way.

Somewhere in the distance, way across the silent city, a dog was barking.

As soon as Ruby opened her apartment door, she knew.

Her eyes went straight to the ofrenda at the side of the room.

The golf bag had fallen over. It had disturbed the books and CDs on the table. A photograph of Luis, in his graduation gown, had slipped over the edge. It lay in the center of the hardwood floor, face-up, with his golf cap on top of it.

It could have been the wind, of course. A strong breeze had been blowing all day, and Ruby could see now that she had left a window open.

Yes, she said to herself, *it could easily have been the wind…*

But today, Ruby Velez chose to believe in something else.

That First Step

by Lorraine J. Anderson

Mary always looked at the dirty wall on the other side of the hall when she walked past the old man's apartment. She was scared of him. He looked mean, he was old—almost forty, she heard Mummy say once—and he always stared at her whenever she passed him in the hall.

Mum and Pop always sighed and told her to avoid him as much as possible. Mum said that they were warned about him in the goddess Dôn's Temple, and that he was a "dangerous influence," whatever that was.

He never talked to anybody and only came out from his apartment to go to work. And he owned a television.

Mary had never seen a television. Nobody they knew could afford one.

Mummy and Pop said he had a funny name, but then they said that she wouldn't get the joke. They said his name was Kenan Meriadoc, but she couldn't say that, so she called him Mister Merry. Which was kind of funny, because he wasn't very merry. He mainly seemed sad.

His parent's laughed at the name, then they started talking about movies and hobbits and rings and barbarians. They were right. She didn't understand it. She wished she could see a movie. But that was another thing they couldn't afford.

At least, that's what Mum and Pop said. They knew all about television and computers and "ranch houses." They lived in the United States when the gods returned. Mummy called Mary her heavenly baby. She was born on the very day, at the very moment Zeus had appeared at the London Olympics ten years ago. They had lived in this tiny council flat since she was a baby, along with her Mummy's Pop and Mum.

Mum didn't like Mr. Merry. She didn't know why. Must be something to do about being a "dangerous influence."

Her little room adjoined the scary neighbor's wall. It was made out of thick woodchip wallpaper that she couldn't poke her finger through. Though she was told it was impolite to listen to the neighbors, she would hear him listen to the television. She couldn't understand the words, but there were a lot of explosions. Pop called them "war movies."

Whatever that was. She knew about wars. The Gods did that all of the time. Except the Goddess Dôn and the God Brân Fendigaidd. Mum said that they had an "alliance." When Mary asked what that was, Mum told her that meant that the Goddess and the God were good friends and would remain good friends in return for certain "favors." Mary asked what the "favors" were, and Mummy said that she would tell her when she was older. Pop looked alarmed, then turned his head away.

Mary wished she were older *now.*

The Goddess Dôn was her favorite. She hoped she could serve in the temple of the Goddess when she grew up. She knew that Dôn was a Goddess of fertility, whatever that was. She had an idea it had something to do with plants; she liked growing plants.

But the movies didn't seem to have a Goddess, or anything like somebody who liked to grow plants. They seemed to have a God, though, because everybody was always saying "My God!" She couldn't understand it, so she listened to his movies whenever she could. She supposed that meant that she was bad, that she was going to the bad Otherworld that she learned about in class, but she couldn't help herself. She was curious. When Mummy said something about curiosity killing the cat, she just nodded her head and agreed, then listened anyway.

There seemed to be a lot of angry people yelling in War movies.

She knew the Gods. She was learning about the Gods in school. The Goddess Dôn had even visited, looked around, gave all of the children necklaces, smiled at them, then disappeared in front of their eyes. She even laid Her hand on Mary's head and told her that if she were very, very good, she might be picked for Her Temple. Mary was ecstatic and her class was all excited after that and they were talking about it two days later. Then the new song by Erik Marrinan came out, and her classmates talked about him and how hot he was and how they all wanted to kiss him. She stopped listening. Not that she didn't not like Erik; she liked him just fine. But he was almost twenty. He wasn't going to date a young girl like her.

When she told her Mummy and Pop about the necklace the Goddess gave her, they smiled at her. Mummy said that it was quite an honor. Then Pop told her not to grow up too fast, and he looked scared at Mummy. Mummy shook her head and said that it would be all right, a lot could happen in six or seven years.

She took one last glance at the old man's door and unlocked her door swiftly. She hated coming home from school alone. Mum and Pop were both at work at this time, and she knew she should be grateful that they were working, but she still hated it. She crawled into her bed in her room. Her Mum said that it had once been a closet in the Before Gods time, but since everybody had moved back to the old country, every bit of space was used and no-one could afford more than a small space. This was why Mummy's parents lived with them and were at work, too.

She turned on the light and opened her homework, but found herself listening at her wall. The old man was listening to movies again and was muttering to himself. She couldn't hear anything, so she sighed and opened her book.

Suddenly, the old man screamed. She jumped and gasped, looking at the wall. He screamed again, then suddenly she heard a thump. Was something wrong with him? Without a thought, she tore out of her apartment to pound on the door. She forgot that she was scared of the man.

The door opened. The old man stood at the door, his face red. Was he—no, he couldn't have been crying. Grumpy old men didn't cry. "What do you want?"

She looked down at her shoes, at the toes sticking out of her sneakers. "I thought…"

He exhaled. "Yes?"

"I thought there was something wrong. I thought you were hurt."

He stared at her a second. "No. I was frustrated."

"Why?"

"You wouldn't understand." He kept staring at her.

She stared back at him. He had a scar on one side of his face. His eyes were brown, and they looked kind. His hair was brown and fell limply past his shoulders. His clothes were dirty and patched. She then looked past him into the living room. The room seemed larger than their apartment, yet it still seemed stuffed. Over in one corner, a box with a picture flickered. "Is that a television?"

He didn't even glance behind him. "Yes."

She stared at it. Men in green clothes were talking to each other in a hole in a ground, and they were holding guns.

"You haven't seen one before?"

She shook her head.

"I wish I had never seen one."

"Why?" she asked. "I think it's just wonderful."

He half grinned. "You would." He stared at her, and she felt like she should go.

"Well, okay," Mary said. She turned.

"What's your name?" the old man said slowly.

"Mary." She turned back to look at him wonderingly. He sounded—lonely.

"Mary," he mused. "So much like…"

He paused.

"Like?"

"Like my own name."

Her eyebrows knit together. "I call you Mr. Merry."

One side of his mouth curved upward. "Have you ever heard my whole name?"

She nodded her head. "I think so. Kenan Meria…" She struggled with the name for a while, then gave up.

"My name—is Conan Meriadoc." He stared at her, as if gauging her reaction.

"I thought it was Kenan."

"Has it been so long?" he said.

"I don't know what you mean."

He turned back into the living room. She followed him into the room. "There was a time, many, many years ago," he said, "that I was King of Brittany."

"Brittany? Where's that?"

He stared at her. "Brittany is now part of France." He flopped down on the couch. "Don't they teach anything in these days?"

"I learn to read and to write and to do math, and I learn about the Gods."

"No—" His face twisted. "History?"

She blinked and shook her head. "Why would I learn history?"

He snorted. "When I was a boy, I learned the art of warfare. I conquered kingdoms, and I died a King and an old man." He turned his face toward his television. "Then I was reborn as a young man in this time of Gods. For what reason, I don't know. But when people heard my name, they laughed. They laughed!"

"Why?"

"Because I shared my name with a barbarian and a hobbit."

She blinked. "Who?"

He smiled. "That's right, you never saw a television. Or saw a motion picture, I suppose."

"You were reborn? What does that mean?"

He snorted. "I died, but then I found myself alive again, in the shadows of the large stone circle in England. You call it Stonehenge." He smiled, genuinely. "I remember dying, but then I was staring at a bunch of startled peasants—you would call them tourists—at the end of my spatha." He pointed at a sword on the wall. He lifted his hands as if seeing the spatha in them. "Apparently, I was supposed to be protecting the Gods who had appeared behind me." He laughed, but he didn't seem happy. "They didn't know me very well. They weren't happy with what I did next."

She clasped her hands. "Oh! I want to see Stonehenge someday."

"A bunch of rocks," he said. "The Druidic Gods may have taken them over, but they weren't Druidic in my day."

"What did you do?"

"What could I do? I thought I was reborn to lead my people to victory. I was famous for a while, then when I wouldn't play the games the Gods wanted me to play, people forgot about me." His shoulders slumped. "Or they laughed at me, so instead, I learned to hide my name, I again swore grudging fealty to Brân Fendigaidd in exchange for my silence...." He stopped, looked at her, then continued, "... and I got a job. And a room. And a television." He looked up at her. "I don't know why I'm telling you this. You don't understand what I'm saying."

"I'm not a baby," she said, glaring up at him.

"No," he said, smiling. "You're not."

"People make fun of my name, too," she said, looking down at the ground.

He snorted. "I suppose they would, 'mother of Jesus.'"

She smiled at him. "You're funny." She hesitated a moment. "I don't know Jesus."

"What God do you follow?"

"I haven't decided yet. I don't have to follow a God until I'm fifteen, my parents said. But I think I'm going to follow the Goddess Dôn. She's the fertility Goddess."

He snorted. "Ah. Dôn. Yes." He frowned, then he turned toward her. "Why did you check on me?"

"I dunno. I thought you screamed."

He sat in the other chair. "I was frustrated."

"Why?"

"I don't know. Of life. At inaction. At my life." He glared at the television. "And I'm tired of television."

"I thought I heard you fall."

"That was on the television." One side of his mouth turned up. "I thought you were scared of me." She stared at him. "I've seen you sneak past my door."

She stared up at him. "I *was* scared of you."

"Well, you're an honest girl, at least."

"Until I started talking to you."

He sat down in a chair, heavily. "How far I have fallen," he muttered to himself, "when I can't even scare a little girl."

"Do you want to scare little girls?"

He smiled. "No. Not really."

"If you came from France, how do you speak English so well?"

"Ten years of television and divine intervention," he said, one side of his mouth curling up. "I originally came from Wales."

"You said you died." She looked him up and down. He was dirty, like he hadn't bathed in a week, but he didn't look dead.

"I was ninety when I died. When I was reborn, I was forty. For a man of over one hundred, I look pretty good."

Mary looked up at the man. She hadn't been scared of him, but now she was wondering if she should leave. He seemed a little crazy. She got up. "I need to do some homework."

He seemed disappointed, and he picked up a glass of water and took a drink. "Yes," he said. "I suppose you do."

She edged out of the room. As she left, she saw the old man look out the window, looking lonely, then she scurried back to her own apartment.

The next day, when she came home from school, she looked at his door and wondered how he was doing. She chewed her lip, dropped her book bag, and pressed her ear against the door.

Yes, the television was still running. She heard some creaks, then suddenly, the door was jerked open. She shrieked and jumped back, her hand over her heart.

Mr. Merry stared down at her, then went back to his armchair, leaving the door open. She stood at the doorway, looking in. "Well?" he finally said. "Are you coming in?"

She walked in the room gingerly.

"I won't bite," he said, "much."

She smiled at him.

"So?"

She sat in the other chair. "I wanted to see how you were doing today."

"I just got paid today."

She shrugged.

"Which means that I'm fine." He looked towards some cupboards. "I bought a Cadbury Dairy Milk. Would you like a piece?"

Her eyes got big. "I only get chocolate on my birthday."

"I never had a chocolate until I was reborn." She stared at him. "We didn't have chocolate in Brittany." He shrugged. "We ate a lot of fish. And some pork from Wales." He stood up and got the chocolate bar, broke off a small piece, and handed it to her. Then he broke himself off an even smaller piece for himself.

"I'm sorry," she said. No chocolate? She stared at the piece in her hand, then started to give it to him.

He pushed her hand back. "That's yours."

"I asked the librarian about you."

"'Librarian?'"

"She takes care of the books in the school."

"Oh. Yes." He shrugged. "I can't read." He hesitated. "What did she say?"

"She said nobody knew much about you. That you were born a long time ago, and that you had appeared out of thin air at Stonehenge."

"I told you."

She took a small bite of her chocolate. "You might have been lying."

He raised his bushy eyebrows. "You are right. I might have been lying." He took a bite of chocolate, himself. "Do you think I am lying?"

"She showed me a motion picture on her computer." She dimpled. "My school has a computer! But only the librarian can touch it." She thought it was quite unfair that only the librarian could touch the computer, so when the librarian was turned, she touched the end of her little finger to it. It was warm.

Mr. Merry shook his head. "And?"

"Oh! And she showed me a moving picture of you appearing out of thin air."

He blinked. "A couple of people were holding up little flat things at me, and I thought they were tiny, useless shields, or some sort of religious thing. I saw those things called 'cameras' later on, but I never connected the two together." He hesitated. "That was really me?"

"You looked a little bit younger," she said. "That was a brilliant sword."

He stared at her intently. "Did it show what happened after we showed up?"

"No. It just showed you and the Gods appearing in Stonehenge."

"Did the librarian tell you what happened after that."

"No. Did something happen?"

He opened his mouth, stared at her, then shut his mouth and looked sad. "The librarian did say something about you." She hesitated, not sure if she should say anything. She hoped what the librarian said wasn't true.

"Really. And what exactly did this librarian say about me?"

"She frowned and said that you cut the tongues out of women."

He snorted. "Well, that wasn't what I expected you to say."

"She said that was the story."

"You should not believe everything you hear. I never," he said, frowning, "cut the tongues out of women. That was somebody else. I was a warrior—a soldier—but I was never cruel like that. Now, the Gods, however…"

"What about the Gods?"

"Never mind. Maybe when you're older."

Mary frowned at that, then she smiled. "I'm glad you didn't cut the tongues out of women."

"Are you now?"

"Because I don't want to be afraid of you." She took another small bite. "Did you have any children?"

"I had two wives and two sons."

"Two wives!" She pulled back from him.

"Not both at the same time," he said. "When my first wife died, I remarried another woman."

"Oh. That's all right, then."

He smiled again. "I'm so glad you approve."

"Who was your first wife?"

"Ursula. She's now a saint."

"A saint?"

"A saint is a good person who follows God."

"God? Which God?"

He stared at her, then he closed his eyes. He looked out the window at the coming rain, and his face was sad. "I think that's a story for another day. You need to study your books now."

"I want to hear…"

"I said," he stood up and sounded angry, "that this is a story for another day."

She got up quietly and went to her bedroom, next door, and listened to him play movies. She thought she heard crying, but she hoped that this was another movie.

The door was open the next time she walked by. She peered along the side of the jamb.

He was looking at the door. "I'm sorry I scared you yesterday."

She slowly moved to the center of the door. "I wasn't scared."

"You looked scared."

She squared her shoulders. "I wasn't."

"What did you do in school today?"

Usually, when her parents asked her this question, she said "nothing," but she didn't think this would work with Mr. Merry. "We learned more about the Goddess Dôn. We learned she had five children, one of which is the tricky God Gwyddion." He laughed at that; she didn't know why. "And her brother was named Math fab Mathonwy, who rested his feet on the backs of women."

"Virgins," he said to himself. "They were supposed to be virgins."

"What's a…"

He stared. "You are an innocent, aren't you? I'm surprised. I thought even a ten-year-old would know what a virgin is. Haven't you heard about it from your friends?" He smiled. "Look it up, but don't ask your parents."

She looked at him, indignant. "Why?"

"Because they wouldn't like it."

"Okay," she shrugged. "Were you going to tell me about Ursula?"

"Actually," Mr. Merry said. "I wasn't."

"Okay."

He went on. "She was a Christian. She was given to me by her father, King Dionotus of Dumnonia, and we were married by the Pope. I wasn't a Christian at the time, I followed Brân Fendigaidd. But he wasn't quite so present in those days; he was a distant God. After we were married, she worked on me to follow her Christian God. Then, when she was on her way to Cologne to visit the church there, she was killed by bandits, along with her traveling companions." He smiled. "When somebody told me after I was reborn that she was considered a saint, and was killed with her eleven thousand virginal followers, I laughed so hard, I cried. Her friends may have seemed like eleven thousand, but there were only twenty with her when they were killed. And I really don't think they were virgins." He fell silent. "She was a good woman, and I learned to love her and embrace her faith. I remarried, but it wasn't the same."

"I'm sorry."

"That was a long, long time ago." He stared out the window and didn't say anything more. She slipped out of the room.

Mary raced into Mr. Merry's apartment. "I saw the Goddess again!"

He looked up from his armchair. He didn't smile; in fact, he looked rather angry. "You did?"

She stopped short. "I thought you'd be happy!"

He smiled, but it seemed to Mary like he took quite an effort. "I'm happy for you. I know you like Dôn."

She stopped and stared at him. "Do you know the Goddess?"

"I've made her acquaintance."

"When?"

"You remember that I was reborn at Stonehenge?"

She nodded.

"You remember that I said Dôn and Brân Fendigaidd were there, too."

"Yes. But she's not a Druid." She went to the other chair in the apartment and sat down.

"Stonehenge is still a place of power, even if it's a Druidic site or not. Many Gods came back from Stonehenge. Most of them came through at London, but…" he shrugged. "I know what I know."

"Including you!"

"But I never claimed to be a God."

"Why were you brought back?"

He sighed. "I wish I knew. I'm just a human."

"Can't you fly? Can you disappear? Are you strong?"

"No more than the usual human. I'm a good fighter with a sword." He shook his head. "Anyway, when I turned around, there was Dôn. And Brân Fendigaidd. And Modron. And Arianrhod. And the rest of Dôn's children. And Llyr. And a ton of the Druidic Gods, most of whom I didn't know."

Her eyes were wide. "You met all of those Gods?"

He winced. "I met the Gods. It took a big chunk of my Christian faith with it when I met them."

"What did they do?"

"Well," he said. "They brought me to Wales. I think they expected me to fight for them. But I couldn't. I was still Christian. I swore fealty to Brân Fendigaidd, just so I could stay in Wales, but I refused to work for them, especially what happened after…" He stopped. "They still keep watch of me, just to make sure I don't do anything. And I keep watch of them."

"Wow." She thought a moment. "What would you do?"

He cocked his head to one side. "I'm not sure. I'm just a man, after all. I have no special powers. I'm not sure what God had in mind when he pushed me back."

"I thought you said—"

"*My* God. The one and only God."

"Oh."

He chewed his upper lip. "The one who hasn't come down to walk among us."

"Why?"

He didn't answer. He got up and looked out the window. He suddenly turned and walked to his kitchenette and got another candy bar. Breaking off a small piece, he gave it to her. "You were telling me about your Goddess?"

"Oh, yeah. She came to school and talked to us again. And she looked at me, and said she thought I would do."

He looked up, startled. "Do for what?"

"I don't know."

"Don't you let her do anything to you." He stared at her. "I've heard what's happened with her handmaidens."

"What happens to them?"

He looked troubled. "Let's put it this way. She isn't as kind as you would like her to be."

She frowned. "She's always been kind to me. The school says that she's good. So does my Mum." She didn't say what Pop had said.

"That's because you don't know her."

"You do?"

"I told you that we were at Stonehenge together."

"Yeah."

"She assumed I was there because of her and her people." He turned away. "In fact, she assumed *all* of the people were there because of her and her friends."

"What happened?"

"People just stared. Actually, a few of them started to laugh, until the Gods got angry and people—died."

Her eyes went big, and she took a bite of candy bar.

"They died?"

"It was a slaughter," he said to the wall, "led by Brân Fendigaidd. You don't hear about it because Dôn—changed the people's minds. But for some reason, they couldn't change me or kill me. So they threatened more slaughter if I didn't keep my mouth shut." He looked scared at Mary. "My God. I shouldn't have said anything."

"They died?"

He turned suddenly toward her, angry. "Yes, they died. For no good reason. And now you need to forget what I just said."

She shrank back into the chair. "I think… I think I had better go."

He turned away. "I think that's a good idea."

She walked quietly out of the room and closed the door.

He was waiting for her the next day. "I'm sorry I scared you yesterday."

"That's all right." She walked up and patted his arm. "I understand."

"Do you?" he said, smiling at her.

"I looked it up." She patted his arm again. "Nobody died. I looked it up in my history book. "

He sighed. "I was there."

"Why would the Gods lie?"

"Why would *I* lie?" He shook his head. "Have you heard what Dôn meant when she said that 'you would do'?"

"Oh!" She did a happy dance on his floor. "I'm going to go to a special school!"

"What?" He looked troubled.

"I'm going away. I'm going to learn how to be a—handmaiden of Dôn."

He was silent, and his face was sad. "What," he said slowly, "do your parents think of this?"

"My parents are happy," she said. She didn't tell him that her Pop looked kinda of sad, and her Grandmum left the room crying, but she came back later and said that she was happy for Mary, never mind her.

"When do you leave?"

"In a few months." She smiled. "I can hardly wait!"

"Are you going to learn more reading and writing?"

She hesitated. "I think so. She said I was to learn other things, too."

"Reading and writing were not important when I was born."

"What would I be doing?"

"Milking cows, baling hay, doing farm work, cooking, having babies." He stared at her, looking startled. "Damn."

"I want a baby."

"You're still a baby." He got up and paced around the apartment. "Damn it."

She ignored his swearing. "I am not! And I want a baby."

He frowned at her. "I was hoping you would learn to think for yourself."

She didn't understand this. "I always think for myself."

"No, you let the Goddess do your thinking for you. Of course, your history books are wrong, too," he mused. "And your parents aren't helping."

"I do not and they are not and my parents do so love me!" She stamped her foot.

He stared at her.

"Well!" she pouted. She was so mad, she didn't know what to say

"I'm sure your parents love you. I would talk to your parents," he said, looking at the sword on the wall, "if I thought it would do any good. Maybe I should talk to Br…" Once again, he shut his mouth and looked at the wall. "I bet you're not supposed to talk to me."

She blushed.

"Right. I know your Mom doesn't approve of me."

She stayed silent.

"Before you go away to your school," he said, "I wish you would read this book to me." He smiled. "It was given to me a long time ago, and you know I can't read. I never learned how." He pulled the book out of the drawer.

She took end and turned it over. "Revised Standard Bible," she said. "What's it about?"

"That's why I want you to read it for me." He sighed. "I would have you read a history book, but I don't have one and I don't know where to find an old one."

She looked at it doubtfully. "That's an awfully big book."

"You're not reading the whole thing. I want you to start with the book of John."

"What's it about?"

"It's about my God."

"Oh. Okay."

He looked at her closely. "Do you think your Goddess will care if you read it to me?"

She smiled. "Dôn is kind. She won't care."

"You just keep believing that," he said. "Can you read it?"

She found the book of John. It was in something called the "New Testament." She started reading. "'In the beginning was the word, and the word was in God and the word was God…'" She looked up. "That's silly."

"It's what they call symbolic." He frowned.

She read further. Sometimes she got bored, but she read a half an hour while the old man listened and looked out the window.

Finally, he stopped her. "Thank you, Mary."

"You're welcome, Mr. Merry."

"Can you read some more tomorrow?"

"Yes." Quietly, she left the room and thought about she had just read. This Jesus seemed like a God, but if he was a God, why hadn't he returned with the rest of them? She shook her head sadly. It seemed like Jesus was about as real as Cinderella, the story her teacher told them last week.

She said her prayers to Dôn, that night, and thanked her for choosing her, of all of the little girls from her school, to be one of her handmaidens.

She wondered what a handmaiden was. Well, she supposed she would find out.

She fell asleep while she was doing her homework and dreamed of serving her Lady.

● ● ●

She read even further in that Book day after day, until she reached the end of the Book of John. Mr. Merry sat back and his chair and stared contemplatively out the window. "Do you want me to go on?" Mary finally asked.

"What did you think?"

"It's interesting," she said. "I don't like Judas."

"You're not supposed to," Conan said. "Is that all you got out of it?"

"Jesus came back to life, just like you!"

Mr. Merry blinked at her. "I never thought of it quite that way." He hesitated. "Do you think he's real?"

"No, I don't," she said. "I think he's like Cinderella. He's not in my history books. I looked. And, anyway, the Gods can bring people back to life."

"Can they, then." He stared at her intently. "Who?"

"You."

He shook his head. "I don't think so. I don't know who brought me back to life, but trust me, your Gods were not happy to have me, after I defied them."

"Do you think your God brought you back?"

Mr. Merry shrugged. "I don't know. I'm beginning to believe so."

"If he did, why don't you go where he is?"

He stared at her until she felt uncomfortable. "He hasn't physically returned, as far as I know," he said slowly. "But you may have something there."

"What?"

"After I first came back, I was taken in by an elderly Christian couple. They gave me that Bible and read the New Testament to me. Before they were ki... passed away, they told me that where two or more gather in Jesus' name, there he is." He sighed. "I never understood that before. I was a King. I had people to pray for me."

Mary smiled. "That's silly."

"Is it? I suppose so. Did you understand anything else in the Book of John?"

She thought a moment. "No. Not really."

He shrugged. "Maybe you're a little young."

She handed the black book back to Mr. Merry. "I need to do some homework."

"What are you learning now?"

"Comparative Gods."

He screwed up his face. "What?"

"They're telling us although some people think that Zeus and Jupiter are the same God, they're actually not."

"What about Odin?"

She laughed. "Oh, he's entirely different?"

"Do they say where they came from and why they've been gone all of these years?"

"They say that the Gods' ways are mysterious, and we shouldn't expect to understand everything."

He barked a laugh. "That's what they say about my God, too. It seems our Gods have something in common."

"No, they're not."

"How do you know? Have you met my God?"

"No." She said positively. She didn't tell him that she didn't think his God was real. "I just know." She hesitated. "You haven't met your God."

"Have you met Zeus or Odin?" She shook her head. "Just because you haven't met them doesn't mean you don't know what they are."

She gave the book back to Mr. Merry. "If you want, I'll read you some more," she said. "Or maybe I can teach you how to read."

He laughed. "I'm too old to learn."

"No, you're not," she insisted.

"I'd rather that you read it to me."

She suddenly felt shy. "I have a lot of homework."

"Of course"

"Maybe tomorrow?"

He looked out the window. "Maybe."

She went back tomorrow. Over the course of a couple of months, she read the Gospels to Mr. Merry. When they had finished, Mr. Merry looked at Mary. "Did you get anything out of that?"

"Yeah," Mary said. "They're good stories."

"Are you sure you don't think that Jesus lived?"

She shrugged. "Yes. I like Jesus. I wish I could meet him. But he didn't come with the gods, so he couldn't be a god, could he?"

The old man looked at her. "That's where faith comes in."

The girl shrugged. "I guess I don't have that kind of faith."

"When you can practically reach out and touch your gods, I guess you wouldn't." Mr. Merry seemed sad, then smiled at the girl. "Thank you for reading."

"You're welcome." She smiled and slipped out the door to her room.

Late that night, she thought she heard him crying. But it must have been the television.

The door was closed the next few days, and no one answered her knock. Finally, on the weekend, when she passed by the day to go to Temple, she saw the door was open. Mr. Merry seemed to be going through his things, and he was lifting up his sword. "Hello, Mr. Merry," she said, stopping just inside the door.

He took a cloth and wiped the blade. It gleamed softly in the daylight. "Hello." He said, then he laid the sword on the table.

"I didn't see you. Were you all right?"

"I had to go see some go… people," he said. "And I found some other believers of Jesus."

"Which people? And why did you see the believers of Jesus?"

He didn't answer that. "I'm thinking about rejoining the other believers," he said. "I'm thinking about moving on."

"Oh."

"What are you doing?"

"Going to Temple. Today's a day of worship for the Goddess."

"Dôn, huh?"

She smiled, radiantly. "Yes."

"Have you asked the Goddess about me?" He stared at her.

"Oh, no! I wouldn't dare ask the Goddess anything."

"I wish you would, someday. I'd be interested in the answer."

"Maybe someday." She smiled. "It's only a couple of weeks until I go to the school."

"Then," he said. "I supposed I won't see you again."

"Oh, no. I'll come home for Solstice and Harvest and those holidays. But if you move…" her voice trailed off.

He snorted. "Like I said."

"I wish you'd be happy for me," she pouted.

"I am," he said. "I'm glad you're doing what you want to do. I just wish…" He shook his head. "Do me a favor. If I leave and never come back, take my Bible."

"Oh!" she said. "I can never do that!"

"You're not allowed Bibles in that fancy school of yours?"

"I don't know." In fact, she did know, because one of her friends told her about a boy who took a Christian Bible to Brân Fendigaidd's school and got expelled. "Probably not," she admitted.

"Then I'll find a good home for it," he said.

"Do you want me to read you something today?"

"No." He went to the counter and found a Dairy Milk. He gave her the unopened bar. "Here."

She gasped. "I can't take that! Those cost a lot of money."

"You can," he said. "But keep it hidden from your parents."

"What if my Goddess finds out?"

"Your Goddess already knows," he said. "That's why she's taking you away from me." He looked sad at her. "I'm sorry."

"Oh, no," she said. "My Goddess wouldn't do that. She wouldn't take me away to punish you."

"Are you so very sure?" He smiled gently. "Are you?"

She saw the old man sitting on the front steps as she returned home from her last day at her old school. She was leaving tomorrow for her new school, and she could hardly wait. Her little bag was already packed, because there wasn't much to pack. Almost everything would be provided for her at school. "Mr. Merry!" she said.

"Surprised to see me out here?"

"Yes," she said. She sat beside him.

"Are you sure you want to be seen with me?"

"You're my friend," she said. "That's good enough."

"I decided that I have had enough of television. I've been watching television for ten years, while working nights in a factory. I wanted to see the sun." He looked at her bag. "So what did you learn today?"

"I learned that Zeus is the father of the Greek Gods and Odin is the father of the Norse gods. And they had a party for me today."

He nodded. "Because you're going away tomorrow." He smiled. "I'm thinking I should go away, too."

"What? Why?"

"To find my God."

"Why?"

"Because I've been running away from Him."

She nodded. "I've heard that the Gods walk amongst us without us seeing them. I just learned that in school."

"They walk amongst us," he repeated, looking up at the sky. "Really."

"I don't always see the Goddess Dôn, but I know she's there." She kicked her heels against the wall. She wished she could give Mr. Merry the same kind of faith that she had.

As if he had heard her thoughts, the old man smiled slowly. "The faith of a child." He looked up. "Maybe that's what I'm missing."

Mary wasn't sure what to say about that. "Do you miss being King?"

"Not anymore," he said. "Besides, this country already has a ruler. I want to know why I'm not dead."

"Oh." She thought a moment. "Can I read my book to you?"

"What's it about?"

"It's about the Gods." She really wanted to read to him. She wanted him to love the Goddess, like she did.

He swallowed and frowned. "Ah." He looked away.

She looked down at her book. "You don't like *any* of the Gods."

"Not particularly. These Gods have feet of clay."

She blinked.

He smiled slightly. "I heard that in a movie once. It means that they are not perfect."

"Yes, they are." Mary was shocked.

"You just keep believing that. You'll get along better in this world than I am."

She looked at him seriously. "Were you hiding?"

"I never was hiding, exactly." He picked up a rock. She waited politely. He stared at the sunset. "I told you the Gods knew where I'm at. They have their spies." He reached around, quick as a snake, and picked something up. Slowly, he opened his hand, and Mary peered into it. A little man stared up her. It was a Brownie. She had never seen a Brownie before, but her Mum told her that they had come back with the Gods and served the Gods and helped people in exchange for cookies and milk.

It had never occurred to her that they talked to the Gods. She smiled delightedly at the tiny man. "You know the Goddess Dôn?"

The little man nodded.

"Brilliant," she said. "Do you take my prayers to her?"

He nodded again and smiled, then glared up at Mr. Merry.

"Thank you," she whispered.

Mr. Merry closed his hand as if he were going to squeeze the Brownie. "And—do you report of my whereabouts to the Goddess Dôn?"

"And to Brân Fendigaidd," the little man said with a sneer. "You know I do."

"I do. Tell him this," Mr. Merry said. "I'm through with the Gods. I throw my allegiance with the one and only God. I revoke my fealty."

"You'll regret that."

"No," Mr. Merry said. "He'll regret that. Especially if the Goddess Dôn hurts my friend. She needs to remember that I know what she did, and especially what Brân did. "

The Brownie looked at Mary. "She is protected by the Goddess. She will not go back on her word."

Mr. Merry raised his eyebrows. "I've seen how Dôn 'protects' humans." He shook the Brownie. "Take him my message."

"All right. All right! Geez," the Brownie said. With a sigh, Mr. Merry placed the little man down gently. The little man scurried into the walls.

The man chewed his lip. Mary didn't know why. "I hope that works. Maybe I should pray to my God."

"I think you should," Mary said. "You should, right now."

"Little Mary, perhaps I should. Lord," he said to the sky. "We are losing. Where are you?" He waited for a moment, then looked thunderstruck, as if a thought just occurred to him. "Oh," he said, slowly.

She stared up at him "Did your God just talk to you?"

"He did."

"What did he say?"

"He said that I've been sitting on my ass long enough."

She frowned. "Your God swears a lot."

He laughed. "He didn't put it quite that way."

She looked out at the sunset. It lit the sky in purple and gold and blue. She wondered which God was there at the sunset. "So what are you going to do now?"

He put a soft hand on the girl's shoulder. "I'm going away to fight your Gods."

She felt a shock go through her. "You can't do that!"

"Why not, mother of Jesus? Gods fight Gods all of the time."

She was confused. "Yes, but…"

"But I'm not a God?" He looked up into the sky. "There is only one God. All these are pretenders. And I can fight against pretenders."

She fingered the necklace she had received from the Goddess. "What are you going to do now?" she repeated.

"My God told me to be like Paul and start spreading the world of God."

She felt sad. "You're still leaving?"

"I need to." He put a hand on her shoulder. "I've known I should for a long time. I just needed someone to give me a push to convince me."

"Did I do that?" She didn't mean to push anybody. She felt empty inside. "I'll miss you."

"Child," Conan said. "You barely know me." He laughed. "And you were going away to school anyway."

A small tear went down her face. "I know you well enough."

He started walking down the street.

She ran after him. "Are you going now? What are you going to do with your stuff?"

He snorted. "I don't need it."

She lunged forward, then the child of the Goddess Dôn hugged a son of God. He hugged her back, then pushed her away. "Go home."

"Who's going live in your apartment?"

"I don't care," he smiled at her, turned a corner, and was gone.

After Mary had been away at school for six months, she wondered less and less where Mr. Merry had disappeared to. But, one day, when she had walked out of the school for a free period, she saw a ragged man by the fence, staring at the school with a frown on his face. The cold, dense fog swirled around him, and she could barely see his face, so she decided to get a closer look. After all, he was behind a fence; he couldn't harm her.

As she walked slowly closer, she recognized the bearded man as Mr. Merry. She looked behind her to see if any of the teachers were looking, then walked along the fence slowly. Mr. Merry walked beside her, walking down the sidewalk. Both looked at the ground ahead of them, seemingly not aware of each other.

"Aren't you going to get in trouble?" he said.

"I'm just walking beside the fence," she said to the ground.

"Yes, of course," he said ironically. "How is school? I've worried about you."

"Good." She hesitated. There were things that she was told she shouldn't share with outsiders. Not bad things, she knew enough for *that*, just things. And ceremonies. And words.

"You don't have to tell me anything," he said.

She relaxed. "I'm sorry. "I can't even tell my parents."

"That's the way they work."

She glanced disapproval at him. He walked even slower.

"Are you living underground?"

He laughed. "I suppose I am. But I'm happy."

"You are? How could you be happy underground?" She had a vision of a cave with an armchair and a television.

"I'm with my people."

"Good." She still didn't understand it, but if he was happy, she was happy.

He looked troubled. "Learn a lot in school," he said. "But just don't let her take your mind. I'm still trying to find you that history book. The one that tells the truth."

She blinked, and her eyebrows drew together. "What do you..." He was gone. The cold fog parted for a second, and she watched him walk slowly down the street.

What did he mean?

She looked up the phrase "take your mind" later in the school library. Surely he didn't mean that she would go crazy—but then she saw another description. Brainwashing. She had heard about that—the madman Jim Jones and Jonestown, the Branch Davidians, all Christian groups—she recoiled from those books. Those Christians were nuts.

But Mr. Merry didn't seem to be nuts. He just seemed sad.

She sighed. The Goddess would take care of her. Mr. Merry just didn't know what he was talking about.

But still, she wondered.

The next time she saw him was three years later. She had almost forgotten the weird old man that lived next to her parents. She and her friends had turned a corner, and there he was, sitting on a wall, looking around.

"Look at that old bum," her friend, Athena, said.

She looked, and a shock went through her. It was him. It was Mr. Merry, the man with the funny name. He was older, greyer, and, if possible, seemed dirtier than the last time she had seen him.

He stared at her, then smiled. "Mary," he said.

"It's all right," she told her friends. "I know him."

They looked at him suspiciously. "You sure?"

"Yeah. Go on."

She looked him over. He was shabbier, but there was a fire in his eyes she hadn't seen when she was a girl. "Mr. Merry." She nodded. "What are you doing here?"

"Actually," he said, sitting back down on the wall, "I was waiting for somebody."

"Me?"

"No," he said. "I shouldn't have said anything, but you startled me."

"Mum and Pop," she said, "told me that you went into the underground. I thought you had died, then when I got older, I found out what that meant."

He nodded, then whispered. "I'm with the Christian Underground."

"I don't understand why there is a Christian Underground," she said petulantly. "The Gods don't stop Christians from worshipping."

"They don't," Mr. Merry smiled slightly. "But they don't make it easy, either."

"I should turn you in for being a terrorist." But as she looked at him, she knew she wouldn't. He wasn't a terrorist. He was just old Mr. Merry.

"For what?" He smiled at her. "For sitting on a wall? For being in a supposed Christian Underground?" He settled himself back further onto the wall. "I'm not going to stay around long enough for you to turn me in," he said, "So you might as well talk with me a while."

She nodded, and sat beside him, like she had when she was a child. He smelled. She hadn't noticed the smell before. She wrinkled her nose, then decided not to say anything. "What are you waiting for?" she said.

"I'm waiting," he said, "for a man to walk by with a white rose. Then I'm then going to follow him to our place of worship for the night."

"Ah. I thought you were a fighter." She smiled. "When I was little, you said you were a warrior. Don't you use your spatha?"

"I am a fighter. But not with the spatha."

"But—it seems that sitting on a wall seems like an odd way to fight."

"One doesn't have to be anyplace in particular to fight," he said. "In my case, I can't stay for long anywhere between Wales and Brittany." He sighed and deep, ragged breath. "Did you know," he continued distantly, "that I'm now a symbol?"

Her eyebrows crinkled. "But you're just a man." A smelly man, she thought to herself.

"I was raised from the dead," he spoke simply, with wonder in his voice. "I had never thought of that before I left here. They call me a miracle."

"Mum said that we are all miracles. That life is a miracle created by the Gods."

"Do your Gods raise people from the dead?"

"No. They judge the dead, but I've never heard of anyone raising…"

"Because they can't. Only the one true God can raise people from the dead."

She got up. "This is heresy. I can't listen."

"Why?"

"It's against our creed."

"The truth shall make you free."

"I don't want to be free. And I don't believe it's the truth." She hesitated. "I'm pregnant."

He opened his eyes wide. "What? Damn. Who?"

"Artificial insemination."

"What does that mean? You mean a man… Did someone hurt you?"

"No," she said. "No man has touched me. The child will be the child of Brân Fendigaidd."

"Were you… hurt?"

"No." She held her hand protectively over her belly. "It's a great honor to carry the child of the God Brân Fendigaidd."

"So," Mr. Merry said, pursing his lips. "He has kept the letter of his word. He did not touch you and he did not hurt you." He sighed. "You are a virgin."

"The God Brân has blessed us."

"And why is he raising such an army?" He looked thunderstruck, then shook his head, then thought again. "An army of true believers…" He shook his head again.

"What did your parents think?"

"Mum was ecstatic." She tried to smile, but she couldn't.

"And your father was less than ecstatic, I'm guessing."

"He wanted to storm the temple. I told him I was happy." She shrugged.

"Are you happy?"

She smiled wanly. "Yes." She was.

He stood up. "Right." He turned and laid his hands her hers. "Remember, if you need me, I am your warrior to command."

"I thought you were God's warrior." She tried to laugh. Although she knew the Goddess would take care of her, she was still scared. "Besides, how will I find you?"

"I have my ways." He studied her closely.

"I'll be fine," she said faintly. "The Goddess won't let anything happen to me. I hope, though," she said, "that you find everything you want. I'll pray for you."

He smiled. "And I for you."

She walked away.

At sixteen, she was serving in the temple of the Goddess when the old man walked in the sanctuary. She barely recognized him. "Mr. Merry!" She smiled and turned coy. "Come to join us?"

"I think you know better than that," he said. "I see you still serve the false gods."

"I follow," she said, turning to light some candles, "the Gods who walk amongst us, not those who keep themselves distant. Or are mythical. Like your God." Her face looked transcendent. "I've seen the Goddess four times. She was there at the birth of my baby." She turned to him and smiled. "I didn't hurt a bit!"

"'I believe,'" he murmured, sitting down in a pew. "'Help my unbelief.'"

She smiled at him, puzzled. "How can I not believe when I've seen the Goddess—and the Gods—with my own eyes?" She cocked her head. "That sounded like a quote."

"It's what a man said to Jesus when he was begging him to help his son." He looked up above the altar.

"What are you looking at?"

"When I was brought back to this world," he said, looking up, "there was a cross hanging up there." He lowered his gaze. "I'm looking at the cross."

"Old man," Mary said, mockingly, "that cross was gone long ago."

Mr. Merry tapped his head. "Not in here," he said. "Not in here."

"Is this part of your unbelief?"

"No, Mary," he said. "That's part of my faith. If I can believe in a God I cannot see, I can see a cross that's no longer there."

She stared at him. "I should call somebody else in to talk to you."

He snorted. "Why? You trusted me as a child, why do you not trust me now?"

"I'm older."

He looked her up and down. "And a bit less wise," he said. "Although still as inquisitive."

She didn't mind the insult. "You don't understand."

"Oh, I understand too well." He looked her over closely. "You turned out beautiful."

She blushed.

"And you're pregnant again, aren't you?"

She stared at him.

He tapped his head. "Faith. Faith tells me things that people do not. Another child of Brân Fendigaidd?"

She stayed silent, but looked away.

"I thought so." He got up and smiled kindly at her. "I think," he said, "that God will make something good of your children." He turned to go.

She suddenly felt desolate. "Mr. Merry?"

"Yes?"

"They took away my first baby. When he was two." A tear came to her eye. "I miss him. I still see him, but I miss him."

"I'm sorry," Mr. Merry said. "I'll pray for him."

"And I'll pray for you." She ran up to his side and hugged him. "Are you coming back?"

"Only God knows." He looked troubled. "I just pray that you and I on the same side."

He walked out the door.

Mary's second son was playing by her side in the playground when she saw the old man again. All of a sudden, her son looked up and smiled. "Who dat?"

She looked up. "Mr. Merry!" He was staring at her child.

"Mary."

"Mr. Merry, this is my second son, Paul."

He snorted. "A name of the apostle to the Gentiles. How appropriate. I take it," he said, "that the father had no input to the naming."

"The God Brân Fendigaidd is busy. And my lady said I could name him what I wished."

"Always an excuse," he said, sitting in a swing.

"Are you off fighting my Gods?" She smiled wryly. "Oh. I forget. You don't fight."

"I do fight. Where ever and when ever I can." He flexed his arms.

"I wish I could fight them directly, but I'm forced to subterfuge." He snorted. "And remember, I'm a symbol."

"A symbol?" She had forgotten what he had said before, then remembered and blushed.

"Of a miracle." He looked around. "There may be many of us in this world. I only know of a couple of people like me."

"Who are they?"

"I've heard of three or four others. Don't know their names." He looked at her shrewdly. "I have no idea where they are, so don't ask."

She looked at her child, who had lost interest. He was playing with a lorry on the concrete. "Vroom," he said.

She looked up and smiled tenderly. "I have my own miracle," she said.

He smiled. "So you do." He bent down and laid a hand on the child's head and whispered in his ear.

"What did you say?"

He smiled gently. "That's between me and him." He walked away.

She stared after him.

The Goddess Dôn appeared beside her. She gasped, then got down on her knees. "I'm sorry, Goddess," she said, bowing her head.

"You should not be talking to that man," the Goddess said, gently. "He is not—nice."

Mary glanced up. The Goddess spoke softly, but her eyes were as hard as coal. "I'm sorry, My Lady. He was my old friend." She sat back on her heels. "He is the one I pray to you about."

"Ah," the Goddess said, almost to herself. "Him. I didn't realize…"

She didn't like the Goddess's tone. "He's just an old man."

"Yes. Yes, he is," she said. She smiled down at the girl. "I shall take care of him."

Mary smiled gratefully.

"In the meantime, I'm planning to send you on a little trip."

"Oh, my Lady!"

"I've heard you say that you wanted to see where we came back to this Earth."

She gazed up at the Goddess.

"Yes, my Lady. I have. Often."

"I think," she said, glancing at the door, "that I shall grant you your wish. I'm going to send you and your friend Athena to Stonehenge to make a fitting offering for me."

"Thank you, my Lady!"

"Now go back to Temple and get ready to leave," the Goddess said, once again gazing after the old man.

Mary up, grabbed Paul, and rushed off, then rushed back. "Thank you, Lady."

The Goddess smiled gently at her. "Think nothing of it."

"Yes, My Lady!"

The Goddess disappeared, and Mary was left. She rushed back to the Temple. She was going to Stonehenge!

She was at Stonehenge! She could barely wait, so she left her friend Athena and rushed through the tunnel under A344 from the car park into the pre-dawn mist, looked up, and gasped. She hadn't seen this from the road, it was hidden by a huge hedge, grown since the Gods had returned. Breaking into a run, she ran to the foot of the crude cross. It was built out of rough-hewn logs, and the bark was slick with blood.

Mr. Merry was hanging from the cross beams.

He looked dead.

At her cry, he looked up.

She could see gunshot wounds on his torso, as if he had been used for target practice, and there was blood on the ground. She screamed for security, but they didn't seem to be around.

He looked down at her. "Sweet Mary."

She couldn't tell if he was seeing her or whether he was swearing.

"Conan," she said. "Mr. Meriadoc. Don't give up. We'll get you down."

He barked a laugh. "Don't." He was gasping. "Your Lady doesn't want me down." He looked past Mary. "I have to admit—she didn't hurt me— but she caused it—just the same."

"We'll get you down and get you to a hospital."

"It's too late," he gasped, then smiled. "Dear little Mary."

"Why?" She knelt at the foot of the cross, crying.

"Your gods," he gasped, "are false gods. I threaten—their existence." He lifted his head and looked into the distance. "I spent my first life-time—at war. I spent—this one—spreading—peace." He smiled. "At last, I see my Ursula."

"Ursula?"

"My wife." He smiled.

Tears fell on her face. "Don't go."

"Why, Mary?"

"Because..." she fumbled for words. "Because I don't want you to."

"Sorry." His head fell, then he opened his eyes, looking beyond Mary, then looked down at her. "Llyfr!" he whispered.

"Llyfr?"

"Bookstore in Cardiff. Go there. Tell Jonah I sent you."

"You're going to live!"

He gasped. "Sorry." He looked up, smiled, and died.

Athena dragged her away from the cross. As she turned, she caught a glimpse of the Goddess Dôn standing a few yards away. She was smiling. When she saw Mary, her smile quickly turned to a frown.

"Why?" Mary cried to the Goddess.

"I didn't do this," the Goddess said, looking at the cross.

"But you let it happen!" Mary shouted. "Why? He was a harmless old man. He was my friend!"

The Goddess laughed. "Not harmless. Oh, no, my dear girl, he wasn't harmless, and I doubt that he was ever your friend." Her gaze turned gentle at Mary. "He was against Us by worshipping Jehovah of the Demiurgos, my daughter."

Mary's eyebrows knit. "Jehovah? We never heard about that God..."

"Nor did you need to," the Goddess said. Her mouth set. "He is not relevant."

He *is* not relevant? Did that mean he existed? She looked closely at the Goddess, and it was as if she had seen her for the first time in her life. Mary had always thought Dôn beautiful, but, with a scowl on her face, Mary now saw that she was rather...plain. Her long hair was a mousy brown, her face was slightly pitted on one side, and she had a small scar right below her right eye. Her aspect was far from perfect.

How could Mary have missed that before?

"But," Mary said, hoping that Dôn would explain this and she could keep her faith in the Goddess, "Why? You said I was to make a sacrifice."

"Yes. You see your sacrifice." She gazed at Mary. "Sacrifices must be made for the greater good. And," she said, with a small smile. "He finally learned what his religion required. Rather fitting, I think."

Mary now knew what sacrifice the Goddess—that Dôn!—was talking about. For a minute, her hate flared up and she jerked upwards, then she looked at the broken body on the cross. She couldn't defy Dôn.

At least, not now. Not now.

She stared at the body. Mr. Merry had died telling the truth as he saw it. Dôn had silenced him because he was trying to spread his truth.

And she was going to find out her truth, even if it meant fighting the gods she had believed in all of her life.

She felt cold.

She couldn't leave her babies, though. Could she? They were innocent now, but they were the children of a God. Would they grow up to be kind, or would they grow up to be cruel?

Not if she had anything to do with it. She swore that on the body of Mr. Merry.

Brân Fendigaidd appeared. For a second, Mary looked imploringly at Brân, then down to the ground. His eyes were as cold as Dôn's.

How could she ever have thought the Gods were kind? They had just allowed her friend to be killed!

How could he be the father of her sweet babies?

She would have to find the bookstore. Conan was right. It was time she decided for herself.

But not right this second.

She lowered her head and fell to her knees again, seemingly submissive. She had her babies to think about. But she could feel her fists clenching.

After five minutes, the security squad ambled up.

Much later, when the Goddess seemed to trust her again, Mary slipped out of the Temple. The night was moonless, and she kept looking around furtively, hoping that the Gods were not following her. She felt guilty for slipping out of the temple and away from her son, but Conan had given his life to give her this advice.

She slipped into the dusty-looking shop called "Llyfr," not seeing anyone around. The light was low, and the man behind the counter looked up, startled. She looked around. It was a bookshop, and it had the standard books—books on herbology and astrology, the latest *Gods* magazine sitting beside the *People* magazine, wands and crystal balls and sachets of fragrant herbs. "May I help you?"

"Are you Jonah?"

The man glanced about, then nodded.

"Conan Meriadoc sent me," she said nervously.

"You are Mary?"

She nodded. He stared at her temple garments, then dropped to the floor on his knees. She gasped, but he was pulling up a floorboard. Getting up, he handed her a couple of old books and blinked. "I heard about Conan," he finally said. "He said you would be coming someday and to leave these for you."

"He was a neighbor," she said lowly. She stared at one of the books. "It's Mr. Merry's Bible. But what is the other one?"

Jonah smiled. "It's a history book from thirty years ago. From before the Gods' return. He said you might come, and he wanted you to have it to learn the truth about the world, or," he grinned, "at least the history that wasn't altered by the Gods. I think he knew he was going to die." He looked her over again. "Keep them well hidden. Start reading where the bookmark is. If you decide not to read it, I ask that you bring them back so that someone else can read it."

Curious, she opened the front page of the Bible. "In the Beginning was the Word, and the Word was with God…" She looked up solemnly. "Are there more books like these?"

"Quite a few. At least those hidden from the Gods." He sighed. "They've destroyed quite a few."

"They did?"

"Yes."

She set her mouth, angry again.

"And people, too? Besides Conan?"

"Oh, yes."

She clutched the books to herself. "Thank you. I vow to read them and learn."

The man smiled and stomped down the board. "That's all he asked. I'll be here."

"I will come back." she smiled back. She left the shop and walked into the night. But, as she walked, she could see Mr. Merry smiling at her, and she smiled back.

"I'm learning about the truth," she whispered.

"Good," he said on the wind, then he was gone.

In Foreign Fields

by David McDonald

The man across the counter from Smythe had no idea how close he was to death.

"I am afraid that you don't have the necessary visa, Mr. Smythe. I'm sorry, there is nothing I can do."

He didn't look sorry to Smythe; in fact, Smythe could have sworn there was gleam of satisfaction in his piggy little eyes.

Smythe tried to be reasonable. He took a deep breath, and counted to ten, taking a brief moment to re-examine the man in front of him, hoping to find something pleasant, some sort of connection. But, try as he might there was nothing about the man he liked. He was dressed in a Customs Officer's uniform that appeared to be at least a size too small, giving him the look of an overcooked sausage threatening to split its casing. Smythe would have been willing to overlook the man's appearance had he been helpful and friendly. Instead the man had seemingly delighted in being as obstructionist as possible, poring over Smythe's passport until he had found an error.

Smythe didn't know whether it was anything personal, or whether the official was one of those men to be found in every city in the world, the sort of man who had been given a small amount of authority and had let the power go to his head. The small golden badge on the man's collar in the shape of a wreath of grapevines led Smythe to think that it might be religiously motivated; the ornament was a sign that the officer was a devotee of Bacchus.

"Look, there has obviously been some sort of clerical mistake. But surely it can be sorted out. I am here on business of the Court of the Tuatha de Danaan, after all."

A red flush had crept up the other man's neck, and when he spoke his voice was thick with anger.

"Look, mate, I don't care whose business you are on. You're in Australia now and we don't take orders from your kind here. You might be a big deal where you come from and able to push people around, but here you're just another Pommie bastard and as far as I am concerned you can get on the next plane back home."

That was enough for Smythe. He leaned forward and placed his hands on the edge of stainless steel counter, and *squeezed*. His fingers dug into the metal, slowly but inexorably crumpling it into a new shape. The customs man looked down and the flush left his cheeks, leaving him a ghostly white. People around them looked up at the tortured screeching of the metal, but they quickly found other things to occupy them.

"Now that you have that out of your system, *mate*, let me tell you how this works," Smythe said. "You have two choices right now. Either you stamp my passport and I go on my way, or I reach over and twist your head around until it pops off your shoulders. What's it going to be?"

"You can't threaten me!" Smythe had to hand it to the man, he was tougher than he looked. There was a hint of fear in his voice, true, but it was hidden under a thick layer of righteous outrage. "I'm an official of the Australian government; if you touch me they'll have your head."

Smythe smiled, the expression completely devoid of humour.

"No, what will happen is that your government will send my government a sternly worded memo, and my government will profusely apologize and give me a slap on the wrist before sending me on my next mission." Smythe leaned even closer to the official, who shrank back. "You, however, will still be dead."

Wordlessly the other man stamped the passport and handed it to Smythe.

Smythe had only been in Melbourne for a day and already he wanted to go home. On the surface, it was quite a beautiful city, particularly by night. The skyline was dominated by the clean lines of modern skyscrapers, glowing beneath the clouds, but many of the older buildings were still in place, adding a sense of history. It was, of course, a mere blink of the eye compared to the weight of history that hung over London, where you could walk the same streets as the Romans once did. Still, Smythe appreciated the sense of continuity. And, whoever had planned the city had allowed for vast spaces of green parkland, tree-lined expanses breaking up the concrete jungle. Other considerations aside, Smythe could imagine himself quite happily living here.

No, it was not the city itself that made him uneasy, it was its inhabitants. Ever since the day the gods returned, London had known only the rule of the Tuatha de Danaan. They had mercilessly driven out any trace of worship of their rivals, and Smythe had grown accustomed to, even fond of, being surrounded by their temples and symbols. But here in Melbourne was only chaos, a melting pot of cultures—and gods. Already, Smythe had seen a group of Maenads heading towards one of their Bacchanalian debauches, averting his eyes from their smoky glances as they giggled and whispered their way past him. He had stumbled through an alleyway into a street that stank of raw meat and incense, only to nearly be run down by a giant paper dragon that writhed and lunged above the legs of the dozen men concealed inside. Everywhere he turned were the worshippers of another set of gods, and it made him realise how alien this city truly was.

At least when he had visited New York it had been divided into carefully delineated spheres of influence. He had spent most of his visit holed up with a family of British expatriates, only leaving their neighbourhood as his duties demanded. But here there were no borders; the devotees of a dozen pantheons were thrown in together. It was unnatural, even blasphemous. No wonder then his quarry had found his way here after fleeing from England. In London he stood out like a sore thumb, but here he was just another lost soul, one man in a population of three million. Fortunately Melbourne had at least one thing in common with London, and with every other city in the world. If you needed information, and you had money, there were always men and women willing to give you one and take the other. It was just a matter of finding them.

He looked down at the piece of paper he had been given. Considering that it had cost him almost a thousand dollars it didn't seem much, merely a first name and address. If it really did lead to information that would bring him a step closer to the Druid then it was worth every cent. If it was a dead end, though, there was a junkie on Flinders Street who was going to receive a rather unpleasant social call.

When he finally found it, after several abortive cab rides, the house could not have been further from the image Smythe had in his mind. Rather than some beaten-down tenement in the middle of a rotting neighbourhood, it was a pleasant suburban home nestled in the leafy streets of the inner east. Smythe walked up the path, admiring the care taken on the garden. So many people neglected the little things but whoever lived here had a real green thumb. Smythe hoped he wasn't going to have to kill anyone who could produce such beautiful roses.

The front door was a work of art, solid oak banded with iron, and an ornamental knocker that leered at Smythe with a gargoyle's snarl. He responded by putting his fist through it, sending pieces of oak and iron flying down the corridor as the door disintegrated. Smythe stepped through the wreckage, walking into the house and past doorways opening into empty rooms. He stopped just in time to avoid the flashing blade as a big man in a sleeveless t-shirt and sweatpants lunged out from behind the bookcase where he had been lurking, hoping to surprise the intruder. Smythe had known he was there from the moment he walked through the door, though, the man's heartbeat thundering in his ears, the smell of adrenaline a slightly unpleasant scent in the air.

Casually, Smythe reached and grabbed the man's forearm before his attacker could pull back, and squeezed, hard. The man screamed as bones fragmented, the noise cut off as the Englishman hurled him into the opposite wall with a sickening thud. He didn't move, and Smythe continued down the passage, emerging into a surprisingly modern kitchen. A man sat at a large dining table, gazing steadily at Smythe. There was a revolver in front of him but he made no move to reach for it.

"So you found me, Mr. Smythe." He gestured at the chair across from him and Smythe took a seat.

"How do you know my name?"

The man laughed. "If an emissary from the Court of the Tuatha de Danaan arrived in Melbourne and I didn't know about it, I wouldn't be much good in my line of business. I make a point of knowing everything worth knowing in this city."

"That's why I am here," Smythe said. "I have some questions for you, Mr.—?"

"Bruce will be fine," the man said. "You come here to ask something of me, but we've hardly gotten off on the right foot. Have you heard of a little thing we call knocking? Or don't you have that in England?"

"Oh, that? That was just me getting your attention, and making sure you take me seriously. No real harm done."

"My guard might have a different point of view."

"He doesn't seem to be saying too much about it."

Bruce started to say something, then seemed to think better of it.

"Let's say that you have gotten my attention. What is that I can help you with, Mr. Smythe?"

"Let's not play games, Bruce," Smythe said. "You know that I am here to find a man, and kill him."

Bruce didn't even blink. "Yes, the one they call the Druid. He's caused the Tuatha de Danaan a great deal of trouble, hasn't he? He created quite a stir in the newspaper, the bold freedom fighter who's dared to take on the mighty gods."

"We prefer the term religious terrorist," Smythe said tersely. "We don't really appreciate the way your press have made him into some sort of hero. He's simply another fanatic who has deluded himself into believing he can overthrow the British government through acts of terror. The name gives him away; he's some sort of Neo-Pagan wannabe."

"You don't really understand Australians, do you? We're all very anti-establishment, here. Just look at our national heroes; we sing songs about sheep thieves and bushrangers and make TV series about drug pushers from the western suburbs," Bruce said with a smile. "The Druid is just the kind of underdog we love."

"And is that why you helped him?"

Bruce stopped smiling. "Don't be silly. I helped him because he paid me. Sentimentality doesn't make for good business."

Smythe reached into his pocket and pulled out a fat envelope. "And how much will it cost me to find out where you sent him?"

Bruce looked at the envelope with naked greed before shaking his head.

"I'm sorry, Mr Smythe, but if word got out that I had told you my reputation would be ruined. My clients pay for discretion as much as for anything."

Bruce seemed remarkably calm for a man in his position. Smythe thought about what the other man must see when he looked across the table at his visitor. Just an average man, of unremarkable height, fit and lean rather than overly muscled, with short sandy hair and nondescript features. Dangerous, yes, given what he had done to the guard and with his reputation, but Smythe guessed that Bruce dealt with a great many dangerous men on a daily basis. He was sure that Bruce trusted his own ability to deal with most situations, especially with a gun within easy reach. Smyth decided it was time for an object lesson.

As quick as a snake, Smythe's hand darted out and snatched the pistol from in front of the other man. Bruce flinched, but relaxed slightly as Smythe hit the magazine release, sending the magazine clattering to the table, then worked the slide to empty the chamber.

"Bruce, what good is a reputation to a man who is going to spend the rest of his life eating through a straw, and using his eyelids to signal a nurse to wipe his arse?"

"What? You can't threaten me, you Pommie bastard." The layer of civility was gone from Bruce's voice. "You aren't in London now, this is *my* city."

Smythe didn't respond, but merely held the gun up in front of Bruce in both hands. Taking a firm grip he twisted, tendons standing out on his forearms, the metal groaning as the frame began to buckle. The walnut inlays of the grip snapped and cracked as he continued to exert pressure, Bruce's eyes bulging as Smythe reshaped the weapon into nothing more than an abstract sculpture of wood and steel.

"So, Bruce, how about you tell me where I can find him?"

There was a cold sweat on the other man's forehead, and he looked as if he was about to throw up. Smythe knew that he had broken him.

"I don't know exactly, I swear," Bruce said. "I arranged transport to one of the smaller cities, but I don't know where exactly he would go when he got there, or whether he would be hanging around."

Smythe leaned forward slightly, and the other man flinched back as if Smythe had raised his fists.

"Are you lying to me, Bruce?" Smythe asked. "I don't like it when people lie to me."

"No!" Bruce sounded as if he was about to cry. "That's all I know, I promise! Please, don't."

Smythe rubbed the talisman hanging around his neck. If he could get close enough to his target its magic would lead him the rest of the way.

"So, Bruce, tell me about this transport."

Even in the early hours of the morning, when most civilized people were in bed, the Queen Victoria's Markets were a hive of activity. Crates of vegetables were being unloaded from the backs of trucks, and harried shopkeepers bustled about getting their stalls ready for the morning crowd. There was an almost tangible aura of excitement that hung in the air, the same feeling Smythe had felt when visiting friends in the dressing rooms before a big show, as if everything was building towards that moment when the curtain goes up. Smythe wondered for a moment what it would be like when the customers arrived, the sound of haggling filling the air and the smell of everything from fish to turnips combining to overwhelm the senses. But, he would be long gone by then, and might never set foot here again.

There was no sense of joyful anticipation amongst the men who shared the flatbed of a battered old truck with Smyth. Benches had been mounted along the inside of the tray, with enough room that each of the four men could sit facing outwards. None of them had spoken to Smythe yet, but hard eyes had measured him as the driver had shown him to his place in the truck. Smythe had seen their kind before, cold, competent men who would still be dangerous even without the sawn-off shotguns cradled in their hands. They were not the sort of men to easily show fear, and the absence of joking or boasting that would usually accompany such a group before any sort of mission worried even Smythe.

The truck started with a truly awful grinding of gears, leaving a thick cloud of smoke in its wake as it headed west out of the city. Smythe had been told that it was heading to the settlement Bruce had mentioned to pick up a load of gourmet olives, and it had been a simple thing to slip a fifty to the driver and hitch a ride. He'd even been given a shotgun of his own. Once he had narrowed the distance enough, his talisman would let him zero in on his quarry.

The men around him were talking quietly amongst themselves, handing around cigarettes and filling cups of coffee from a battered thermos. The man next to Smythe looked at him and hesitated, then passed the Englishman the flask.

"I'm Harry," he said, extending his hand.

Smythe took it. "Smythe."

"So, Bruno finally loosened the purse strings enough to hire another gun." Harry shook his head. "Wonders will never cease. Still, I'm not complaining, the more the merrier as far as I am concerned."

"Sorry, but I'm just along for the ride. I won't be hanging around."

"That's a real shame. The last trip was pretty hairy—we only just made it back in one piece."

Smythe leaned forward. "Is it really that dangerous out there? I thought it was just the usual old wives' tales."

Harry shuddered. "Oh, they have no idea here in the city what it is like out there. I mean, we do our best to keep the roads clear, and the towns and the bigger farms are pretty well warded, but once you get out in the bush then it's a different world. There are things out there that hate us. Sometimes, if you are unlucky, they get sick of waiting and they try attacking travellers."

Smythe gestured around him. "Hence the guards, and the guns?"

"Exactly! But, we really shouldn't be travelling alone like this. I keep telling Bruno that, but he is too much of a tight arse to pay the caravan fees." Harry spat on the floor of the tray. "It's not Bruno who is risking his life on a run for olives though, is it?"

Smythe looked around. Each of the men wore the emblems of a different pantheon. Smythe could make out the thunderbolts of Zeus on one man's collar, while another had the sinuous golden form of a celestial dragon tattooed around his neck in such elaborate detail that it seemed ready to fly away—or strangle its host. Harry wore a pendant of golden wire, bent into a complex knot, that showed that he and Smythe shared allegiances.

Smythe made sure that his voice was low enough that only Harry would hear him.

"And it doesn't bother you, working with heretics?"

"You'd think it would, but out here it doesn't seem to matter as much. The gods of this land don't make any distinction between someone who follows Zeus or Ogma, they hate us all equally. To them we are all invaders; no, we are vermin to be wiped out." Harry shrugged. "I can't say I blame them, really. Imagine if you were invaded, your country taken away from you, and you were forced to eat shit for hundreds of years. And, then one day, you were given the power to take some sort of revenge. Wouldn't you use it?"

Smythe had no answer to that.

Smythe was half asleep when the talisman suddenly flashed red hot, the pain jerking him into awareness. He scrabbled desperately at his chest before he realized that the heat had already dissipated and that there was no physical damage. Even after all these years he still wasn't used to the way magic ignored the laws of the real world.

"Stop the truck!"

It took a few more hard knocks to the rear window of the truck's cabin before it came to a stop. Smythe noticed that the driver didn't pull it onto the shoulder, but left it idling in the middle of the road.

"What in the hell?"

Smythe could tell the driver was angry, but frankly he didn't care. The Druid was close, ten miles or so, which meant that Smythe would now be able to use the talisman to track him. Already he could feel it tugging at him, trying to lead him into the bushland, which meant from here he would have to rely on his own two feet.

"Thanks for the ride, but I'm getting off here."

As Smythe prepared to leap to the ground below a hand grabbed his sleeve. He spun around, ready to strike out, then relaxed as he saw Harry's concerned face.

"Man, you don't want to do that. Do you have a death wish?" Harry asked. "There are things out there that will love chowing done on you."

Harry recoiled from the expression on Smythe's face. Behind him, the Zeus worshipper forgot his new god and made a much older sign to avert evil.

"It's not me that has to be scared, Harry."

With that, Smyth handed his gun to Harry, then vaulted over the side of the truck bed and was gone into the darkness.

It didn't take Smythe long to realize that there were other things that walked in the darkness around him. His skin crawled from the feeling of hostile eyes on him, and he could sense their wariness towards the stranger in their midst, and an uncertainty about what his capabilities might be. They could feel the power that he harbored, and for now seemed unwilling to risk confronting him. But, he could almost taste the malice that bore down on him, the way that he was out of place, an interloper. It was all the same to Smythe, he had his mission and he didn't care whether he was welcome or not. Still, the cold weight of the machete in his hand was a comforting presence.

But, if he were to be completely honest, the aura of hostility made him a little uneasy. Back home Smythe was used to nature being his friend. The woods of England belonged to the Tuatha de Danaan and as their instrument he was an ally. Had he been on his home turf the birds themselves would have brought him news of his prey, and the trees would have whispered where to find sweet fruits and pure water. Here, though, the world around him seemed to be actively against him, branches falling just so to block his path and vines tangling around his feet as he pushed through. With each swipe of his blade he carved through wood that seemed to be screaming just below the range of even his hearing.

These were more inconveniences than anything, though, and only once did he feel any real sense of danger. As he walked along the banks of a reed-choked lake he became aware of two lambent green eyes the size of tea saucers that glowed with a ravenous hunger. A coughing roar echoed across the water, there was the sound of splashing as if some huge bulk was moving towards him. Judging by the space between those eyes, whatever it was it was *big*, and tangling with it was not going to help him fulfil his mission. Smythe decided to move on quickly, and the sounds receded into the distance.

Smythe approached the next water hole he found with a little more caution, but pulled up short as he was confronted with the sight of four beautiful young women frolicking in the water. Forgetting stealth, he hurried down the banks, twigs snapping under his suddenly clumsy feet. Gay laughter cut off abruptly as the girls looked in his direction and suddenly they were gone, in their place four black swans launching from the water on beating wings. By the time he reached the bank only ripples remained, and he could merely watch as they wheeled across the sky, silhouetted against rapidly lightening sky. Pulled onwards by the urging of the talisman, Smythe continued on his way.

As the sun rose, so did the temperature and Smythe was soon dripping with sweat as he walked on. Compared to home, this place was a desert, instead of cozy woods and lush green fields he was surrounded by wild scrub that looked like it had never known the hand of cultivation. The occasional towering gum tree punctuated low, squat trees with vicious thorns, and soil was sandy and unwelcoming, barely covered by scraggly dry grass. Even in the shade there was little relief from the heat, and Smythe found himself growing faint. Staggering, he threw out a hand to steady himself against a tree. Within seconds, he felt as if red-hot needles were piercing his skin, and looking down he saw that his hand was covered in ants.

As he frantically brushed them off, Smythe did a double take, his jaw dropping. Each of the ants had a human head, tiny faces mouthing words in a language he could not understand, the angry looks making the meaning clear. Swearing, he trampled as many of them as he could reach into the dust, ignoring their high-pitched squeals of pain. Finally, he had removed the last one, leaving his hand covered in rapidly swelling lumps. What sort of country was this, where everything seemed determined to do him harm? Shock flared as he realized what the throbbing in his hand meant. Nothing this side of a demigod should have been able to break his skin. Thinking back, Smythe realized he had been growing weaker, and more vulnerable, with each day he spent in this godforsaken country. The sooner he could go home, the better.

His thoughts were brought to a crashing halt as his talisman flared with radiant heat at the same moment he stepped into a large clearing amidst the trees. There, in its center, the Druid waited for him.

"So, they sent the Sword of Ogma to deal with me. I guess I should be flattered."

His voice was a flat rumble, exactly what Smythe would expect from a man who looked like that. The Druid was truly imposing. At six and half feet he towered over Smythe, and he had stripped off his shirt to reveal his massive build. His muscles were the thick slabs of a man used to backbreaking physical labor, not the carefully sculpted and molded muscles of a gym junkie. Every square centimeter of skin from his collarbone to his belt and down his arms to his elbows was covered in intricate tattoos, angular runes and stylized animals fighting for room. But it was the large serpent on his chest that drew the eye, tail clasped in its mouth as it devoured itself. Elaborate in its detail, it was a true work of art. Above it, in sharp opposition to the flowing lines of the tattoo, his face was all planes and angles, like a sculpture hewn from living rock by a particularly angry stonemason. In a strange contrast, intelligent eyes took in everything around them from under heavy brows and a completely shaven head.

"It's nice that my reputation has preceded me," Smythe said. "Professional pride and all that. But you must have known they'd send me. Blowing up a few barracks is one thing, but when you struck down Cocidius you sealed your fate. No one harms a god and lives."

"If you are proud of being a lap dog to false gods, then good for you." The big man crossed his arms over his chest, muscles writhing under his skin. "I'd be too ashamed, personally."

Smythe couldn't help himself, and started laughing.

"False gods? That's a bit rich. After all, my gods have revealed themselves, and shown their powers for the entire world to see. I've seen them with my own eyes, even touched one or two of the friendlier ones." Smythe took a step closer. "But your gods? These nature spirits you revere? They've been rather quiet, don't you think? How many of your fellow believers have to die before they show their faces?"

"I don't feel a need to question the workings of the gods. I simply obey."

"Really? 'Ours not to reason why, ours but to do and die?'" Smythe held out a hand, palm facing the other man. "Seriously, I am not taking the mickey here, but can I ask you a question?"

The Druid smiled, the expression somehow wrong on his face. "Please do. I am always happy to instruct."

"Well, it's like this. After seeing the glory of the Tuatha de Danaan I can't imagine how anyone can think that they can be defeated." Smythe asked. "To do the things you've done, to pull off some of the attacks you've managed, you can't be stupid. After all, they supplanted your gods once when the Celts chose to exalt them as worthy of worship and stamped out the old ways. Why would things be any different now?"

"You're assuming that the things you call gods are the same Tuatha de Danaan worshipped in the old times. Just because these beings style themselves gods doesn't make them divine. Neither do their powers. They could be aliens for all you know. Another quote for you—'any sufficiently advanced technology is indistinguishable from magic.'" The other man's voice hardened. "But all I really need to know is that long before the Tuatha de Danaan were even whispered of, my masters were ancient and even those who served your gods still feared mine. They were the reason the Romans built their wall, why they wove spells into the very stone to try and keep the nameless powers of the north at bay"

"If they are so powerful, why is it that you had to flee to the arse end of the earth?"

The Druid laughed. "Flee? You think I was running? I was *sent* here."

"Why would you be sent here?" Realization dawned. "You heard about the old gods here."

"Exactly. My masters thought that we might find allies here, who would have joined us on that day we will rise up and sweep away the creatures that have infected this world. But whatever this country's gods are, old or new, they hate me as much as they hate you. Fools."

"When you rise up and sweep us away? How quaint. Well, I'm not holding my breath. Neither should you—you certainly won't be around for it."

With that Smythe launched himself at the Druid, hoping to catch him off guard. Big as the man was, Smythe was confident that if he could get in one good blow the fight would be finished right then. The other man might outweigh him, but the Tuatha de Danaan had blessed Smythe with strength and speed beyond any mortal man. No matter what powers the Druid might have, Smythe doubted that a man carrying so much muscle could be that agile anyway; his speed should make it no contest at all. He clenched his fist and swung it at the Druid's face, but before his blow fell a sickening impact sent him tumbling across the clearing, only to be brought to a sudden stop by a tree trunk as thick as his waist. Despite its girth, Smythe left a dent in its trunk, cracks radiating out in all directions.

Smythe staggered to his feet, spitting out blood. The big man was *fast*; Smythe had not even seen the blow coming. This time as he approached he was much more circumspect, keeping his weight on the balls of his feet in readiness. As he got within arm's reach of the Druid, the other lashed out with fists that seemed the size of bowling balls. Jerking his head back, Smythe managed to avoid the first punch, the air of its passage fanning his face. Throwing his arm up he was able to deflect the second one, most of its energy deflected away from him, but still powerful enough leave his forearm unpleasantly numb. But now he was inside the other man's reach and he unleashed a series of quick, short jabs. Solar plexus, over the heart, then throat and chin. The Druid staggered back and shook his head, trying to clear it.

"Not bad for a little man like you," he said, his voice hoarse from the blow to his throat. "But you will have to do better than that. The nameless ones have made me their instrument. If gods fall before me, how will you stand?"

With an angry growl he came at Smythe again, fists held in front of his face, boxing style. His first jab missed Smythe's chin, but it was only a feint, the second one catching Smythe under his arm. Smythe gasped as he felt ribs crack, and he staggered backwards, desperately trying to keep out of reach. The Druid was like a machine, moving forward with terrible and implacable purpose, fists crashing down on Smythe's arms as he sought to defend himself. Again, Smythe ducked in under the bigger man's arms, trying to land blows to the man's kidneys or ribs or groin, anywhere vulnerable. But the short jabs meant he couldn't get enough power behind them to do any real damage, and the other man kept on coming. Suddenly, the Druid's arms were wrapped around him, and horror dawned on Smythe as he felt the true power of the man's embrace.

"Now I have you!"

The Druid began to squeeze, his arms like bands of iron crushing Smythe's back and chest. He could feel the air being forced from his lungs as his ribs creaked beneath the strain, and no matter how he struggled he could not break the bigger man's grip. As black spots began to blossom before his eyes, he pulled back his head, and with one last convulsive heave brought his forehead crashing into the bridge of the other man's nose. The Druid let out a roar of pain and his grip relaxed slightly, just enough to allow Smythe the leverage to bring his knee up into the other man's groin. The Druid's arms went limp as he fell to his knees and Smythe broke free, taking a few steps back and watching his opponent carefully. To Smythe's disbelief the other man slowly rose his feet, face bleeding and creased in pain.

"Oh, you are going to suffer for that."

The Druid staggered toward him, but he had slowed down considerably and Smythe dodged to the side, driving his boot into the side of his enemy's knee. There was a terrible crunch and the Druid screamed, falling to the ground. Smythe darted in, intent on finishing the fight there and then, but in his eagerness he had misjudged his opponent and left himself open. Even after the punishment the big man had taken, the fist that crashed into Smythe's solar plexus had enough power behind it to drive the air from his lungs and double him over retching. Somehow, he found the strength to move away from his enemy, and for a moment they paused, each watching the other, waiting to see who would recover first.

It was Smythe who looked away first, suddenly aware of the deathly silence that had fallen, unnoticed in their blood lust. The everpresent sound of cicadas was silenced for the first time he could remember; even the wind seemed to fall still as a figure stepped from trees at the edge of the clearing. From the waist down it looked like any other man, but from the chest up it was covered with a fine fur, reddish brown with a scattering of white spots. The creature had a head that reminded Smythe of a cat but with a more pointed snout, and a long, prehensile tail whipped back and forth angrily behind it. Meeting his eyes, it hissed at him, revealing rows of sharp teeth.

Smythe tried to rise as a movement to its left drew his gaze, and he felt his heart skip a beat as another creature entered the clearing. This one was obviously female, proud breasts covered in the same fine fur distinguishing it from the first. Then another male appeared, and another female, until at least ten of the creatures, an even mix of gender, stood in an ominous circle around him and the Druid. Behind them, back amongst the shadows, he could make out smaller shapes peering around the trunks of trees.

"Something tells me that we are in a spot of bother," Smythe whispered.

The Druid nodded. "Perhaps we should think about a truce for the moment?"

For a moment, the balance held and all was still as the creatures simply watched the two men, unblinking eyes giving no clue as to their intentions. Then, as if some signal had passed between them, the stillness broke and the creatures fell upon the invaders.

Ash had had a gutful of patrol duty. Six hours a day for the last two weeks, stuck doing a circuit of the stockade that had been erected around the farmhouse and outbuildings. Not that he wasn't grateful for the walls, twelve feet tall and made of sturdy trunks of red gum that had been lopped off into rough points and carved with blessings from half a dozen different pantheons. This far from town you wanted something between you and all the things that would happily tear you to shreds. But why was he the one who had to do the afternoon shift, during the hottest part of the day? It wasn't like anything ever happened then, anyway. It was the night time patrols that got all the action. Just because he was only sixteen didn't mean he couldn't shoot as well as the older men.

A wide walkway ran along the inside of the wall, wide enough for three men to comfortably walk side by side. Every thirty feet was a round platform, roofed over to protect from the worst of the elements and offering welcome shade. Ash stopped beneath one and looked out into the bush. Nothing stirred except for the breeze in the gum leaves, and the occasional bird flicking from branch to branch. Inviting shadows pooled about the trunks of trees, looking cool and welcoming in contrast to the glaring sun. Ash was not fooled; he knew that beneath the peaceful exterior, hidden dangers lurked. No one ventured out past the stockade except in force, heavily armed and surrounded by friends. Ash steeled himself to step back out in the sun, knowing that staying still too long would earn him a clip over the ear if he was noticed. He stopped, and tried to focus his hearing. What was that he had heard?

The sound came again, and Ash felt a chill run through him, causing him to shiver despite the afternoon heat. There it was again, screaming, faint and in the distance but unmistakably human. The screams rose and fell as the wind ebbed and rose, the pain and fear in each note holding Ash captive, unable to run and raise the alarm. He didn't even notice the trickle of urine that ran down the inside of his leg, splattering on the rough timber beneath his feet. The noises went on and on, and Ash wondered how anyone could live through the pain that would produce such sounds. As he sobbed with horror, the tranquil bushland around him seemed to be watching him, biding its time, pregnant with promise and threat. In that moment he knew that the land would always see him as an invader, and that this would never be his home.

Evidence of Things Not Seen

by Kelly Meding

Not all stories have happy endings. Few stories ever truly end. This story's conclusion I will leave for you to judge.

● ● ●

I trim my fingernails three nights a week.

It must sound like a random, banal chore, but it is a useful grooming habit. I'm a baker by trade, and it's easier to keep my nails short than to dig dough and batter out from beneath them every night. I work in the North Bakery with my sister Jocelyn, as we've done since the bakery opened eighteen years ago. Almost two years after we settled here, because it took that long for everyone to organize and turn our temporary settlement into a community—or as close to a community as possible, for all three thousand displaced immigrants who live here in Shanty-Dusseldorf.

Despite its proximity to the outskirts of Dusseldorf, none in the Shanty are born Germans. My family is American. The manager of the bakery is Australian, and his wife of five years is from Canada. As disparate as our countries of origin, we are bound by our ancestral blood. The blood that Odin called back to his claimed parts of Europe twenty years ago, only to leave us here to scratch out a place for ourselves in a country that was ill prepared to accept so many new occupants.

Odin expects loyal worship, and yet he does nothing to prompt loyalty.

I'm grateful for my job at the bakery, as is Jocelyn. Our earnings pay for food and for our half of a house we share with the Burkholders, our neighbors from America. We were separated from the rest of the congregation during the journey to Germany, but the Burkholders remained by our side. And we by theirs. Their eldest son Jaime is my age, and we're expected to marry soon—only we do not love each other. It's expected because of our secretly shared faith.

Odin forbids open worship of anyone except his pantheon. Churches and synagogues have been turned into houses for Asguardian worship. Odin's Wolves are rumored to roam the countryside, slaughtering those who would meet and worship the "Christian God" in secret. So many worship Odin out of fear of having their throats ripped out by Wolves we've only seen in news clips—huge, angry, devilish.

I have no desire to see my throat ripped out, but I will not be bullied into giving up the faith that has sustained my family for hundreds of years. Faith that sustained us through my brother's murder, on the long voyage to Germany, and for those first two grueling years while the German government juggled their responsibility to their native residents, to the influx of immigrants, and to the pagan gods demanding subservience. Faith in the one and only God and the power of His love.

Faith is, according to His word, the substance of things hoped for and the evidence of things not seen.

I cannot have faith in a god who shows himself so blatantly to the world and demands our submission through cruelty and death. And in that, I am not alone in Shanty-Dusseldorf. Be they Mennonite, Anabaptist, or Brethren, the Faithful meet twice a month, for one hour, to worship God and give thanks as we should.

Not even the threat of Odin's Wolves will steal those two precious hours from me. My faith is all I have left of the home long ago left behind in a haze of fire and blood.

My earliest and most treasured memories are of the family farm in Lancaster County, United States. I still see the old farmhouse that housed seven generations of Braders, its wide sweeping porch made for rocking chairs, sewing baskets and hours of friendly gossip. The red barn that smells of manure and straw, its packed earth floor trodden by hundreds of cows and horses. The cross-stitched pillow on my bed, a gift from my grandmother, decorated with flowers and green grass and my name, Robin Brader, in red thread. I can taste the sweetness of iced tea and the sharpness of fresh, uncooked snap beans. I feel the sun warming my skin on many summer afternoons spent shucking corn and playing with my siblings.

I treasure these memories of a simpler life—a time long gone that we'll never see again. Not since the pagan gods returned and destroyed everything that used to be.

We, of course, didn't know they had returned right away.

Rumors of their appearance at the Olympic Games ran through our small Mennonite community like influenza, hitting everyone hard and fast. My parents said little to us children. The middle of three, I was almost ten and therefore deferred to my elder brother Jacob for guidance. He told Jocelyn and me not to worry, so I didn't. At the time, I knew little of the machinations of the gods, or of the changes they wrought on the outside world. I didn't care.

In our small town, only one thing mattered to me: my approaching tenth birthday.

My Aunt Tilda was sewing me a brand new dress made of a blue floral print we chose together several months earlier. My mother was baking her special corn cake for the occasion. My brother, who couldn't keep a secret in a lockbox with a key, was carving a bookcase for my bedroom. We'd have lunch outside with all of our neighbors and church friends, and then Father would play the harmonica. I went to bed the night before my birthday with these pleasant thoughts racing through my mind, so excited I had trouble falling asleep.

I was awake to hear the first scream.

I shot up in bed, heart pounding in my ears, straining to hear the unusual sound again. It wasn't close by, and for a brief moment, I thought I'd imagined it. Or I'd mistaken a dog's howl for a woman's scream. My fingers went numb clutching the patchwork quilt I'd bedded with since I was a toddler. I glanced at the dark lump of my little sister Jocelyn, asleep in the other bed. She hadn't been disturbed.

My exact thought processes in those precious final moments are unclear to me, lost behind so much confusion, fear, and time. I recall hating Jocelyn for being able to sleep so soundly while I tossed and turned, and for not being awakened by the strange scream. I know I made the decision to lay back down and try to sleep again.

And that's when the world I knew shattered.

Hours later, as our house burned and our livestock scattered, we succumbed to the will of Odin and his decree that our people return to Europe and worship him. I didn't understand why we had to leave, but I believed my father when he promised a good life for us in Germany. Not once in my life before that moment had he lied to me.

We fled before the sun rose on my birthday. I had no dress, no party, no cake—only a long trip across an unfamiliar ocean, crammed on a ship with hundreds of strangers. That day my family left behind more than possessions and a way of life. We left behind our dignity, our free will...and the body of my brother Jacob, who was killed as an example to the others.

Jacob is why I chose to resist them.

Kit first approached me after an early morning worship meeting. Our forty-seven Faithful had gathered in the ground floor of Shanty-Dusseldorf's sawmill, long before dawn would streak light across the sky, and there we knelt in the sawdust to worship God. Led by Minister Bucknell, we sang our hymns quietly, but with love and thanks, and we recited Bible verses long ago committed to memory.

The last townsperson to be caught reading from a Bible, print or digital, was hung in the square by the throat for two weeks as a warning. The Brader family Bible had managed the journey to Germany, only to be burned with thousands of others a year after the return.

We became as our ancestors had been before the printing press: a people of oral history. My children, should I ever have them, may never see an expansive field of corn or taste my mother's corn cake, but they will know that it once existed in a far off place that is no longer home.

The sawmill is on the edge of the community border, far from the heart of Dusseldorf and its native citizens. All immigrants are sequestered in Shanty-Dusseldorf, a collection of quickly-built homes and businesses meant to house the newcomers to Germany and somewhat appease the Asguardians. Other major cities such as Berlin, Hamburg, Munchen, and Frankfurt, have a Shanty built on the outskirts—the name coined from American history and another time of great social upheaval.

Despite our disparate origins, many immigrants to Germany found others like themselves and small communities sprang up within the Shanties. A large number of Catholics live in Shanty-Frankfurt and still swear their allegiance to the Pope. And like our small collective in Shanty-Dusseldorf, the Faithful worship in secret.

We also communicate in secret now, from Shanty to Shanty, because of brave men like Kit.

After worship, I left the sawmill alone, one of the last to vacate before the workmen began their day. I love the smell of fresh wood shavings, and the peace in my heart from the hour of worship allowed me to linger longer than was wise. I brushed pine shavings off my linen skirt as I trod up the path to the edge of town, intent on arriving at the bakery early to begin another day of kneading risen dough and knotting fresh pretzels.

He emerged from the shadows between two homes, silent as a thief, and yet not startling in the least. Violence was next-to-nonexistent here, and no one had been physically attacked in years. We were united as a people, in our faith and in our dislike of Odin. Transgressions were dealt with swiftly and harshly by the constable.

"You have a lovely voice," he said. His own voice washed over me like a balm, warm and inviting and infinitely gentle. Eyes flashed a brilliant shade of emerald, almost too bold to be real. His hair was reddish-bronze, and his face beautiful, if a man can be described as such. All sharp angles and smooth, closely-shaven skin.

Still, the compliment did not endear this stranger to me. It made me instantly cautious. "When have you heard me speak?" I asked. "I do not believe that we're acquainted."

"Just now, for a start. And about an hour ago when you sang 'What A Day That Will Be' with your fellow Faithful."

He was smiling as he spoke, but my blood froze at his bold words. He'd eavesdropped on our service, and he was a stranger to me. I didn't recognize him from Shanty-Dusseldorf, and his accent was strange. He wasn't native German. He sounded clipped, like someone trying very hard to hide an accent by overcompensating the loss of it.

"Thank you for the compliment," I said, "but I must get to work. If you'll excuse me?"

"I'd like for us to speak at greater length. Perhaps when your workday is over?"

"We have nothing to speak about, Mister...?"

"Call me Kit. All of my friends do."

"Then perhaps I should call you something else."

He laughed, and the sound caressed my nerves. "Perhaps you should. In order to win you over, allow me to buy you supper at the café? At five o'clock?"

"Save your money, Mr. Kit. I'm promised to another man."

"I don't wish to marry you, Ms. Brader." My surprise at hearing my name on his lips was demolished by his next words: "I wish to recruit you to fight against the Asguardians."

No one actually fights against the Asguardians. Fake gods or not, they still possess unearthly powers that human beings are ill-equipped to battle. I cannot call a lightning strike from the sky. My sister cannot create thunder with the bang of a giant hammer. We fight best through secrecy, through words, and through our numbers. There are millions of us to a handful of them. These so-called gods disappeared from the world once before. With time and patience and carefully planned strikes, defeat is possible.

Consider termites.

Termites are miniscule creatures compared to humans, so miniscule that we give a single termite little thought—much like the pagan gods give little though to a single human. A single termite will do very little damage to a home's structure. A hundred termites working independently may do a bit more damage, a bit more quickly. Take thousands of termites, working as a collective, and they'll weaken the structure from the inside out. Add enough exterior pressure and down it falls.

The trick is to remain undetected until enough damage has been done.

I did not meet Kit for supper that night. I didn't know him, and I didn't trust his intentions. He could have easily been one of Odin's spies sent to trick me, only to have me publicly killed as an example to others. I had no intention of dying slowly and being displayed in the square for a fortnight.

He found me again, after the next worship, and the next after that. For three months, he slipped from the shadows and asked me to meet him. No man planning an ambush would be so persistent, not when other, more gullible marks wandered all around the Shanty.

After his seventh consecutive appearance, I took a chance and asked him to meet me the following evening in the woods south of the Shanty's border. He agreed.

"I'm glad you're willing to listen to me," he said later, beneath the silver light of the half-moon. It peeked through the branches of trees just losing their leaves, casting stripes across his angular face and making his emerald eyes shine. An owl hooted nearby, but we were otherwise alone.

"You have five minutes," I replied. The cool steel of a serrated bread knife pressed against my forearm. I'd tucked it into my shirt sleeve before leaving home, unwilling to meet Kit without some sort of weapon. I simply did not trust him.

He didn't look eager to attack. Physical altercations did not appear to be his forte, given his slim stature. He had certainly never spent a summer tilling a field, or an autumn harvesting the crop. Perhaps he was a teacher of some sort.

"I work for a woman who wishes to see Odin and the Asguardians fall," Kit said. "She dislikes their reign here in the west, and I've been sent to usher her plans forward."

"Who is this woman?"

"I can't tell you that. You'll need to trust me, Ms. Brader, and my intentions."

"I don't."

"Give me time." His lips twitched, almost revealing a smile. He made the termite metaphor, almost exactly as I told you, and I began to see his employer's vision. "I have contacts in many other Shanties around Germany, but not yet here in Shanty-Dusseldorf."

"Why me?"

"I've watched various groups of Faithful this past year, observing as they worship, listening as they speak to each other, and your heart is impossible to hide. Your convictions run deep. I trust my instincts when it comes to hum—people, and I believe in your ability to be discreet and keep this a secret."

My skin crawled moments before something rustled the underbrush nearby. My insides lurched with fear. I studied the shadows around us, alert for unwanted lurkers. Kit seemed foolishly unconcerned. When I was certain nothing larger than an owl was watching, I turned to study him. On the surface, he seemed completely genuine, almost guileless, but no one was such things these days. Everyone had an agenda, or they worked for someone who wrote their agenda for them.

"How do I know this isn't a trick?" I asked. "As soon as I agree, you'll arrest me in the name of Odin and I'll be publicly punished as a traitor to the Asguardian rule."

"Never." The ferocity in his voice quelled all ideas of such a scenario. I may as well have suggested he boil an infant in goat's milk for the reaction I received. He looked both furious and confused.

The intense emotions shamed me and quieted the storm of uncertainty in my heart. "Then help me trust you, Mr. Kit. Tell me something about yourself."

"It's simply Kit." He smiled, and the fury melted from his beautiful face, leaving it smooth and kind. "And I'm not terribly interesting."

"You seem to know much about me. Please."

"I'm not a native German."

"I could have guessed that."

His slim eyebrows arched. "How?"

"Your accent. You don't have the inflections of an American affecting a German accent, or vice versa. You sound...distant."

"You're right. I was born in Japan."

"How long did you live there before the return?"

"Are you trying to make me tell you my age, Ms. Brader?" His smile grew wider, teasing me, almost flirtatious in a way that warmed my chest and cheeks.

No, he wasn't flirting. Impossible. "My apologies."

"No need. I'm actually older than I look, but that's all you get for now. I came to Germany because of The Return, and I've worked for years to create a network strong enough to one day crush Odin and his puppets."

"Do you hate them?"

Kit blinked hard, several times in succession, as if he didn't understand the simple question. "What are you asking? Do I hate all of the returned gods, or do I hate Odin in particular?"

I knew very little about the other gods and their methods of rule in the parts of the world they had stolen. We received only select international news in the Shanties, filtered down from the cities, which was filtered to them through the government leaders loyal to Odin. In some ways, we in the Shanties are little more than serfs to the nobles of the native Germans who live within city limits. We work the mills, work the fields, do the baking and laundry and goods-making. My entire existence, while very much like how I was raised in America, is done here with an invisible chain around my neck.

Odin called himself a god and forced this life upon me. Even the true God has never forced His will in such a way. We are free to choose our faith in God, or to deny it—and God Himself made free will. He made an opportunity for Eve to curse it to her children by telling her of the Tree of the Knowledge. God allows us our lives, asking only our faith in return for His love.

Odin throws tantrums like a schoolyard bully, casting himself lower than even Beelzebub.

I didn't know which question I wanted Kit to answer, so I said, "Tell me whichever is your truth."

"The gods are not equals, and some are worse than others. Odin's fate is intertwined with mine at this moment, so he and his pantheon are my focus. And yes, I hate him."

"As do I." My voice was cold, even to my ears.

Kit flinched as if my anger had physically struck him. He reached toward me, as though to lay a comforting hand on my arm. He froze, then drew back. I was grateful for his discretion.

"I was barely ten years old the night Odin's Wolves drove my family from our generational home and forced us to come here. My brother Jacob was fifteen. He'd always looked after my sister and myself."

"You admired him."

He didn't phrase it was a question. The admiration and love coated my words. "Jacob tried to stop Odin's soldiers from burning down our house. I saw him torn to pieces by one of Odin's Wolves."

Even twenty years later, Jacob's death ached like a festering sore that never rose close enough to the surface to be lanced. I had no relief from the pain of losing him. No respite from the assaulting images in my mind—Jacob's flesh torn from bone, screams that never ended. The odors of blood and burning wood so overwhelming that I smelled them in my dreams for years afterward.

I still smelled them then, lingering in the woods beyond Dusseldorf.

This time, Kit's warm hand did land on my arm. I tensed momentarily, and then allowed the comforting touch. "I'm sorry you had to see that," he said.

"As am I." I titled my chin, raising my eyes to meet his, as confident of a decision as I'd ever been in my life. "Tell me how to help you defeat Odin."

"You were distracted at breakfast," Jaime Burkholder, the man I was promised to in marriage, said to me the next evening. "And you've been distracted since you arrived home from work. What's wrong?"

I'd retreated to the front stoop of our shared family home in order to avoid the chaos of people within, some preparing supper and others relaxing after a long day's work. The air was chilled, almost too cool to be comfortable without a coat, and getting colder as the sun continued its downward path.

I was far from alone on the stoop. We lived on a busy street, with homes built so closely together that only weeds and moss grew between them, and a car could only drive one-way. Fortunately, few families within the Shanty could afford a car so this was rarely a problem. Across the lane, Daniel Brenneman swept his stoop with a handmade willow limb broom. Next door to him, the three Baker children played some sort of game with sticks and pebbles. To my own left, two doors down, a small crowd had gathered for some purpose which was likely juicy gossip.

I'd barely slept the night before and my mood was surly all day as my thoughts remained distracted by my conversation with Kit. My first task would occur early next week, and if I was to be a termite, I had to be much stealthier with my feelings.

Jaime knew me too well to be put off by my bad mood. Friends since childhood and promised in marriage at sixteen, we'd spent nearly the whole of our lives in each other's company. We loved each other dearly but had never been shy in declaring our lack of romantic love—to each other only. We knew better than to say such a thing to our parents. They wouldn't care. Arranged marriages had fallen out of style generations ago, until our scattered Faithful made it necessary again.

We could be excellent spouses to each other one day, when I finally consented to marry. My thirtieth birthday approached, and my parents insisted on an official engagement that day, followed by a proper wedding within two weeks. Kit had seemed to know all of this the previous night, and it hadn't upset me as it should have. He was correct in that marriage would only help my cover.

I hated that my cover would put Jaime in danger.

Jaime sat on the stoop next to me, his long, lean body a familiar presence by my side. He placed a comforting hand on my shoulder and squeezed. "Please, talk to me, *Schatzi*."

"I'm all right. Tired, I suppose."

"Has your mother been pressuring you about the wedding?"

"Somewhat. She doesn't understand why we've waited so long, but the world is very different from when she was young. There is no guarantee of safety here."

"There was no guarantee of safety in America."

I pulled away from his touch, hands tightening into fists in my lap. "We were perfectly safe until the Wolves came, or have you forgotten that night?"

"None of us have forgotten it." He spoke with an anger he rarely showed, and my annoyance wilted under the strain of memory. Jaime had lost his grandparents and his baby sister when the fires began. We had all lost something precious thanks to the greed of the pagan gods.

"I'm sorry. Sorry for my mood, and for resisting our engagement for so long."

"Don't apologize for that, Robin. You know better."

"We should have been married years ago."

He studied my face, and I allowed it. I hoped he saw everything I couldn't say—that I wanted to marry him, even if I could not admit why. I could never tell him about Kit. Entering marriage on a bed of lies carried the potential for disaster, but I had no choice. I'd do almost anything to see Odin ruined.

Jaime shifted down to the lower step, not quite kneeling, but giving the impression. He wrapped his cool hands around mine and squeezed them gently. "Robin Brader, will you honor me by becoming my wife?"

My heart thudded. As a little girl, I had long dreamed of marrying a man for love and raising a family in our generational home. Those dreams burned to the ground with that home, and now there was only a marriage of convenience and a life of espionage. "Yes, Jaime Burkholder, I will become your wife."

We didn't hug or kiss. We were simply agreeing to a course of action that had already been shown to us. Our parents, when we told them at supper that night, were thrilled. In two weeks time, Jaime and I would be married.

"You don't seem happy, Robin," my sister Jocelyn said the day before my thirtieth birthday—the day of my wedding. I was sitting in a chair so she could loop my long hair up into fancy ringlets, which would all be covered by a simple white veil and make her careful work for naught. But she loved hair-styling, and though untraditional, this was her gift to me.

"Nerves, I suppose," I replied. The answer was a half-truth. I was nervous, in some manner, about my first night sharing a bed with a man. Mother had prepared me as best she could for what was expected of a wife, and I knew Jaime would be gentle. As loving as possible with a woman he was not in love with, nor was in love with him.

The full truth was that I was entering into this marriage with a very large, very deadly secret that my new spouse could absolutely not know. Twice this week I had passed along a small parcel for Kit, never asking why or what the transaction meant for our cause. I did as I was told, and so far I had not been caught.

"Do you suppose I will soon be married?"

I had no mirror, no way to see my sister's face and understand the question. She sounded sad, almost wistful. She added a final pin to my hair, securing the short square of white cloth serving as my veil. I turned in my chair and looked up at a younger version of myself—same brown eyes, thick brown hair, oval face. She was pretty, she had a good job, and she possessed a lovely singing voice.

She was also painfully shy. Jocelyn was only six during The Return, and she often has nightmares of the Wolves. She trusts very few outside of our family. Finding an eligible man within the faith is difficult. Finding one with the patience to court Jocelyn will be next to impossible.

"Any man would be lucky to have you as his wife," I said.

"The unmarried men in the Shanty don't seem to share your opinion."

"Most of the unmarried men in the Shanty are idiots."

"Then how am I to meet a proper husband?"

I had no answer for her.

My dress was a simple white frock that I sewed with my mother's help, and I smoothed down the stiff material as I stood. I crossed the small bedroom to the mirror by the door. I certainly looked the part of the faithful bride.

"I'll tell father that you're ready," Jocelyn said.

She left the room and moments later, my father entered. He wore a simple black suit over a crisp white shirt. His whiskers were trimmed and his gray hair cut for the occasion. Behind the scent of tar soap, I caught the familiar biting odor of moonshine. It was his comfort most days now, after losing his job at the mill to younger, faster workers. In some ways, I think Father also lost his faith that day—faith in himself and his ability to provide for his family, as well as faith in the God who allowed The Return to destroy everything we had in America.

No one speaks of the drinking. It's been outlawed in the Shanties, and while no one is likely to cast the first stone, it's better to simply not voice a sin lest you give it more power.

"You look lovely, Robin," Father said.

"Thank you."

We went downstairs together, and into the family gathering room. A few white drapes had been hung along the walls, and in the next room a pretty white cake sat in the center of the dinner table. Jocelyn and Mother stood to the side next to Jaime's parents, his brother, and Jaime himself.

The only person in the house not part of the family was Jonathon Bucknell, the leader of our group of Faithful worshipers, and the only surviving son of our minister from America. He would marry us.

A traditional wedding would be held in our church, with the entire congregation in attendance, followed by a large dinner with friends and family. This was impossible now, but our people in the Shanties found new traditions. Small gatherings, simple ceremonies, promises made to the one and only God and to the spouse, and then a prayer.

Minister Bucknell had married dozens of Faithful couples in the past few years, and today he would secretly marry Jaime and me, in the eyes of God and our family.

Father led me to stand beside Jaime, and we joined hands in front of Minister Bucknell. I tried to pay attention as a hymn was softly sung and words were spoken. I tried to think of the man next to me, soon to be my husband, but my mind wandered to Kit. His other-land accent and unnatural green eyes, and the way I felt in his presence—important, needed, treasured.

I was important to my family. They counted on me for love, support, and my bakery income. I did my best to offer them my faith and counsel, as well. All of that was different, though. It was expected, part of my role as a Brader woman in this household. Kit saw me as something more. An important part of a larger machine working to tear down a false god. He offered me a chance to make a real difference in this ever-changing, dangerous world of ours.

He offered something that felt real.

We ate supper in somber silence, as though too much excitement would draw the attention of the Wolves and put eyes on our religious ceremony, and afterward we cut the wedding cake. Mother and Jocelyn moved into the kitchen to clean up the remnants of supper. Father retired to his rocking chair near the room's only window.

My husband led me upstairs to our bedroom for our first night in our marriage bed.

The dreams woke me. My screams woke my husband.

He held me in his arms while I shook, unable to stop the tremors coursing through my body, as I sifted through the images from my dreams. They had come so fast, one after another, that most were out of focus, grainy pictures long faded. The parts I remembered haunted me.

A woman in white is burned alive on an alter of stone. Three men crouch in the woods around a mangled, bloody body. Something resembling a man-sized cobra stands outside a fancy building and sneers at passersby. A young boy is dragged screaming from his weeping mother, who is held back by two large, inhuman police. A grotesque creature with bat-like wings flies high above a dark, sleeping city. A beautiful white fox the size of a stag darts through a dark, dreary forest.

So many more, and none of them made any sense. Death, destruction, and monsters that had returned along with the pagan gods.

"I'm here, *Schatzi*," Jaime said, over and over.

"I'm sorry," I replied when I found my voice. "I rarely have such violent nightmares." And when I did, they were often about Jacob's death. None of the images tonight involved my family or our violent past.

"It's all right." He kissed my temple. The gesture was meant to be comforting, but I found it irritating. "Yesterday was a day of changes. It stands to reason that your subconscious mind would exorcise some of that."

Getting married and experiencing sex for the first time were important changes, yes. However, I could not assign the intensity of my nightmares to those two things. These were too immediate, too specific.

A woman my age with raven-black hair huddles in the dark, weeping.

"Perhaps you're right," I said. A lie to add to the others. "I'm grateful I didn't wake the entire household."

"Do you remember the dream?"

"No." The small ache I'd felt in my gut the day I accepted Kit's proposal burned hotter with each new lie I told my husband. I despised deceit in others. How was I to reconcile this abhorrent thing I was becoming?

He watched me in the near-dark, as though studying a puzzle to be solved. "Would you like a glass of water?"

The question was so odd that I could only nod. It also gave me a few moments alone with my thoughts. Never in my life had I experienced such dreams as these, and never did I want to experience them again. They were too real, too immediate.

A minotaur pauses at a city crosswalk.

I pressed the heels of my hands against my eyes, hoping to stay the replay of images. Only this one felt new, unfamiliar. Surely I was awake and no longer dreaming. I attempted to clear my mind of anything outside of this house. I thought of my husband, my steadfast Jaime, and the life we were beginning together.

Jaime clutches a glass of water as he stands by the kitchen sink, staring out the window into the darkness.

The image of him, perfectly clear in my mind, startled me out of bed. I stumbled on the rag rug and pressed my back to the wall, my gaze fixed on the open bedroom door. The slight ache in my body disappeared behind a curtain of fear. I had not simply imagined what Jaime might be doing at this moment. Even though I knew it was impossible, I had seen him as he stood now. But how?

"How?" I asked the empty room.

The room did not answer.

We didn't speak of the nightmares the next morning, and I didn't tell Jaime about the constant play of images that haunted me for days afterward. They came at night when I tried to sleep, long barrages of faces, monsters, and places I had never visited. They came during the day when I allowed my mind to wander, to lose focus on a task or action.

I often saw Jaime—working, speaking to his parents, playing cards with his friends—when I thought of him. I never heard conversations or words, only saw actions. Several times I saw my own family engaged in mundane tasks. On the third day, while kneading biscuit dough at the bakery, I saw a clear image of my mother scrubbing the kitchen floor. When I returned from my work, I found the kitchen floor diligently clean and shining.

That day I decided I was going crazy.

"Am I possessed?" I asked.

Minister Bucknell watched intently from one side of his kitchen table. I had gone to him for counsel on the fourth day of my visions. I didn't know what else to do, or where to go. He had listened as I described everything, nodding on occasion, but not speaking.

"Forgive me, Sister," the Minister said, "for I am untrained in the ways of demon possession. Are you certain these episodes are not simply from over-stimulation?"

"From what would I be over-stimulated, Minister?"

He blushed. "The duties of a wife—"

"No, that is certainly not the issue." While Jaime and I had consummated our marriage that first night, we had yet to engage a second time.

My nightmares were certainly a factor, but our marriage had never been about love or passion.

"Perhaps other stress?"

The visions began only a few weeks after I commenced my work with Kit, but I had participated in only a handful of exchanges. None of them had produced high levels of anxiety during or afterward. Everything had been moderately normal until my wedding day. Or more precisely, on my birthday, as the nightmares had begun after midnight.

"No other stress," I said.

Bucknell studied his hands for a long while, and I struggled to keep my mind clear. Any wandering would produce a vision and—

"Are you seeing anything right now?" he asked.

"I'm trying not to. It happens when I stop concentrating, or if I think of a specific person."

"Think hard on your sister Jocelyn. Do you see anything?"

I did as he asked, picturing my lovely sister easily. The first image flashed to life immediately. "She's at the bakery, forming loaves of bread."

"Isn't that a task she performs every day?"

"Yes, but—" The image flickered, changed. *Jocelyn's left arm moves too close to the open oven door. She screams and jumps away.* "No."

"Sister?"

"She's burned her arm. Her left arm, on the oven door."

He squinted at me, as though deciding if he believed me or not. "Shall we walk to the bakery together and see?" He didn't believe me.

"All right. You can see for yourself."

We walked in silence, three streets down to the North Bakery. As usual, it was a hub of activity and consumers, all come for something delicious and filling to eat. I made my greetings to the owners, then led Bucknell into the rear kitchen where most of the ovens were kept.

Jocelyn was sitting on a stool while Annabelle, another baker, wrapped a bandage around her left forearm. Her eyes were wet, and they widened in alarm when she saw me.

"Oh, Joss, what happened?" I asked.

"I burned my arm on the oven door," she replied. Her wary gaze flickered past me to the Minister. "It was a stupid accident. I always pay better attention."

"Is she all right?" I asked Annabelle.

"The skin is blistered," Annabelle replied. "I applied ointment for the pain and to prevent infection. She'll need to keep it clean and dry for a few days."

"I'm really not this clumsy," Jocelyn said. She was speaking to Bucknell this time, though, and her amusing reassurances quelled my concern.

"She truly isn't so clumsy," I said for Jocelyn's sake. She seemed determined to make a good impression on the Minister.

"How long ago was she burned?" Bucknell asked, oblivious to my sister's emerging crush.

"Only a few minutes," Annabelle said. "She'll feel the pain soon enough."

Jocelyn pulled a face, and I smiled. She was fine.

"Mrs. Burkholder, thank you for our conversation," Bucknell said to me. "Have a pleasant day, ladies."

He hustled out of the kitchen without a word about my vision. He'd seen it proved true with his own eyes, and he looked frightened. I suddenly regretted my decision to confide in him. We had no real system of church elders, not like our ancestors had. Bucknell was alone in the Shanty, with no other ministers close by to counsel him. He could shun my company, or he could turn me in to the Dusseldorf authorities—despite The Return and the magic it brought, magic use among human followers was forbidden by Odin.

I could be executed by the Wolves as a witch.

"Robin?" Jocelyn came into my space and slipped her arm around my waist. "What's wrong?"

I hugged my sister, so grateful for her. "Nothing, dear one. Everything's fine."

Another lie twisted the dark feeling in my gut.

Kit emerged from the darkness behind the shed the Faithful had used for our early morning meeting. He was a familiar, lithe shape, but I had no thought or patience for his spy games. The last two days had been spent in a state of constant anxiety, always worried that Bucknell would reveal my secret. I thought of him often, caught glimpses of him during the day. More than once, during those odd windows into his life, he looked up, as if sensing he was being watched.

In some ways, spying on Bucknell was helping me control the visions. I saw fewer at night when I dreamed, and my daytime hours were more focused than ever.

Perhaps personal anxiety was an antidote for second sight.

The other Faithful were long gone, and the street was silent. I ducked into the shadows with Kit, intending to brush him off and leave. In his presence, however, a sense of peace washed over me. Peace I hadn't felt in the week since the first barrage of visions had changed my life. I leaned against the shed, grateful for the peace when it should have scared me.

"Something's wrong," Kit said. "What is it?"

I found myself unable to lie to him, as I so easily lied to others. "I've been having visions since my birthday."

His green eyes glittered in the dark. "What do you mean, visions? What sort of visions, Robin?"

I didn't correct his familiar use of my name. As a married woman, he should address me as Mrs. Burkholder. He wasn't of our faith, so I forgave the slip. "I see things as they are happening. People I know, and people from all over the world, in places I've never even seen in pictures."

"You're seeing the present?"

"Yes. I know it's strange, frightening, even—"

"Since your birthday?"

"As I said before. I've had them all week, and I don't know why."

Instead of being wary or scared, Kit seemed...intrigued. Almost happy. "That's a very useful talent, Robin. Useful and dangerous."

"I know. If the Asguardians discover this, I could be executed."

"Or stolen away for their use."

I shivered. "I'd rather die than be a slave to the pagan gods."

"I won't let it come to that." The ferocity in his words warmed the cold left inside by the grim future awaiting me. Kit was brave and protective, but he was one man against an army. "Who have you told?"

"Minister Bucknell."

His eyes widened briefly, and his nostrils flared. "Why him?"

"I thought I was going mad, Kit. I needed to confide in someone, and he seemed the best choice at the time. I proved my visions to him and, in some ways, to myself. I'm not crazy."

"No, you aren't. You've been very brave, but telling anyone about this was a mistake."

"I know that now. If he turns against me, I'll be hunted down. My family could be punished because of me."

Kit raised his hand, as he often did when he wanted to comfort me with his touch, only to drop it back to his side. He seemed to struggle for words, and I didn't blame him. I had put his network of termites into jeopardy and become a liability, rather than an asset.

"You don't have to say it, Kit."

He blinked hard. "Say what?"

"That you wish for me to step aside as your contact in the Shanty."

"I don't want that. That's far from what I was thinking."

"But—"

"No." He shook his head emphatically, the decision made in his mind. "I have another solution."

"Which is?"

"Meet me tonight, in our usual place in the woods. Midnight."

"I can't."

"Robin—"

"I'm married now. My husband shares my bed. He'll notice if I leave."

"Can you leave the house in the evening? After dark?"

My behavior this week had been strange enough that going out for an evening walk would unlikely elicit comment. "I believe I can, yes. Nine o'clock?"

"All right. Until then, be careful, Robin. Keep an eye on that Minister."

The double-remark nearly made me smile. "I will."

He disappeared into the shadows. Some of my energy returned, and I began the long walk to the bakery and another long day of work. Kit had a plan, and I trusted him enough to see it through. I only needed to survive another day.

Concentrating on Minister Bucknell and dipping into his life left me with a headache by noon. Every time I checked in, he was doing some mundane task, such as reading, scribbling notes, or visiting households of faithful around the Shanty. At lunch, I ate slowly and concentrated on absolutely no one. Food and some aspirin helped ease the tension in my head, and I returned to work.

Bucknell's visits continued into the afternoon, and as my last hour of work wound to an end, I realized his path was moving closer to my house. Jocelyn was not working in the bakery today, because Mother was ill and needed someone to help her take care of Father. My shifting thoughts gave me a new vision focus.

Jocelyn fixing tea in the kitchen, her expression anxious as she glances over her shoulder. Her hair is done up, and she's wearing a nicer dress than

Saturday at home deserves.

The odor of burning cloth jolted me back to my own present. I jerked my dishrag away from the hot oven it had caught on, frustrated with myself for not focusing on the now. My personal now, not on the actions of others a thousand yards away. Jocelyn's dress meant nothing. A ruined dishrag would come out of my pay.

I finished my day without another incident, and I didn't think to check on Bucknell again until I'd walked halfway home.

He reaches across a wooden table and clutches Jocelyn's hands in his. He smiles. She smiles. They have tea set up, but do not drink.

I stopped walking so suddenly that a woman behind me almost ran into my back. She tossed me a dirty look as she passed, struggling to hold onto a large basket of laundry.

My sister and Bucknell were having an intimate moment in the kitchen, without an adult supervisor. Granted, he was a minister, and therefore allowed to be alone with her, but Jocelyn was young, she liked Bucknell, and in that way, Bucknell was more a suitor than a minister. My instinct was to run home and interrupt them. Had this happened a week ago, I'd have done just that.

Except a week ago, I wouldn't have known about the meeting before stumbling upon it. And I couldn't face Bucknell today, not until I'd met with Kit and heard his solution to the problem. I took an about route home, stalling my arrival as long as possible, but Bucknell wasn't budging from the kitchen table. The closer I got to the house, the more it became obvious to me that he was waiting.

At last I arrived, steeled my spine, and walked into my home. Father was asleep in his chair by the window, an empty glass clutched in his hand. Voices trickled from the kitchen, followed by a feminine giggle.

"Jocelyn?" I said.

A chair scraped, and then my rosy-cheeked sister stood in the kitchen doorway. "You're home," she said, oddly breathless for having been sitting a moment ago.

I didn't respond to her observation. "I heard another voice. Do we have a guest?"

Minister Bucknell appeared behind her, his face impassive. "Good afternoon, Mrs. Burkholder."

"Minister. Have you been here long? May I offer you some tea?" As the eldest daughter, it was my duty to ask these things of a guest—even though I knew the answers, and he suspected as much, I had to play along for Jocelyn. She was completely innocent, and I'd protect her with my life.

"Ms. Brader was very kind to offer me tea when I first arrived."

"When was that? If I'd known to expect a visit, I would have left the bakery sooner."

"It was no trouble," Jocelyn said. "Father is in the family room."

"Asleep," I said. Before she could get more defensive, I continued. "Is your visit nearly over, then, Minister Bucknell?"

"I'd hoped we could speak in private, Mrs. Burkholder," he said.

My heart jumped. "Certainly."

I followed him into the kitchen while Jocelyn excused herself to check on Mother. Once her footsteps receded on the stairs, I gave Bucknell my blandest smile.

He remained on the other side of the kitchen table, as if nearness would somehow infect him with my second sight. "Have you had more… incidents this week?"

"Incidents? I'm not sure I understand." I knew perfectly well what he meant, but I was not going to make this easy on him. I'd found some measure of courage in Kit's support, and I held tightly with both hands.

"These so-called visions," he said quietly. He glanced over his shoulder, as though uttering the word would wake up Father and cause him to care about what was happening in his own household.

"Of course, my apologies. No, I haven't."

His eyebrows furrowed in a deep V. "Are you being truthful?"

"Why are you concerned?"

"Because visions like these come from one of two places, and neither is from the Lord."

"And what places are those?"

"Satan and his followers."

The words fell like a blow to the face and hurt all over. I was devout in my faith and my love of the one true God, and Bucknell knew this. Hearing him accuse me of consorting with the devil was cruel—as well as an outright lie. "I am no worshiper of Satan, and I resent the accusation, Minister."

Bucknell barely blinked. "It was an answer to your question, ma'am, not an accusation. And if this curse is not from Satan, then it is given by the pagan gods themselves. You're one of theirs."

I backed up until my rear hit the counter, and I could go no further.

I hated the Asguardians with my entire being, and I was no more theirs than I was of the devil. "I am no one's puppet. I am God's instrument."

"I'm less certain of that."

To hear the minister of our Faithful doubt me scraped my soul and left weeping gashes behind. My eyes stung with tears that I refused to shed in front of him. I had not asked for these visions. They came to me at a time when, perhaps, I could use them to battle the pagan gods laying waste to our planet and our faiths. The visions were frustrating at times, but they were a gift. I knew it in my soul.

A gift from whom seemed to matter not at all.

"Please leave my house, Minister," I said, my voice impressively calm.

"Do not come to our Faithful meetings again, Mrs. Burkholder. You are no longer welcome."

"Leave."

After he'd gone, I shut myself into the bathroom and wept silently. I wept for the loss of trust from a man I'd looked to for guidance. I wept for my sister whose feelings for such a hateful man would likely be spurned. I wept for an uncertain future, and I silently prayed that Kit found a way to fix this.

For my own sake, as well as my family's.

Supper was quiet, as usual, in our joined households. Jaime tried to engage me in conversation, the dear man, and I did my best. He knew I was troubled. We'd been friends for far too many years for my mood to go unnoticed. He also knew when not to push. I wanted desperately to confide in him, for him to take me in his arms and tell me everything would be all right. Even if I didn't believe it, I needed to hear someone say it.

No, that wasn't correct. I needed to hear Kit say it. If he believed, then I would believe.

I helped Jocelyn clean up after supper. She hummed nameless tunes, and I envied her the optimism of the young and innocent. She didn't remember the way Jacob had been torn apart. She didn't understand the loss of basic freedoms we'd endured by coming to Germany. She was so young when we sailed across the ocean, too young to know the difference in the air, in the soil, and in the stars overhead.

In my sister's eyes, Shanty-Dusseldorf was home. In her eyes, Minister Bucknell carried our faith and united the community. I hoped she never saw beyond the veil of youth. Perhaps one of us could live happily.

Jaime excused himself at seven-thirty. He'd been invited to a card game at a co-worker's home, and I wished him luck as he left. He would be gone for several hours, easing my ability to escape for my meeting with Kit.

Everyone had retired upstairs when I left the house a little after eight. The night air was chilly and each breath released clouds of vapor. I took an indirect path to the Shanty limits, weaving down narrow streets like someone on an aimless walk. I didn't know what Kit's plan would entail, and some small part of me wondered if I would ever see my family again. Would Jaime know what became of me?

I hated the idea of breaking his heart so thoroughly, but if leaving my family behind kept them safe, then I would do it without hesitation. Jaime would take care of my sister and parents. As my thoughts turned to him, an image flashed that made my blood run cold.

Jaime tied to a post, a cloth over his mouth, another over his eyes. A cut on his forehead is bleeding. Equipment behind him is silent, still for the night.

I stopped in the middle of the street, skin prickling with alarm, my entire body tense. My heart slammed against my ribs. Jaime wasn't at a card game. He was at the sawmill. I'd been there several times for meetings of the Faithful. I knew the interior well.

Bucknell knew also the interior. He was setting me up. He knew I would come and bargain for Jaime's life. He probably assumed I had no allies, no others who shared my secret. No one knew about Kit. I concentrated my thoughts on Bucknell.

He's standing in front of the saw belt, hands tucked into the pockets of his overcoat. He seems sad, troubled. Nervous.

He also seemed to be alone. I stared down the quiet street, in the direction I'd been going. I should meet Kit and enlist his help. But Kit cared nothing for the people in my life. He would do whatever he thought best in order to keep me safe and to ensure his mission to overthrow Odin—my family be damned.

No, as foolish as the decision was, I went alone.

A word about law enforcement in the Shanties.

As Odin and the Asguardians settled in to rule this part of Europe, they made their power known through demonstrations intended to scare followers into obeying. Heads of police organizations were publicly executed and Asguardians put in their places. Police departments still run

much as they did before the Return. Shanty's have a single constable who
responds to trouble and reports back to the city's main department. Laws
have become stricter, punishments more severe. Most fell into line and
crime rates dropped in every country Odin ruled.

Such an oppressive system only lasts so long. As a species, human
beings are prone to rebellion, hence people like myself and Kit. However, we stay hidden, working as termites do, because we fear the Wolves.
Odin's Wolves roam the countryside, and no one knows where they are at
any given time. We aren't equipped to fight the Wolves because firearms
have been banned, unless granted special dispensation by the city.

No one in the Shanty has ever been granted permission.

Weapons of other sorts abound, though, because we in the Shanties
are the working class. We have tools and raw materials, and we have the
inner strength to do what we must to survive.

The sawmill itself was full of weapons, but I didn't wait to arrive before
finding one. I committed a crime by breaking into a shed behind someone's home and relieving them of a shovel and trowel. I tucked the trowel
into the waistband of my skirt. The cold metal poked into my ribs as I
walked. The sawmill was on the opposite side of the Shanty from my
meeting place in the woods, but I couldn't think about that. I had to concentrate on Jaime.

The hulking building came into view in the light of the half moon,
silent in the gloom of night. The rich scents of pine shavings made my
nostrils tingle with the urge to sneeze. I paused near the door and focused
on Jaime and Bucknell in turn.

Nothing had changed in their positions or their surroundings.

I drew in a long, shuddering breath and held it, hoping to both calm
my anxiety and steel my nerves. All I managed to do was become light-
headed and exhale a bit too loudly.

The sawmill door was not locked. The hinges squeaked. I opened
it enough to slip inside, the shovel up by my shoulder, ready to swing. I
knew the dark interior well from our Faithful meetings. The long hallway
ended on the cutting floor, where long belts carried trees to be shaved,
cut, and sawed into planks. A layer of shavings covered the floor and
cushioned my steps.

I squinted through the gloom, past machinery I couldn't name, and
spotted two figures near the loading doors. Bucknell's back was to me.

Something dark and ominous rippled down my spine, a sense of not being completely alone. Instead of ignoring it, I latched onto that feeling. I allowed it to sift freely into my mind.

It stalks its prey, closer. The prey doesn't notice, doesn't know. Must succeed. Reward.

I wanted to weep at the intensity of hate coming from that vision. I'd never felt emotion from my sight, never had a point of view I couldn't recognize. The creature was made of shadows, of power, and of strength. It terrified me with its shapelessness.

And it was coming closer.

I moved again, only to freeze mid-step.

Bucknell was gone.

I crept forward, keeping close to the largest machines, listening, anticipating. I was no spy, no fighter. I was a wife desperate to save her husband. My focus narrowed in on him, tied to a support beam at the opposite end of the mill floor.

"I know you're here, Robin," Bucknell said. His voice bounced around the mill floor, its source impossible to determine.

I stopped, momentarily frozen by fear. I wanted to duck beneath the equipment and hide, to cower there until the bogeyman went away. But I'd cowered twenty years ago while my brother paid the price. I wouldn't cower tonight.

"What do you want?" I said.

"I'm sorry. They already knew."

"Who knew what?" Speaking to a disembodied voice was beyond confusing. I began inching closer to Jaime, hoping he was tied with simple ropes that could be unknotted.

"About you."

Jaime's head strained toward me and he tugged against his bonds. I wished he could see me, so I could comfort him somehow. So he knew I was trying to help him.

"They came to me first, Robin," Bucknell said. "I swear they—"

His words cut off in a scream, followed by a chillingly familiar growl. A growl I hadn't heard with my own ears in twenty years.

I surged forward, running as fast as I could to Jaime's position. I dropped the shovel at his feet, then tugged off his blindfold. I paused for the split second it took for him to recognize me, and then yanked on the ropes binding his wrists behind his back. The knots were tight, but not hopeless. I was muttering apologies, an endless stream of frightened nonsense that was impossible to edit. Jaime tried to speak against his gag.

The first knot loosened. "Almost there, *Schatzi*," I said.

Jaime roared a noise of alarm. A shadow moved above us. Instinct drove me forward, toward the shovel, in the same instant a hulking, furry shape dropped to the sawdust strewn floor. Wood shavings puffed up, clogging my eyes and nose, and I coughed. I grabbed the handle of the shovel and swung blindly outward as the Wolf lunged.

Metal cracked against bone, and the impact jolted through both of my arms. I fell sideways, away from the snarling Wolf. Jaime jerked free of the support beam and scrambled to me. He reached for the shovel, his instinct to get between me and the Wolf, to protect what was his.

The Wolf lashed out with a massive paw. Jaime yelled as he was flung sideways. He crashed into the side of a machine with a dull thud, then lay still. Fear and anger warred inside me, and I used both of them for all they were worth. I slashed the shovel at the Wolf's head. It reared back and snarled, showing off gleaming white teeth each the size of my thumb. Its lips were stained red. Blood.

Bucknell's blood.

"You murdered my brother," I said, uncaring if this was the exact Wolf who'd killed Jacob. They were all monsters.

The sound the Wolf made could easily be some kind of laughter, and I wanted to scream at the hideousness of it. It snapped at my heels, darting in close enough for me to swing but not connect. It dashed to the side, then back. My arms began to ache, and I realized its game—it was wearing me out. Playing with me before it struck the killing blow.

I was sweating despite the cold, and frustrated tears leaked from the corners of my eyes. If I gave up, it would sweep it to kill me and Jaime. But I was only prolonging the inevitable. The Wolf would outlast me. I couldn't win.

We were going to die.

Accepting this only made me fight harder, swinging widely enough to connect several times. The Wolf whined once as it bounced away, its shoulder bleeding. The blow should have angered it enough to go for the killing stroke, but it didn't. What sort of creature tortured its prey, only to avoid the kill?

I pulled the shovel back to my shoulder and glared at the oversized monster. "What do you want?"

Its large, red eyes seemed to say, "Why you, of course." Its lip lifted up in a snarl that could easily have been a sneer.

"Kill me and be done with it!"

A sharp, furious bark echoed through the mill. The sound was unfamiliar, unlike anything I'd ever heard from a dog or wolf. It repeated, and this time the Wolf's hackles raised. Its ears twitched.

With a vicious snarl, a white-furred beast bolted from between two saws and barreled directly into the Wolf's chest. Brown and white tumbled together, legs kicking, teeth snapping. The Wolf's deep-chested growl was a stark contrast to the higher, shorter grunts and barks from the other animal. Not quite as large as the Wolf, but shaggier and a longer face, it moved too fast for me to identify it.

The focus was off of me. I fell to my knees next to Jaime and pressed my fingers to his throat. A steady pulse beat under my touch, and I nearly wept for joy. He had a lump on his forehead next to the cut. I touched his face and hair, whispered to him, tried to wake him so we could run. I wouldn't leave him behind to be murdered by the winner of this canine battle.

"Please, Jaime, we have to go."

One of the monsters let out a long, pained whine. They'd moved out of sight, and I strained to hear the thuds and scrambles of fighting. Instead, I heard the gentle patter of feet moving toward me through the shavings. I struggled back up on aching legs and lifted the shovel, ready to fight to my own death.

The white creature emerged from the shadows and stopped a few feet away. In the dim light, in stillness, I saw it clearly. An impossibly-sized white fox watched me with glittering green eyes as sharp as emeralds. Blood streaked its muzzle and more colored its front paws. Its ears twitched as it looked from me to Jaime and back to me. It took a single step closer, sniffing. I pulled the shovel back a fraction, prepared to swing in our defense.

The fox huffed, then retreated a few steps. It sat on its rear and closed its eyes.

In my lifetime, I'd never seen true magic with my own eyes until that moment. The white fox's entire body shimmered like sunlight on fresh snow. Its shape expanded into a mist that reformed smaller, narrower. The air snapped and crackled with invisible power that seemed to reach out and caress my skin. The hair on the back of my neck prickled with awareness as the white mist faded, leaving behind a man.

Dressed in white linen pants and a white shirt, his reddish-bronze hair a stark contrast, and even before he raised his head, I knew.

Kit's emerald eyes flashed with anger and concern as he unfolded from his crouch. "Are you hurt?" he asked as he stood.

"You're a fox," I said.

"Only part-time."

"I don't know what that means."

"I'll explain, but first we have to leave."

I agreed. Leaving was a very good idea. "Jaime's hurt. Help me, please."

"No, Robin, we have to leave him here."

All of the fear and shock of this evening collided inside of me, and I began shaking. I marched across the wood shavings and grabbed the front of his shirt—the first time I had ever laid my hands on another person in anger. "He's my husband, Kit. I won't leave him for Odin's Wolves to find and kill."

"The Wolf who was here is long gone. We'll send the constable to collect your husband. As long as your family believes you're dead, they'll be safe from further interference from Odin."

My thoughts stuttered. I released him and stumbled back. "Dead?"

"I thought we had more time, or I never would have left your side this morning. But they found out about you before I could get here and warn you. I'm so sorry I was late."

"I don't understand. Please, make some kind of sense."

Kit glanced behind me, at Jaime, who was still deeply unconscious. And then he told me a story.

The end of the world will be heralded in threes. Three winters of war, followed by three more winters of bitter, unrelenting cold. All will be trumpeted by the arrival of the Norns, the three maidens of Fate. Born from the homeland of the Asguardians' enemies, the maidens each possess a gift of sight: past, present, or future. From the moment they arrive in the world, the fate of the gods is sealed and actions put in motion cannot be undone.

The moral of the story: forces exist before which even the gods are helpless.

"Do you understand?" Kit asked.

I understood the myth well enough. Some of the literature we'd been allowed to read here had alluded to something similar, the three sisters of Fate, always in a different form. It was only a myth, though.

Just as the pagan gods were, until twenty years ago, only a myth.

"What are you saying, Kit?" I needed him to be clear.

"Your visions are that of the present, Robin. You see what is happening, and you see it all over the world. I knew you were special, and I was right. I believe you're Vedandi, seer of now."

"That makes no sense."

"It makes perfect sense."

"I don't believe in the power of the pagan gods, or in their rule. How can I accept that I'm a reincarnation of one of their own deities?"

"You believe in your one true God, correct?"

"Of course."

"Forces exist before which even the gods are helpless, do you remember that?"

I nodded, unable to force words out beyond the lump in my throat.

"The gods ruled once, and they were defeated," Kit said. "They will be defeated again. Can you believe that your God has put measures in place to assure that?"

He spoke so strongly, with such conviction that I found I could believe it. "You're saying that I'm an instrument of my God? That these visions will serve a purpose in removing the pagan gods from power?"

"Yes."

"But why now? Why this past week, on my thirtieth birthday?"

"I cannot answer that. I don't know why. I can only offer you my help, and a place where you will be safe while we collect your sisters."

"Jocelyn?"

He shook his head, his expression turning sad. "No, your Norn sisters. They're being watched, just as I was watching you, and we need you three together. I'm sorry, Robin, but you must leave your human family behind."

Grief squeezed my heart and wouldn't let go. It became difficult to breathe. "I can't."

"Odin's Wolf knows your scent, Robin. If you go back to your family, it will track you there. It will kill them all to get to you."

"Then take us all with you."

"I can't. I wish I could, for your sake, but they will be safe once you're gone. You'll still be able to see them. With your sight."

I'd be able to see them grieve my death. To see them moving on without me, ruled over by a pantheon I hated. No. If I accepted Kit's words and left, I'd leave for good. I wouldn't look back, even through my mind's eye. "No. No, I have to live in the present." Tears tracked warm lines down my cheeks. "I have to give them up, don't I?"

"I'm sorry." Kit reached for me then, and I allowed the embrace. He smelled of pine and moonlight dew and so many wild things I couldn't name. His skin was warm, his hold true. He could protect me, as he promised. I had faith in that—but first I had to know.

"What are you?"

He pulled away far enough for our eyes to meet. In their emerald depths, magic sparkled. "I was careful to never lie to you when we met. All I ever wanted was your trust."

"I accept that."

"I am Kitsune, a servant of Inari, a Shinto goddess."

I knew little of the other pantheons who'd returned, but could identify Shinto as Japanese. I didn't know the names of their gods or goddesses, but Kit spoke with respect when he said Inari's name. "Why are you in Germany?"

"Because Inari learned of your existence, and the existence of your Norn sisters. She didn't know when your sight would develop, only that it would be soon, and she sent me here to watch you, as my brothers watch your sisters."

"Why?"

"To protect you from Odin. Once your sight manifested, he would want you dead or imprisoned, so as to halt his fall from power." He traced a fingertip down my cheek, his caress warm and protective. "My inattention nearly got you killed tonight, and for that I am truly sorry."

"You saved us." I looked behind me, at Jaime's unconscious form. "In order to protect my family, I have to die. In their eyes."

"Yes. I know it's a lot to accept, but we don't have much time before a proper retreat is made impossible."

"All right, I'll go with you. Please, give me a moment?"

Kit tilted his head in deference, then backed away. I knelt next to Jaime and gathered his hands into my lap. Kissed their work-hardened surface. Kissed both of his cheeks that I would never again seen widen into a smile meant just for me. He might remarry one day, now that he was free of our promised union. He might remain a widower and be happier for it. I didn't know. Mine was not the gift of future sight. I could only see the present, and my present was full of heartache.

"Be happy, *Schatzi*, please."

As I stood, some of the fear in my heart hardened. Emotion turned to stone. And my burning need to see Odin's fall fueled each step I took toward a new, uncertain future.

Kit and I leave for Denmark tomorrow. He's lost contact with his Kitsune brother who was sent to watch over my Norn sister, Elsa, the seer of the past. Our third sister, Caitlyn, seer of the future, is already in hiding. Safe.

With the power of the Shinto gods behind us, Kit and I will do whatever it takes to unite we three Norn. You cannot fight the sisters of Fate.

My story has no happy ending, because it is not over.

The future conclusion is only for my sister to see.

In the House of Osiris

by *Janna Silverstein*

"What do you know about Osiris?" Nahktinebi asked. Ellie Bhukari and Halima Ahmad sat in the high priest's study, a spacious, modern office on the 15th floor of a tower in downtown Cairo. Big picture windows overlooked the new temple complex in the heart of the city. Ellie's eyes were sore from crying and worry, and the afternoon light blazing through the windows didn't help matters.

"I know that Osiris is the god of the dead. I know that Isis was his sister and his wife." Ellie paused, thinking, then added, "I should probably know more than that." She sipped her tea to cover her embarrassment. A voice in the back of her mind, the practical side, said, *Don't be embarrassed, not now.*

Fat, bald, and well-manicured in his Western suit, Nahktinebi smiled. His collar was sharp, buttoned, and set off with a perfectly knotted red tie; his French cuffs were pressed and fastened with gold cufflinks. "Do not worry, Mrs. Bhukari. Even my wife is not very conversant in the ways and stories of the gods. It is important to know something, of course; one never knows when the gods may decide to intervene—as we have learned."

Ellie shifted in her padded chair; she had learned very well just this afternoon. That was why she was here. Her husband was missing, and because the temple had summoned her, she knew it had something to do with an intervention. She pushed back her anxiety. The priest would get to the point; she'd known him long enough that she knew he liked to talk. Even after all this time he wouldn't call her Ellie, always Mrs. Bhukari, formal, old-style. She was no one except in relation to her husband.

Kamal said that formality was one of the reasons that Osiris had chosen the old economist as his high priest. He was known then as Mohammed Bousaid. The man knew how to do business. She had no doubt that he wore his business suit as comfortably in the temple as he had in the bank. And one did not rush into business in this culture, something she always had to remind herself, even after years of living here.

"It pleases their vanity to think that we are all intensely consumed with their history," the priest went on. "But only a very small number of us are scholars. It is either our job or our eccentricity. My scholarship was my eccentricity and it has become my job." He leaned forward and sipped his tea. Ellie noticed his delicacy: he picked up the bone china cup to sip so carefully, one pinkie extended and everything, though he did it with two hands. He hadn't been able to lift a cup with one hand since the stroke. But she couldn't wait on his delicacy any longer.

"Please excuse my anxiousness, but . . . the intervention you mentioned—it was Set who appeared yesterday, wasn't it? I saw pictures on the web. He was . . . huge. The police cordoned off all the streets around the temple and I couldn't get anywhere near there. Did Kamal get caught up in all that? He's been gone more than a day and if you know anything . . . "

She knew it wasn't polite to push the man, but when Kamal hadn't come home from the temple, where he was a junior priest, she made phone calls all afternoon and through the evening but got no answers. When dawn came without news, she called in sick. It wasn't until 1 PM that the phone rang; it was Halima, the high priest's administrative assistant, to tell her when to come to Nahktinebi's office. Halima sat by her now, an old friend whom she'd known since before the gods' Return, apparently to be a calming presence for a difficult conversation.

The priest's smile faltered. "Of course. No apologies are necessary. It's just that, if you know the god's tale, you will better understand Khamweset's situation." Nahktinebi used Kamal's priestly name.

Ellie knotted up the hem of her shirt in her lap. "What is his situation?"

Halima slurped her tea and Ellie glanced her way. She looked worried, uncomfortable.

Nahktinebi leaned forward and folded his hands upon his desk. His gold signet ring flashed in the light, the cartouche detailed with precision. He looked first at his hands, as if considering his words. Sunlight glinted off of his shaved head. Ellie swallowed the lump forming in her throat. Whatever he had to say, it obviously wasn't good.

"The gods are both spirit and flesh. Sometimes they walk the Earth in their physical form. Sometimes, they choose the spirit way. And some-times they inhabit their servants. They do this to gain perspective, to see the world through another's eyes. Sometimes they do this to demonstrate their power—to inspire faith or awe or perhaps to bless the servant with whom they join."

Ellie didn't like the sound of that. She interrupted. "Did some god choose to—" She almost choked on the word. "—bless Kamal?"

"Indeed. Osiris chose his servant, Khamweset."

"And what happened?"

"In the old stories, Osiris was a good and powerful king with a loving wife and loyal subjects. His brother Set, in a jealous rage, tore him limb from limb and scattered his parts to the four corners of Egypt."

"Oh my God. What—?"

Halima put her hand on Ellie's shoulder. "Ellie—"

"What happened?" she asked.

"Set descended upon the temple even as Osiris inhabited his servant. Set chose that opportunity to . . ." Suddenly the high priest averted his gaze.

Ellie finished the sentence for him. "He chose to reenact that old story, didn't he? He . . . killed Kamal."

Nahktinebi sighed and looked at her again. "That is correct."

Ellie's stomach lurched and her bile rose. She swallowed, and her breath came in fits and starts. Halima took her hand.

"But it is not that simple," the priest said. "In the old stories, Isis gath-ered the pieces of Osiris' body, breathed life into him, and he became the god of the dead. The gods move quickly, and as soon as Set had spread Khamweset across the land, the goddess stepped in. Even now, the pieces of his body lay in the temple of Osiris."

"I have to go to him," Ellie said. She shook her hand loose of Halima's, grabbed her purse from the floor, and gathered her sweater from the back of her chair.

"You must not . . . " Nahktinebi said, as Halima said, "Ellie, what are you . . . ?"

She put her bag on the chair and, as she pulled on her sweater, said, "I have to go to the temple. I have to go to Kamal."

"Mrs. Bhukari, I am not finished. You must sit down."

"What more is there to say?" Ellie demanded. Her eyes filled with tears but she felt oddly in control.

"We have engaged a priestess of Isis to help complete the cycle," Nahktinebi said. "Tonight, Isis will inhabit her priestess and they will finish what Set has started."

"What does that mean?"

"Isis will resurrect Osiris and mummify his human shell."

"His human . . . You're talking about Kamal. She can't do that." Ellie felt dizzy and grasped the back of the chair. This whole thing was so absurd. She wasn't sure what Isis couldn't do. But if Isis could resurrect Osiris, why couldn't she resurrect Kamal? Why should he die because Set had had a hissy fit?

"Mrs. Bhukari, please. This is the way of things. Death and resurrection are the way of the world. The cycle must be complete." Nahktinebi made it sound so reasonable, so obvious to anyone who thought about it. "The gods reenact this cycle every year, as winter becomes spring and spring becomes summer. It is a necessary thing."

"It was never necessary before these . . . creatures came. I have to talk to Isis." She said it before she even realized the words were coming out of her mouth. She grabbed her bag and headed for the door.

Nahktinebi met her there. His hand was on the doorknob as she reached for it.

"I beg you," he said. "Don't do anything rash. You can't just go talk to the goddess, command her as if she were your servant. And please . . . don't call the gods 'creatures.'" He glanced at the ceiling as if he was concerned their conversation might be overheard. "In just two hours, the sun will set. Isis and her priestess will come to the temple of Osiris to complete the cycle." He released the doorknob and took her hand in his. "If you must go to Khamweset, go in good faith. Go to let him go."

"I can't let him go, not like this. If these . . . gods are gods, then they can do anything. They can change the rules, they can bring Kamal back." She tried to loose her hand from the high priest's, but he wouldn't let go.

"Mrs. Bhukari—Ellie. I beg you, calm yourself. Come to the temple, yes, please. But let us handle this. This is priestly business. If anything can be done, let us do it."

Ellie read Nahktinebi's face. He looked sincere. He also looked worried. Something about this wasn't right. She didn't know why, but she had the sense he wasn't telling her everything. Maybe she could get her answers at the temple. She took a deep breath and released it. She subsided and he loosened his grip.

"All right," she said. "I'll be there at sunset." She glanced out the window and her breath hitched as she thought of Kamal's dark eyes in sunshine. She had to stay focused, think about practical things. "This time of day with the traffic, it'll take me two hours to get there anyway."

"I'll have one of our drivers take you," the high priest said.

"No," Ellie said too quickly and wasn't sure why. She looked to Halima, still seated by the desk. "Halima, would you drive me?"

"*Aywa*," Halima said. *Yes.*

"*Shukran*," Ellie said, relieved. *Thank you.*

"I am so sorry for your loss, Mrs. Bhukari," Nahktinebi said. "If there's anything I can do . . ."

Ellie walked out without giving the man a second glance. Halima grabbed a book off of one of the shelves by the door and followed Ellie out.

Having Halima drive made Ellie feel like she really would get there. As she and Halima walked down the hall away from the high priest's office, Halima linked her arm through Ellie's; Ellie was grateful for that act of solidarity. She realized that she hadn't trusted that one of the high priest's regular drivers would have gotten her to the temple at all.

The drive over the Amun-Ra Bridge across the Nile from Cairo to the west temples at Giza proceeded at a crawl, just as Ellie knew it would. She pulled down the visor to keep the setting sun out of her eyes. In her lap rested the book Halima had taken, a primer on the story of Isis, Osiris, and Set. It was all pretty visceral stuff: passion, incest, jealousy, murder, magic, and resurrection. Halima wanted Ellie to have some grounding before she witnessed the ritual at the temple. Ellie skimmed the story, but her grief and the vague sense that something just wasn't right gnawed at her. She couldn't focus. And then a thought occurred to her.

"Halima, did you know about Kamal?"

"I knew something had happened at the temple, but I didn't know what. When Nahktinebi asked me to call you, I suspected. I'm so sorry." Ellie couldn't see her eyes behind her dark sunglasses, but her lips were pursed. Ellie could tell she was upset.

"I don't trust him," Ellie said, looking out the window. "I never have."

Shadows grew with sunset, later every day in early spring. As she looked across the landscape, the white facades of the Great Pyramids facing her were bathed in blue shadows as the sun sank, refaced with marble as they had been in ancient days. Scaffolding scaled the smallest pyramid, where workmen hammered a golden cap into place at its top, echoing the look of its two larger companions. The Sphinx, restored and newly painted, peered with black eyes out across the sands. New temples with tall pylons huddled in a wide radius around the colossal tombs, modern structures built in the ancient style, bright with fresh paint and inscriptions in hieroglyphics, Arabic, and English. It was the first time in the all the years she'd lived in Cairo that the sight didn't thrill her.

Ellie stewed, unsure what she was doing. Nahktinebi was right: she couldn't just order the gods around. If Isis really was a goddess, then anything should be possible, she reasoned. Maybe she'd need to just ask reasonably, person to . . . what? Goddess? Alien? Force of nature? She didn't know.

And little was reasonable where gods, for lack of a better word, were concerned. Upon their return, Set had laid waste a giant swath of downtown Cairo to make way for new temples before Amun-Ra had stopped him. Ellie and Kamal had been honeymooning in Hurghada on the Red Sea, a brief weekend away when all hell broke loose. The destruction in Cairo caused grief and chaos and revolution for months afterward. All these years later, Ellie still wasn't sure Egypt had seen the last of what had come to be called the Cairo Intifada, the uprising against the gods. So many were lost; so many were stunned and angry—or converted in the end. The gods' supernatural powers had subdued a large portion of the population. Maybe there *had* been reason in the madness after all.

Many of the gods who had Returned elsewhere had been quick to adapt to new ways of doing things—but the Egyptian gods wanted things to be familiar and structured. They'd adapted to the many languages they'd encountered in this new world, but they bristled at new technologies. They had to be shepherded, much to their dismay and irritation, toward taking advantage of the reach and influence that things like the internet could provide. Nahktinebi and Kamal had been instrumental in that work.

At the same time, over the last couple of years, rumors proliferated that Nut, goddess of the night, had shown up at nightclubs in Alexandria and danced the night away. Horus, with his distinctive, hawkish features, had turned up at the Ministry of Defense to discuss the country's security. Thoth had been seen at the new library in Alexandria and near the universities in Cairo, Luxor, and Aswan, taking an interest in the latest scientific research and in education policy. So the gods were coming slowly to the new world. But old passions and old caprices still ruled them.

Kamal, who had been Mohammed Bousaid's wonder-boy Chief Technology Officer, practically an adopted son, had hitched his wagon to the high priest's star when the changes came. Did he believe in these old gods? Ellie didn't think so, anymore than she believed Bousaid worshipped Osiris or any of the other gods without question. They were practical men in difficult circumstances. Ellie had wanted to flee to her parents in Manhattan when the gods Returned. Kamal insisted they stay in Cairo, where they'd met at American University in the computer science program and married soon after. She'd stayed at on the school; database administration paid well, even in Egypt's struggling economy.

So here she was, inching her way toward a temple to a god she didn't believe in to stop or change or interfere with a ritual she didn't understand in a land that still wasn't hers.

She closed her eyes against the last, late light of the day and tried not to think about anything.

"Do you want me to come in with you?" Halima asked when they arrived at the temple.

"No. I need to do this myself." She opened the car door and started to get out when Halima put one hand on her arm. Ellie turned back toward her, and Halima took off her sunglasses.

"Ellie, listen to me. Nahktinebi is a powerful man. He gets what he wants. If he feels threatened, he will defend himself."

The idea didn't surprise her, but Halima's saying it just now did. Halima squeezed her arm, then let go.

Ellie climbed the stone steps to the house of Osiris. She walked past the soaring pylons into the open-air courtyard, and then between two carved and painted columns into the deeper shadows of the wide vestibule. Silent attendants met her there, taking her sandals, sweater, and bag. She walked between another pair of columns into the hypostyle hall. The floor was layered in thick, rich, hand-woven carpets piled three and four deep, soft and giving like velvet beneath her feet. Subtle lighting illuminated carved figures marching across painted walls and pillars. Men and women in simple sheaths flitted from side chamber to side chamber on unaccountable errands. The silence made Ellie self-conscious.

From out of the shadows, Nahktinebi appeared, followed by two attendants. He wore his temple garments, a white, belted shift, a broad, richly beaded collar of lapis lazuli, carnelian and jasper, golden bracelets and anklets. In the dim light, he looked as though he'd stepped out of the very walls that surrounded them.

"Ellie, thank you for coming," he said and took her hands before she could pull away. He didn't look pleased, despite the welcome words. "Please follow Meryt. She will give you temple garments so you may attend."

Once Ellie had slipped into a white shift of her own, belted with a golden cord, she was escorted into the inner sanctuary, a tall rectangular room. Her heart beat hard and fast in her chest. The air smelled of burning incense, and off in a side chamber male voices chanted softly.

She had never seen the inner sanctuary before. Only the priests and temple attendants were allowed in the room. Like the outer rooms, the walls were carved and painted—white backgrounds patterned with hieroglyphs told the story of the god Osiris, dead and reborn. At the center of the room, light from above illuminated a stone plinth.

And there, on the plinth, lay a body: Kamal.

Ellie launched herself at the platform. He lay unclothed . . . in pieces. His hands, arms, legs and feet, though placed beside his body where they were connected in life, were severed, the edges ragged. His torso had been torn in half at the waist. His head lay at his shoulders, severed as well. His eyes were half open. She recoiled, tripped, fell back and landed on the carpeted floor.

She couldn't breathe; she sucked at the air even as darkness teased the corners of her vision. How could anyone revive what was left of the man before her? Her beautiful Kamal.

Chanting voices approached. Ellie turned toward the sound. Nahktinebi lead a procession of junior priests and attendants into the sanctuary. All but two of the attendants stationed themselves around the room. Those two followed the high priest to the plinth—one male and one female. The man carried a tray upon which a number of implements lay. The woman, a girl really, was adorned with jewels as rich as Nahktinebi's, and wore a golden headdress of a disc between two horns; she must be the priestess of Isis. Another attendant approached from the shadows and helped Ellie to her feet, drawing her backward, out of the circle of light bathing the plinth, the priest, and the priestess.

The attendant tried to withdraw, but Ellie held on to him. She didn't trust her knees not to buckle. Her breath came in fits and starts; her chest was tight. She pressed it with the heel of one hand, trying to calm her hammering heart.

Nahktinebi stationed himself by the plinth, the priestess to one side, the attendant to the other, their backs toward Ellie. The chanting around them stopped. The high priest took what looked like a small gold lamp from the tray and raised it over his head.

Light suddenly filled the room. Ellie winced and shut her eyes at the heat that enveloped her. When she opened them, the giant goddess Isis stood on the opposite side of the plinth surrounded by an aura of golden light. She must have been 30 feet tall: a lean woman in a skin-tight dress. Her arms were multicolored falcon's wings, with shimmering feathers that reached to delicate fingertips. Her brown eyes were outlined in jet, her lips closed in a benign, gentle expression. This was Isis the protectress, Isis the creator. Ellie was breathless at the sight. The whole chamber vibrated with electricity; static teased at her hair.

Isis looked down. In a voice like the wind through a valley, she said, "Eleanora, wife to Khamweset, priest to my beloved Osiris, I am here to task you, if you would be tasked."

Ellie's heart skipped a beat; she fell back a step. "What . . . ?" Suddenly her mind was blank and her throat was tight. The attendant wrested away from her grasp and ran.

"Great lady Isis!" Nahktinebi's voice sounded tiny as he interrupted. "Mother of Horus, your priestess is here to do your will."

"This priestess cannot help me. And you . . . " The goddess turned her gaze on the priest and her eyes turned orange, the color of flame. She roared, "You do not interfere!" The volume left Ellie's ears ringing. Isis swept one hand out. A coruscating ribbon of orange energy shot from her fingertips. It lifted Nahktinebi off the ground and thrust him across the room. He slammed against a column and crumpled in a heap on the floor. The priestess and the attendant ran, the girl's headdress toppling as she fled. The attendant's tray clattered away, spilling its contents toward the side of the room.

The goddess turned her attention back to Ellie.

"I know what you want," she said. "You want the priest."

"Where is he, Lady?"

"He is beyond my influence. He was taken by Osiris in the midst of service, and Set took them both. My beloved is trapped in the flesh that Set rended. That body is broken, but Osiris holds his spirit. Help me resurrect their power. Together we will renew this world."

Ellie didn't know what to say. She didn't know any of the rituals the gods required; what she knew of them she'd only learned in the last two hours.

"What are we going to do here?" she asked finally. "How can we possibly do this?"

"You must join with me, as your husband joined with mine. We must heal the body and infuse it with air and life."

"That's . . . not very specific," Ellie said. She straightened up and smoothed her shift to give herself time to think. She took a deep breath and she suddenly felt clear and present. "The legends say that when you revive Osiris, you use your wings to push air into his lungs and then"—she thought for a moment—"you make love to him to bring him back to life. They don't say how you rejoin all these pieces."

"A god doesn't need a fleshly form. We will wrap him as servants of old wrapped the pharaohs for their journey to the underworld."

Ellie knew what that meant: mummification. She squared her shoulders and steadied her gaze, even if she was gazing at a woman six times her size.

"Why do you need me?" she asked, the seeds of a plan forming. "Why not the priestess?"

"As I am to my beloved, you are to yours. No power greater than that kinship can complete the cycle of death and life."

Ellie paused before she said the next words. They might be the last words she ever spoke—but she had to try.

"A god may not need a body, but my husband does." Ellie couldn't show weakness, even though her heart beat wildly in her chest. "He must be complete and whole. To be resurrected, he needs his body—his fully healed, fully functional, living physical form. You say you can't do this without me. I can't do this without Kamal's full resurrection. He must be the man he was—body and mind and soul—before Osiris took him, and before Set tore him to pieces."

Isis' eyes widened, the first truly human expression Ellie had seen on the goddess' face. "What?" The giant hands sheltered by bejeweled feathers curled into fists.

Ellie swallowed and resettled her footing. She put her hands on her hips. Sweat broke on her forehead. Red heat rose off of Isis' wings.

"Are you not the Goddess of Life as your hymns proclaim? Can't you do this?"

Ellie felt heat behind her, and she turned to see another great flash of blinding light. A strong gust of hot wind knocked her up against the plinth and off of her feet again.

"Who dares task a goddess?" The deep voice was so loud it left her ears ringing. Another god stood before her—as tall as Isis, a brown human male body dressed in a white kilt overlaid in gold. His head was unlike any creature Ellie had ever seen, with skin like obsidian, a long bent snout, narrow eyes with epicanthic folds, and tall ears with sharp corners. He held a slim, black staff that reached from the floor to his shoulder.

"Set, this is not your concern," Isis said.

Ellie clambered to her feet.

"Who stands between my brother and his birth to the underworld? A mortal?"

"I do!" Ellie cried. And then she froze. Her voice sounded impossibly small to her ears. *What the hell are you thinking?* she wondered. She craned her neck to look at the great, beastly head.

"What right have you to interfere with the business of the gods?" Set lifted the staff and slammed its tip against the floor. Its effect was muffled by the carpets he pounded. Unbidden the thought occurred to Ellie, *That'll leave a mark.* She stifled a giggle. *A little hysterical, are we?* she asked herself.

"The right of a wife to defend her husband!" she yelled. *What the hell? You've got nothing left to lose.* "The right of the wife of a priest of Osiris to demand his return. Restore him to me!"

"Wife of Khamweset, stay out of this!" Isis commanded. "Set, return to Chaos. You have no place in this ritual."

"This mortal interrupts nothing less than the cycle of the world. What a mortal wants is immaterial to our purpose. Osiris must proceed to the underworld."

Set lifted a foot. He moved the foot toward Ellie, and with a cry she dodged away. She rounded the plinth, closer to Isis. Set put his foot down. The whole building shook.

He then lifted his staff and pointed it toward her. Lightning surrounded its length and she dashed away again. The flash struck the spot where she'd stood, leaving a smoldering hole in the piled carpets. The air crackled and crisped with ozone, the smell of burnt wool in the air.

"Set, enough!" Isis cried. "The human speaks reason." Ellie looked up at Isis, shocked. The goddess' agreement was the last thing she'd expected—and so quickly. She frowned. What was Isis playing at? "You came for Osiris before his time . . ."

"Only days. He knew my return would come."

"It does not matter. You were the one who drew this human into the cycle. We cannot deny her. This ritual must continue."

"But everything is changed."

"You changed it when you involved the priest." The room got warmer. Isis' wings glowed. The light was too hot for such a small space. Energy crackled off the edges of her wings and ricocheted around the room. Ellie ducked and ran toward the far wall. She hid in a side chamber door, half behind the doorframe to see what would happen.

Set raised his staff and then pounded it down again. An explosion of light and heat erupted from the point of impact. Ellie was knocked off her feet. The light fixtures exploded; sparks cascaded from the ceiling.

Silence from the sanctuary.

On hands and knees, Ellie crawled to the doorway and peeked around it. Set was gone. But there was still one source of light. At the plinth stood a woman, no more than 6 feet tall, graceful, with bejeweled wings like a cloak over her slender, powerful arms. Those wings glowed a golden light that illuminated her smooth, high-cheekboned face, the plinth, and the body that lay upon it.

Ellie rose to her feet and stepped across the scorched carpets. She took the two steps up the platform to stand beside Isis and look at her husband in pieces. His brown skin was ashen. She touched his poor, loose hand, dislodging it slightly from where it lay. It was cold.

Looking at Kamal, she said to Isis, "What do we do now?"

"We merge and breathe him into being."

Ellie made the goddess meet her gaze. "And we bring him back to life, full and whole and as he was? No tricks. He never should have been a part of this."

"As you wish. I warn you: you will not understand everything that you see. And you will see truth that was hidden."

"As long as you keep your word, we're good," Ellie said. She took a deep breath and braced herself. "What do I do?"

Isis moved to stand behind her and put her feathered hands on Ellie's shoulders. "Stand before me like so." The goddess ran her fingertips down Ellie's arm; the sensation was almost erotic. Isis folded her fingers between Ellie's and leaned her body against her. "Close your eyes. Be still," she whispered in Ellie's ear, an intimacy she hadn't expected.

Ellie closed her eyes. Isis leaned into her. The sensation was like a hot tide, water soaking into and through her skin. Ellie felt Isis' fingers melt into her palm, felt Isis' arms enfold her own, felt Isis' torso meld into hers as though her own body were a sponge, absorbing Isis in a slow wave.

Like waking from a dream, Ellie realized she wasn't alone in her own head. "Open our eyes," a voice inside her instructed. Ellie opened her eyes. The whole world had changed.

Kamal's body glowed red on the plinth, brighter and deeper wherever his body had been severed. She saw the ghost of another face there, above, behind, around his own.

"You see Osiris' spirit imprisoned in this shell," Isis told her.

"And Kamal?"

Isis did not respond. She lifted Ellie's head and looked around the room. The air was thick with spirit, a sea of souls rocking in the echoes of the energy that so recently split the air.

In the shadows at the corners of the room, black, opaque figures huddled in the deepest recesses, sour and rotten smelling, and dashed from corner to corner. They chittered and whispered. They chilled Ellie, and her stomach tightened. Hands clawed at her arms and she lifted them, trying to shake off the intruders. But her arms were wings, light and feathered, heavy and bejeweled; the sound of her feathers rustling unnerved her. One moment she filled the whole room. The next, she stood, a woman beside a plinth, staring at her husband's dead, pieced-out body. A million voices filled her head, the clamor of the city, the power of centuries of souls assaulting her. She panicked; she felt nauseous; she wanted to scream.

Isis wrapped her in her wings, bowed her head and closed her eyes. The voices faded, the nausea subsided, the fear quelled. "Do not try to control this experience. What is it your people say? You're along for the ride. And you are . . . bait. Every fish needs a lure. You are Kamal's lure. Just. Be."

And there was that warm tide again. She was lifted up as if she were in a dense salt sea. Isis spread their wings and began to flap. Power rose inside them. She, Isis, her body, lifted off the floor on power far stronger than anything natural. Heat swept through her wings. They glowed from within as they beat the air, creating a wind that filled the room. They hovered over Kamal. The light enveloped him and the severed chasms between each body part. Those chasms glowed more intensely than before. Isis beat their wings harder, forcing the air into Kamal's nose, his mouth. His chest rose and fell in a strange, lurching rhythm—artificial respiration.

Her body began to vibrate. Power surged through her and out of the tips of her feathers in a wild blast. It poured into Kamal. Like a welder's torch, the light fused his body together. Each chasm closed in a fiery burst.

He was perfect, whole, glowing red like a sword pulled from the forge. Breathing. Silent. His face changed; as though the bones moved beneath his skin, his features smoothed out, flattened and reshaped themselves. His skin darkened, lightened. "You see my husband-brother's face," Isis whispered inside her mind. "He is as beautiful to me as your Kamal is to you. And as precious."

And suddenly they were moving together over their husbands' body—two spirits in each form. Ellie felt four hands on her body, felt Kamal's body with four hands of her own. It was when she felt Osiris' power enter Isis' awareness, so enormous that she sensed time slipping through her fingers, stars passing through her body as though she were made of the gossamer stuff of the universe, that she was swept away.

In the darkness, in a quiet grotto in a corner of the goddess' spirit, Ellie heard the voice of Isis. *One final truth: Beware Nahktinebi. His word is not pure.* The goddess placed visions into Ellie's memory for her to find when she woke from her dreams.

"Ellie."

She woke with a jolt. Kamal.

She lay on the plinth in the middle of the temple. Kamal was beside her, propped on one elbow, smiling at her, his big dark eyes filling her sight. His hand rested on her stomach—she was naked! Her eyes widened a moment. She didn't remember getting undressed—and then she decided she just didn't care.

Kamal was here. Kamal was alive and whole. She threw her arms around him as tight as she could. He was warm, almost hot enough to have a fever. She soaked it in.

"Baby," she whispered. Her chest heaved with her breath and her tears.

"That wasn't the homecoming you expected, was it?" he said.

"No," she said. "Nothing like it." She pulled back from him and stroked his cheek. "I don't . . . I can't—"

"I think they call that a religious experience," he said.

"Is that what that was?" She smiled a little.

"I believe resurrection falls into that category, yes." He was trying to be light—that was Kamal, always keeping it light, especially when things were difficult—but she was still recovering.

"Are you OK? I thought you were dead."

He leaned his forehead against hers. "I feel . . . like me. I feel . . . alone in my head."

Ellie understood what he meant; she was keenly aware of Isis' absence, the sudden quiet and privacy of her own mind, without the multifaceted dimensions of the goddess' perspective. Only two arms held her, not four, and she had only two arms to return his embrace. The whole world felt small, and her body too confining to hold her. She could only imagine what it must have been like for Isis to be inside her, restricted to her torso, her limbs, her tiny awareness. "I know," she whispered. "I know that feeling. Do you know what happened?"

"I think I do. I remember coming into the temple and preparing for service and Osiris . . . appearing . . . " His voice trailed off and his eyes became distant.

Ellie ran her fingers along his neck and shoulder, now scarred with a tidy red seam where he'd been healed by Isis.

And Ellie remembered things she'd never seen.

Nakhtinebi bargaining with Set: Kamal's life in return for a temple to the chaos god. Nahktinebi pointing out Kamal. Nahktinebi lighting incense in a bowl and breaking a scepter over a flame. Seeing Set through Isis' eyes. Understanding an attack timed to Osiris' habitation of Kamal, days before Osiris typically gave himself in spirit to their cycle, which always turned at the spring equinox.

"He made a deal," Kamal said, incredulous.

"Did you see that?" Ellie asked. "Did you . . . ?"

"I remembered it. He made a deal with Set to kill me."

"But why? Kamal!"

"I don't know. . . . I . . . wait, I *do* know." Kamal thought for a moment. "He had a stroke last year, do you remember?"

Ellie did remember. He'd been away from the temple for two or three months recuperating—his hands still shook, a remnant of the nerve damage—and Kamal took over for him while he recovered.

"I saw the truth. Osiris gave it to me," Kamal said, apparently remembering it as he said it. "Nahktinebi felt threatened because I served in his place. He thought Osiris would replace him with me. He wanted to get me out of the way."

Ellie realized it even as Kamal did, remembered it—a vision given to her by Isis. The goddess didn't like Nahktinebi and never had. But she hadn't known the whole truth until she'd laid eyes on Set.

And then Ellie remembered Halima's warning. A stroke could make any man feel vulnerable. But rage rose in Ellie. Kamal had trusted Mohammed Bousaid. They'd known him for years. Feeling vulnerable was one thing; attempted murder was another.

Ellie pushed herself up to sit and looked toward the pillar where the high priest had landed earlier. He was gone. He was out there, somewhere, she knew. What would he do now?

Kamal sat up and swung his legs over the edge of the plinth. He rubbed his forehead with one hand, clutched the edge of the platform with the other.

Ellie sat up beside him, put a hand on his back. "Kamal, you can't stay here. You can't keep working with this man." Even as she said it, she felt an unexpected grief at the thought of parting herself from the goddess. If they left Egypt, she'd be beyond Isis' reach. But of one thing she was sure: she wanted that communion again if she could have it somehow.

But . . . Kamal.

His gaze rose to hers then, tired, sad. "No, I'm not going to run away." He slid off the plinth. His landing was unsteady and he grabbed the edge again. "Whoa." He took a moment to get his footing. "What he did to me, he did out of fear."

Ellie's eyes widened. "Kamal, he tried to kill you."

"Shhh." He tried to soothe her, ran one hand down her arm, and then quickly leaned it on the plinth again. "He did, yes." He rubbed his mouth. "Ellie, the truth is that Mohammed was right. I am to be his successor, but it wasn't to be now. It was to be when he died or when he chose to leave the priesthood. Osiris is not a vengeful god; he believes in the cycle. The trouble is, Mohammed didn't." His eyes filled with regret, and that's when Ellie understood that if Kamal hadn't believed in the gods before this, he did now. "Osiris will deal with him."

With a certainty that echoed with Isis' awareness, Ellie knew that was true. The idea chilled her. She swallowed. Was some part of the goddess still in her?

Kamal looked around the room at the parade of pictures that told the story of how, in the underworld, a man's heart was weighed against a feather, a test that Nahktinebi would fail without a doubt. "He'll deal with him sooner rather than later. And he won't be gentle. The other gods will deal with Set." He put his arms around her and held her tight for a long time. She reveled in every breath he took. "You know what?" he said finally.

"What?" Ellie asked. Kamal pulled back and looked at her.

"I think we should go visit your parents for a while."

She liked that idea, but there was that grief again, a tug at her heart that she didn't want to resist.

Kamal continued. "And I think that things will be very different when we come back."

"As long as we do come back," she said.

Singing for the Man

by Lawrence M. Schoen

Twenty-one years ago Mat had retired from academia and set off on the first leg of what should have been a global-spanning retirement. The Return had come two months later, sending him back to the new Mexican state that had once been a piece of southern California. Now he was finally crossing the Atlantic ocean again.

International air travel had suffered in the past two decades. Even with the various divine subsidies provided by one or another god located in the destination city, flights out of New York could cost years of income, and that was traveling coach. Matlal Alejandro Garcia y Fuentes had a ticket for an aisle seat in the plane's second row, right-hand side, first class all the way. His two travel companions, the teen popstar Zyanya and Javier, her bodyguard/composer, had seats in same row on the other side of the aisle.

Zyanya's visit to New York and her planned trip out of the country had filled the tabloid press, and her ever-increasing popularity with worshipers of the gods of several pantheons meant a crowd of eager fans congregating at the departure terminal hours before they arrived. Javi kept a protective arm around his charge, but airport security in the form of a dozen nonhuman servants of various gods serving time as airport security kept the fans behaved and behind a rope line. Just another day in New York.

Mat had grown up under the standards of pre-Return bureaucracy, and insisted they arrive two unnecessary hours before the flight boarded. Zyanya used the time to sign autographs while Javi glowered. Moments before the boarding call, a trio of Aztec priests approached Mat. They wheeled a smallish steamer trunk with his name printed on a laquored seal stuck to the top. The lead priest showed him a ticket indicating the trunk had the window seat next to his. "Checked baggage can be lost or tampered with," said the lead priest, speaking to him in Nahuatl. The trunk even came with its own passport, listing its point of origin as Atlanta, Georgia rather than Mexico.

Lacking tickets themselves, the priests nonetheless followed Mat and his companions through the airport, pulling their charge after them. One positive aspect of the diminished volume of air travel in the new age, the arbitrary and intrusive regulations of airport security had become a dim memory. Who needed the TSA when the gods made it their business to ensure each flight arrived at its destination? The priests boarded the plane just long enough to secure the trunk in first class, seat belt tightly fastened, and then departed.

Mat never said a word to any of them. By some means known only to themselves, they had recognized him as the emissary of Huehuecoyotl, the god a few of the better educated English-speaking Americans called "Old Man Coyote," when they weren't confusing him with his less civilized cousin of the northwestern plains, the trickster god Coyote. The priests merely served the god, but Mat represented him, had met him several times (in both male and female guises), and for the past year received almost daily visitations in his dreams. Those conversations had lessened once he'd traveled beyond the borders of the Aztec pantheon, north and east across the remapped United States.

Mat had endured several encounters with similar priests during the months of Zyanya's tour. They were men who endorsed the ritual sacrifice of his people, tearing their chests open atop the rebuilt pyramids of Mexico to offer up still-beating hearts to keep the sun in the sky. He grappled with the cognitive dissonance on a daily basis, working to achieve the goals of his patron god, an individual he had come to know personally, while recoiling from the necessities of a religion that insisted on murdering its own worshippers.

"So what's in the trunk?" Zyanya's question pulled Mat from his conflicted thoughts. The girl had piled her waist-length blonde hair atop her head in a coiffure of looping coils that made her look older than her fifteen years. Despite her obvious Swedish ancestry, she'd been born and raised in Durango. Since the beginning of their tour she'd taken to using her natural vocal gifts and Mat's phonetic lessons to mimic regional dialects at every stop, and assaulted him now with a question phrased in

Zapotec with the unique accent of a native of Brooklyn, New York.

"I don't know. But apparently Old Drum wanted us to have it." Mat used one of his patron's titles, having learned the hard way not to 'name drop' gods, especially in New York. "I'm guessing it's something we need and can't get where we're going."

She nodded, smiling as she turned to Javi seated by the window, switching to a Brooklyn-Spanish. "I'm just glad to go somewhere where they don't know me. It will be nice to getaway from the crowds for a few days."

The trip was a break from Zyanya's tour of the continental United States. They'd been criss-crossing the country by bus for months, the young girl singing songs of Aztec mythology, both in some of the indigenous languages of Mexico and others translated into English. Matlal had written them all, with Javier Salvador Salvador composing the music. At each venue the audience had grown. Zyanya was filling baseball stadiums now, topping the charts in several demographics. Her songs put names like Huitzilopochtli and Tezcatlipoca on the lips of English-speaking American youth, teaching them catch phrases in Nahuatl and Mixtec, Totonac and Zapotec.

They were all tired, and during a recent dream conversation with the god, Mat had suggested a vacation. When that had proved agreeable, he specified a destination: the Isle of Man.

Only now, with the exit hatch sealed less than fifteen minutes after the initial boarding call, the plane easing back from the gate, and the flight attendant going through the tedious routine of emergency procedures, did Mat notice how tightly both Zya and Javi gripped their armrests. Neither had ever flown before.

They flew nonstop to Ronaldsway, the only commercial airport on the tiny Isle of Man. With fewer than a hundred thousand residents its history nonetheless dated back more than six thousand years before Christ, and in the days prior to The Return had been a haven for independent agencies competing to carry humanity into space. That portion of the economy had vanished, as had the tourism revenue and any income from the film industry. Nowadays every other inhabitant either worked the land or fished the Irish Sea for a living. It offered little in the way of vacation splendor for a tour-weary popstar and her retinue, but in his dream Mat had insisted—to the extent one can insist when dealing with a god.

"You've asked me to help you expand the popularity of Mexico's original languages," he'd told Huehuecoyotl. "This will help me do that."

"Explain it to me," the god had said, appearing in his dream as a beautiful woman clothed in a flowing dress of green feathers. "It's not as if any Aztec traveled there, built a home, and taught his children a forgotten dialect of Ixcatec."

"The official language of the Isle of Man is Manx."

"And this concerns me how?"

"It went extinct in 1974."

The dream image of Huehuecoyotl pursed her lips. Her brows lowered. "Which is it? Official language or dead one?"

"The last native speaker, a fisherman named Ned Maddrell, died in 1974. In the decades that followed, there were enough speakers who'd learned it as a second language to bring it back. Before The Return it was being taught everywhere on the island from preschool to college and a small number of new native speakers had been created, making Manx a living language again. Those speakers are adults now, many with children of their own. I want to talk to them."

"You speak Manx?"

In his dream Matlal shook his head. "I've only dabbled. But most of them speak English as well. They've already accomplished what you're trying to do, they've brought their language back."

"Mmm. Perhaps. Certainly on a smaller scale. Still, I see the allure, though what you ask may be difficult. That island is under the domain of the Tuatha Dé Danann, Irish deities who prefer battle to civilized conversation. Still, most of them keep to Ireland, proper. I share certain traits with Manannán, the main god watching over the island. And, we have a friend in common, and that might be enough. Let me see what I can arrange. A little flattery regarding their linguistic accomplishments will likely open the necessary doors."

The dream had ended and Matlal began to hope. While he did have a legitimate enough interest in studying the ressuerection of the Manx language, he had another reason for visiting the island. There were stories of an ancient harp, the Uaithne, that could stop the sun in the sky. For the past twenty years all the world's ancient stories had been made true again and the harp was said to be on the island. Since he'd learned of it, Mat had dreamed of using it to save his people. Maybe a mythological Mannish harp could accomplish once and for all what the Aztec gods managed by blood sacrifice. No matter how slim the chance, he had to try.

A tall and slender man met them as they deplaned. He was dressed casually, black boots, black jeans, black sweater, the colorlessness of his clothing dimmed the brilliance of his chestnut hair and short beard. He waited until they had cleared the landing gate and stood staring at the signs trying to determine the direction for baggage claim. He advanced upon them with a distance-devouring stride, stopped directly in front of Mat and appraised him.

"Ah, your old pup is sly, but I see his handiwork in you. I don't know why you had to arrive by air though; it would have been my pleasure to meet you at sea. It's not natural for mortals to fly. And speaking of unnatural, since when do the Aztec count little blonde European girls among their number?"

As quick as thought, Mat was shoved aside. He stumbled; a fall that a year ago would have broken a hip merely landed him on his ass. Javi had vanished from Zyanya's side and a large dog stood in front of her, blocking the newcomer from the singer with bared teeth and an unmistakeable growl. The other travelers in the area departed at a run, most letting go of their carry-on bags for the sake of greater speed. The man in black didn't so much as flinch.

"Javi, back off. He's not a threat." Mat struggled upright and tried to push the dog back. It neither budged nor stopped growling.

"A threat? Me? Don't be ridiculous. I'm your host."

"We don't have a host," said Zyanya, staying well behind the snarling dog. "We're staying in a hotel."

"Child, I am the host to all who stand upon this island. But moreover, I am bound to my fellow psychopomp, Xolotl, who calls your patron his best and truest friend, and thus I set myself at your service on his account."

"You're saying you're some kind of psycho?"

Mat glared at the girl and waved her to silence before things went further askew. He cleared his throat and with a small bow of respect began introductions. "Manannán mac Lir, may I present Zyanya, songstress of Mexico and destined tribute to Xochipilli. And Javier Salvador Salvador, composer and protector. Zya, Javi, this is Manannán, god of the sea, and the being for whom the island is named. He also escorts the dead to the afterlife; that's what 'psychopomp' means."

"Please, call me Manny. And you are Matlal, yes?"

Mat nodded and spoke words he'd rehearsed in Manx. He was confident of his pronunciation, but less certain of the intonation contour of the language. Nonetheless, the god grinned like a child opening a birthday present and slapped him a mighty blow upon the shoulder that nearly sent him staggering again.

"I knew I would like you. Now, come along. No doubt you're tired after your travel."

A pair of flight attendants chose that moment to come bustling through the terminal, pushing a luggage cart loaded with a small steamer trunk. "Sir, you forgot your trunk!"

Without another word Manannán placed both hands upon the trunk and lifted it up onto one shoulder. "This way, if you please. Our transportation is waiting just outside."

The most beautiful woman Mat had ever imagined waited for them outside the airport. The perfection of her face and figure screamed godhood and more. A stretch limo had parked next to her, right on the sidewalk. A uniformed driver had already liberated their luggage from baggage claim and was busy loading it into the vehicle's rapidly filling trunk.

Javier, still in dog form raced forward as if to supervise the placement of their bags, then whimpered briefly as he turned back to Manannán who stood with the mystery steamer trunk over his shoulder.

"Too right, not enough space for this in there." Manny drummed his fingers over the boarding pass taped at one end of the trunk. "Not to worry, it traveled here as a passenger so we'll continue to treat it as such." He flung open the car door, and as effortlessly as if handling sea foam placed the heavy trunk across one of the limo's broad seats before climbing in after it.

The driver held the door, and the rest of them followed the sea god. The old man, young girl, and the dog took the bench seat opposite Manannán and the trunk. The stunning goddess joined them in the limo, closing the door behind her. She tapped the smoked glass partition separating them from the front seat, a signal for the driver, and they were off.

Manannán took the goddesses's hand in his, raised it to his lips for a quick kiss, and regarded his guests. "My wife, the goddess Fand, formerly of Faery, and the brightest spot in my life lo these many centuries."

Fand smiled and looked directly to Matlal. "Tell me, is your own prankster such a flatterer? I assume he must also have the gift of pretty speech to disarm and beguile."

"Trickster?" Zyanya's normally angelic face scrunched up in confusion.

"The one you call 'Old Drum'. Do I have it wrong? Nearly every pantheon assigns the role of trickery to one of their own, for balance, to keep things interesting both among gods and mortals, sometimes even to play the fool." She paused, blinking eyes that any man could lose himself in without regret. "I had thought your patron occupied that position as well."

"Huehuecoyotl has been described as a trickster," said Mat. "But I understaood Manannán to be the sea god of the Tuatha Dé Danann. Surely he doesn't…"

"Oh, yes. I blame his father—"

Manannán snorted, but Fand ignored her spouse and continued as if there'd been no interruption.

"—Lir, now there was a sea god. But that was back at the beginning, leaving Manny free to get into other sorts of trouble. Formative trouble, if you ask me, and that's what stuck. They made him the guide for the dead hoping it would teach him to be serious, and he is when he's performing that duty, but I think he'd prefer to spend his time being a rogue, carousing with men, seducing women, and shrugging innocently with boyish charm when it's time to pay the piper. Is it any wonder he keeps a sea between himself and the rest of the gods on Ireland's shores?"

"Have a care, wife," said Manannán. "You'll be giving our guests the wrong idea."

Zyanya blushed, one hand resting lighting on the neck of the big dog at her feet. Mat managed a careful smile, a new idea forming in his mind, creating a new hope.

Manannán had canceled their hotel reservations, insisting they accept his hospitality instead. The accommodations blended the best of early 21st century comforts with the pinnacle of feudal architecture, which basically meant a stone castle complete with bulwarks and buttresses as well as modern plumbing and high speed wireless connectivity. Unlike most of the returned gods, Manannán seemed to appreciate technology.

Javier finally shifted back from dog form after the luggage had been transferred to their respective rooms. Fand promised a tour of the castle and then left to allow them time to settle in and refresh themselves. Mat waited just long enough to confirm that his companions had whatever they needed before locking himself in his own room. His modest suitcase had been set on a stand at the foot of a kingsize bed, its contents distributed to the drawers of an immense armoire that looked to be carved from a single piece of dark wood. The steamer trunk sat in the corner, unopened. It called to him.

The trunk's seal remained intact. It tore easily under his hand, the various fastenings offering no resistance. Inside, individually swaddled in a double layer of bubblewrap, three dozen eight-ounce bottles lay nestled in tiers of shock-absorbing webbing and globs of dry ice. Ice-cold coca cola.

Smiling as he liberated a bottle and popped the cap, Mat searched the armoire for his personal effects and located the earthen mug Huehuecoyotl had given him on their third meeting. He held the empty cup upside down in one hand, the bottle of soda in the other. With a flip of the wrist he turned the cup rightside up. By some divine quirk of his patron, it had half-filled with steaming xocolātl. As he'd done every day since receiving the mug, Matlal topped it off with cola, cooling and sweetening the mix. He drank it down in a series of five gulps. A little over a year ago, he had been eighty-five, all but blinded by cataracts, and nearly crippled by arthritis. One cupful at a time that had changed. Today he looked about fifty, had the eyesight of his youth and the agility and stamina of his college days. Huehuecoyolt had promised him his heart's desire, to travel the world. That dream that had been crushed by The Return, and while the god's promise hadn't come for two decades, it had included the rolling back of those years and more.

Mat was nobody's fool. Things that seemed too good to be true always turned false. And how much more so when they came from a deity known for playing complex games of manipulation and trickery. He couldn't hope to grasp anything close to the full scope of Huehuecoyotl's plans, but felt confident that they involved much loftier goals than playing on an old man's vanity or promoting mythologically-based pop songs. He hoped they included causing mischief among the other members of the Aztec pantheon. Whether his patron knew his own plans, or had simply helped to position him in the right place, Matlal intended to do more than prank the gods. The Uaithne might end their blood sacrifice once and for all, and perhaps not even Old Man Coyote himself had anticipated *that* trick.

While leading them on the tour of the castle, Fand insisted they consider it their home for the duration of their vacation. She promised to show them everything the island had to offer over the next few few days. Zyanya and Javier readily accepted, but Matlal demurred, citing other plans. After learning the location of such essentials as the castle's kitchen and dining room he excused himself and went to bed.

The linguist was up shortly before dawn. Whether it was the specific cup of cola and xocolātl or the rejuvenating effects of a year and more of the brew, he felt unburdened by jet lag. He dressed, gathered up his tablet and stylus, as well as the simpler notepad and pencil that were the tools in trade of linguists back in the day, and left to find some of the new generation of Manx speakers.

As befit a god of the sea, Manannán's castle stood a stone's cast from the water. Mat walked along the shore until he encountered a small pier and a handful of fishermen preparing to cast off and begin the day's work. Ned Maddrell had been a fisherman, so where better to start? Mat clambered onto the pier and called out in Manx, a phrase he'd put together with care, syllable by unfamiliar syllable.

"Could you use an extra pair of hands in exchange for some conversation?"

Whether due to the oddness of the offer or the peculiarity of his accent, the fisherfolk made room for Mat and welcomed him aboard. Introductions passed back and forth. The crew consisted of three men and one woman. Two of the men were middle-aged, with weathered faces and calloused hands. The remaining man and the woman were younger, somewhere in their early twenties, clearly accustomed to the labor of fishing but without the physical signs of having done it their whole lives. The older men were brothers and used English, dropping the occasional Manx word or phrase into their speech. The younger pair were the children of two of the brothers' other siblings, making them cousins to one another; they spoke Manx and English with equal fluency, and happily took turns translating anything their elders said in English over into Manx for the benefit of Matlal's notepad.

Mat passed the long hours of the day working the nets, hauling in fish, asking questions, and listening to tales of the history of the Isle of Man. These last were told alongside stories of the island's current life and the blend of myth and reality they had dwelt in since The Return. When the boat docked at the pier just ahead of sunset Mat could barely hold his pencil. He had filled his notepad from end to end, but his weariness came from a day spent in the slow physical labor of the fishing boat. It was one thing to see himself in the mirror, getting younger day by day, but it was something else again to find himself sore from pushing his body to do the kind of honest work he hadn't experienced since before he'd entered academia more than half a century ago.

He returned to the castle, using the walk to stretch his aching limbs. In the kitchen he put together the pieces of a cold dinner, helped himself to some ibuprofen from a medicine cabinet, and took both back to his room. After laying out his clothing for the next day, including two fresh notepads, he went to bed, awaking even earlier the next morning to set out for the pier once again, delaying only to prepare his morning libation with the cup Huehuecoyotl had given him and a bottle from the steamer trunk. A different crew accepted his services and he spent the second day as he had the first, filled with stories and notes, as well as bits of grammar and vocabulary. If he took a perverse pride in the aches and pains that spread throughout his body he quickly dismissed it as the whimsy of an eighty-six year-old man caught up in forces beyond his control. What he was learning—both about the island and its reborn language—was what was important.

Matlal continued this pattern of fishing with the local speakers for a full four days. On the fifth day he slept in past dawn, drank his blend of cola and xocolātl, and sat in the castle's breakfast room transferring material from half a dozen notepads to his tablet as he waited for the others to awaken. Javi came in still half asleep and searching for coffee. Mat sat him down and poured the younger man a cup. A few sips later he'd stirred enough to start asking questions.

"Where have you been? Zyanya and I have toured the island twice. She's visited nearly every school and all the stores worth seeing. Fand took her under her wing and has been introducing her to everyone who's anyone here, from local artists and musicians to folks who fought the last battle against the Fomor to the layers of politicians that Manannán allows to run the island."

"And what have you been doing?"

Javi shrugged. "I kept an eye on her at first, but it got pretty clear that she didn't need a bodyguard. And even if she did, having a goddesses treating her like a younger sister was more protection than I could provide.

Since then I've been exploring the music scene, jamming with some of the locals. It's not like anything I'd ever heard before. It's been great."

The linguist smiled. "Glad to hear it. Think you could get some of them to come here this morning? I know it's short notice and that musicians aren't usually morning people, but we have work to do."

"Work? I thought we were on vacation?"

"'Were' being the operative term. You and I are going to do something completely new. We're writing a song about the gods."

Javi finished the rest of his coffee in a long, thoughtful sip. "How is that new? We always write songs about the gods."

"Not in Manx we don't."

Javier delayed just long enough to have a second cup of coffee before heading out, promising to return by lunch with a representative sampling of local musical talent. Matlal used the time to finish the lyrics, modeling the cadence on several ancient songs he'd heard from among the oldest of fisherfolk he'd met, men and women who spoke little Manx excepting the words to songs they'd learned from their own grandparents as children sitting in front of a hearth repairing the nets that would be used the next morning. He printed out a copy of the finished lyrics for Javi to find when he returned—Manannán's network supporting wireless printers throughout the castle. Then he went looking for his singer.

Whether Zyanya had been blessed by the gods with musical talents or had drawn the blessings and attention of the gods because of talents she'd been born with had always struck Mat as one of those unanswerable questions that existed to confuse college freshmen in introductory philosophy courses. The reality of it was that she could memorize a song's lyrics after a single read through, whether English, Spanish, or her native Zapotec.

Manx had some sounds and combinations not found in those, or any of the indigenous languages of Mexico that she'd been learning under Matlal's tutelage. It took her five runs through the lyrics to land all the phonemes right, and ten before she hit the strange syllables with the kind of stress that a native speaker would have. He had translated the words for her but she didn't have a clue what they meant, only how to make them sound. After a couple hours her mimicry duplicated Mat's own all-too-limited facility with the language. He had to hope that the idiomatic usages he'd included would make up for substituting rote memorization for fluency. That, and Javier's music.

Matlal found his composer in the castle's music room, a large performance space with added soundproofing beyond just the stone walls. He was jamming with seven men and women on instruments ranging from electric harp to drum kit, some sort of tin whistle to base guitar. Javier sat at a grand piano, playing a haunting melody that both suited the lyrics and blended the rhythms of local tunes that were part of the bone and blood of everyone on the island. He reached the end of the melody and a harpist sitting nearby took it up, her fingers dancing over the strings in a blur. Mat stood transfixed, not only by the music but also the appearance of the woman playing the harp. It wasn't simply that she was attractive—the goddess Fand's beauty didn't allow for real comparison on the island—but her expression gripped his heart. He saw passion in her violet eyes, a hunger for the music that somehow tapped into her very soul and allowed room for nothing else while she played. Golden hair surrounded her face, cascading in gentle waves over her shoulders and down her back. Mat shook his head but couldn't clear it. The harp continued, its melody proclaiming a romantic ballad that needed no words to convey the purity of feeling it spoke. When the tune came to an end, he found himself applauding, the feeling of romance lingering long after the notes had stopped.

The room of musicians looked up at the applause. Javier grinned and jumped from the piano to rush over to Matlal. "You liked it?"

The linguist couldn't find any words and had to settle for an enthusiastic nod, his eyes still locked on the harpist. Javi followed his gaze and the young man's grin widened. Everyone in the room was looking at them now, staring openly at Mat and then following his gaze to the harpist who in turn was focused on Javier, eyebrows raised in a question.

"Oh. Sorry, sorry. Laurie, may I present Professor Matlal Alejandro Garcia y Fuentes, our lyricist and leader. Mat, this is Laurie Golden, the Uaithne."

Other introductions followed, this man on drums, this woman playing guitar, but Mat heard none of them. He stood transfixed, nodding slowly. When Javier stopped speaking, words slipped from Mat's mouth. "The Uaithne is a harp." He gestured to the modern instrument in the woman's hands. "An ancient harp."

Violet eyes twinkled up at him. "More specifically, it's the Dagda's harp. But the name also applies to the one person, other than the Dagda himself, who can play it. And for some reason that only Manannán knows and hasn't bothered to explain to anyone, that person is me. But please, call me Laurie." She had risen, set aside her instrument, and crossed the room to offer her hand. Automatically he reached out to clasp hers, inhaled deeply as the scent of her reached him. The world tumbled away, but only in his own head, and the moment passed. He was shaking hands with a charming woman. He remembered how to speak again, even as he tried to recall if he'd ever met anyone with violet eyes. "I'm Mat."

Matlal didn't understand why, but Laurie Golden projected his attraction back. Nor did it occur to him to question it. While Javier helped the other musicians pack up, Mat escorted her out of the music room and, by mutual silent agreement, out of the castle. They wandered down the shore, in the opposite direction Mat had taken for his linguistic fishing trips, and found themselves walking down the streets of the neighboring community that lived in the shadow of the island's namesake. Soon after, they landed at an open cafe, took a table for two in the back, and finally broke their silence by ordering lunch. As the waiter took their menus and his leave, they returned to staring at each other like smitten teenagers. After two full minutes of this they both managed to blush, mutter, and look away.

"You've been god-touched too," said Laurie. "Is that it?"

"God-touched?"

She made a rapid gesture with her hands, similar but different to the way they moved upon her harp strings. "Singled out by one of them. Favored. And used."

"Oh. God-touched. I never thought of it that way. I…I guess I am."

"Umm… do you mind if I ask how?"

Mat stared down at his silverware, then turned his gaze to the fascinating water glass in front of him for a time. When he looked up, Laurie stared back at him, her hands folded under her chin. He swallowed hard. "I'm eighty-six years old."

"Excuse me?"

Mat only nodded. Her lovely eyes had acquired a new gleam.

"And Javier, he said your name was Garcia y Fuentes?"

"Yes."

She thumped the table, laughing with delight. "I thought I recognized the name, but you looked too young. I know you!"

"You do?"

"Well, no, not really. I know *of* you. My pop-pop, he used to tell me stories about his college roommate. My favorite was the time you pranked the Dean of Students. Did you really send him bogus letters from every registered student, demanding a honorary doctorate for Elwin Ransom, the philologist from the C. S. Lewis books?"

It was Mat's turn to thump the table as his memory tumbled back through time. "Your grandfather was Chuck Golden? Oh my god! We were thick as thieves back then. I haven't heard from him in ages. How is he? Does he still smoke those ghastly Turkish cigarettes?"

Laurie's smile faded and her eyes misted. "He passed away just after The Return. Lung cancer."

"Oh. I'm… I'm so sorry. God, and that remark about the cig—"

"No, please, he loved those things, even when he had cut back to just one a day because of the coughing. He said they reminded him of the best days of his life. Back at university, in that basement apartment the two of you shared. I've heard enough stories of you from that time to fill a book shelf. And now here you are, looking not all that much older than me…"

The silence surrounded them, a funeral shroud made of bright memories and blameless cruelty, leaving them with their own thoughts.

"Old Man Coyote. The Aztec call him Huehuecoyotl. He came to me the night of The Return. I was there, at the Olympics. I didn't know I was talking with a god, and nothing came of it for another twenty years. Then last year, he showed up again, wanting me to write songs in the old languages of Mexico. Songs of the gods. He teamed me up with a singer and a composer, and together we've been bringing back nearly forgotten languages, and revitalizing the old stories and myths of the Aztec throughout not only Mexico but all of North America. And in exchange, he's been making me younger, a little bit more each day."

"Manannán plucked me from the streets of New York; he insisted I was the reincarnation of the original harpist who had been killed by the Fomor, the dark gods that battled the Tuatha Dé Danann. And the harp, it's like it came alive in my hands. It does things when I play it that are impossible. Puts armies to sleep, calms weary spirits, and—"

"—and stops the sun in the sky," finished Mat.

"How did you know that?"

"It's part of why I'm here."

"I don't understand."

Mat reached across the table and gathered her hands in his. "In Aztec mythology, we're told that our gods demanded blood sacrifice. This wasn't for the gods' own needs though. Our bravest warriors and most treasured artists willingly presented themselves to the high priests to have their beating hearts torn from their chests. The gods required this in order to make the sun rise every day. Without this sacrifice, there would be no sun."

"But—"

He shushed her. "I know, it makes no sense. It's the 21st century. Even in Mexico every school child knows the Earth revolves around the sun, that it rotates on its axis to create day and night. But when the gods returned, they brought the ritual sacrifice with them. I came here for your harp. I thought if I had the Uaithne, I could use it to keep the sun up, and maybe then Tezcatlipoca, Xipe-Totec, Quetzalcoatl, and Huitzilopochtli would stop the slaughter."

Mat let her hands fall from his; he slumped back in his seat.

"You're here to steal my harp?"

"I'm here trying to save my people. Will you help me?"

Their waiter arrived, putting their plates down in the ensuing silence.

Mat paused in the double doors of the music room, listening to Zyanya and Javier. The young singer stood alongside the piano while her nahual bodyguard played. The melody managed to be both haunting and delicate, and Zya's voice swelled with emotion, despite the oddity of some of the consonants and having no clue what the words meant. He applauded softly as the song came to an end, entering the room.

Javi studied him. "You left with Laurie hours ago. Is everything all right?"

"Fine. She's an amazing musician. Which reminds me, how would you both feel about a small concert before we end this vacation? As a thank you gift to our hosts. I wrote that song just for them."

Zyanya glanced at Javier then back at Mat. "A concert? I thought we were on vacation?"

"We'll keep it simple, I promise. The current hit in Nahuatl, a few of Zya's most popular songs in English, and then finishing with this new one in Manx."

The composer chewed his lip. "You want us to perform for gods?"

"Don't think of them as gods. It's not like they're *your* gods, right?

Think of them as Manny and Fand."

Zyanya grinned. "I've had a difficult time remembering Fand is a god. We've had so much fun. She's like the big sister I never had. I'd love to do something nice in return."

"I'll set it up. Tomorrow night. We're already booked on a flight back to North America around midnight. We can head to the airport after the performance and be on our way home while they're all still humming your music."

Javier pushed back from the piano and stood, placing himself protectively between the girl and the linguist. "Old Man Coyote sent us to you. We understand that it's your words that drive everything. But he also charged me with Zyanya's safety, and that comes before anything else, including you. We trust you but… You had us come here for our break. You wrote a song in a language that won't be understood anywhere else. You vanish with the harpist that ended the war with the Fomor. And now you want us to perform in the last few hours we're on this island. What's really going on here?"

Mat didn't even try to keep the wistful sound from his voice. Javi was both romantic and perceptive enough to detect and be distracted by it. "Though neither of you have said anything about it, I know it's been obvious to you that Huehuecoyotol has been erasing my years. And, well, Laurie Golden is an amazing woman…"

Zyanya giggled. "Are you going to start writing love songs for me to sing?"

"We can talk about that on the plane ride home. Okay? Now go pack."

Grinning, Zya practically skipped from the room, singing teasingly as she passed Mat. "Professor's got a girlfriend, professor's got a girlfriend."

He turned back to Javier. "There are a couple things you need to know…"

Manannán welcomed the idea of a concert, but demurred at keeping it small. "That won't do, not at all. Everyone on the island should get to hear it!"

"We'd like to keep it acoustic," said Matlal. "Just Zyanya singing and Javier accompanying her on the piano, maybe a local musician stepping in on a number or two. Something we could do in the castle's music room, to show our appreciation to you and your people for your hospitality."

The god's eyes twinkled. "I think we can have it both ways. That space is completely wired."

"Meaning?"

"Unless you have an objection, I can have the performance broadcast live to every household on the island. All of the people will get to enjoy your gift without altering the intimacy of the actual concert. Tomorrow night is a bit short notice, but I can make a couple calls and send my boat to bring in any engineers I need. Yes, thank you, Mat, this is a wonderful idea. Fand in particular will be delighted; she's grown quite fond of your little singer."

"Both of you have been incredibly generous, Manny. You have a very different relationship with your people than the gods back home."

"A lot of it is having elbow room," said the god. "If I was constantly bumping into the rest of the Tuatha Dé Danann it would all be different. With just Fand and me here, we're better able to appreciate what we have, including the people around us. That said, it's been a delight having a few new voices around, even if you are leaving us so soon. Speaking of which, if you and yours are to catch the weekly flight out after the concert then I need to get on with those calls so it all comes together. But don't make any plans for dinner tomorrow. I'm sure Fand will want to send you off in style."

Dinner the next night was a quiet affair. The three mortals and two gods gathered around the castle's simple breakfast table. A dozen large takeout bags with a familiar fastfood logo occupied a near counter and Fand bade everyone sit while she fussed about, filling platters with fried chicken, corn on the cob, mac and cheese, green beans, mashed potatoes, and honeyed biscuits.

"Manny wanted to give you a banquet in the main dining room, a huge, ostentatious send-off. I told him that was crazy. On the one hand it would have kept the staff busy with cleaning and all that afterwards, and you made a point of wanting them to be able to enjoy your concert. Besides, you've been stuffed with local food all week. I knew you'd prefer some simple and familiar fare. Comfort food served up without any fuss."

Manannán pretended to grumble unhappily, muttering about his reputation as a god and a host, but Mat saw the way he smiled as he tore into his meal, licking his fingertips between pieces of chicken. Javier also displayed a robust appetite. Zyanya ate sparingly, but she always did before a show and more than made up for it afterwards. Mat had no doubt that Javi would set aside a little bit of everything from dinner and see that she had plenty available to devour on the plane ride home.

After they finished eating, the gods presented them with gifts. Fand gave Zyanya a gold necklace of two seabirds flying together, wing to wing, and told her that she had flown so with her sister long ago. She leaned close and whispered something in the girl's ear that made her eyes pop, but Mat only caught one word of it. Magic. Manannán handed Jaivier a wooden flute inlaid with silver, assuring the musician that he had carved it himself from a dark wood that only grew on the Isle of Man. Whether it had any other properties he didn't say. When it was Mat's turn, Fand took Manannán's hand in both of hers and smiled brightly at her mate.

"Matlal Alejandro Garcia y Fuentes, you bear the mark of your patron, a powerful deity on the other side of the ocean, and though your presence on my island has been a source of great pleasure to me and mine, it is not proper that I gift the servant of a brother god, particularly one whom I understand is as fond of his tricks as I am of mine. And yet, what kind of host would I be to let you leave my shores empty-handed? And so I offer you a boon. Whether or not you ever choose to claim it is on you, but should there be cause, you have only to speak my name, Manannán mac Lir, and give voice to your need, and I will be at your side."

Zya and Javi looked to Mat to express the right words of thanks. "Though the three of us has each been touched by gods of our home, we hope you will accept the gift we have made to celebrate our time on your island. I have cobbled together some words, Javier has lent them music, and tonight Zyanya will give them voice for you, the first audience to hear them. May you find them worthy."

Fand clapped her hands. "A new song?" and Manny grinned.

"Let us delay our guests no longer. No doubt they have final preparations to make before their concert. Mat, be assured, the engineers inform me that all is right and ready and you will not so much as notice their presence. Our entire household will attend you in the music room, and should you run overlong, have no fear of missing your flight. My word on it, your plane will not leave without you."

"A sea god has such power over a machine of the air?"

"Not any divine power, no. But I have a controlling interest in the airline. A phone call will do quite well enough. Now, go. Prepare yourselves as you need. My lady and I are expecting to be dazzled!"

True to his word, the entire staff of Manannán's castle had piled into the music room. To Mat's eye, it seemed as if the back wall had somehow been moved further from its opposite number to make more space. The god's other guests, notables from every area of life on the Isle of Man, had also been crammed in. The front row of seats, which included Manannán and Fand, stood barely five feet from the piano. Matt stood in the corner of the room behind the instrument, lost in shadows and with a clear view of the room.

At the appointed time, Javier entered. He wore a simple black silk shirt buttoned with rounded chips of obsidian, black jeans and black boots. When he glided into place at the piano only his hands and face seemed visible. Then Zyanya stepped in from the hall. Her hair shone in a gleaming blonde array that showcased her bright, young face and left her shoulders bare. She wore a strapless gown of pale blue silk that cinched slightly at her waist. Her only adornment was the gold necklace of twin seabirds. The audience hushed as she began to speak.

"This is the first time we've been to the Isle of Man. For me, this trip has meant a lot of firsts. The first time I'd ever been on a plane, or crossed an ocean, or met so many wonderful and friendly people. Thank you so much for making my world a larger place, and for showing me it is filled with such beauty and generosity. Before we leave, we wanted to take this time to repay some of that."

She signaled to Javier and he began playing the introduction to her latest hit, a song in Nahuatl about Chalchiuhtlicue, the Aztec goddess of water, rivers, and storms. Only she, Mat, and Javi understood a word of it, but the audience hung on every syllable as Zyanya sang of the cruel balance of drought and rain, the patterns that defined the world and all too often yielded heartache. Javier's music at times summoned the thunder of the storm and Zyznzya's voice was sweet as rain. By the song's end, a third of the audience had been moved to tears and weren't certain why.

One of the men that had earlier jammed with Javier stepped up, a small stick in one hand and a traditional Irish bodhran in the other. He looked once to the piano and then began drumming. Javier brought the piano in next, and soon after Zyazya began a song in English about the Centzon Totochtin, the four hundred drunken rabbit gods of pulque. The song started light and slow describing a friendly gathering and shared cups of the fermented beverage the Aztecs had made for thousands of year. The tempo of the music increased, paralleling the growing acts of ribaldry as more and more of the rabbit gods arrived to the party and those already present kept drinking. Soon Zyanya was singing as fast as humanly possible, Javier's fingers flew across the keys, and the drummer beat upon the bodhran with a stacatto pace that ran together into a nearly continuous beat. By the end, all of the audience was in tears, but this time weeping with laughter and delight, applauding wildly. The drummer bowed to the audience, and then to Javier and to Zyanya before he departed, giving the singer a few extra moments to catch her breath.

He was replaced by another local musician who accompanied Zyanya's next song on the fiddle. A woman with guitar joined in for the song after that, and then Zya sang two more with only Javier's playing. When she finished the last of these she glanced back at Mat in the corner before addressing the audience once more.

"I'd like to sing one last song, something that we wrote during our time here. I'm a little nervous because I've never performed it, so we've asked for some special help and she's graciously agreed to be here with me. Laurie Golden."

As if conjured by her name, the harpist stepped into the music room. She had her golden hair down around her shoulders and the emerald dress she wore was the twin in cut to Zyanya's own. In her arms she carried a harp of ancient wood, the Uaithne. The audience recognized both harpist and harp, murmuring with hushed awe. Javier stood and brought his piano bench forward, placing it alongside the singer before leaving the room. The harpist seated herself and settled her harp into place. Zyanya addressed the audience once more.

"We came to the Isle of Man because my lyricist likes languages. Back home, he's always going on and on about how few people are left who speak this language or that language. He told me that Manx had officially died off back in 1974, but that you brought it back. I guess that made him really happy because he wanted to come here and learn enough about it to write this song. I hope you like it."

Laurie's fingers stroked the strings of the Uaithne and Zyanya began to sing. Though only about half the people in the room spoke fluent Manx, all recognized the words from a story as old as the island itself, the legend of how Manannán met and wed Fand. Where before Zyanya had song of sadness and heartache, of riotous fun and partying, of gods interfering in the lives of mortals in tones of irony and frustration and incredulity, now her voice took on a purity of sound. She sang of love, of its power to render even a god helpless, of the perfection of finding that other person who completes and fulfills, of sharing endless years that begin and end every day with joy.

When the last notes of her voice died away, the audience surged up as one with thunderous applause. In the front seats Manannán and Fand clasped one another in a teary embrace, murmuring words meant only for the other's ears.

The applause continued for several minutes but eventually everyone sat. Blushing, Zyanya thanked them all again. Matlal stepped out from behind the piano, stopping next to Laurie Golden. She looked up at him as he placed a hand upon her shoulder. In response she mouthed a single word. "Now?"

"Now."

Thousands of years earlier the harp had been bound so that it would only play for the Dagda, the high king of the Tuatha Dé Danann, only him and one other. Laurie Golden was that other. When she'd first come to play the harp it had taken a miracle for harp and harpist to recognize one another, to allow music to pour from its strings. Now that sound came as easily for her as with any harp. But accessing the instrument's deeper magic took more effort. When she had accompanied Zyanya's song, Laurie's eyes had been wide open. Now she let them close, looking deep inside herself she made contact with something she knew lived within but which she seldom had cause to touch. The connection flowed outward, into her hands, and she began to play.

As if recognizing a melody they could only have heard in dreams, everyone in the room fell deeply asleep.

Still playing, Laurie rose to her feet and nodded to Matlal and Zyanya. All three left the music room and walked quickly through the castle and outside to where Manny's limo awaited them, packed for a drive to the airport with Jaiver at the wheel. They climbed inside and only when the car had pulled away from the castle's grounds did the harpist stop playing. As one, Matlal and Zyanya began tugging at their ears, pulling out the industrial-grade earplugs that had kept them awake. Mat checked his watch.

"We're twenty minutes from Ronaldsway, and if I've timed this right our flight should start boarding within minutes of our arrival. In a little over half an hour we should be airborne and on our way. Before any of our audience wakes from their impromptu naps."

Zyanya burst into tears. "Why, Mat? Manny and Fand were so nice to us. What are you doing all of this? And why is *she* coming with us?"

"Zya, you know what happens at the Temple of the Sun, right?"

The singer wiped at her eyes, blinking back tears. "The best of us offer our lives to the gods."

"And do you know why?" Mat kept his voice level, watching Laurie watching Zyanya, hearing the words from a girl who had never known a world before The Return.

"Duh. To keep the sun in the sky. So the world isn't plunged into eternal darkness."

Mat nodded. "And have you wondered why, with all the billions of other people in the world, all the other pantheons of deities watching over them, why the Aztec people alone do this? Why we murder our own sons and daughters?"

Zyanya paled. "Murder? Mat, don't blaspheme!"

Mat reached out a hand to Laurie who took it, holding it tightly. "Her harp has the power to stop the sun in the sky. Just like it put everyone to sleep. She's the only one who can play it, and she's agreed to help."

"Why didn't you tell me this before?"

"I told Javi. And I'm sorry, but we decided it was better if you didn't know. We didn't want to hinder your performance. We needed to catch Manny off-guard to be sure he'd fall asleep with the rest of them."

The partition separating them from the driver's compartment lowered. "We're almost to the airport. If you really want to do this, it's time to get ready, professor."

Mat squeezed Laurie's hand. "We're not your people. Are you sure?"

"More than anything. I think I've been living here on the island for years, just waiting for you to show up." She leaned forward and kissed him full on the lips, making both of them blush. "For luck," she said.

When they reached the airport, Javi leapt from the car. He signaled a porter who came running with a cart and together they unloaded the luggage from the trunk while Mat flagged down a second porter and cart to handle the steamer trunk from the passenger compartment. Overhead a loudspeaker announced boarding for their flight to New York, informing them of the gate number.

Javier stuffed money into the hands of both porters, sending one to see their bags quickly stowed in the plane while the other followed them with the trunk as they raced to board their flight. They left the limo at the curb without so much as a backward glance.

As on the flight out, they had only to show their tickets to a bored airport employee and they were waved past. Less than five minutes after arriving at Ronaldsway they were buckled into their seats on both sides of the aisle in the first row of first class: the teen singer, her bodyguard, the linguist, and his trunk. Mat's eyes were locked on the exit, willing the crew to dog and latch the door, seal out the world and mark the start of their flight. It was only after the flight attendant had done so that he realized he'd been holding his breath.

The usual patter and pantomime followed. Seat belts, oxygen masks, floatation devices, no smoking signs. The sound of the engines changed, and a moment later the plane began backing away from the gate. When it had enough room to turn it stopped, changed direction, and made its way to the runway where it picked up speed for takeoff. Matt looked over at Zya and Javi and ventured a smile.

And then the plane slowed, slowed, stopped. The engines died.

Illuminated sporadically as he passed the runway's lights, the silhouette of a man strode toward the plane. While still fifty feet or more from the plane it leaped into the air and closed the distance. A dull thud came from the exit and the plane's captain came out of the cockpit to unseal the door himself. He moved back, and Manannán stepped onto the plane; his eyes found Mat in an instant.

"You have something of mine." His words were cold, devoid of inflection.

"I took nothing of yours." For the second time in his life Mat found himself disagreeing with a god. It was over. And he'd been so close.

"I didn't say you took it, I said you had it. Open the trunk."

Knowing the futility of argument he turned in his seat and began working the latches and fastenings. When he had finished with the last of them, the trunk opened on its own to reveal Laurie Golden swaddled in foam and bubblewrap, the Uaithne clutched to her breast.

"You left a stack of soda bottles behind," said Manannán. "Did you think them a fair trade?"

Before Mat could respond Laurie spoke. "I don't belong to you, Manny. I'm not one of your worshippers. I've been a guest in your land these years, and now I'm going home."

He shrugged, a gesture full of a weariness Mat had never seen on the god before. "The harp belongs to me."

"No, it belongs to the Dagda. He's gone. You escorted him beyond this world yourself. Ownership reverts to the only person who can play it. You named me the Uaithne when you first brought me here. Besides, you gave the harp to me when I ended your war with the Fomor."

Sighing, the god leaned against the plane's bulkhead. "I'm trying to spare you both pain."

"You don't understand," said Mat. "I need to do this. It's important."

"I do understand. And I understand why you believe it's important. But… it won't work."

"What?"

"You are a scholar, Matlal. A man of great learning. Your mind was shaped in the twentieth century by reason and science. You cannot help yourself from seeing the world through such lenses. You think if you can use the Uaithne to stop the sun that your own gods will have no reason to continue their tradition of blood sacrifice."

"They won't! The whole point of it is to keep the sun in the sky—"

"Mat, listen to yourself. You know that makes no sense. All the centuries since your gods first departed and before The Return, the sun rose and set, day after day. You cannot apply reason to religious ritual."

"But—"

Manannán pressed on. "Maybe once it truly worked that way. Maybe the blood of your people was needed to keep darkness from the world. I don't know. But the practice continues today because of divine inertia, not because of rational explanation. You won't change anything. At best you'll only piss them off. The sacrifices will continue and you'll have two hundred deities angry with the mortal who presumed to tell them how the world works. Crafty as he might be, not even Huehuecoyotl could save you from that. Don't throw everything away."

"What do you expect him to do then, Manny? His own gods are killing his people!" Laurie's hands had found Mat's. They clung to one another as if the god might try to pull them apart.

"If I thought you might really hear me, I would tell you to ignore the spectacle and drama. I would point out that the number of worshippers who willingly give themselves over to sacrifice is less than a hundredth the number who died from hunger and disease and mundane traffic accidents in the years before The Return made those deaths a memory."

"Now who's pitching a rational argument?"

The god let his gaze fall upon Zyanya and Javier for a moment before turning back to Mat. "Your patron has done you a great disservice. Not only has he restored your youth, but in the process he has managed to kindle the spark of hope in you, the one gift that no god can stand against. Worse still, you have spread it to others. These two who would follow you from their own true paths."

Mat took a deep breath. "Why are you telling me this?"

"I should stop you. Even though you bear the mark of another god, I should smite you and put an end to this before it goes further. For even knowing your plan with the Uaithne cannot work, you will seek some other means, try some other scheme. Almost any god who recognized what you are—the danger you pose—would kill you here and now. Do you understand me?

"And yet... I am not almost any god. As psychopomp, were you of mine it would be my honor to name you hero and escort you beyond this world. But no, you are marked by a trickster god, and as one of that kind myself I know that we stand between mortals and our fellow deities. Twas ever thus. I am sending you home, Matlal, in the company of my island's beloved Laurie Golden. With all my heart I advise you to give up your pointless scheme to have her stop the Mexican sun in the sky; it will not accomplish your goal and will only destroy you and those dear to you. And I would not wish for that."

"Is this the boon you gave me? You letting us leave?"

Manannán laughed. "No. You retain that, and I have no doubt you will have need of it. What I do now is repayment for your gift to Fand and me." He gestured, including Zyanya and Javier in his words. "Your song, your words, reminded us of a time long gone. What Huehuecoyotl has set before you as a task for the millions of people in your homeland, you have done for the entire people of my island. I am deeply in your debt, Matlal. Please do not bring about your own destruction and leave me in that state. Seek another way, and perhaps in time I will be able to restore the balance between us."

He nodded one time more, turned, and stepped off the plane. The captain quickly dogged the hatch and fled back to the cockpit. Moments later the engines started up again. Mat and Javi wrestled the steamer trunk into the aisle and a pair of flight attendants took it away.

As they settled back in their seats, Javier looked grim. "What do you plan to do when we get home? Will you use the harp as you intended?"

"What would be the point? No, I'm going to take Manny's advice and come up with another plan." As he said these words, Mat felt his heart lighten at a sudden realization. A smile burst out on his face, bright as the sun.

"I don't get it," said Zya. "We failed. Why are you grinning?"

He turned to Laurie, sharing his smile with her, squeezing her hand, then spun back to face the singer and her bodyguard. "I'm seeing things more clearly. And I've just been handed an even more powerful weapon than the Uaithne."

"What's that?"

Mat let the smile envelope him in its warmth as he answered. "A second trickster god just implied that there's a way to get what we want. And he owes us a big favor. We haven't failed. Far from it, I think we've just had our feet set on the right path."

A Clockwork God

by Paul Kupperberg

Sumer, 2334 B.C.E.

An was alone in his temple.

A situation due to change quite shortly.

He imagined he heard the scrape of his destroyer's sandals on the stone steps of the great Ziggurat that dominated the northern quarter of Ur, the soft squeal and squeak of the Akkadian's leather armor and scabbard as he climbed.

The time had come. *His* time.

An had sent his priests and servants away and barred the doors to the faithful. This place of prayer and contemplation was soon to become a battleground. It had tasted the blood of sacrifice and betrayal in the past, but never that of its host, and for what was to come, only the gods may remain to witness.

Except there were none left, not to bear witness nor stand by his side against the destroyer. None of his own. He, An, god of the heavens and creator of the universe, was the last standing of his kind. All along the great valley of civilization between the Tigris and Euphrates Rivers, the temples of Sumer stood sacked and soaked in the blood of the gods. Gone were his beloved Ki, their son Enlil, his mother Nammu. Gone were Enten of the farms, the water god Enki, his daughter Uttu, goddess of the plants. Dead too were Ashnan of the grains, Kabta of the bricks, Inanna of the granary. Nanna. Ninhursag. Ereshkigal, Ningal, Enkimdu, Ninshebargunu.

An did not fear death. He, from whose hand had sprung the Sumerian world and afterworld, was the All and would remain so, whether in this form or another. But...he had grown fond of this incarnation as flesh and would miss it so. It offered pleasures for which those at Oneness no longer had need but which he could not imagine existence without. The sights, the smells, the *sensations* of man, those fragile beings created by the gods to be servants! No wonder that after they created man, the gods assumed human form so that they might experience the gifts they had given these beings but did not themselves possess.

But the flood of sensations must surely have been more than humans could contain and they proved too stubborn and unreasonable to make proper servants. Reason demanded the gods destroy these disobedient apes, but the same gifts they acquired by becoming as humans themselves overwhelmed them with compassion for these quarrelsome creatures. So was man given voice in his worship, but contempt soon followed familiarity, and the people of Sumer began turning their backs on their gods and reaching towards the deities of Akkad in northern Mesopotamia. While the mortal leader Sargon sought to unite the Akkadian speaking Semites and the Sumerian speakers under his rule, his gods promised Sumerian worshippers places of honor in their temples to worship and a happier life after.

And old gods to mourn.

This time, the sound of leather scraping over stone was real, not imagined. Behind him. A footstep. And another. And another.

An drew in a deep draught of air and grasped the hilt of his bronze great sword. With defiant slowness, he turned to face his end on this physical plane.

The boy's dark eyes grew wide with awe as he peered from behind the altar. From where he crouched in hiding and in defiance of An's command to leave the temple, he could see the god where he stood, without armor, in the center of the great atrium, open to the sky above. He wore the robes and symbols of his godhood, ceremonial garb and delicate jewelry crafted of gold and precious gems, but in his hand he clutched a war sword.

The boy knew what was happening. Sheltered though he was supposed to be in the company of the women, the human wives and concubines of their god, the world as they knew it collapsing was not an event that could pass unnoticed. And the boy, all of eleven summers old and on the cusp of manhood, could not sit huddled in fear with the women while their gods faced extinction at the hands of usurper gods.

So he stayed behind and hid behind the pedestal of the great statue of An, where he could watch and wait with An for the pretender god to come. And, when the time came, to strike! He did not lie to himself that the iron dagger he had snuck days before from the belt of a sleeping harem guard would prove particularly lethal against a god, but it might be distraction enough to enable An to strike the killing blow.

For as long as he had even a single worshipper left, An was yet the Creator of the Heavens and God of the Skies and All Heavens Yet Unseen.

Anu said, "You are the last of your kind, my lord."

An bowed.

"Though I am the last of the First, as long as I am, what was can be created anew."

"You are the last because the age of the gods of Sumer has ended," Anu said. He raised his own sword, polished bright and so sharp as to divide day from night. "Now man will say, 'Bless you, great Anu, who made the universe and spread over us the Endless Heavens above.'"

An brought up his blade.

"Or shall they sing the tale of An in memory of the day he carved a pretender god from the soul of his people?"

Anu laughed. "Your day is over, old one. You have heard your *last* song!"

And then the gods did battle.

Fire and sparks erupted from clashing blades that rang like thunder in the boy's ears. An was at once on the defensive, his sword coming up to parry Anu's and forcing him back one step, then another, and another.

"My lord!" the boy whispered and began to pray. His fingers closed around the hilt of the dagger at his waist. He could feel the slow progress of a single bead of sweat that dripped from his shaved head, down behind his ear and onto his neck.

He was frightened. He was a boy, a child. A child armed with nothing but a dagger with which to do battle with a god.

Perhaps it was just as well the gods were gone. They would laugh at him for his arrogance and his fear.

In combat, An staggered towards the boy's hiding place, Anu in pursuit. He could hear the gasps and grunts of the old god in his desperation to fend off the new. To him, his gods were creatures of eternity...until they began to die.

"Who can say what lies beneath their human features?" his mother said to him when once he had asked. "They were here before the world existed and they will witness its end. Man may do them no harm, but it is whispered that one god may slay another, but when they clash, the Earth will shake and mankind will know the end is near."

The Earth did not shake, but all else his mother had said seemed true.

Now An alone survived, but for how long? And when the Creator ceased to be, would not his creations follow him into oblivion?

The boy prayed but An weakened still. The power of prayer was said to strengthen the gods. The more who prayed to him, the greater his might. Where were the prayers of the people of Sumer? Was his the last voice in all the land to speak the name of An with reverence?

Or had the time come for the boy to become a man and defend his faith with actions rather than words?

"I am coming, my lord!" he whispered. The boy drew the dagger from his waist.

And, as the interloper god thundered past his hiding place, driving the ever weaker An before him, the boy leapt from concealment and plunged his blade into Anu's broad back.

Anu barely paused, glancing back over his shoulder before slicing his blade through the air and through the neck of An, separating the head and body of the Creator of the Heavens and God of the Skies and All Heavens Yet Unseen.

An's head rolled across the stone floor, its eyes wide and staring, and the boy was certain its lips moved and it continued to speak, but Anu had turned with eyes wide and blazing of his own.

"Boy!" the conqueror rumbled. "I'll not bother to ask upon whose side you stand!"

In two great strides, great Anu was upon the boy, one massive hand closing around his arm. He lifted him from the floor and tossed him, like a well-gnawed joint of mutton, out a window. The all-father of Akkad, the new god of the heavens and skies, did not wait to hear the soft thud of impact on the cobblestones far below of the boy's body before turning to claim his throne.

Jerusalem, Today, 2033 A.D.
If at any point in his life Irwin Benjamin had been asked for a list of twenty

places he wanted to visit before he died, the Middle East wouldn't have made the cut. He acknowledged it was old, it was fascinating, it reeked with history as the cradle of civilization and birthplace of the world's major religions...but he just never really cared enough to want to go there. Besides, people were always shooting and blowing each other up in that part of the world, usually taking innocent bystanders and visiting American Hebrew school students with them.

So, naturally, here he was, making his third visit to this ancient land since 1998, when he was thirteen.

He forced himself to remember that none of those trips had been made voluntarily. The first had been out of guilt and misguided filial obligation (or were those the same thing?). The other two were strictly business, both the result of the Bureau loaning him out to other agencies to assist in their investigations.

At least this time he was being put up at the elegant King David Hotel overlooking the Old City and Mount Zion. That was a definite step-up from the youth hostels and Tzahal barracks he'd stayed in on previous visits, but hardly enough of a perk to make up for having to make the trip in the first place.

"And let's not forget the two days under Palestinian guns in the rubble of the old synagogue in Sderot," he said to himself as he reached for his morning orange juice.

No, on second thought, do forget that.

After a lifetime of being an obedient Jewish son, five years of marriage, and eighteen years as a government employee, FBI Special Agent Irwin Benjamin was accustomed to taking orders. He took them well and he took them without qualm. "The world is made up of two kinds of people; the ones who give the orders and the ones who take them," his great Uncle Milt used to say. Milt was full of such generalizations and pronouncements; he was also usually full of shit. But in this particular instance, he was, in Irwin's experience, dead right. Otherwise, how was it that he had spent most of his forty-eight years largely doing what other people told him to do?

He obeyed his mother (*everybody* obeyed his mother!); he obeyed his wife for the five years they were married and continued to allow her to call the shots in the eighteen years since their divorce; he obeyed his supervisors at the Bureau, his performance record a perfect reflection of his get-along personality, containing no black marks and just enough low level commendations to keep his career from stalling out entirely; and now, he obeyed the gods.

A god, at any rate.

God*dess*, pardon me. The Egyptian goddess of harmony, justice, and truth, to be precise.

Irwin glanced around the hotel's bustling terrace dining area as he sipped his juice, then checked his cellphone for the time. Both his breakfast companions were late and neither had sent an explanation, a irritation he let pass after a brief and satisfying flare of resentment. He hated to be late himself and was habitually early; he also hated waiting for others, who were invariably tardy, but in his best passive-aggressive manner he preferred to stew rather than confront.

"Been through much therapy, have you?" he muttered.

"I'm sorry, Agent Benjamin, did you say something?"

Irwin pushed back his chair and rose, smiling quickly at the short, stocky woman who was approaching the table.

"No. I mean, yes, I did," he said quickly. "But I was talking to myself."

"I do it, too. All the time. It's a bad habit we acquire when we spend too much time alone, I suppose," Gloria Rowe said. She took the seat to his right. "Sorry I'm late, but I was stuck on a call from New York. It's so hard to get an open long distance line in the first place, I try to make the most of it when I do get through."

"No problem, Father," he said, feeling as he always did a little awkward addressing the woman by the masculine pronoun. But she was a priest in the Roman Catholic Church. Woman had only started being ordained about a decade ago, so the Church (with, admittedly, bigger issues to deal with in this new religious age and a track record of being slow to adapt to change) had yet to find a fix for the title conundrum.

The waiter came by to take their order, and just as Irwin was telling him that they were still waiting for one more in their party, the devil of which he was speaking appeared.

"Excuse my tardiness, my friends," Eric Strobe boomed in lightly accented English as he slid past the waiter and into the chair across from Irwin. "If you have ever experienced the Jerusalem morning traffic, you will understand." He turned to the waiter. "Coffee, my good man. Hot, thick, and strong." He found his napkin which, with an elaborate flick of his wrist and a loud snap, he unfolded and dropped in his lap.

"Yes, Mr. Strobe," the Arab waiter nodded, then looked expectantly at Irwin and the lady priest. "Sir? Ma'am?"

"Turkish coffee," Strobe explained to them. "Guaranteed to strip the lining from your stomach."

Irwin ordered the coffee. Father Rowe had tea.

Once the waiter had taken the rest of their order, Strobe said, in a voice loud enough to be heard halfway across the terrace, "Welcome again to Jerusalem. I trust you slept well and have had time to overcome your jetlag?"

"Not me. That's why I'm having the coffee," Irwin said with a weak grin.

Strobe laughed, loud. Others around the restaurant began to look his way.

"Excuse me, Mr. Strobe, but I was under the impression that we were supposed to maintain a...well, a low profile," Gloria Rowe said, looking around nervously at all the staring tourists.

Eric Strobe was, Irwin thought with amusement, the *least* low profile individual that he could recall meeting in a long time. At six foot three inches tall, the dark-haired Israeli came with an athlete's physique and a model's chiseled good looks. He was going to attract attention whether he stood stock still in the corner or shone a spotlight on himself atop the Wailing Wall.

"From whom?" Strobe said.

Father Rowe leaned in and lowered her voice to say, "From...from the killer."

Strobe leaned in and moderated his own volume to say, "I assure you, Father, he is not here. He is not within one hundred kilometers of here. And the habitués of this establishment are, in fact, accustomed to boisterous Eric Strobe always speaking too loud and laughing too hard."

"We're not undercover, Father Rowe," Irwin said. "Eric is with the *Sherut HaBitahon HaKlali*, the General Security Agency, commonly known as the *Shabak*. They're like Israel's FBI, responsible for internal security."

"And like my new good friend Irwin, I have been placed on loan to the security office of the Hall of Gods and Division G, under the command of...," Strobe looked quizzically at Irwin. "Captain Mayer?"

"Not quite...it's Mayat. She's an Egyptian goddess, not a *lanzman*," Irwin grinned.

"A...what?" Father Rowe said.

"An Egyptian goddess," Irwin said with a shake of his head.

"No, the other word you used...?"

"Oh, *lanzman*. It's Yiddish. It means 'lands man,' like someone from your hometown, or in this case, a fellow Jew."

"So, you. *Lanzman*," Strobe said, pointing his chin at Irwin. "What do you think? These...beings, these creatures, whatever they are. Do you think they're gods?"

Irwin Benjamin's eyebrows rose in surprise behind his horn-rim glasses.

"Hell if I know," he said. "That sort of thinking's way above my pay grade."

"You must have an opinion," Strobe said.

The waiter returned to slide their coffees and tea before them and Irwin said, "I don't spend a lot of time thinking about it."

"Really?" Father Rowe said, surprised.

"Really. I never was particularly religious, and it's just as easy to *not* worship a thousand gods as it is not to worship one."

"I think you're being slightly facetious, Mr. Benjamin. I assume you had some religious background and training as a child," she said.

"Sure, the standard Jewish middle class, non-observant route of after school Hebrew school and Bar Mitzvah."

"But it must have meant something to your parents that you followed in their heritage?"

Irwin sighed. The inevitability of his conversation, or some form of it, had been hanging over his head from the moment he had been told by his supervisor that the Bureau had requested the priest's help as a technical advisor on the case. Gloria Rowe was some sort of world-class Biblical and Church scholar, a leading expert with a several advanced degrees and at least one doctorate each in history, theology, and archaeology. And a priest. Her vocation may be as a historian, but her avocation was saving souls and his, if it existed, was no doubt in desperate need of salvation.

"It's a tradition, Father, that's all. Protestants have coming outs and cotillions, Jews have Bar Mitzvahs. For me and my friends, they had about as much to do with religion as a sweet sixteen party."

"That's so sad," Father Rowe said.

"For who?" Irwin snapped, feeling a flash of irritation at her condescension.

"Excuse me," Strobe said. "As fascinating as this is, it is all beside the point. Our mission is a secular one, yes? We have a killer to catch."

"But he's killing gods," Father Rowe.

Strobe shrugged. "So? He is a killer. We are in the business of hunting killers. Man, god, it makes no difference to me."

"He's racked up thirty-two victims so far. Looks like he's going for a record," Irwin said. "All I want to do is find him and stop him and go home. I'll leave religion to the politicians."

"Don't you mean the clergy?" Father Rowe said.

"Religion *is* politics, Father. Always was, but these days more so than ever." Irwin threw back the little cup of syrupy black coffee, trying not to cough as the harsh brew raked down his throat.

"Something I said seems to have struck a nerve with you, Agent Benjamin," she said gently. "Whatever it was, I meant no offense."

"Sure," he said and took a deep breath. "Sure," he said again, this time meaning it. "I get a little touchy on the subject. And being back in Jerusalem doesn't help my mood any either."

"You've been here before?" Father Rowe said in surprise.

"Twice. Once on Bureau business and once as a kid."

"What happened?"

Irwin pushed back his chair and stood. "I was shot and killed when I was thirteen years old by a Palestinian during a hostage situation."

Gloria Rowe's eyes went wide. "I'm sorry? You were...what?"

"Pissed at my parents, for one thing," he said. "I wanted to go to Disney World instead that summer."

Back in his hotel room, Irwin Benjamin washed his hands and face and threw up his coffee in the toilet. When he was a kid back in East Flatbush, one of his Hebrew school friends used to call vomiting "praying to the porcelain *Messiach*." It used to crack them all up. No one in any of the classes of eleven, twelve, and thirteen year old boys he studied the Hebrew language and religion with gave any serious thought to the lessons being taught by old Rabbi Schindler, prune-faced Mr. Zindel, or any of the other instructors. You went to Hebrew school, you had your Bar Mitzvah, and then you could be done with temple and prayer and god if you wanted, just like your parents. And they all wanted. Religion was just that thing that interfered with after school activities Monday through Thursday all through middle school.

He had grown up never thinking about but accepting of some abstract concept of "god." A Big Brother who watched over mankind—usually in wrathful disapproval, if the Bible stories were to be believed—but who otherwise didn't seem to have much impact on life. He joked that his father's idea of observing the High Holy Days on the Jewish calendar was to park his car around the corner so the neighbors couldn't observe him driving.

A week before his thirteenth birthday, some scared shitless Palestinian kid not much older than him but with a cause and an AK-47, had been startled and shot him in the chest. Irwin's last thought, as the bullet interrupted his loud and frantic screams to god to please, please save him, was, "What a load of crap."

And then he died.

New York City, Six Weeks Ago
Special Agent Benjamin kept quiet during the more than hour long staff meeting in the Hoover Building's fifth floor conference room. The participants were agents who, like him, headed up special units or oversaw task forces. Unlike him, his fellow supervisors had command of *other* agents that made up their various units and forces. Irwin Benjamin was a special unit of one.

And even in that set-up, he commanded nothing. His fate was, quite literally, in the hands of the gods. Or one god*dess*, Mayat, who headed up the security office of Hall of the Gods.

And his mission was classified. Only the Director's office knew he had been loaned out to the Hall, and only the Director and his first deputy knew exactly why. The gods wanted a lid kept on his investigation and the Bureau was eager to cooperate. For his part, above and beyond his personal policy of never rocking the boat, Irwin wasn't eager to learn what the gods did to whistleblowers. He wouldn't have been surprised, in fact, to learn that was one of the reasons he had been chosen for this assignment. The gods did like their humans obedient, although matters of low self-esteem aside, Irwin did recognize the other factors that contributed to his being where he was.

And yet, with all that, he was still required to be at the hour long weekly staff meeting in Washington, D.C. where he could *not* report his progress on a case that was not officially open. But, he was classified as holding a unit command, and all unit commanders were required to attend the meeting.

So Agent Benjamin attended and pretended to listen as his colleagues outlined the progress of their cases and to watch them wonder why the he was there every week but never spoke.

It was, he had to admit, kind of fun knowing something that none of them knew. And after seventeen years without any sort of ripple in his career, it was an interesting feeling to be the subject of speculation. The FBI teaches its investigators to look for patterns and, more importantly, *changes* in patterns. The radical change in his pattern must have been driving the rest of them crazy.

After the meeting, he chatted briefly with the others, enjoying their conversational feints at his business, then walked with them to the elevators. The rest of them were going down; he hit the "up" button and mumbled something about seeing them later, he had a meeting "upstairs."

He rode the elevator up three floors, chuckling. He knew he was showboating, but all of a sudden, being the object of speculation didn't seem like such a bad thing. He was forty-eight years old, with three years more years to go until he hit the magic twenty year retirement mark. If he was ever going to make a move up in grade to beef up the coming pension, it had to be now.

He had been handed the opportunity on a golden platter. Nineteen gods dead (and counting), and Special Agent Irwin Benjamin was the only law enforcement agent to not only have seen the killer, but to have spoken to him as well. So now he was not only the killer's favorite Feebie, but a favorite of Captain Mayat's as well. Her Division G was under the auspices of the Hall of Gods, which used to be known as the United Nations and now served the same function for the celestials as it once had for the countries of the world. But as supreme and infallible as they liked to appear, apparently what the gods knew about forensics and modern criminal investigative techniques left a lot to be desired, so she handed her divine serial killings off to the experts.

And, somehow, it wound up in his lap.

Assistant Director Pyle had Irwin brought directly into his office and seated with offers of coffee or bottled water. From the A.D. himself. The newly appointed number two man in the Bureau.

"Special Agent Benjamin...may I call you Irv?" Pyle said once the beverage orders had been all sorted out.

"Irwin. Sir," he said. "My name's Irwin."

"Irwin," Pyle smiled awkwardly, glancing quickly at Irwin's file in front of him. "Of course. Irwin." He went back to the file, flipped through a few pages, his forehead creasing into a frown as he went along.

Finally, he looked up.

"I'm puzzled, Irwin," he said.

"Sir?"

"I may be new to the A.D.'s desk, but I do know my way around a man's jacket," Pyle said with no small pride and even larger smugness. "I was associate director of human resources for six years, and yours isn't the jacket of a man who gets an assignment like this."

Pyle was a gray Washington bureaucrat, a FBI lifer who spent his entire career on the administrative side and who had never had to pull his weapon except to qualify on the range. The organization was lousy with the type; they were the ones who felt like they had to come thundering into new commands to prove how tough they were to the guys out in the field actually doing the job.

So Irwin just said, "Yes, sir."

"Then how do you explain the assignment, Irwin?"

"I can't, sir. Other than Captain Mayat requesting me."

The A.D. slid a second folder out from under Irwin's file. This one had a brick red cover and the words "EYES ONLY" stamped on it.

"I see that. What I don't understand is why you, Irwin?"

"Look, no disrespect, sir, but what difference does it make?"

Pyle looked up sharply.

"What I mean is," he went on quickly, "I don't know if it's because she likes my face or thinks I know something I don't know I know, but we've been ordered to cooperate with Division G and Division G wants me to investigate."

Assistant Director Pyle didn't like the agent's tone, but apparently he was, for a Washington gray man, enough of a realist to see the point.

"Jesus Christ, nineteen dead gods," he muttered. "Why aren't they handling this internally? I thought only gods can kill each other."

"They did their own investigation, just before the fifth killing, according to Captain Mayat. She said they concluded none of the gods in the known pantheons was the killer."

"Based on what?"

Agent Benjamin shrugged.

"Her answer pretty much boiled down to, 've haff our vays!' She didn't seem to think there was much room for argument. And the fact that the killer is using crosses carved from the wood from the alleged 'True Cross' to kill his victims has lead them to believe that he's a follower of what she called one of the "new faiths," Christianity...a conclusion with which our profilers agreed, by the way, and which my conversation with him confirmed."

Pyle found the transcript of the conversation the agent mentioned in the red folder. While he read it through, Irwin said, "Also, they may be gods, but murder investigations are out of their league. Mayat's operating on the idea that you set a 'new faith' mortal to catch a 'new faith' mortal, and since I was the closest one to the investigation..."

The assistant direct laid the transcript in front of his agent and said, "Is this an accurate account of that conversation?"

Irwin glanced at it. Not that he needed to read it again. He had it memorized by now.

TRANSCRIPT OF SUSPECT INTERVIEW
UNSUB KNOWN ONLY AS "JUNKER GEORGE" OR "GEORGE"
LOCATION: (Former) NEW YORK CITY PUBLIC LIBRARY, 42nd Street & 5th Avenue, New York, NY
TIME: 8:10 P.M. EST (APPROX.)
AGENT ARRIVES ON SCENE. OBSERVES SUSPECT EXITING BUILDING.

FBI: Excuse me, sir, I'm with the FBI. May I have a word with you?
"GEORGE": You can see me?
FBI: Yes, sir. Any reason why I shouldn't?
[SUBJECT IS NON-RESPONSIVE]
FBI: Would you stay where you are, sir? I'd like to talk to you... Please, George...
"GEORGE": I don't answer to earthly authorities.
FBI: I'm under the authority of the security office of the Hall of the Gods, George. They're on their way over.
"GEORGE": Nor do I answer to the false gods. That [REFERENCE TO AGENT'S WEAPON] won't do you any good either. Let me pass, please. I don't wish to harm you.
FBI: You won't. Last warning, George. Put your hands behind your head and turn around.

"GEORGE": You shall have no other gods before him.

FBI: Right now the subject's murder. We can talk comparative religion later, once I've got you cuffed. Hands behind your head. Turn around.

[SUBJECT RESISTS. AGENT FIRES HIS WEAPON.]

"GEORGE": Since you've chosen to cast your lot with the heathens, you can share their fate.

[AGENT'S RELIGIOUS MEDALLION IS UNCOVERED IN FIGHT]

"GEORGE": The star of David. *Baruch Hashem.* [TRANS.: Hebrew, "Blessed be God"]

AGENT: Who are you?

"GEORGE": I am Junker George, the Lord God's instrument on Earth. You've spoken with Father Rowe, I take it?...What is your name, brother?

AGENT: Benjamin. Irwin Benjamin. Look, whoever you are, you can't...

"GEORGE": I can. I must. Tell Father Rowe I will see her again. You too, brother Benjamin. We have much work to do, we three.

AGENT: Wait! You...you're under arrest!"

[SUSPECT FLEES.]

END OF TRANSCRIPT

"Yes, sir. Word for word. Our conversation was picked up by a tourist's camcorder that was dropped when George and I had our scuffle."

The gray man nodded thoughtfully and drew the paper back towards him.

"He sounds like he thinks you're on his side. 'We have much work to do' and he calls you 'brother.' And *this*...he asks if you can *see* him? What do you think he meant by that, Irwin?"

"I don't know, sir. He's delusional, maybe he thinks he's invisible? He also calls himself 'the Lord God's instrument on Earth.' The psych boys think one possibility is that when he saw I was wearing a Star of David, he thought he'd found an ally in his holy war against the Returned gods."

"He hasn't, has he?" Pyle asked, trying hard not to sound as though he were serious.

"No, sir. I wear the Star of David because it belonged to my father, that's all. I'm not religious, and don't follow any faith, old, new, or ancient, and even if I did, it wouldn't make any difference to my investigation."

"Did psych cite other scenarios?"

"A few, but they all amounted to pretty much the same thing...except for one: George really is God's instrument on Earth."

Pyle leaned back in his seat and drummed his fingertips on the desktop.

"How did I know you were going to say that?"

"We've got to at least consider the possibility. If the Returned gods are real, the Biblical god could be as well."

"My entire life," Pyle said, slowly, "I never doubted that He was, Irwin. But not in any...*tangible* way, do you know what I mean?"

"Um, yes, sir." Was the A.D....*confessing* to him?

"Then these...the Returned gods came along, and it shook my certainty. I mean, where *was* God, anyway? It sounds like a question a five year old should ask, but it's still a good one. *Where* was He? Why had He allowed these false gods to take his place without so much as a struggle?"

Irwin, who had formally stopped believing in God a week before his thirteenth birthday, wanted to say, "Maybe because he doesn't exist. Or, if he does, he's a Clockwork God, one who built the mechanism, wound it up to set it going, and then went away...or stayed around just to watch, either with indifference or sadistic glee."

Instead, he said, "He supposedly gave us free will. Maybe he didn't abandon us."

"Crap," the A.D. sighed. "I miss the good old days when all we had to deal with was the Unabomber and Waco."

New Vatican City, Kentucky, Three Months Ago

"I don't think the Jesuits like me, Mother," Father Rowe said in a whisper to the woman walking alongside her.

"Oh, I'm sure of it," Mother Camille said with a hearty chuckle. "I believe they disapprove of women in general, but definitely of lady priests in particular."

"Well, it is a lot to accept, I suppose," Gloria Rowe said, trying to be charitable.

"They're a bunch of buffoons with minds stuck in the sixteenth century," the khaki-clad Mother Superior said. "It's the twenty-first century, and if it hadn't been for the Sisters, most of the men would have had their heads stuck up on the pikes of the heathen gods on the Vatican border."

Her hostess, however, did not belong to a charitable order. In fact, the Mother Superior headed up an order rather more militant than the Church had seen since the Crusades. The Sisters of the Knights Templar had formed on their own, a group of like-minded nuns, many with military backgrounds prior to taking their vows, pledged to the salvation of the Church's accumulated knowledge and history. The Church had initiated a program of scanning and digitizing its vast library in the early-1990s, an effort that escalated into a Biblical Manhattan Project after the Return and the Vatican had sealed itself against the siege of the pagan gods that went on to this day.

For years and at the cost of uncounted lives, the digitized data was smuggled out of the Vatican and handed off to the protection of the Sisters of the Knights Templar. The flow of data had begun to slow three or four years earlier, the tiny stick drives and memory cards containing hundreds of thousands of digitized pages slowing to a trickle, until now, when nothing new had emerged from the besieged city for almost a year. Had those who stayed behind to do the scanning finally completed their task? Or had the noose around the Papal city finally drawn so tight that even information was choked off?

The Sisters had found a sanctuary for their order and the precious heritage they guarded in the U.S. military base and official gold repository formerly known as Fort Knox. The impregnable fortress had been built nearly a century ago to house the countless tons of gold bouillon that America once held in reserve, but which had been looted in early 2014 by the local gods in what they called "tribute." The collapse shortly thereafter of a central government and a functioning military command structure left Fort Knox open and unattended. The Sisters moved in, cleaned up, set up a localized power grid and defense perimeter, and stood guard over the isolated, offline servers that stored the Word of God and the wisdom of mankind, as well as the sect of Jesuit priests who were organizing and cataloguing the data.

Rumor had it the Sisters had also secured two other self-contained locations to warehouse duplicate and triplicate back-up copies of the data, but those locations, if they existed, were just rumors. Cheyenne Mountain. The Federal Repository Vaults in New York City. The Large Hadron Collider complex near Geneva. Spain's Torca del Cerro del Cuevon, one of the deepest and most treacherous cavern systems in the world. Somewhere. Under the ever-watchful eye of the heavily armed Sisters.

The Sanctuary of the Holy Word, or New Vatican City as it was commonly known among its inhabitants, wasn't just a repository of knowledge. It was an active library, open to acknowledged and recognized scholars like Father Gloria Rowe. Once she had explained her mission to New York's Archbishop McClellan, he had authorized her unlimited access to the digital stacks.

Each morning, Mother Camille, in boots and a freshly starched ABU (Army Battle Uniform) with a clerical collar and sidearm and half a dozen assault weapon carrying nuns, escorted Gloria Rowe to her workstation inside the vault. The priest couldn't quite understand the need for an armed squad to follow behind her inside the heavily fortified Sanctuary, but she supposed every Order had its own traditions and litanies that might seem strange to the non-initiated.

Mother Camille and Father Rowe came to the great vault door, its exterior as plain and functionally unadorned as it had been during its days under military control. The sisters escorting her took up positions behind them, facing out and away from the vault and its contingent of standing guards. The Mother Superior nodded to the squad leader, who began the process of opening the twenty-one-inch thick, twenty-ton Mosler Safe Company vault door.

"The Jesuits aren't the only ones who should be grateful, Mother Superior. Humanity itself owes the Sisters a great debt," the priest said.

"We're just doing the Lord's work," the nun said humbly.

"Amen," Father Rowe said and smiled.

Her workstation was a twenty-year-old MacBook from which Wifi, Ethernet, Bluetooth, and any other form of connectivity or communications hardware or software had been stripped. The laptop had one point of entry and that was for data via the USB cable that connected it to Church's isolated, offline servers. There was no way for outside computers to detect or locate the activity inside the closed off bubble of the Sanctuary.

Father Rowe's search here had begun as soon as she came to the limitations of her own library back home in New York. She had almost two thousand volumes on Church history and archaeology on her shelves, and while they had yielded some tantalizing hints and clues to what she sought, she quickly concluded she needed to dig deeper than any individual library likely went.

The Church collection was vast...and disorganized. The early years of scanning had been orderly and organized, books and papers catalogued and cross-referenced, key words highlighted to optimize search results, subjects and authors indexed, and files properly labeled.

As neat as the first twenty years had been, the second twenty were chaotic. Most things had been scanned without proper, or in many cases, any labeling. Hundreds of thousands, millions, of pages were pushed across scanner beds and left to be saved automatically under file names that had no relationship to their content. With the pagan gods seeking to tear down the Church battering at its doors, all that mattered was getting them scanned while there was still time. It could all be sorted out later.

"Later" was now and Father Rowe was reduced to the slow, laborious task of opening each and every one of the tens of thousands files of books and documents that were *likely*, as best her Jesuit hosts could determine, to be from the time periods she was looking for. Many were; most weren't. The tedium was, at times, mind-numbing.

But then...she would make a find. A local functionary's report to his superior; a cleric's entry in his registry; an illuminated manuscript referencing the objection of her search; even what she could only call "alternate drafts" of the early Gospels, including passages excised by the Church and earlier, often multiple interpretations of Biblical tales long considered chiseled in stone. Well, in a way they had been...but only after the authors had gotten them exactly right.

The finds were scattered though, and open to interpretation. What she was looking for would have been considered, in the era between the Biblical Age of Miracles and the Modern Age Return, the stuff of fiction: A piece of the One True Cross, taken and guarded since 325 A.D., when the Cross was supposedly unearthed by workers who uncovered Jesus' burial site, the Holy Sepulchre in Jerusalem, to build a church there ordered by the newly converted Emperor Constantine.

This piece of ancient wood from an olive tree had been, according to the story she was told, entrusted to a small sect of priests who swore their lives to its safeguarding. What made this two thousand year old relic worthy of such protection was that it was a piece of the Cross stained with Christ's own blood, giving it special powers that the sect had either kept hidden from the world, or was keeping safe until it was needed.

But more, beyond the Relic and the sect which protected it, Father Rowe was searching for ancient evidence of a man. He would have been present at the discovery of the Cross in Jerusalem. He would have shown up at pivotal moments in Church history, he might have marched in the

Crusades, watched as the Reformation took hold and Enlightenment swept across Europe...

The stuff of fiction, she reflected.

Junker George had sat across from her in her own Church and had her bless six small wood crosses which he claimed to have been carved from this bloodied Relic. He didn't exactly claim to be some sort of... immortal warrior, but he spoke like a man telling his own story and not repeating tales of others. Whatever he was, he was killing the gods of the Return with these crosses, eliminating their scourge from the world. "I want to return Christ's light and glory to a world that's been eclipsed by the darkness of false gods and idolatry," the god-killer had told her, but at the time she thought he was a madman.

The FBI came along to assure her that, mad or not, he was doing as claimed. Gods were dying. And each divine death brought humanity one step closer to the elimination of the pagan gods. How could even murder be a sin when it was being done in support of the very first of God's own commandments, "You shall have no other gods before me"?

Was an immortal slayer of gods any more far-fetched than the gods themselves with whom she shared the world?

But she was a scholar and she needed evidence to be convinced, not myth. And, as her hunt through the random assortment of fact, theology, and theological conceit of two thousand years of Church history was proving to her, it was often difficult to tell the difference.

Sderot, Israel, June 1998

"I still don't know why we couldn't go to Disney World," Irwin grumbled into his chest as the old bus bucked and creaked along an unpaved and severely potholed dirt and stone road more than sixty kilometers from Jerusalem and less than five kilometers from the northeast tip of the Gaza Strip.

It was summer and he was in the Middle East where the sun and the heat were merciless and he was forced to spend every waking hour with his parents doing boring crap like riding un-air conditioned buses out into the freaking desert to look at broken down old piles of stone and rubble.

"What is this place anyway?" he said, this time in a voice meant to be heard by his mother, who sat across the aisle from him.

"It's a synagogue, from the time of the Roman occupation," she said, fanning herself with her ever-present guide book.

"Big whoop," he said, trying desperately to pretend the Israeli dust drifting through the windows were actually the cooling spray of Disney World's Typhoon Lagoon's waters, but his imagination wasn't good enough.

"It is a big whoop," his father, next to his mother, growled. "In the states, some place's been around a hundred, two hundred years, we think it's ancient. Over here, people are living in places put up a *thousand*, two thousand years ago."

Why his dad thought it was so cool to live in a two-thousand-year-old house he couldn't understand. Their house in Brooklyn had been built in 1963 and all he ever did was complain that it was old and broken down. But that was his dad, N.Y.P.D. Patrolman Daniel Benjamin; always ready with a contrary opinion or better idea if it would make someone else feel like a schmuck. Especially his children.

Especially Irwin.

His older sister Doris was spending the two weeks in Israel working on a kibbutz, a collective farm, where she was picking tomatoes eight hours a day. At first, Irwin thought he was the one getting off easy by not having to spend part of his vacation playing migrant farm worker; but now, by day four, he recognized the truth. Sure, maybe Doris had to spend part of the day laboring in the hot sun...but she spent the other sixteen hours hanging out with kids her own age...and her parents nowhere to be seen.

He hated her. And he hated his parents, and Israel, and sweaty Jewish tourists, and ancient history, and rubble...and dust. He hated the dust most of all.

The old synagogue at Sderot was everything Irwin had expected it to be.

Which was a few partially standing old stone walls, sections of a roof, and a lot of what used to be the rest of the walls and roof. But it had a story, of course. Something about a small band of heroic Hebrews holding off there against the Philistines or the Palestines or something army.

Irwin hadn't paid attention to anything a tour guide said since about five minutes after the first one they followed around Jerusalem started droning on and on. He knew what he was listening to, though. It was a lecture, so he could learn something, just like in school. Well, fuck that noise! This was summer vacation and no matter what his location, his brain was officially switched to "off!"

So he tried to hang around the fringes, hopefully in some sort of shade, and pretend he was listening, just to avoid a harangue from his father about his pathetic lack of interest in the world around him, or maybe one of his mother's favorites, his inability to appreciate anything nice or fine in his life, or his acting as though he wasn't part of the family.

It was torture and at times over the last few days, he had prayed for sweet death to release him from the agony of boredom and the endless heat rash of Middle Eastern tourism.

When he first heard the automatic weapon fire, he thought he was imagining it as an answer to his prayers. Later, he wouldn't be able to stop thinking about one of his grandmother's many admonitions, this one about being careful what one wished for...!

Paris, France, One Month Ago
Irwin Benjamin hadn't been home for any longer than it took to exchange clean clothes for the dirty ones in his travel bag since the night Junker George killed the Native American deity Hu Nonp in what used to be the third floor reading room of the Stephen A. Schwarzman Building of the New York Public Library at Manhattan's Forty-Second Street and Fifth Avenue. Victim number six. The night he and the killer met and spoke.

His last visit to the one-bedroom condo in suburban Maryland he called home had been a little over eleven hours earlier. Shirts, socks, underwear, a fresh toothbrush, and he was out the door and driving to Baltimore Washington International Airport, where his FBI credentials impressed no one, but his temporary Hall of the Gods I.D. landed him a first class seat on the very next Air Lugus (formerly Air France, renamed post-Return in honor of the Gallic god of light and the sun) flight to Paris.

Where the latest victim was waiting for him. Nemausius, Roman-Celtic in origin, the god of the sacred spring at Nimes.

The first victim outside the North American continent, number twenty-three. He'd been kept busy enough hop scotching the U.S. and Canada; they had no idea how George traveled, but he sure got around. Phoenix. L.A. Calgary. St. Louis. Toronto. Atlantic City. Las Vegas. Thunder Bay. Newark. Quebec. Baltimore.

He'd reached a point where he knew what to expect even before he got to the crime scene. There would be little or no sign of a struggle, just a dead deity with a crudely carved wood cross clenched in his or her hand, and no other mark on them besides a cross burned onto the chests. He would show witnesses a composite photo that both he and Father Rowe agreed was a good likeness of Junker George, but which no one could ever identify. He didn't appear on any video surveillance footage recovered from several of the scenes; each video, however, was similarly marred with the same vague, almost imperceptible smudge that traveled across its field of vision immediately preceding and after the killings.

"You can see me?"

Those had been George's first words to him outside the library. Of course he could see him, Irwin had thought at the time. Who's this guy think he is, Caspar? But the presumption of invisibility was the least of the tall, gaunt man's abilities. There was also his strength, which was impressive, but what had really gotten through to the agent was the ability to shrug off the 9mm slug he had fired pointblank into the man's chest. Junker George hadn't been wearing Kevlar under his clothing; Irwin had been up close and could see flesh—unharmed flesh!—through the blast scorched hole in his shirt.

A couple of weeks back, he told A.D. Pyle that George was likely delusional.

He hadn't really believed that then and he definitely did not believe that now.

"Don't get me wrong, inspector," Irwin said to the Interpol agent who had met him at the airport and now drove him into Paris in her well-worn but solid sounding Renault, "I still think this guy, whoever he is, *whatever he is*, is a few lines short of a psalm...but that doesn't mean he can't be who he claims he is."

Chief Inspector Isabelle Martel didn't take her eyes off the road as she deftly wove through the late-day traffic on the A1 from De Gaulle Airport to Paris, so he watched her frown in profile.

"God's instrument of vengeance on Earth," she said. The agent was tall, dark haired, and as solid as the proverbial brick wall. She drove with the seat pushed all the way back, one elbow out the window, and a Galois, unlighted he assumed, out of respect for his presence in the car, stuck in the corner of her mouth.

"I can't say whether the big man actually gave him the job or not, but there's no denying he's been performing like employee of the year."

"Incredible," Martel said, sighing it with Gallic fatalism. "Just when we think we have grown accustomed to the world's latest insanity, it throws its next psychotic fit at us."

"Have you had much contact with them before?"

"*Les dieux?* No. Most of the time I am tracking fugitives or smugglers. Strictly down to the earth crimes." The Renault was starting to slow as traffic ahead thickened up as they got closer to the city.

Martel glanced at him and smiled. "Do not worry. One of the rewards of the job, eh?" she said and flipped on her lights and siren. The traffic parted for them the rest of the way into Paris.

Nemausius was probably the most perfectly formed individual Irwin Benjamin had ever seen. Though male, the only word to describe him was beautiful, so beautiful that he continued to radiate life and light even almost a day after his death. His only imperfection was the dark, ugly cross burned into his sternum.

"You can't go by the human model for the gods," FBI Agent Irwin Benjamin was explaining, with Inspector Martel's assistance as interpreter, to the bespectacled and baffled French medical examiner. "As it was explained to me, they've assumed human forms to live among us, but these bodies are more or less impervious to harm."

The coroner blinked and looked quizzically at the blond god stretched out on his stainless steel table.

Irwin nodded. "Right," he said to Martel. "Impervious to anything *we* can do to them. But the gods are all equal as far as it goes for being able to kill each another."

Martel said it again, but in French. The coroner responded in kind.

"He says, they do not go into rigor, or show lividity or decay. How is that possible?"

Irwin's word-weary Hebraic shrug translated effortlessly into French ennui. The coroner nodded and said, "*C'est un mystère.*"

"The doctor has not touched him, waiting for your arrival, per instructions," Martel told him. "Is there something specific you are looking for?"

He nodded. "Just one thing."

Irwin pointed to Nemausius' clenched left fist, laying at his side.

"Could you please ask the doctor to open his hand?"

Isabelle Martel relayed the instructions and with gloved hands, he slowly uncurled the fingers of Nemausius' hand.

"*Qu'est-ce que c'est?*"

"This," Irwin said, trusting scant memories of barely passed high school French classes to interpret the doctor's surprised utterance, "is the specific thing I was looking for."

"A cross?" Martel said.

"A cross. Hand carved from olive wood, approximately three inches tall, and, I'll bet the Eiffel Tower against the Statue of Liberty that analysis will turn up traces of holy oil on it."

"You have seen this before?" the doctor asked through Martel.

"Nineteen times," Irwin said. "Looks like George has gone international."

Agent Irwin spent the next eight hours in the Paris offices of Interpol waiting for the French coroner to perform the autopsy and write up his preliminary findings. Unlike the typical American squad room, Interpol's coffee was superb and the pastries several light years ahead of the box of stale Dunkin' Donuts that he was accustomed to. The fact that he could have been wandering the streets of Paris and taking in a few sights while he waited never even occurred to him; he hadn't come three thousand miles to play tourist.

In spite of their funny accents, Inspector Martel and her colleagues were cops like cops everywhere else. Most of the Interpol agents spoke English—along with at least one or two other languages in addition to their native tongues—so the America fed felt right at home amongst his European counterparts, swapping war stories and laughing at tales of their bosses' bonehead moves.

Inspector "call me Isabelle, please, Irween" Martel was proving particularly charming company. Hidden by her bulky leather coat and black beret was a tall and, as previously noted, solidly constructed young lady, an athlete of some sort, with a pageboy haircut framing a face rife with imperfections that seemed to add up to a beauty all its own. He didn't know if all French women were so effortlessly seductive, but the inspector certainly seemed to have that trick down pat. And, after hours of sitting in her office, feet up on opposite sides of the desk, talking about the job while waiting for the phone to ring, the conversation turned to their personal lives and those points of commonality shared by too many people in their line of work.

Divorce. Insomnia. Instability. Stress. Crap, the job was an ongoing case of PTSD, too often self-medicated with alcohol, drugs, or self-pity.

"I used to drink," Isabelle admitted, "perhaps a little too much at times. Well, this is France. We take wine with breakfast, yes? Regrettably, I do not handle moderation very well, so it was all or nothing for me. I chose nothing; total abstinence. Instead, I started lifting weights. It is much healthier for me, I think."

That would explain the shoulders, Irwin Benjamin thought with a mental sigh of admiration, and not for the athletic accomplishment. He said, "It seems to agree with you."

"*Merci*," she said. "What is your substitute, Irween? Presuming, of course, you have one."

"I never really had to substitute. I don't drink much outside of social occasions. I guess I don't mind *getting* drunk, but I've never liked *being* drunk, if that makes sense."

"Completely. But the worst is having *been* drunk, yes?"

"Oh, yes. The hangover. I decided somewhere along the line in college that nothing was worth the hangover, so I started drinking in moderation and just pretending to be drunk with my friends."

Martel laughed. "So you had your cake and ate it too!"

"You mean, I got to stay sober, still act like an ass, and use being drunk as an excuse for my bad misbehavior?"

"*Exactement!*"

"I hate to tell you, but no excuse was ever good enough to override my own teenage Jewish guilt."

"Ah, yes. My grandmother was Jewish. I saw what she did to my father." She smiled mischievously. "Are you still burdened by your guilt?"

"I'm not a teenager anymore," he said.

"No, but you are still Jewish."

Irwin grinned. "Touché. But, I've learned to deal with it just fine."

"I am pleased to hear that, Irween," she said in a way that left him no doubt of her intentions, and Irwin thought, holy crap! Is this really gonna happen? He'd never, not once in seventeen years on the job, scored with a hot colleague, although he'd heard plenty of stories from others who claimed they had. Well, everyone always said Paris was the most romantic place on Earth. He just hadn't realized that would include its law enforcement agencies.

But, of course, that was when the telephone rang.

Special Agent Benjamin and Inspector Martel never did get to consummate anything beyond the official transfer of evidence to his possession ("one (1) hand-carved wood cross, origin unknown; one set (1) forensic images, crime scene / autopsy photographs, seventy-two (72) total; Police Nationale and Interpol dossiers"). It hadn't been the coroner calling but Isabelle's superior, telling her that the second European killing (number twenty-one, worldwide) by Junker George had just been confirmed in Spain. Irwin saw she was ready to hop into her little Renault and drive off to take charge of the scene.

And he saw her face fall with disappointment as she was told to stay put. Agent Benjamin was in charge of the investigation; Interpol was to play a strictly advisory role. He didn't need to speak her language to know she was telling her boss that it wasn't right; she had caught the case and should be allowed to stay on it. That would last a few rounds, depending on her tenacity, before she would give in, coldly, and with deadly formality. The order came from the top, at the directive of the Hall of the Gods.

She hung up and turned her glare on Irwin.

"Apparently, you are a lone wolf and you and your god masters wish no interference from lesser beings, especially agents of Interpol."

"Is that what they told you?"

"No, just that you were to be given our fullest cooperation and to involve myself only at your request," she said. "I inferred the rest."

"You infer wrong, mademoiselle. I could use all the help I can get, but the deities upstairs want this to be a one-man operation for reasons that I can't even begin to guess, and if it's got to be one man, why me?"

Isabelle smiled. "Oh, I can think of some reasons I might choose you, Irween, but, for now," she said, plucking a business card from a box on her desk and holding it out to him, "here is my number. Use it if you wish to request me...for your investigation."

His next stop was Spain, where an Iberian weather god named Eacus had been found minus his heart and clutching a wood cross atop the Alcazar of Toledo, the stone fortification at the highest point in the city. From there, Junker George traveled back north to the Pyrenees to dispatch Dercetius, a mountain god, then to Italy to take, first, the heart of Carna, goddess of the preservation of the heart and other internal organs (was he trying to be funny?), then those, following in rapid succession, of Tibernius, the river god, Nixi, goddess of childbirth, and Hilaritas, the goddess of humor and rejoicing. He then crossed the Adriatic, killing one god in the Croatian coastal city of Zadar, then hop-scotching his way through Hungary, Austria, Bulgaria, Slovakia, and Turkey, leaving a trail of dead gods and crosses. With Irwin always only a day or two behind him.

Then, two days ago, Junker George announced his arrival in Jerusalem.

Jerusalem, 325 A.D.

The overseer roughly shoved the kneeling workers pressed shoulder to shoulder around the excavation aside as he waded through them, snarling curses and cuffing at the backs of their bowed heads.

"I'll give you something to pray for if you don't get back to work, you lazy bastards! Why have you stopped digging, damn you? Do you expect the emperor's church to build itself?"

No one answered. No one made a sound, as if everyone but himself had been struck dumb.

He reached the edge of the gaping wound opened in the middle of Jerusalem by the workers' picks and shovels. Hadrian's temple to Aphrodite had stood there for almost two centuries before they had demolished it to make way for the church ordered built there by the Holy Roman Emperor. It was a sacred spot, the place where Jesus had died and had been buried, and the newly converted Christian monarch wished erected there a basilica worthy of its holy nature.

The overseer peered down into the excavation. Only one man was in the pit, and he was kneeling and praying with the others. His shovel lay at his side. Before him, the apparent object of his devotion, was a partially exposed wooden beam.

"You!" the overseer roared.

The worker didn't respond.

"I'm talking to you!"

The worker ignored him.

"Jesus Christ almighty!" the burly master bellowed. He hopped down into the excavation and unhooked the curled up whip from his belt as he strode towards the man. "I told you to get on your feet and get back to work. What the hell's holding things up?"

At last, the worker's head lifted and he turned pale gray eyes on the overseer.

"I have found something," he said.

The overseer looked at the tall, gaunt man and tried to remember his name. He knew he was employed as a digger, a strong, diligent worker who showed up daily and made no trouble, but his name and his face seemed to hover just beyond the man's memory. This was the first time he had reason to pay any heed to the worker; any previous remembrance of him was dim and nebulous.

"An old beam? What's so goddamned special about that? We've been digging up debris since we began."

The worker rose, towering over the burly overseer.

"It is not a beam, sir. It is a cross."

"So? Dig it up and throw it on the scrap heap!"

The worker said, "Upon this site was Golgotha, where our Lord Jesus died."

"So?"

"Where our Lord Jesus died upon a cross."

The overseer shook the whip at the gaunt man. "You'll get this out of the way and get back to work or die under the lash!"

The worker shook his head. "This is a sacred place."

The overseer let the whip uncoil from his fingers and the woven leather lash trail onto the damp earth.

"It's my work site, dog," he snarled. He flicked the whip to his side, once, then started to bring it up and around at the worker.

The gaunt man stepped towards him, reaching out to catch the descending lash as effortlessly as retrieving a line tossed to him by a co-worker. He wrapped it once around his fist and tugged; the overseer, holding tight, was pulled towards him. The worker caught him by the throat and squeezed.

"Give thanks to the Lord this is his sacred place else I'd snap your vile, blaspheming neck here and now," he said, releasing the boggle-eyed overseer to slip to the ground.

"*You!*"

The woman's voice was strong, commanding, and accustomed to obedience. And known to all who labored on this monument to the life of Christ.

The worker turned and knelt to the speaker, who now stood at the lip of the excavation.

"I have found something, your highness," the gaunt man said, his eyes averted from her royal presence. "A cross." He looked up then, into the eyes of Helena, the emperor's mother. "*The* cross."

Helena turned quickly to the nearest laborers and pointed at them.

"Get down there and help him," she commanded. Then she said to the worker, "The overseer. Did you kill him?"

"No, my lady," he said.

"When he is able, send him to me. In the mean time," she said to the rest of the workers, "Resume your labors!"

The emperor's mother turned to leave, but looked back at the worker. "What is your name?"

"Joshua, ma'am," he said.

"I am holding you personally responsible for conducting the artifact safely to my care, Joshua."

"I am humbled, your highness."

She regarded him coolly from under a raised eyebrow. "Yes," she said, and left.

Sderot, Israel, June 1998

Irwin, Mr. and Mrs. Popkin, Mr. Schwartzberg, and Rebecca, the bus driver, had been in the wrong places at the wrong time when the four AK-47 wielding Palestinians converged on the old synagogue. It was apparent even to Irwin that the gunmen should have gone for the bus first. The way they did it, though, most of the tourists, including his parents, had enough warning and time to get on the bus and haul it out of there.

Unfortunately for Irwin and those other four, they had wandered away from the main group and were cut off from the bus by the attacking terrorists.

There was a lot of gun fire and screaming and shouting and a general air of unreality about the whole scene. He remembered feeling the sting on his legs of high velocity debris thrown up the rounds peppering the ground around his feet. He remembered diving for cover behind some rubble, Mrs. Popkin landing on top of him, screaming, but he could still hear his father yelling for him and when he peered out from his cover, he saw some of the other tourists and the tour guide were holding his old man back from racing into the gunfire to save him. They had to drag him onto the bus and keep him from leaping out the still open door as the bus lurched forward and sped away in a cloud of dust and gunfire.

His dad could be a real pain in the ass, but at the moment, Irwin never loved him more.

Mrs. Popkin didn't stop screaming until one of the gunmen slapped her across the face. Mr. Popkin was indignant but not enough to risk their AK-47s, and they were all rounded up and prodded by gun barrels and rapid fire commands in Arabic and broken English onto the flatbed truck that raced in from out of nowhere.

But no sooner were they loaded face down on the filthy truck bed that smelled like livestock and covered with a stiff, gritty canvas than new shouts arose from the gunmen and the truck rocked to a stop. Without warning, the canvas was ripped from them and they were hustled off the truck and made to race towards the ruins of the old synagogue. Inside, they were herded into the one part of the ancient structure where the walls on three sides still stood and a portion of the roof remained intact.

Before he was pushed inside, Irwin thought he caught a glimpse of an armored personnel carrier. The tank-like buses were parked all over Jerusalem and the countryside through which they had driven. They belonged to the Israeli Defense Force, who would, he realized with relief, of course be somewhere in the area. They were only like three miles away from the Gaza Strip! There had to be a ton of soldiers nearby, against the five Palestinians who were now skittering from window to window to cracks in the wall to watch as, from the sounds of it, about a dozen armored personnel carriers or tanks rumbled and creaked into position all around the tumbled down structure.

Irwin exchanged looks with the Popkins, Mr. Schwartzberg, and Rebecca, each of them hearing the same thing he did. The Israeli army, heroes of the Six Day War, the Yom Kippur War, rescuers of the hijack hostages in Entebbe and countless other military victories, were there to save them. Their worries were practically over.

Forty-three hours later, Irwin and the other four Americans were still being held by the Palestinians, who were trying to use them to negotiate their own escape and freedom. Irwin didn't quite know what the problem was between the Jews and the Palestinians beyond both of them claiming the same chunks of territory for themselves, but he didn't know why he, an American, had to be in the middle of it. For the last two days almost, he'd been scared, hot, tired, uncomfortable, hungry, bored, and angry... and he wished everybody would just work out their shit and leave him out of it. He wanted a cold glass of lemonade. He wanted a shower. He wanted to be at Disney World instead. He wanted his mommy and his daddy and even his stupid sister.

He wanted to go home!

But these AK-47 assholes just didn't get it. Israel didn't negotiate with terrorists. Ever. It just waited them out and killed them. Sometimes, a couple of hostages got killed too, but that was the price of being a Jewish state surrounded by Arab enemies. The I.D.F. was just waiting for the bad guys to get tired and sloppy. Then they were going to come rushing in with guns blazing and kill every single last one of the Palestinians. The old man in charge of this failed operation, the two middle-aged men Irwin thought were probably his sons, the truck driver, and the truck driver's grandson, a tall, gangly wide-eyed boy probably the same age as Irwin and, if possible, even more frightened. They were all going to die...and for what? Real estate? Religious differences? *Politics?*

So Irwin waited it out. He sat as still and as quiet as he could, not even making eye contact with his captors. He didn't want to get to know them, not under these circumstances. If he knew them they'd become "people" in his mind and he'd have to care about them. But why let that happen? They were all going to die, weren't they? So, let them be strangers when it happens...and hope he didn't get killed with them in the crossfire.

The first flash/bang grenade caught everybody by surprise. One hundred and eighty-five decibels of sound and a light as bright as the sun exploded in their midst to stun them all, terrorists and hostages alike.

A second flash/bang erupted, followed by a tear gas canister that filled the confined space with dense, choking fumes. The hostages screamed, the terrorists yelled and scrambled around, the old man, wheezing from the gas, breaking for some fresh air at the door, his head exploding from a sharpshooter's round the second he showed himself. Irwin rolled into a ball and buried his head under his arms, squeezing himself into the corner and trying to be the smallest target possible. Fuck the tear gas, just stay down, stay low, under the gas, away from the bullets.

Over the screaming and shooting, the mechanical rumble of a personnel carrier drew closer to the ruins. More guns. Explosions. One of the terrorists grabbed Irwin by the arm and tried to drag him to his feet, probably to use as a shield against the I.D.F. guns.

"*And fuck you!*" Irwin screamed. He kicked wildly at the figure, smashing a foot into his face, kicking at the guy's crotch, clawing at the hand that grasped him.

The man, one of the sons, suddenly stiffened and grunted, then toppled forward on top of Irwin. He'd been shot in the back by a stray round.

Irwin tried to wiggle out from under the dead weight, but he was pinned. Maybe he should just stay there, use the dead guy the way as a shield the way he'd planned to use Irwin, and pretend to be dead. This couldn't go on much longer...he just had to survive a few more seconds and he'd be okay, he'd be...

The Palestinian kid was suddenly looming over him, shouting in Arabic and gesturing wildly with the gun. Irwin pushed at the dead man on top of him and gestured his helplessness. The other kid was wild with fear and wasn't about to let go of his weapon, but he did transfer it to one hand and use the other to pull at the bloody shirt while Irwin pushed from below. The body rolled over. Irwin started to get to his feet.

A third flash/bang landed two feet behind the Palestinian kid, and Irwin started screaming, "Oh, god, oh, shit, please god, oh please!" but the thing exploded anyway and caused the kid's finger twitched. One shot. Blam, like a punch to the chest, and Irwin went flying backwards, shocked and surprised, his ears ringing with the almost simultaneous grenade blast and shot. But mostly he was shocked, wishing he could stop screaming to god to help him...if there was any help coming from that quarter, it would have helpful *before* he got shot.

Holy fuck, he realized. I've been shot.

In the chest.

Isn't that where I keep my heart?

"Ogodogod," he cried out loud, but as he died, he thought, "What a load of crap."

Jerusalem, 2 Days Ago

Father Rowe waited just until she had buckled her seatbelt to say to Irwin in the back seat of the jeep, "I'm sorry it's taken me so long, but the archives are a mess. Everything's grouped roughly by era, but there's no organization and hardly any labeling of the source material and..."

"Look, Father," Irwin said, "I know you went through a lot of time and effort to find this material, but I don't need the whole making-of documentary, just the facts, ma'am, just the facts."

Eric Strobe, behind the wheel of the jeep, was maneuvering out of the pick-up lane and trying to merge with the traffic leaving Jerusalem Airport. He had been assigned to pick up the FBI agent and the priest, who had both just arrived in Israel, albeit on separate flights within an hour of one other.

"Be kind, Agent Benjamin," the burly man said as he stomped on the gas to roar in ahead of a bus. "The good father is on our side."

"I know, I'm sorry," Irwin said. "Please go ahead, Father."

"No, you're right. My travails in the trenches of academia aren't relevant and probably only interesting to another historian," she said gently. "But, to the point...I was searching for historic and biblical references to the True Cross and to individuals or groups within the Church involved with it. The literature on the Cross is quite extensive, beginning around 325 B.C. when it was said to have been discovered by workers excavating for the Church of the Holy Sepulchre. Since, it's been broken up and the pieces, most of them holy relics spread around the churches of the world. But enough of the Cross's estimated volume is unaccounted for that it's quite feasible a piece the size of George's description could be in private, or even clandestine Church, hands."

"Any evidence that might upgrade feasible to reality?" Irwin asked.

"I'd have to stop short of calling it actual 'evidence,' Agent Benjamin. There are rumors of religious orders growing up around pieces of the Cross, some said to possess special powers, but no first hand documentation of any that I could find."

"Are you saying your research was a dead end?" Strobe said.

"No, not at all. I did come across references to one order, never named, that was said to hold the Holy of Holies, the piece of the Cross stained by the blood of Jesus where the spike that driven through His hand or feet. The pope heard about them, around 700 A.D. and decided that a relic of this importance to the church should be in the hands of its leader, but the order refused to turn it over so, so the pope sent some people to take it. The renegade order fought back and most of its members were killed or captured, but someone got away with the piece of the Cross.

"What makes this one stand out is that references to this order and that piece of the Cross keeps popping up, here and there, across the centuries. The first official reference was in a dispatch sent to Pope Alexander III in 1172, which seems to have been turned over to the Office of the Inquisition and, at some point before the fourteenth century, was opened as an official investigation."

Irwin shook his head. "A seven-century-old lead? That's what you're bringing me?"

Father Gloria smiled. "The investigation was still ongoing and active as of 2012. The last report was filed in February of that year, a few months before the Return."

"Ah, but a seven-century-long investigation…!" Strobe exclaimed. "Can you imagine the paperwork, Irwin!"

"There's not a lot of that, or at least not a lot that I've found yet."

"I don't suppose there was any helpful mention of Junker George in those later reports," Irwin said.

"No, nothing in the later reports, but several earlier mentions," Gloria said. She pulled a folder from her bag.

"Can't be too much earlier. George didn't look much more than forty-five or a well preserved mid-fifties."

"*Much* earlier," she said, and handed him the folder.

Inside were four laser printouts of images that had been scanned into the Church archives. The first pre-dated photographic imagery, a portrait of a stern, hard-eyed cleric from the fifteenth century. The next was a story from a 1906 American so-called 'men's adventure' magazine accompanied by an illustration of the Mad Monk of Morsberg. The third was a faded fax image from the early days of the technology in the 1940s, and the final was a copy of an Italian police report and mug shots from 1963.

"It's George," Father Rowe said when Irwin, stunned, didn't respond. "All of them. It's Junker George!"

"Victim number thirty-two is Tawaret, an Egyptian goddess of fertility," Strobe said, flipping through the file as he spoke. "It's the work of your man…the carved wood cross and missing heart confirms that, but there are some interesting deviations here."

Irwin Benjamin was working off the borrowed corner of Strobe's desk in the downtown offices of the *Shabak*. He had the images Father Rowe had found spread out in front of it. He was trying desperately to find the *differences* in the four pictures, anything to indicate that they weren't all the same man. So far, he had been entirely unsuccessful. Strobe had sent copies of the photos to the identification unit to run through their computerized files for matches, and to match the images themselves up with one another to check for variations in certain unique and unchangeable facial characteristics, like the shape of the skull, bone structure, eye shape and location, the angle of an ear relative to the rest of the head, and about a hundred other points of comparison, great and small.

As stuck as he was on the riddle of the four faces of George, he did hear his Israeli counterpart when he said there were deviations.

"That'll be a first. George's been about as regular as the tide up till now."

"Two significant differences. First, Tawaret is his first non-humanoid victim. She had," he said, pausing to find the description in the report, "the head of a hippopotamus, the arms and legs of a crocodile, and the torso of a pregnant woman."

Irwin reached for one of the crime scene photos, not really wanting to see the creature Eric had described, but knowing he had to. It was every bit as hideous as Irwin had feared it would be, a frightening nightmare of a thing that looked more likely to cause fear-induced early labor than protect the pregnant. He knew it had once been a living, thinking creature, but it was hard to look at the dead thing sprawled in the desert dust as anything but a Frankenstein-like monstrosity assembled from spare parts.

"Christ," Irwin muttered.

"Hardly," Strobe said.

"No kidding. What's number two?"

"The vic was killed at another location and moved to where we found her."

Irwin raised an eyebrow.

"Do we know that location?"

Strobe shook his head. "Her temple was in Luxor, but as usual we are having trouble getting straight answers out of the gods. She was known to spend most of her time there, so we are assuming that is where she was killed."

"Then why leave her in Israel to be found?"

The Israeli dropped the Tawaret file on his desk. "The very question I had been asking myself, but I believe I may have found an answer." He reached for another folder, this one with official looking seals and warnings in Hebrew stamped on its cover. "In your dossier."

"What the hell do I have to do with it?"

Strobe said grimly, "He left her body outside the old synagogue at Sderot."

Jerusalem, Today

It had taken two days to get clearance for Strobe and his companions to travel to Sderot. The Return of the ancient local gods may have put an official end to the religious conflicts between Israeli Jews and Palestinian

Muslims, but it hadn't even slowed down the thousands of years of cultural differences between the two peoples. Strobe had to wait for official word that there were no current military actions in the area before setting out from the relative security of the open city of Jerusalem.

They traveled in silence for the first few miles, the Israeli at the wheel of his jeep, Father Rowe riding shotgun, and Irwin jammed into the backseat, hidden behind sunglasses and a cap to protect his balding head from the Mediterranean sun.

Finally, Irwin said, "How many gods do you think there are?"

Father Rowe turned and hooked her arm over the back of her seat. "Speaking again, are we?" she inquired sweetly.

"You sound like my mother, Father. Any idea? Has anybody counted them?"

"There's no complete divine census that I know of, but I've heard estimates of anywhere from two to as many as five thousand individual gods across the various pantheons."

"And George is...what? Planning on killing them all, one at a time?"

Strobe's eyes found Irwin's in the rearview mirror. "He is a fanatic. Logic doesn't apply."

"*Our* logic doesn't apply, Eric. But *his* logic, whether we get it or not, does and it's not going to change, not after all this time."

"Don't tell me you believe that nonsense about this George being immortal," Strobe said.

"Your own ID unit confirmed those four images were of the same man. Besides, how is our killer being immortal any more outrageous than the fact that our killer, immortal or otherwise, has been the killing the *gods* we're currently sharing the planet with us?"

"I thought you were an atheist, Agent Benjamin," Father Rowe said with a small smile.

"Just because they call themselves gods doesn't make them so," Strobe said.

"I don't really care what they call themselves or who they are," Irwin said. "My job's to find the guy who's killing them and stop him."

"Even if he's fighting a war against humanity's common enemies?" Strobe said.

Irwin stared at the back of the man's head. "We'd all like to see them gone, Eric, but if you're intimating that there's some sort of anti-gods underground..."

Strobe made a sound of disgust. "There are thousands of them, all over the world, and they all stand the same chance of bringing down the gods as my bubbe and her sister Tillie."

"And it's all beside the point anyway," Irwin said. "George is one man with a hit list of several thousand names, minimum. He's killed less than three dozen of them in a few months. If he plans on hitting them all, he's going to need to be not only immortal but also pretty damned lucky. I mean, Mayat's set me on George's tail, but I don't for a second believe she doesn't have her Division G security forces also working on it full time through the Hall of Gods. Someone's going to tweak to him sooner or later, and when they do, he's going to have everybody from Zeus, Odin, and Jupiter on down falling on him hard and for good."

"So where does that leave us?" the Israeli asked.

"You've talked to George," Irwin said to Father Rowe. "He may be a fanatic, but two things he ain't is stupid or irrational."

She nodded.

"So he knows he can't keep going this way if he really does intend to wipe out all the false gods. In fact, I think he's known it since he started his crusade."

"Then why is he doing this? What is he after?" Strobe wasn't happy with this line of inquiry. He liked his serial killers to be single-minded and straightforward, regardless of how their motivations twisted the boundaries of logic and reason.

"Fear and intimidation. He wants the gods to know he's out there, capable of doing what he threatens, and after them all. That's why he's hop-scotching the world. North America, Europe, now the Middle East, hitting only one or two gods from the local pantheons, then moving on to the next location."

"No matter what their other differences, all the pantheons would have a common enemy in Junker George," Father Rowe said slowly, beginning to understand where Irwin was headed.

Strobe began to nod. "And the gods would no doubt wish to deal with it as a group, wouldn't they?"

Irwin said grimly, "Yeah, he's putting them on notice and on edge. He's not going to keep on picking them off one by one much long. He's got a bigger plan in mind. Everything up till now's just been the lead up."

"Let us say I accept your premise," Strobe said, "where do you fit into his grand scheme, Irwin?"

Irwin shrugged. "I dunno. Maybe it's got something to do with my having been another Jew who got killed and resurrected in this general vicinity."

Sderot, Israel, June 1998
Irwin didn't remember being dead. He remembered everything up to and including being shot and dying, but nothing of being dead itself, which would have been the cool part and maybe even almost worth the whole trauma.

"You were dead for almost three minutes before the medic got to you and got your heart beating again," his father told him, two and a half days later in the hospital in Jerusalem where he had been brought for surgery and recovery.

"It's a miracle," his mother said, sitting next to his bed holding his hand. "The bullet missed your heart by millimeters."

"That little terrorist bastard was the last one the I.D.F. took down, so they got to you almost immediately after you were shot. The shock put you into cardiac arrest, but they got your pump restarted with artificial respiration," his father said.

Irwin, in pain and still groggy from the aftereffects of surgery and medication, smiled goofily and mumbled, "Artificial nothin', I need the real thing," the punch line to some old Three Stooges bit that used to crack them both up when he was younger.

It was apparently the right thing to say. It made both his parents smile and his mother lean back in her chair and, suddenly, relax. He was going to be okay.

Mr. Schwartzberg had been killed in the rescue operation and Rebecca, the bus driver, had been wounded in the leg but had been treated and released from the hospital the previous day. After the army medics had stabilized him at the scene, he had been taken by helicopter back to Jerusalem for surgery to remove the bullet. He was disappointed that he'd been unconscious for that part, too.

Two days later, Irwin was able to sit up in a chair instead of spending all day in bed and even take short walks, as long as someone was there to help him. This time, it was his mother who was escorting him, holding him by his right arm while he wheeled the stand with his intravenous bags of antibiotics, saline, and who knew what else with his left.

For some reason, his mom thought she had to keep talking the whole time she was alone with him. He knew how scared and nervous she was, even though he was back on his feet and the doctors were assuring the family that he was fine and would make a complete recovery. But she kept talking, even when she didn't have anything to say.

"It's a miracle," she repeated. "It's a miracle."

It wasn't a miracle, Irwin thought. A miracle should have a *good* outcome, and while he couldn't argue with a complete recovery, he had to wonder why any reasonable God would opt for that as His miracle over, say, Irwin's never having gotten shot at all!

But he didn't say any of that to his parents, or to anyone, not for a long time. There was something shameful about being an atheist in the culture he was raised in so he kept those ideas to himself. He didn't know whether or not God actually did exist; that wasn't the point. Because even if He did, sitting up there on a big throne in heaven, whether He was just watching what was going on or actively directing things like AK-47 bullets to miss some kid's heart by a whisper, Irwin didn't want any part of Him. This "God," both as an idea and the reality, was an insecure bully and thug, demanding worship in return for a lifetime of heartbreak and misery that He not only failed to stop, but which He was causing in the first place.

As he got older, Irwin Benjamin would now and again find himself in a spot where he almost wished he could believe in God. But any time he reached that point, all he had to do was look at the now faded scar on his chest to remember that there was no such thing as divine intervention. Then came the Return and the thousands of gods that brought. If God was such a glorious thing, shouldn't *thousands* of gods multiply the wonder exponentially?

It would...if He was. But Irwin believed he, and the rest of the world, had the scars to prove just the opposite...

Jerusalem, Today

He hadn't thought about this place since he and his family left Israel behind on July 4, 1998. He had overheard a doctor warn that he might suffer from nightmares or some other form of post traumatic stress syndrome, but once he had seen the last (he thought) of Israel, the dusty, rocky, rubble strewn terrain and the battered old synagogue never crossed his mind again.

He returned home a hero in his neighborhood, all the kids wanting to see his scars and tell how he'd been shot and killed and brought back to life. He told the story so often in so short a time, it quickly lost its power and became in his mind, incredibly, no greater in significance than the time he'd broken his wrist falling out the first floor window of his uncle's house in New Jersey. He rode that story through middle school and into high school.

But being there now, thirty-five years later, it all came flooding back. The heat, the dust, the desolation. It was all pretty much the same, maybe a bit more the worse for wear from the constant warfare that raged around it, but he could, suddenly, remember every detail of the attack, see it in his mind's eye, a silent movie superimposed over the rough landscape.

"Agent Benjamin?" Father Rowe asked gently. "Are you alright? You've been standing there staring for the last five minutes."

"Yeah, I'm fine. Just remembering...guess that can't be helped, huh?"

"I know it must be difficult for you," she said.

He shook his head.

"It's not, really. I mean, the memories are all there and very vivid, but it's more like I'm remembering something I saw in a movie. All very realistic, but happening at a distance, you know?"

Strobe consulted a diagram from the Tawaret file and, after getting his bearings, lead Irwin and the priest over to the spot where the fertility goddess' body had been found.

It was a spot different from any other spot around it only in that it happened to be the one on which the body had landed. Otherwise, it seemed to hold no significance or message they could decipher. It was just a place, visible from the rarely traveled road.

"Israel's not so big that his leaving Tawaret here to be found is a coincidence. He wants me here," Irwin said.

"Why?"

Irwin shrugged.

"Dunno. Let's ask him."

Irwin took a few steps away from his companions and shouted, "George. If you're here, we've come to talk."

Strobe and Father Rowe exchanged looks.

Then looked back to see a tall, gaunt man dressed in black walking towards Irwin.

"Where did he come from?" Gloria Rowe gasped.

"You can't see him unless he wants you to see him," Irwin said, watching Junker George draw closer to him. "You two hang back and let me take the lead on this for now."

"Why not?" Strobe grumbled. "If what you have told us is true, he has nothing to fear from us."

"Hello, brother Benjamin. Father Rowe," he said, stopping half a dozen yards from Irwin. He looked at them in turn as he said their names, nodding silently in acknowledgement to Strobe.

"I'm here," Irwin said.

George nodded.

"I am pleased you came."

"Well, you haven't exactly left me much choice. You've been leading me around the U.S. and the world since New York. If you've got something to say to me, just say it. You didn't have to leave me a trail of thirty-two bodies to get my attention."

"You've changed, brother," George said.

"Me? I haven't changed. This is how I always get when I'm tired, cranky, and fed the fuck up."

George's sharp, hard features softened into what must have passed for a smile from him.

"You've found your strength. The last time we met, you were soft and confused. Now, you are a leader. You needed the battles to fight to become strong. I provided you with those."

"Please, can't you just give me a straight answer."

"Not all answers are that easy."

Irwin threw up his hands in defeat and turned his back on George, looking at Strobe and Rowe in frustration.

"See what we're dealing with here, folks? We need answers but all he's got to offer is platitudes. Just like the Bible."

"Irwin," George said softly. "God knows your pain and He understands your anger."

Irwin spun quickly back to face him. "Who the fuck says I'm angry? Don't presume to know me just because I've been forced to hunt you and..."

Without raising his voice, George interrupted him. "You haven't been hunting me. You have been following my trail of breadcrumbs."

"You mean corpses."

"They are false gods, blasphemers against the Holy Spirit. God commands they die for their sins."

"'God commands,'" Irwin snared. "God commands we kiss his ass or suffer his wrath. God commands babies in the womb develop cancer. God commands madmen go into schools and theaters and malls and kill people by the score. I don't want to hear God commands."

"He also commanded that a thirteen-year-old boy be shot and nearly die at this very place, only to be resurrected..."

"Re*suscitated*," Irwin corrected.

"...Revived," George conceded, "moments later so that he might live to come back here so we would meet today to work towards the banishment of the false gods from our world. Cause and effect, from the divine perspective."

"I suppose God told you that personally?"

"God doesn't speak to me directly, but He has granted me the wisdom and perception to divine His wishes. And to understand the human heart."

"What's that supposed to mean?" Irwin snapped.

"Our Lord sent His son to suffer for our sins, yet He also sent terrorists to shoot your father's son for the sin of being in the wrong place at the wrong time. He knows you resent Him, brother Benjamin. He knows you doubt His very existence and think you would turn your back on Him even if offered proof. But He needed you to doubt Him so that when the time came for you to believe, your belief would be absolute and true."

"Is that supposed to pass for impressive? Five minutes internet research would have told you what happened to me when I was a kid and your conman's intuition and dime store psychoanalysis fills in the rest. Anyway, how am I supposed to help you kill gods? I'm only human."

"You have already begun," George said.

"*Who* are you?" Father Rowe cried out, unable to hold back any longer.

"I am a humble servant of God, Father. Just like you."

"You know what I mean," she insisted. "Who *are* you, George?"

"I am exactly who you know I am to be."

"Where did you get the piece of the True Cross?"

"I...found it," George said.

"Where."

"In Israel."

"You want us to believe you and your mission, George, stop beating around the bush and answer her questions. Where's that chunk of wood from?" Irwin shouted.

"I found it in Jerusalem, while I was a laborer in the employ of Helena, mother of the Emperor Constantine, digging the foundation for the Church of the Holy Sepulcher in the year 325 A.D."

"Judas Priest!" Strobe exclaimed. "You're trying to tell us you're over seventeen *hundred* years old?"

Father Rowe shook her head, her eyes locked with George's. "No, he's much older than that. Aren't you, George?"

A single nod.

"Yes."

"And...," she said, licking her lips, almost afraid to ask the question, "you knew *where* to dig...because you were there, weren't you? When... when..."

"When our Lord was made to suffer and die upon the Cross and when He was laid to rest," he nodded. "I was a wanderer, seeking a path which would enable me to cease wandering and find a direction. The words of Jesus, His sacrifice, His radiance..."

Strobe looked wildly at Irwin. "You're not buying this, are you?"

Irwin didn't take his eyes off of George as he said, "I think maybe I am, Eric."

"Why you, George? Out of all of humanity, why *you*?"

"I am not quite human or god, but something between. That's why I can not be seen unless I will it; being neither one or the other, I slip between the perceptions of both."

"This is madness," Strobe shouted.

"Agent Benjamin said it before, why should his immortality be any more ridiculous than a world full of living gods?"

"So, let's say I buy your story," Irwin said. "What do you want of me?"

"I want to free you from the shackles of authority and beg your help in returning the world to the one, rightful God."

"What if I don't believe in that God any more than I do Apollo or Jupiter?"

"You were given free will to believe or disbelieve, as you choose. You don't have to believe in the one Lord to crusade against the false gods. I am sure He will reward you, either way."

The world was a worse place for the Return of the gods. As divisive as the split between the Abrahamic religions of Judaism, Christianity, and Muslims had been, those were minor compared to the rifts between a hundred pantheons or more and all their petty, jealous little gods. Freedom was impossible when subjugated to religion, and peace was impossible when no two religions could agree on which hat to wear or what day of the week to celebrate their worship. A man wasn't free to live where he wanted or worship as he saw fit.

What choice did Irwin have?

George looked almost pleased when they first heard the helicopters approaching from the east.

"Captain Mayat is coming for me," he said.

Irwin was confused. "What? No, that can't be. I didn't even tell her we were coming up here."

"She's been using you as a Judas goat, brother Benjamin. While you've been hunting me, she's had you followed. You led her and her forces straight to me."

The blood drained from his face and Irwin's ears began to ring. "Crap, I never even thought of that...!"

"It's all right, my friend. I have been aware of her plan all along. She is coming for me with a squad of young warrior gods from many pantheons, likely as many as forty or fifty from the number of helicopters coming our way. It's much more efficient to kill them in large groups rather than one by one."

Irwin said, "Hey, wait, what about us...?"

"You can run. Captain Mayat will understand. What chance did you three stand against the killer of gods? Besides, you will have served your purpose by drawing me out into the open, so whatever the outcome of this encounter, you can not be blamed."

"But...what about you, George?" Father Rowe said. "Can you stand up to so many?"

This time, George did smile. From his pocket he drew one of his wood crosses and held it up to them.

"I am well protected. Now, you and brother Benjamin had best be going. It would not be wise for you to be caught in the middle of this battle."

Strobe frowned, "What about me?"

George took several steps towards the Israeli. "Your time ends here, with the other false gods."

"What the hell are you...?" Irwin said, startled, but before he could finish the sentence, a blast of brilliant, pure white light erupted from the cross in Junker George's hand and enveloped the screaming Eric Strobe.

When the light faded, Strobe was gone. Laying unmoving on the ground was a humanoid being with a bizarre bird-like body.

"He was Ka-poe-kino-manu, a Hawaiian *kupua*, or trickster demigod," George said. "That is how Mayat knew to spring her trap."

"But...if he's been Eric Strobe, where's the real Eric?" Irwin asked.

"There never has been an Eric Strobe. Such are their powers that they can make those around them believe they have always been known to them as who they say they are, even if just born of the moment." George tilted his head, listening. "They're almost here. You better hurry."

"Are you sure you're going to be okay? You've only ever faced them one at a time," Irwin insisted.

"That's because I wanted the pagans to *believe* those were the limits of my capacity," George said. "You will hear from me soon. Now, go."

They went.

As he guided the speeding jeep down the rocky road, Special Agent Benjamin saw in his mind's eye the Hall of Gods assault squad's attack on George. He imagined the tall, gaunt gray-eyed man standing out in the open, completely exposed as the choppers did their creepy, appearing out of nowhere thing, their rotors battering the hot, shimmering air with a steady, thunderous thrum.

If Captain Mayat's people—or whatever they were—were on the ball, they would have dropped ground troops to encircle George and hold him in position for the helicopters to do their work.

Father Rowe was holding tight as the jeep jostled and jumped over the rough road but she never took her eyes off Irwin. He ignored her, concentrating on his driving, and listening, like she was, to the sound of what they had left behind.

First came the clatter of heavy caliber machine gun fire, then the concussive slam of air-to-ground missiles being fired and exploding. One. Two. Three. He wondered if the old synagogue would survive this and was surprised to find he hoped it did.

More machine gun fire. The missiles had missed...or hadn't done their job?

George must have been waiting, likely for all his attackers and their machines to come into range, because next came silence.

And light.

They were over a mile away from the fire zone when the light rose like a bubble through water into the sky. He could feel its heat on his back and see its brilliance all around and ahead of him. Through the smothering light, he heard four dull, muffled thumps. The helicopters' fuel tanks exploding from the heat, he decided. It probably didn't matter though; whatever kind of beings were aboard them would have been wiped out by the first touch of the light.

Father Rowe, her eyes squeezed shut and her lips moving in prayer, crossed herself.

"Do you think he could have survived that?" she said at last.

Irwin nodded. "Yeah, otherwise he wouldn't have gone into the situation. I don't think he's got any sort of death wish."

"I've said a prayer for him...and for you too, Agent Benjamin," she said.

"Does a Catholic's prayers work for a non-believing Jew?"

"Dear God! How can you still cling to your atheism after what we've just seen and heard? Can't you at least give the Lord the benefit of the doubt?"

"I'll do better than that," Irwin said, taking his eyes off the road to give her a hard look. "I'll concede that yeah, there is a God. I just choose not to *believe* in Him."

"But...the two can't be separated..."

"Why not? There are thousands of living, breathing gods all around us, but you don't believe in any of them. So all that really separates us is the disbelief in *one* god, isn't it?"

"If none of this matters to you, why have you thrown in with George?"

"Because of the one thing that I *do* believe in, Father," he said, his eyes set on the hard road ahead of them. "Us."

ABOUT THE AUTHORS

LORRAINE J. ANDERSON ("That First Step") has been experimenting with many different kinds of fantastic fiction, including comic strips with the artist Sherlock, fantasy stories, science fiction stories, fictional newspaper columns, and Young Adult paranormal fiction. She hopes to someday make fiction more than a hobby. Her stories can be found under "Lorraine J. Anderson" at Amazon.com, BN.com, and Smashwords.com.

A Pennsylvania resident, PHIL GIUNTA ("Root for the Undergods") graduated from Saint Joseph's University in Philadelphia with a Bachelor of Science in Information Systems. His first novel, a paranormal mystery called *Testing the Prisoner*, debuted in March 2010 from Firebringer Press. His second novel in the same genre, *By Your Side*, was released in March 2013. In August 2012, Phil's short story about the Celtic gods, "There Be In Dreams No War", was featured in the anthology *ReDeus: Divine Tales* from Crazy 8 Press.

Phil is currently editing a short story collection titled *Somewhere in the Middle of Eternity* for Firebringer Press and working on a paranormal thriller called *Lineage* intended as an eBook-only novella. He is also the narrator of an audio version of *Testing the Prisoner*, which can be heard for free at Podiobooks.com. The audio version of *By Your Side* is forthcoming on the Prometheus Radio Theatre feed: http://prometheus.libsynpro.com. Visit Phil's website at http://www.philgiunta.com.

Having grown up on fantasy, science fiction, and comic books, ROBERT GREENBERGER ("The Wanderer") has reveled working in these fields as an adult. He has worked as an editor or executive for DC Comics, Marvel Comics, Starlog Press, Gist Communications, and *Weekly World News*. As a freelance writer, he has written for all ages and numerous genres, notably the media tie-in field with several *Star Trek* novels to his credit. He won the Scribe Award for his novelization of *Hellboy II: The Golden Army* and has gone on to co-found Crazy 8 Press. His recent works include *After Earth: United Ranger Corps Survival Manual*, *After Earth: A Perfect Beast* (co-written with Peter David and Michael Jan Friedman) and two *After Earth* digital short stories, one of which can be found in *Beast* and the other in the *After Earth* novelization.

Having received his certification to teach English, Bob now makes his home in Maryland where he hopes to teach. For more, see www.bobgreenberger.com.

PAUL KUPPERBERG (**"A Clockwork God"**) is the author of the Archie Comics young adult novel, *Kevin*, featuring the first openly gay character in Archie Comics' history, Kevin Keller (as well as the upcoming *Kevin Mad Libs*, both published by Grossett & Dunlap) and the writer of the 2012 Eisner Award nominated monthly *Life With Archie: The Married Life* magazine for Archie Comics, which featured the bestselling marriage of Kevin Keller and Dr. Clay Walker. Paul has also written almost a thousand comic book stories, from Batman to Bart Simpson and Superman to Scooby Doo, and is the author of more than two dozen books, including the comic book themed mystery novel, *The Same Old Story* (available in August from Crazy 8 Press). In addition to being a co-creator and contributor to *ReDeus: Divine Tales* and *ReDeus: Beyond Borders,* he also has stories in the young adult anthology *Latchkeys: Splinters* (also available at Crazy8Press.com) and in the Hellfire Lounge books (Mariettapublishing.com). You can follow Paul at Paulkupperberg.com.

WILLIAM LEISNER (**"Sestercentennial Day"**) is pleased to return to the ReDeus universe, following "The Year Without a Santa Claus," the lead-off story in *ReDeus: Divine Tales.* He has also written several novels, novellas, and short stories in the *Star Trek* universe, most recently the Original Series novel *The Shocks of Adversity.* He is currently at work on a new tale for the third ReDeus collection, *Native Lands,* due later this year, as well as other original projects. He is a second-generation American, born in Rochester, New York, and currently residing in the Twin Cities, home to one of the largest Hmong populations in the U.S. William would like to acknowledge Mai Neng Moua, editor of *Bamboo Among the Oaks* (Minnesota Historical Press Society, 2002), as well as the contributors to this anthology of work by Hmong American writers, for the insight and inspiration their stories, essays and poems provided while writing this story.

STEVE LYONS (**"Dia de los Muertos"**) is the author of over twenty-five science-fiction novels, as well as radio plays, comic strips, short stories and more. Quite a few of these stories have been set in the *Doctor Who* universe, both old and new flavors. He has also "worked with" such popular characters as the X-Men, the *Stargate SG-1* team, the Micronauts, Strontium Dog and DC Comics' Steel. He has written non-fiction books about TV shows and films, and contributed to many magazines. He is a regular writer of the *Doctor Who Adventures* comic strip, aimed at younger readers. He is also currently working in the war-torn worlds of *Warhammer 40,000* and has a couple of Blake's 7 adventures in the pipeline. Early 2013 sees the release of his audio drama, *Destiny of the Doctor: Smoke and Mirrors*, part of a special series to celebrate the fiftieth anniversary of *Doctor Who*. He lives in Salford, near Manchester, in the United Kingdom.

DAVID MCDONALD ("**In Foreign Fields**") is a professional geek from Melbourne, Australia who works for an international welfare organization. When not on a computer or reading a book, he divides his time between helping run a local cricket club and working on his upcoming novel. He is a member of the Australian Horror Writers Association, the International Association of Media Tie-In Writers, and of the Melbourne based writers group, SuperNOVA.

A Ditmar Award-winning writer, David's stories appear in anthologies such as *The Lone Ranger Chronicles* from Moonstone Books, *Epilogue* from Fablecroft Publishing, and *Deck the Halls* from eMergent Publications. He is also a regular contributor to the *Tales of the Shadowmen* series from Moonstone Books.

You can find out more about David by visiting his website, www. davidmcdonaldspage.com, where he blogs about writing, pop culture, sport and all things geek, including his series of conversational reviews of New *Doctor Who*, which has twice been nominated for the William J. Atheling Jr. Award for Criticism and Review.

Born and raised in Southern Delaware, KELLY MEDING ("**Evidence of Things Not Seen**") survived five years in the hustle and bustle of Northern Virginia, only to retreat back to the peace and sanity of the Eastern Shore. An avid reader and film buff, she discovered Freddy Krueger at a very young age, and has since had a lifelong obsession with horror, science fiction, and fantasy, on which she blames her interest in vampires, psychic powers, superheroes, and all things paranormal.

Three Days to Dead, the first book in her Dreg City urban fantasy series, follows Evangeline Stone, a paranormal hunter who is resurrected into the body of a stranger and has only three days to solve her own murder and stop a war between the city's goblins and vampires. Additional books in the series, *As Lie the Dead*, *Another Kind of Dead*, and *Wrong Side of Dead*, are available in both digital format and mass market paperback from Bantam.

Beginning with *Trance*, Kelly's MetaWars series tells the story of the grown-up children of the world's slaughtered superheroes who receive their superpowers back after a mysterious fifteen-year absence, and who now face not only a fearful public, but also a vengeful villain who wants all of them dead. *Trance* and *Changeling* are available now in both digital format and mass market paperback from Pocket Books. *Tempest* is available in digital format only via Pocket Star, with *Chimera* (book four) following Nov. 11, 2013.

You can find Kelly on Twitter (@KellyMeding), Pinterest (http://pinterest.com/kellymeding/), and Facebook, as well as her website (http://www.kellymeding.com/) and her blog Organized Chaos (http://chaostitan.blogspot.com/).

SCOTT PEARSON ("A Medieval Knight in Vatican City") was first published in 1987 with "The Mailbox," a short story about an elderly farming couple. Over the last quarter century he has published a smattering of humor, poetry, nonfiction, reviews, and short stories, including three *Star Trek* stories, a couple of mysteries, and "The Tale of the Nouveau Templar" in *ReDeus: Divine Tales*. His first novella, "Honor in the Night," is in the *Star Trek: Myriad Universes* anthology *Shattered Light* from Simon & Schuster. Upcoming later this year is "On My Side" in *A Quiet Shelter There* from Hadley Rille Books. Scott lives near the banks of the mighty Mississippi River, fabled in story and song, in personable St. Paul, Minnesota, with his wife, Sandra, and daughter, Ella. He and Ella host Generations Geek: A Father/Daughter Nerdcast on the Chronic Rift Network at chronicrift.com. They talk about the geeky things they do and interview cool geeky guests like sci-fi writers and space shuttle astronauts. Please visit Scott on the web at www.yeahsure.net, www.facebook.com/yeahsure, and @smichaelpearson, as well www.generationsgeek.com, www.facebook/generationsgeek, and @generationsgeek.

AARON ROSENBERG ("What Remains Is Light") is an award-winning, #1 bestselling novelist, children's book author, and game designer. His novels include the DuckBob series (*No Small Bills, Too Small for Tall,* and the upcoming *Three Small Coinkydinks*), the *Dread Remora* space-opera series, and the O.C.L.T. supernatural thriller series, plus novels for *Star Trek, Warhammer, WarCraft,* and *Eureka.* His children's books include *42: The Jackie Robinson Story, Bandslam: The Novel,* books for *iCarly, PowerPuff Girls,* and *Transformers Animated,* and the original series Pete and Penny's Pizza Puzzles. His RPG work includes *Asylum, Spookshow,* the Origins Award-winning *Gamemastering Secrets, The Supernatural Roleplaying Game, Warhammer Fantasy Roleplay,* and *The Deryni Roleplaying Game.* He is the co-creator of ReDeus and a co-founder of Crazy 8 Press. Aaron lives in New York with his family. You can visit him online at gryphonrose.com and follow him on Twitter @gryphonrose.

LAWRENCE M. SCHOEN ("Singing for the Man") holds a Ph.D. in cognitive psychology and psycholinguistics. He spent ten years as a college professor and has done extensive research in the areas of human memory and language. This background provides a principal metaphor for his fiction. When not writing he works as the director of research and analytics for a series of mental health and addiction recovery facilities in Philadelphia.

Additionally, he's one of the world's foremost authorities on the Klingon language, and since 1992 has championed the exploration and use of this constructed tongue throughout the world. He's also the publisher behind a speculative fiction small press, Paper Golem, aimed at showcasing up-and-coming writers as well as providing a market for novellas. On top of that, he's also a hypnotist, but uses his powers of manipulation and mind control to help other writers.

In 2007, he was a finalist for the John W. Campbell Award for Best New Writer, was a finalist for the Hugo Award for Best Short Story in 2010, and this year received a nomination for the Nebula Award for Best Novella. He's hard at working writing the third novel in the ongoing adventures of the Amazing Conroy, a stage hypnotist traveling the galaxy in the company of Reggie, an alien buffalito that can eat anything and farts oxygen.

Lawrence lives near Philadelphia with his wife, Valerie, who is neither a psychologist nor a Klingon speaker.

JANNA SILVERSTEIN ("In the House of Osiris") is a science fiction and fantasy writer and editor with a number of short story publications to her credit. Her writing has appeared in *Asimov's Science Fiction*, Orson Scott Card's *Intergalactic Medicine Show*, *10Flash Quarterly*, and in the anthologies *Swordplay* and *The Trouble With Heroes*, among others. She was twice a Writers of the Future semi-finalist. Her editing career includes ten years at Bantam Spectra working on both original and licensed fiction, stints at Wizards of the Coast and WizKids Games producing game-related fiction in print and on the web, and freelance projects for publishers including Pocket Books, Night Shade Books, and Kobold Press. Among recent projects, she is pleased to have edited the Gold ENnie Award-winning *Complete KOBOLD Guide to Game Design* and most recently *The KOBOLD Guide to Worldbuilding*. She has a lifelong interest in ancient Egypt and traveled to the Middle East in 1997 to walk among the temples at Luxor and Karnak, and to stand before the Sphinx in its crumbling glory. She came away from that trip crushed out on the Egyptian goddess is Hathor but decided that Isis is much more of a badass. Janna is a native New Yorker living in Seattle whose day job is in technology. She lives with two rambunctious cats and a great many books.

STEVEN H. WILSON ("Axel's Flight") has written for *Starlog*, DC Comics' *Star Trek* and *Warlord*, and, most recently, served as principal writer and director for Prometheus Radio Theatre and publisher of Fire-bringer Press. His original science fiction series, *The Arbiter Chronicles*, currently boasting nineteen full-cast audio dramas and the novel *Taken Liberty*, has won the Mark Time Silver Award and the Parsec Award for Best Audio Drama (long form). His third novel, *Unfriendly Persuasion*, was released in 2012. As a podcaster, besides hosting the Prometheus Radio Theatre podcast, he has recorded Lester Del Rey's Badge of Infamy for podiobooks.com, performed multiple roles in J. Daniel Sawyer's production of *Antithesis*, and contributed narration to the audio novel *Geek Love*. Active in science fiction fandom since 1984, he has written, drawn, edited and published fanzines, acted and directed with a comedy troupe, and served as a gopher, a con chair or a guest at roughly a hundred conventions. Wilson, who works as an IT manager, holds degrees from the University of Maryland College of Journalism and the Johns Hopkins University Whiting School of Engineering. He lives in Elkridge, MD with his wife Renee and sons Ethan and Christian. His weekly blog of ramblings on various topics, plus all kinds of information about his work, past, present and future, is available at www.stevenhwilson.com.

ABOUT THE ARTIST

Ever since she was a kid, LORRAINE SCHLETER drew all the time, becoming her strongest skill. She received her degree in Studio Art at Indiana University and worked various part-time jobs to support herself while continuing to produce commissioned art. Recently her freelance career has started to take off. Lorraine has produced works for Wizards of the Coast, Fantasy Flight, and other game companies and individuals. "Hopefully, as I continue to grow as an illustrator, doors will continue to open up for me," Lorraine says. We agree.

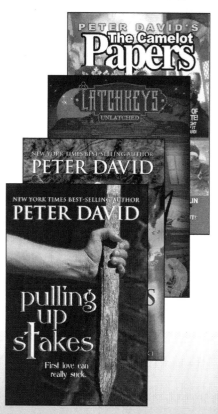

Made in the USA
Charleston, SC
18 August 2013